Gia said, and then switched on the TV.

Bennett rolled his eyes. "Right. God forbid
actually get to know someone or, I don't know
the best orgasms you've ever had in your life."

"Are you offering?"

Was he? *Shit.*

She waggled her eyebrows. "If it makes a difference, I'll
tell you that two times is my max with the same guy. It's
kind of a rule I have."

"A *rule*?" Jesus Christ, she was a complicated woman.

She shrugged. "Keeps me honest."

"What the hell does that mean?"

"I don't want to be anyone's girlfriend. I also don't want
to mislead anyone. So I make sure I don't."

"That sounds awfully lonely." Jesus, it sounded terrible.
He might not have found "the one," but sex aside, he
couldn't imagine having gone his entire life without a real
romantic relationship.

She looked at him a long time, and just as she was about
to speak, the lights went out.

Everything went out: lights, TV, the hum of the air
conditioner.

"Fuck me," Gia said.

I'm trying not to.

PRAISE FOR THE BRIDESMAIDS BEHAVING BADLY SERIES

IT TAKES TWO

"Jenny Holiday turns up the heat and the charm for a summer read more satisfying than a poolside popsicle.... It's hard to imagine finding a more delightful summer escape."
—*Entertainment Weekly*

"This is romantic comedy at its best, complete with clever, sexy banter, a vibrant cast of characters, [and] a wedding that is a character in itself."
—*Washington Post*

"A witty, sexy and wonderfully entertaining romantic comedy."
—*USA Today*, *Happy Ever After*

"Holiday combines class and sass with a hefty dose of humor.... This winning hero and heroine will take up residence in readers' hearts."
—*Publishers Weekly*

"[An] irresistible mix of lively, piquantly witty writing; sharply etched, marvelously memorable characters; and some completely combustible love scenes that are guaranteed to leave burn marks on readers' fingers."
—*Booklist*, starred review

ONE AND ONLY

"The perfect rom-com."

—Refinery29

"A satisfying iteration of the contemporary bridezilla subgenre."

—*New York Times Book Review*

"When it comes to creating unputdownable contemporary romances, Holiday is in it to win it."

—*Booklist*, starred review

"Delightfully sexy and sweet, Holiday knows how to deliver the perfect combination of sexual tension and happily-ever-after."

—Lauren Layne, *New York Times* bestselling author

"*One and Only* is fantastic! A great start to a new series. Compelling characters, tons of heat, loads of heart. I highly recommend!"

—M. O'Keefe, *USA Today* bestselling author

ALSO BY JENNY HOLIDAY

THE BRIDESMAIDS BEHAVING BADLY SERIES

One and Only

It Takes Two

three little words

BRIDESMAIDS BEHAVING BADLY

JENNY HOLIDAY

FOREVER
New York Boston

Forever
Hachette Book Group
1290 Avenue of the Americas, New York, NY 10104
forever-romance.com
twitter.com/foreverromance

First Edition: January 2019

Forever is an imprint of Grand Central Publishing. The Forever name and logo are trademarks of Hachette Book Group, Inc.

The publisher is not responsible for websites (or their content) that are not owned by the publisher.

The Hachette Speakers Bureau provides a wide range of authors for speaking events. To find out more, go to www.hachettespeakersbureau.com or call (866) 376-6591.

ISBN: 978-1-4555-4246-8 (mass market), 978-1-4555-4244-4 (ebook)

Printed in the United States of America

OPM

10 9 8 7 6 5 4 3 2 1

This book is for Audra North. I'm so glad you didn't sue me. But I accept that you still might. #CauldronYears

Acknowledgments

Lorelie Brown and Sandra Owens read an early draft of this book, and their comments helped me see what wasn't working and where my blind spots were.

Amber Belldane and Robyn Barnes helped me enormously when this book was in the planning stages and I was thinking of having Bennett be the minister at Wendy's wedding. (Can you believe it? I had this "the minister + the bad girl" thing in my head, but it wasn't going to work for a variety of reasons!) I'm so appreciative of the time they took to help me understand how that might have worked...even though it ultimately didn't.

I don't think I would have finished this book without Christine D'Abo doing morning sprints with me.

As always, Audra North kept me laughing.

Courtney Miller-Callihan rocks. That is true in a general sense, but in this case specifically she read a partial draft when I was stuck and convinced me that I was not, in fact, writing the most boring book in the history of books.

And last but not even remotely least, my thanks to everyone at Forever Romance. Estelle Hallick is my capital-*F* Forever friend but also my small-*f* forever friend. Elizabeth Turner Stokes has made this series beautiful with her cover artistry. Lexi Smail continues to blow me away by doing her thing where she sees what I meant instead of what I said, and making everything better for it.

Chapter One

*T*he woman throwing a hissy fit at the gate had to be Gia Gallo. She looked the part: tall, thin, and in possession of one of those huge, ugly handbags that cost more than most people's rent.

She was also stunning, but that wasn't relevant.

Helming a successful Manhattan restaurant in an increasingly hip neighborhood meant that Bennett Buchanan had encountered his share of models. The funny thing about models was that they usually weren't that good-looking up close. They were all angles and bones and overly exaggerated features that photographed better than they came across in real life.

Gia, though, with her shoulder-length, wavy, honey-brown hair, her heart-shaped face, and her plump pink lips, was almost unnaturally beautiful.

Or she would have been, if she hadn't been using that gorgeous mouth to yell at the poor beleaguered gate agent who had just announced that their flight to Tampa was canceled.

Bennett didn't go for entitled. He'd seen enough spoiled princesses in his old-money southern youth to last a lifetime. New York might rub him the wrong way a lot of the time, but one thing it had going for it was that debutantes were few and far between. Or at least their New York equivalent, the society ladies, didn't make their way up to his little Cajun place in Washington Heights.

"Listen to me," the bad-tempered beauty said to the gate agent as she held up a garment bag. "This is a wedding dress. It needs to get to Florida *now*."

Yep, that was definitely Gia, one of the bridesmaids in his friend Noah's wedding.

Bennett got up from where he'd been sitting and headed over to the desk to try to run interference.

A second agent had joined the first. He looked as if he had a lower bullshit threshold than his colleague and was rolling in to play the role of Bad Cop Gate Agent. "A bridezilla. My favorite kind of customer," he said under his breath, but not really, because Bennett, who was still a few feet away, could hear him.

"I am not a bridezilla," Gia said.

"Honey, that's what they all say."

"I am not a bridezilla, because I am not the bride. I *am* a bridesmaid, though, so if you want to call me a bridesmaidzilla, go right ahead. I will totally own that." She leaned over—she was taller than both the agents—and got right in the face of the one who'd called her a bridezilla. "This is my friend Wendy's wedding dress. Actually, it's her *dead mother's* wedding dress. And Wendy? She hasn't had the easiest time of it. So I have made it my personal mission to make sure her wedding goes off without a hitch.

This dress will make it to Florida if I have to walk it there myself." She sniffed and straightened to her full, imposing height. "And *don't* call me honey."

"Well, you'd better start walking, *honey*, because they're about to close the airport."

"What part of don't call me—"

"Gia?" Bennett interrupted, pasting on his "the customer is always right" smile. "Are you by chance Wendy's friend Gia?"

She whirled on him, and she was *pissed*. Her eyes, a gorgeous amber that reminded him of his nana's cinnamon pecan shortbread, narrowed. They were topped by long lashes and heavy eyebrows. The powerful brows contrasted sharply with pale, flawless skin marked by two blotches of angry pink in the centers of her cheeks. Jesus Christ, that kind of beauty was a shock to the system, equal parts invigorating and painful, not unlike when you burned yourself in the kitchen in the middle of a manic dinner shift.

"And *you* are?"

The question dripped with disdain, which was good because it reminded him that the karmic scales tended to balance beauty with sourness. She was like the abominations northerners called peaches: vibrantly pinky yellow and fragrant on the outside, hard and woody and unyielding on the inside.

Still, he would do what he could to rescue these poor gate agents from her clutches. The monster storm bearing down on the eastern seaboard was going to make their lives unpleasant enough without the addition of an indignant model who believed that the laws of nature didn't apply to her.

He stuck his hand out. "Bennett Buchanan at your service, ma'am." He let his drawl come on strong. That always charmed people.

Gia was not charmed.

She rolled her eyes.

But she did step away from the counter, enough that the next customer in line took her place.

"You're Noah's friend."

"Yes, ma'am."

"Don't call me ma'am."

The thing was, he was pissed, too. She wasn't the only one whose flight had been canceled. She wasn't even the only one who had been charged with transporting an item essential to the wedding ceremony.

Noah and Wendy had spent the last six months traveling. They had a system in which they jetted to a far-flung locale for two weeks and then spent two weeks at home in Toronto, where Wendy's aunt was recovering from a car accident and Noah, who was moving to Canada to be with Wendy, was studying to transfer his legal credentials.

It was like a honeymoon in reverse—the final trip would be their wedding in Florida. They'd dropped in to New York a few months ago for dress and ring fittings and had left the properly sized final products in the custody of their friends. He wasn't really sure why they hadn't done that stuff in Toronto, but he didn't ask questions. He did as he was told.

Which meant he had the rings in his pocket. He, however, was not throwing a hissy fit over this fact.

So, yeah, he was pissed.

And cold. So freaking cold.

Top of that list of things about New York that rubbed him the wrong way?

Winter.

You can take the boy out of the South...

Damn, he hadn't realized how much the idea of getting on

that plane and emerging in a few hours into the warm, humid air of a *civilized* climate had gotten its hooks into him.

But unlike Gia, he was capable of holding his temper when things didn't go his way. He was an adult. A fact of which he reminded himself as he checked the impulse to start calling her *honey-ma'am*.

"The wedding isn't for a week," he said. "We'll be able to rebook. Let's head back to the city, and we can try again when this storm passes. We can share a cab."

Which was the last thing he wanted to do, but if they were closing the airport, taxis would be in short supply, and Bennett was a nice guy.

Well, okay, he *wasn't* a nice guy, but he'd grown adept at faking it. And if he could behave, so could she.

Instead of answering him, Gia elbowed her way back to the counter and started demanding a hotel voucher.

"We don't give vouchers for weather delays," the first agent said.

"Good luck finding a hotel room anyway," said Bad Cop Gate Agent. "Storm of the decade, they're saying."

Gia puffed up her chest and opened her mouth. Bennett cringed. What did she think? That they could wave a magic wand and, like Harry Potter, repel the foot of snow that was set to be dumped down on them?

He would just leave her to her little tantrum, then. He could only fake this nice-guy shit for so long.

But before he turned away, something interesting happened. Something subtle that probably no one else noticed. Gia's body, which had clearly been ramping up to escalate her fight, just sort of...deflated. Her chest sagged as her spine rounded, and her chin came to her chest. He didn't miss her eyes on the way down. They were filling with tears.

Shit.

When someone needs help, you help. That's what separates men from monsters.

Chef Lalande's refrain echoed through Bennett's brain. His mentor's mantra was a giant pain in the ass most of the time, but it was the philosophy that had saved Bennett and that Bennett had embraced. Pay it forward and all that.

It wasn't a philosophy that could be invoked selectively—that was the pain-in-the-ass part. When you changed the kind of person you were, you had to be all in.

"Hey, hey, Gia. It's going to be okay. I promise." He moved toward her, compelled to touch her for some insane reason, but he checked the impulse.

"How can you promise that?" The belligerent tone from before was gone, replaced by resignation. "Can you make this plane go?"

"Look." He pulled a small velvet pouch from his pocket. "I have the rings." He wasn't sure what his point was other than that he was on the hook for getting there as much as she was.

Whatever point he was making she ignored anyway. "Can you divert this storm?" She started walking.

He followed. "It can't snow for a week. Worst thing that happens is we miss a few days of lying on the beach." Which was a goddamn tragedy—he shivered thinking about heading back out into the winter—but it was what it was.

She started walking faster. She was almost as tall as he was, yet he had to hoof it to keep up with her.

"Can you make a hotel room magically appear in an overbooked New York City?" she snapped as she pulled out her phone. The pissiness from before was creeping back into her voice.

"No," he said sharply, suddenly done with her—he tried, but even on his best days, he was half the man Chef Lalande was. He wasn't responsible for this woman. "I can do none of those things." He stopped walking.

It took a few seconds before she realized he wasn't with her anymore. She stopped and turned. Looked back at him.

Then she did that deflating thing again. She reminded him of a pizza oven. You opened it and a blast of heat escaped and the temperature inside dropped by several hundred degrees.

"I'm sorry," she said. "I don't even know why I'm being like this. I'm just so..."

Mean? his mind supplied. *Arrogant?*

"...hungry."

He barked a surprised laugh. "Well, ma'am, that I can fix."

—⟋⟍—

Gia wasn't really sure why she was letting this man she'd never met before shepherd her out of the airport. Sure, he was Noah's best friend and former neighbor—Wendy had told her they'd be on the same flight—so he probably wasn't going to ax-murder her, but was she really going to just let him take her home without even throwing up a pro forma protest?

It was just that she was so tired. God, it felt as if she'd been working for months nonstop. Of course, her last job had only lasted three days, but it had been miserable. It was an editorial shoot, a feature on summer dresses—for *Vogue*, which was *great*, because those kinds of jobs were becoming fewer and further between. But damn, it had been a punishing gig. Long days—they were always long, but these had bordered on abusive—and the dress they'd wanted her in was too tight on her ass and she'd had to swap with Lily Alexander, the modeling world's seventeen-year-old wunderkind. Which had thrown a huge wrench into the proceedings because it had been one of those stupid "dress for your age" features that showed a woman in every decade. So Gia, who'd been cast as the "thirties" model, had to swap with Lily, which meant the "twenties" dress ended up being tea length and the "thirties" dress ended up being strapless, *God forbid*.

Throw in an extra-bitchy art director and an extra-dickish photographer, and you had a perfect storm of toxicity.

But when you were twenty-nine years old and your job was to be a human coat hanger, you didn't complain. Not when there were any number of younger, skinnier human coat hangers—witness Lily Alexander and her small-enough ass—nipping at your heels. Many of them would take the laxatives offered by bitchy art directors and the sexual harassment dished out by dickish photographers, too.

Gia had gone right from that horrible job back to her hotel to retrieve Wendy's wedding dress, which the hotel had been storing for her, and then on to the airport. If only she'd been smart enough to hold on to the room for one more night, just in case.

But she hadn't been smart enough. So here she was. Instead of on a plane bound to join her best friends at the wedding site, she was on a shuttle to the Newark Airport train station—there were no taxis to be had—with the best man.

She was so hungry.

The other thing she should have been smart enough to do was grab something to eat on their way out of the airport. She could let up on herself a little bit. The job was over, and she'd booked a month off after the wedding. Though maybe she shouldn't have. It wasn't as if it were raining high-quality jobs these days.

Regardless, she needed this little problem of hers to stay little. To not become a *thing*.

While they waited on the platform for a city-bound train, she called last night's hotel and pleaded her case up to and including the grossest kind of name-dropping, but they were resolute about being full. Several more places said the same thing.

She had options. She could call her agent. He would figure something out. Or she could call any number of models—or bitchy art directors, or dickish photographers—she knew who lived in the city and find somewhere to bunk for the night. But the logistics of it suddenly seemed so incredibly, bone-crushingly daunting.

So instead she was apparently going home with Mr. Mint Juleps and Moonshine here, at least for now.

Bennett Buchanan, though? Seriously? Who named their kid that? Gia was Canadian, so admittedly, her impression of southern American culture was based on *Duck Dynasty* and the William Faulkner novels she'd read in her one year as a literature major, but this dude, with his drawl and his falsely pretty manners, sounded like he belonged in a rom-com romancing Reese Witherspoon.

He kind of looked like it, too.

He had a ridiculous smile, to begin with. Smug, slightly arrogant, and studded with perfectly straight, sparkly white teeth, it was the kind of smile people in her industry paid big money for. He had short black hair, too, and deep-blue eyes that looked at everything, including her, several seconds longer than seemed necessary.

And the drawl.

Oh, the drawl.

But the world was full of good-looking guys with charm to spare. And Gia had seen a lot of the world, so she could make herself immune to any man, even one whose voice sounded like slightly scratchy honey. Which wasn't a thing, but whatever.

So, deflector shields engaged, she would go home with Bennett Buchanan long enough to get her bearings and make a plan. She would eat something, because half her problem right now was blood sugar.

She would *not* sleep with him.

"Put this on." He shrugged out of his parka and placed it over her shoulders—she had not been prepared for the storm. Then he produced a baggie. It was full of pecans. He opened it and held it out to her.

Her mouth didn't just water; it did this weird gushing faucet thing. She actually had to sort of suck up a big pool of spit so as not to drool on the floor.

She bit into one, and flavor exploded on her tongue. It was unexpectedly spicy. But after the burn, underneath it, there was something else. A deep, caramelized, smoky sweetness that felt like a reward.

He shook the baggie to indicate that she should take some more.

All right, who was she kidding? She probably would sleep with him. If they were going to be snowed in, what else were they going to do?

"Did you make these?" The baggie, and the absence of an artisanal tin from some SoHo gourmet shop, suggested the answer was yes.

"I did."

That was…interesting. Reese Witherspoon's southern rom-com boyfriends usually had monogrammed hankies in their pockets, not pecans.

By the time they reached Penn Station, where they changed to the subway, she'd eaten the whole baggie.

Sixty-seven pecans to be precise—she'd counted. A plain pecan contained ten calories, and who knew what was in the magical elixir he'd coated them in.

She refused to think about it. She had some breathing room. She was on vacation.

And she felt better for having eaten.

Because that was how food worked. Your body needed fuel, and food was that fuel.

She almost fell asleep on the subway, lulled by the infusion of calories and the rumbling of the train.

"Next stop is us," Bennett said, seemingly minutes but actually almost an hour later.

She shook her head to rouse herself as he hoisted his duffel bag onto his shoulder and reached for the handle of her suitcase.

Us.

He hadn't meant anything by it. In fact, what he had meant was *me*. *Next stop is* me.

What must it be like to have a house—or an apartment, or whatever? When Gia was working, she lived out of hotels. When she wasn't, she went back to her parents' place or stayed with her friends in Toronto. But that was a far cry from having an apartment you came back to so frequently and repeatedly that the nearest subway stop was "yours."

They emerged on 181st Street, and holy crap it was *snowing*.

It hadn't started yet when they'd left Newark under a white sky—which was why she'd been so annoyed at the airline. Why cancel a flight when there wasn't a speck of snow on the ground?

As they'd trained in, though, it had started—big, fat flakes falling leisurely against the windows, so pretty that Gia had half wished she could open the window and stick out her tongue to catch them, let the cold, metallic taste of them merge with the spicy sweetness of the pecans. And, judging by how much was accumulated on the sidewalk, it must have really started coming down in earnest while they'd been underground on the long subway ride to Bennett's.

Gia loved snow. When she was a kid, snow had meant escape. She'd bundle up and go outside, which was one place her mother, ever concerned about ruining her makeup, wouldn't follow. And when Gia was bundled up, she was just one of the kids. What she looked like didn't matter—in their small Ontario town, they all wore the same face-concealing uniform of hat and scarf.

So snow lifted her spirits, usually. And this was pretty snow. Clean, insistent, country-like snow. Snow that wasn't messing around.

She probably would have started twirling like Maria von Trapp: Maria Takes Manhattan Edition if she hadn't been so worried about getting Wendy's dress to Florida.

And, you know, if she hadn't been trailing along behind good ol' boy Bennett Buchanan.

"Damn, that took forever." He stopped in front of a restaurant. "You must be starving."

"I'm sorry I ate all your pecans."

"Plenty more where they came from."

She glanced up at an awning bowing under the weight of half a foot of snow. They were at a restaurant called Boudin.

"We don't have to eat out," she said. "We can just go to your place."

As soon as the words left her mouth, she regretted them. She'd only meant that she didn't need a fancy restaurant meal—she'd be perfectly happy to hit a bodega and hunker down at his place while she called around to figure out where she was going to stay tonight.

Or, you know, decided whether she was going to sleep with him.

Honestly, it was the path of least resistance, and that was usually how it went. Some dude would make advances, and if she had the itch, she would assess suitability. If the guy in question was being too over the top about her beauty, or about the fact that she was a model, she might deflect, but sometimes not, because really, beauty was what she had going for her, and there was no point in pretending otherwise. She had learned her lesson on that front. What do they say? *Fool me once, shame on you. Fool me twice, shame on me.*

Gia wasn't the kind of person who needed to be fooled twice.

But she didn't want to make it *sound* like she was entertaining the notion of sleeping with him, so *Forget the restaurant; let's go to your place* probably hadn't been the smartest thing to say.

He didn't seem to take it the wrong way, though, just held the door open for her and said, "This *is* my place."

"Oh. You live here?" She craned her neck—there did appear to be apartments above the retail level.

"Nope, but if you want food, we're better off here than at my apartment. I think I have tea and mustard in my fridge there, and that's pretty much it." When she didn't answer—she was confused—he said, "Come on. We're letting the snow in."

She obeyed, and was hit with a wall of the most wonderful smell. It was some kind of garlicky roasting meat, maybe, mixed with . . . something kind of herby and green?

A hostess approached. "Welcome to— Chef! I thought you were in Florida!"

Chef.

Ah, everything suddenly made sense. His claim that this was "his place." The incredible pecans.

"Flight was canceled." He shoved his bag and Gia's suitcase to one side of the vestibule. "Can you get one of the guys to take this stuff downstairs?" He took the garment bag Gia had been carrying and handed it to the hostess. "And make sure they hang this up?"

"Sure thing."

Bennett scanned the room, his eyes moving back and forth like he was reading something that required his utmost concentration. Gia followed his gaze. The place was narrow and deep—home to maybe twenty tables along a banquette that ran along one side of the place as well as a bar. It was dark and cozy, lit only by candles. And that *smell*. Oh, God, that smell. Gia wanted to bottle it so she could spritz it around at will.

"What the hell is Eddie doing behind the bar?" Bennett called after the retreating hostess.

"Blanca called in sick." She shot him an anxious look over her shoulder.

"Blanca called in *snow*, you mean." His pacifying tone from the airport was gone, replaced by something rigid and sharp and unforgiving. The hostess grimaced, and he waved her on.

"Come on." He gestured for Gia to follow him into the restaurant's dim interior. At the bar he pulled out a stool for her. Then, eyeing her handbag, he pulled out another one. "I think that bag is going to need its own stool."

She shrugged. "I like big bags and I cannot lie."

The corners of his mouth turned up. She was proud to have made him smile. Which was strange. Usually it was the guy making lame jokes at her.

"Chef?" said the man behind the bar, presumably Eddie. "Oh, thank God. Everyone keeps asking me how oaky the chardonnay is and shit. The only reason I haven't totally ruined your rep is that it's pay-what-you-can night, so the bar is lower."

"The bar is *not* lower on pay-what-you-can night," Bennett said sharply, and there was so much barely tethered ire in his voice that Gia winced on the bartender's behalf.

"Right. Sorry, Chef."

Bennett walked behind the bar and rolled up his sleeves. "I imagine they're behind back there without you?"

Eddie nodded.

Bennett sighed and hitched his head toward the rear of the restaurant, which was all the urging Eddie needed to hightail it back to the kitchen.

Then he turned to Gia. "What are you drinking?"

"This is your restaurant," she said, stating the obvious, because standing behind the bar with a sense of ease that couldn't be faked, he looked like the king of the castle.

"Yep." He must have decided he wasn't going to wait for her drink order, because he reached for a bottle of wine from a rack above the bar and set to work uncorking it.

"I need those juleps, Eddie." A frazzled-looking server set a piece of paper down on the bar, not realizing Eddie wasn't bartending anymore. "And two glasses of sauv blanc."

"You got it." Bennett set a wineglass in front of Gia and poured a generous amount of ruby liquid into it.

The server looked up, startled. "Chef?"

"Hey, Tosha. We're a bit behind here, but I'm gonna get us caught up."

"You'd think we'd be dead in this weather," Tosha said.

"Nah. Not on pay-what-you-can night. Do me a favor and put in an order of the boudin—straight up and balls—

for me, will you? Tell them to rush it. I'll have your juleps up by the time you're back."

"Pay-what-you-can night?" Gia asked as he produced a bowl of the magical pecans and slid them across to her. "What does that mean?"

"Exactly what it sounds like. You order, we feed you, you pay what you're able to. If you can't pay, that's okay— you can still eat."

He set a bunch of other stuff in front of her, too: a cutting board, a bowl of limes, and a small knife. "Some people—like you—pay in labor." He took one of the limes and demonstrated what he wanted her to do—cut it into sixths but cut off the pointy ends first, and then spear a cocktail skewer through each of the resulting wedges. His hand moved fast, producing six perfectly shaped wedges in a matter of seconds.

She opened her mouth, but then she closed it when she realized she had no idea what she meant to say. Her impulse had been to object, but why? The place was clearly slammed. And if the rest of whatever he was planning to feed her was as good as those damned pecans, she'd gladly work for her supper. This was certainly more interesting than the usual "You're so gorgeous; I can't believe I'm out with an actual model" date.

Not that this was a date.

She took a drink of her wine. She wasn't a connoisseur, but as with the pecans, there was a layered complexity to the wine that was both startling and delightful. It started out tasting like berries but deepened into something darker, almost smoky. It was an unexpected juxtaposition. It was also utterly delicious.

Well, hell. She took another drink—tried not to make it too obvious a gulp—and picked up a lime.

They worked in silence for a few minutes, Gia chopping, Bennett...dancing. It was really the only word for it. He moved quickly but with laser-like precision, every reach, pivot, and pour perfectly calibrated to achieve his aim with both economy and grace, his concentration unshakable. He was utterly in control of himself and his surroundings.

When she finished with the limes, she pushed the cutting board forward slightly—not more than an inch or two. But he noticed and wordlessly replaced the limes with a bowl of lemons with one hand while he garnished a margarita with the other.

She paused for a moment, part of her still feeling like she should be objecting to being put to work like this, but when she cast around for a reason, she couldn't come up with anything, so she picked up the knife again. She was probably still on the defensive from the shoot, where she'd had to accommodate all manner of unreasonable requests, from "Can you try to stop shivering, because your nipples are showing" to "Can you stand on one foot while we do this next section of shots because your one leg looks weird like that and it will be better if it's not in the shot."

Bennett was already back to his work anyway, so the window for her to object had closed. He'd made an astonishing number of drinks in the ten minutes they'd been here. Currently he was methodically dividing a bunch of mint he'd muddled among four glasses.

This would be perfect for today's picture. On the train she'd thought idly about taking a picture of the snow later, but suddenly she wanted to capture the image of his calm, masculine grace at the center of all the kinetic energy of the restaurant.

She dug in her bag for her camera, looked through the viewfinder, overrode the flash so he would be lit only by the candlelight, and took her time waiting for the perfect shot. She would only have one chance, because that was how her system worked but also...

"Did you just take a *picture* of me?" He turned to her, his brow knit in bewilderment.

...because you couldn't be stealthy with a Polaroid camera. Especially this old-school one—it sounded like an old man wheezing when it took a picture.

"Yep." She stuck the camera back in her purse and set the photo on the bar.

His bewilderment turned to amusement as he bent over the photo, which was doing its wonky slow-mo developing thing. "Why?"

Usually people commented on the Polaroid aspect of things, the retro novelty of an instant camera.

"I do this thing where I take one photo a day."

"And what do you do with the pictures?"

She dug around in her bag and extracted a Sharpie. Careful not to touch the still-developing image, she wrote the date on the white bottom part. "I do this, and then I stick it in my bag. I keep meaning to get organized and get a scrapbook or something, but I'm not very crafty." She chuckled, thinking back to her friend Elise's wedding. Maybe she should get the Queen of Pinterest on the case.

Bennett was back to work, pouring shots of whiskey into the mint- and ice-filled glasses. "So is your bag one of those bottomless Mary Poppins–style ones?"

Her bag was legendarily large, and there were a lot of photos rattling around in there, but her Polaroid habit was pretty new. She'd stolen the camera from a job about three months ago. It had been another unpleasant shoot. The photographer had been going for a retro look, so in addition to the regular setup, he'd been shooting "candids" with the Polaroid. But when "candids" turned out to also mean creeping on the girls while they were changing, he'd suddenly discovered his camera had gone missing.

The server called Tosha reappeared at the bar, and as if on cue, Bennett garnished the last of the mint juleps he was making for her and set it on a tray with the wine she'd ordered.

"How are they doing in the kitchen?" he asked.

She just rolled her eyes, said, "Pay-what-you-can night," hoisted the tray of drinks, and took off.

"So," Gia said, "how often do you do pay-what-you-can night?"

"First and third Sundays." Bennett wiped his hands on a towel and leaned over the bar to look at the still-developing photo.

She turned to take in the full room. "So all these people can order whatever they want and pay you literally nothing."

"That's right."

"Sounds like an excellent business plan," she teased.

He was still hunched over looking at the picture. "It's not business. It's charity."

Huh. Of course it was charity, but honestly, she'd expected him to have some other angle. Everyone had an angle in this city—or at least in her slice of it.

"But not of the bullshit, society-pages variety," he added, his lip curling up in a sneer. "Not that kind of charity."

"What kind, then?"

He looked up suddenly and met her gaze. His stillness, after he'd been in motion for so long, was jarring. His *attention* was jarring.

The candles on the bar bathed his face in warm light. He looked like he belonged in a painting. "'If anyone has the world's goods and sees his brother in need, yet closes his heart against him, how does God's love abide in him?' *That* kind."

Was he...quoting *the Bible* at her?

Bennett craned his neck toward the kitchen. "Where the *fuck* is the boudin I ordered?"

Yeah, there was no "probably" about it anymore. She was definitely going to sleep with him.

—⁂—

Bennett shouldn't have come back. He should have just taken Gia to the Mexican place two doors down. It was better that he not know what a shit show his place became in his absence, despite the fact that they'd gone over and over how everything was going to operate while he was out of town.

And the way everyone kept saying, *Oh, well, it's just pay-what-you-can night.*

Fuck that shit.

Someday Boudin would be a full-time pay-what-you-can restaurant—a place where anyone could come for a meal, regardless of their ability to pay. A community restaurant. He had to believe that. He forced himself to keep the faith even when it seemed like no matter how much money he managed to save, it would never be enough to make it happen. It was what he'd been working for all these years. Why he was living in one room. Why, Noah's wedding aside, he never went on vacation.

But until then, he was doing this high-low thing, where he hosted fancy people most of the time and opened the doors to everyone a couple of times a month. The juxtaposition made for some snobbish remarks, even from his own staff, which made him irate.

When he'd caught up on the drink orders, he burst through the doors to the kitchen and shouted, "I ordered boudin, y'all. Where is it?"

"Shit—that was for you?" said Izzy, the kitchen's expediter, whose job was to stage-manage the employees during rushes.

"Yes. And I also want a large house salad."

Without waiting for a response—he tried not to be as much of a dick as most chefs, but he knew how to keep a kitchen in line—he picked up a couple of plates that were ready to go and headed back out.

He pasted on his game face. Years of practice had enabled him to tamp all his shit down and present a calm, welcoming face to customers.

"Gumbo." He set the first dish down in front of a man who didn't meet his eyes. "And the snapper." The man's companion was a thin woman with deep lines around her mouth and eyes.

"Thank you," she said, the two words infused with more feeling than the usual throwaway expression of gratitude. When he let go of the plate and started to retract his arm, she laid her hand on his forearm and said it again. "Thank you."

He knew how she felt. He knew that when you were hungry and someone did you a solid, it felt important to thank them.

He also knew his response should be casual, that he shouldn't call attention to the charitable aspect of the evening. "You're most welcome. I hope you enjoy."

He noticed that neither diner had a coat warm enough for a regular February day in New York, much less this particularly nasty one.

You know who else hadn't dressed for the weather?

Not to mention seemed like she hadn't had a decent meal in a week, given the way she'd demolished his pecans?

He turned, taking a moment to study the model at his bar.

The difference between Gia and his customers this evening, though, was that her situation was entirely self-inflicted.

Which was not something he had a lot of sympathy for.

But Lalande would have fed her just the same, so Bennett would, too.

He and Tosha walked up to the bar at the same time. Bennett hitched his head toward Gia, and Tosha set down the plate of food in front of her. Bennett went back behind the bar to refill Gia's wineglass and to pour himself a glass of tea.

"I can't possibly eat this all," Gia protested.

"You don't have to." He produced a side plate from behind the bar. "I'm going to help you."

He was starving. He stabbed a ball and took a bite. There it was. Things might be a little unbalanced in terms of the service this evening, but the food was absolutely up to snuff. His shoulders relaxed a little.

"Meatballs?" Gia peered at the plate like it was rotting roadkill. "And..." She furrowed her brow. "Some kind of pâté?"

"Kind of. It's all boudin, which is a traditional Louisiana sausage."

"Same as the name of the restaurant."

"Yep. We serve a few different kinds. It's all based on a pork-and-rice filling." He pointed to what she'd thought was pâté. "This is boudin blanc. Loose sausage—no casing— which is how it's traditionally eaten." He picked up a piece of baguette. "You spread it on bread. Maybe add a little mustard if you're into that. Which you should be because we make our own, and it's pretty amazing if I do say so myself."

"And these?" She pointed to his most popular menu item.

"Boudin balls. Deep-fried sausage balls, basically." He picked one up and broke it in half to show her the darkly hued interior. "Made from our boudin noir."

"You *dye* them?"

He barked a laugh. He would personally murder anyone he caught with food dye in his kitchen. "Nope, the red is from pig's blood."

He eyed her. Was she going to be the kind of person who would happily eat one part of an animal but blanch at eating another?

Yes, yes she was, judging by how quickly the fork that had been on its way to her mouth reversed direction.

"Deep fried isn't really my thing." She pulled the fork out of the meatball and made a fake apologetic face. "Kind of a job hazard."

He tried not to sneer as he turned to fill a new drink order, but damn, he had *no time* for people who were afraid of real food. "I ordered you a salad, too," he said, forcing his tone to be neutral. "It should be here soon."

"It's here now." Ruben, Bennett's sous-chef, came up behind Gia and set down the restaurant's house salad, which was Bibb lettuce, roasted beets, shaved fennel, and some of the pecans Gia had hoovered earlier, with a creamy tarragon dressing served on the side.

Ruben wasn't wearing his whites, and he stepped behind the bar. "Everything's under control back there now. Let me do the bar, and you can enjoy your evening."

Bennett didn't argue. Ruben had been with Bennett for years—he'd come up from New Orleans after Bennett opened Boudin—and was a trusted deputy. He wouldn't jeopardize the evening's service by bailing on the kitchen if he was needed there.

"Thanks." He came around to sit next to Gia. "Ruben, this is Gia, one of the bridesmaids in Noah's wedding. Our flight was canceled."

"Oh, shit!" Gia said, cutting off Ruben's attempt to greet her. "We should be on the phone trying to rebook!"

She whipped out her phone, and Bennett saw Ruben stiffen. Ruben knew how Bennett felt about phones in his restaurant. All his staff did. He made them go stand out back when they wanted to use theirs.

"I'm not picking up a cell signal," Gia said. "Must be the storm. What's your Wi-Fi password?" She didn't look up as she asked, so she didn't see Ruben grimace.

"No Wi-Fi," Bennett said mildly.

She did look up then, her face composing itself into an expression that would have been a more appropriate response to his confessing he murdered puppies in the kitchen. If he'd entertained the notion that someone who carried around a Polaroid camera might be refreshingly low-tech in other ways, that look of hers crushed it. "You don't have Wi-Fi here?"

"Nope." Bennett speared a bite of her salad and swallowed it along with his anti-Wi-Fi rant. It would only fall on deaf ears. Cute ears, he noticed, as Gia tucked her hair behind one of them—it was small and perfectly shaped and sported a tiny ladybug earring that was completely incongruent with her prickly personality.

Ruben moved aside and pointed behind him to a sign that said, "Wi-Fi Password: Eff off and talk to each other." Everyone always thought it was tongue-in-cheek, but Bennett was dead serious about it.

"Wow." She blinked several times. "Wow."

He took pity on her and got out his own phone, but he had no service, either. "I have a landline at my apartment. Finish your dinner, and we can call when we get home."

She looked for a moment like she was going to argue some more, but then she stabbed a beet and popped it into her mouth.

"Oh my God." She blinked rapidly. "This is a *beet*? I've never tasted anything this delicious. What did you do to it? Give it a hand job?"

Ruben burst out laughing.

"They're lightly smoked, then roasted." Bennett tried not to smile, but damn, Gia was funny. "Glazed with a little raw macadamia oil." At least she had good taste in root vegetables.

"Try the dressing," Ruben said, because in Bennett's restaurant, even a lowly salad dressing was given the star treatment.

But what did you want to bet Miss No Blood in My Sausage wasn't into fatty, creamy dressings with her beets?

Gia speared another beet and barely dipped one end of it into the dressing. It emerged with the tiniest speck of dressing on it, and she ate it. It would be enough, though.

As if on cue, her eyes widened. "Oh my God. That *is* good."

She redipped the beet—more generously this time— but then said, "Oh, sorry. If we're sharing, I shouldn't be double-dipping."

Bennett made a "go right ahead" gesture. "We take double-dipping as a compliment around here." They ate in silence for a minute, until he remembered the photo, which was on the other side of her. "Hey, can I see that picture? Is it done developing?"

She slid it over to him. He was at the center of the image, in profile. The focus on everything else was soft.

The candle flames at the edges looked like small, fuzzy, yellow suns. It was hard to say why, but the picture evoked energy and activity.

He liked seeing himself this way, at the center of this place he had built. Inhabiting this life he had made out of nothing.

He wanted to ask if he could keep the photo, but that would be weird. Anyway, she'd already labeled it. It was destined for her bag.

"So you gonna make it to this wedding?" Ruben asked, drawing him from his thoughts.

"We have to," Bennett said. "I've got the rings."

"Eh," Gia said dismissively. "They can buy cheap stand-ins for the ceremony. I have the *dress*."

"And they can't buy a cheap stand-in for that?"

"No, because the whole point of a wedding dress is that you wear it at your *wedding*. That's its one and only function. The rings you wear forever."

Bennett opened his mouth to argue, but actually, she was right.

"Besides," she said, "the dress belonged to Wendy's mother. Wendy's parents are both dead. And Wendy is...well, she's one of those people who really had to work for her happily ever after, you know what I mean?"

"If she's anything like Noah on that front, I do know."

"You've met her, right?"

"Yeah—a couple times. Noah was a regular here before he hit the road with Wendy, and we lived in the same building, too." Bennett missed Noah. He hadn't really realized how much he'd relied on him until he was gone. They had a similar outlook on life, because they'd both had to work hard to get where they were. Neither of them took things— or people—for granted.

"Actually," Bennett went on, "the first time I met Wendy, she was sitting right where you are." He chuckled, thinking back to the night Noah first brought Wendy in. Anyone with eyeballs could see that they were perfect for each other, but Gia was right about their happily-ever-after being hard won. It had certainly taken them long enough to catch on to how well suited they were. He looked down at the untouched sausage plate. "She ate an entire order of the boudin balls, in fact."

"Aren't Chef's balls amazing?" said Ruben, who had been following their conversation. But then, belatedly, he grimaced as he realized he'd phrased the question awkwardly.

But it was too late. Gia did not miss a beat before calmly informing him, "Actually, I haven't tasted Chef's balls." Then she paused ever so slightly before adding, "Yet."

Bennett laughed even as a flare of heat traveled through his body. "Well, you haven't lived until you've tasted my balls. They're legendary. They get rave reviews."

He thought it would stop there—that was probably about enough suggestiveness, given that he and Gia didn't really know each other—but she looked right at him and said, "I bet they do. Engorged with all that blood."

Damn. Was she…propositioning him? He would think so, except for the fact that she'd spent the previous several hours of their acquaintance acting like she was barely tolerating him.

He had to admit, she was tempting. Despite her appalling lack of taste—she hadn't even tried any of the sausage. And her appalling manners—he thought back to her behavior at the airport.

She was just so goddamn *pretty*. Pretty and picky and entitled.

It was more than pretty, though. Beauty was ultimately superficial. There was something else about Gia that pulled him in, something hard to put into words. It was like there was a mystery simmering under the surface, a restlessness—like she was floating above the world rather than actively participating in it. He wanted to know why. Even her dead-pan humor, as funny as it was, seemed a way for her to keep the world at arm's length.

It would have to remain a mystery, though, even if she *was* hitting on him. Bennett didn't do casual. Not anymore.

But Jesus Christ, when she picked up a boudin ball—with her fingers, not her fork—and slowly brought it to her mouth, her eyes on him the whole time?

He kind of wished he *did* do casual.

She licked her lips before the ball made it to her mouth. He expected her to take a bite. His balls were pretty big—ha. But no. She opened her mouth wide and carefully placed the whole thing on her tongue.

And gasped as her eyes widened.

"Oh my God," she said, the phrase barely recognizable through the mouthful. "Oh my *God*."

Well.

Shit.

Chapter Two

*I*t was totally immature. And mean. Bennett didn't have a coat—Gia was still wearing his—but she couldn't help it.

Bennett's back, as he trudged ahead of her, made such a perfect target.

Since she'd decided she was going to sleep with him, she could consider this foreplay. He'd gotten her to eat deep-fried pig's blood—no, to *enjoy* deep-fried pig's blood—so she was pretty sure he could coax out other forms of enjoyment as well.

There were lots of ways to seduce men, if you could even call it that. Not to be conceited, but it usually didn't require too much effort on her part. And hey, if you were going to be blessed/cursed with looks that matched the current cultural norms for beauty, why not use them? Especially if they were the only currency you had.

Still, she hadn't resorted to throwing a snowball to get a

boy's attention since, oh, about fifth grade. What was next? Was she going to pull his hair?

An image arose in her mind's eye then, unbidden, fully formed, and a little bit shocking: her hands tangled in his hair, pulling his head between her legs.

She shivered, not from the cold, and let the snowball fly.

"Ooof!" He whirled, surprised and indignant. He took a moment to assess the scene, to confirm her guilt, then said, "You are going to regret that." His voice was low and sure and so very...southern. It carried through the fast-falling snow and lodged deep in her core.

She was pretty sure she was *not* going to regret it.

Bennett had no free hands—he was carrying his bag and her suitcase. So she stooped and scooped up a bunch more snow. She got another two balls—what was it with them and balls?—off before he abandoned their luggage to a snowdrift and started retaliating.

"Ahhhh!" Gia used Wendy's garment bag to block his first volley, only belatedly realizing that using the priceless family heirloom wedding dress as a shield probably wasn't helping on the "make sure the wedding goes off without a hitch" front.

She looked around and, spotting an awning extending from a shuttered grocery store, ran for it, shrieking as several incoming missiles hit her back. Once there, she hung the dress and her purse on the awning's crank and ducked behind the wooden structure that would have been used to display produce in more agreeable weather. Conveniently, there was a huge snowdrift within arm's reach—in the ninety minutes they'd been in the restaurant, the storm had positively dumped snow.

Sheltered as she was, she was able to get off several direct hits while avoiding most of the incoming ones. She also had the advantage of knowing her way around a snowball fight. You didn't grow up in Canada with an older brother and survive otherwise.

Bennett wasn't packing his balls tightly enough—ha!—so they often disintegrated before they reached her, and when they were still intact, they were mere puffballs. Hers, on the other hand, were well packed and lethal.

As she pummeled him, she erupted with laughter, and wow, it had been a long time since she'd laughed like that—probably not since the last time she'd gotten together with the girls. Bennett's sputtering and empty threats only made her laugh harder. She ignored her frozen hand and kept up the onslaught until he approached with his hands up, like she had a gun. "I surrender!" he said, his deep-blue eyes dancing under snowflake-studded lashes.

I surrender.

That phrase always had the effect of immediately jolting her back in time...

She was nineteen and in Ibiza on her first big overseas job. Savoring the taste of money and youth and freedom. Dancing in a dress a designer had given her that retailed for more than a semester's tuition had cost.

I surrender was the first thing Lukas ever said to her. It was his opening line as he approached her on a dance floor, hands up. Then, as he'd come closer, he'd mimed being slain by her beauty.

She had found it all charming. But she'd been nineteen and naive.

"You okay?" A hand appeared. A gloved one. It was Bennett, postsurrender, reaching down to help her up from her battle station.

She reminded herself that she was no longer nineteen and naive, and took Bennett's hand. As soon as she was on her feet, she dropped it and went to retrieve the dress. She waited, squinting up the street, while he collected their luggage. Visibility had noticeably decreased, even since they'd left the restaurant. She'd been telling herself all night that they'd be able to get on a flight out tomorrow, but she was going to have to face facts. No one was getting out anytime—

"Ahhhh!" A wall of snow rained down on her from behind. So much snow that she couldn't see.

"You bastard!" she yelled, whirling on him. How had he done that? That had been a wheelbarrow's worth of snow.

Or, you know, a recycling bin's worth.

"Oh, shit, sorry, that was too much, wasn't it?" He dropped the bin, contrition written all over his face, and started brushing the snow off her hair.

She should have told him there was no such thing as "too much" in a snowball fight, that it was every man for himself, and that he'd just made a genius move. Instead she stood there and let him stroke her head. After he'd brushed off as much snow as he could, he lifted her hair from the neck of the coat and tried to turn the collar up to better shield her from the storm.

"Crap." His face fell when he came around to stand in front of her. She must look like a drowned rat.

"I'm okay," she said, suddenly seized with the desire to reassure him.

"Let's get you inside and warmed up."

She couldn't argue with that plan. Couldn't even work herself up to retaliating. Though she bore him no grudge as it related to the snow, she was suddenly freezing. Like, wet and miserable and cold-inside-her-bone-marrow freezing.

"Come on." He slung an arm around her shoulder and angled his body against the wind, which was a chivalrous but futile gesture given the relentlessness of the storm.

They turned a corner, and he pointed. "It's just up there."

Wow. "Up there" was a giant, Tudor-style building that looked like a castle.

But the castle was an apartment building, and Bennett's unit was...not the palace Gia had expected.

Well, okay, not that she expected anyone in Manhattan to live in a palace. But according to her observations—and her taste buds—Bennett was an exceedingly talented chef. And those pay-what-you-can nights would suggest that he did well enough with his restaurant that he could afford to literally give food away at least some of the time.

But he lived in a studio. A big studio, but it was still only one room.

But then again, her impression of how top chefs lived was based on Food Network shows, so who knew?

As she shrugged out of her wet coat and toed off her boots, she scanned the space, which grew more interesting upon further inspection. It was small, but it was far from your standard bare-bones bachelor pad. It was exquisitely decorated. The walls were paneled with whitewashed wood, and the furniture was light, too—a pale beige sofa, a fluffy armchair, and an artfully distressed trunk repurposed as a coffee table made up the living portion. A narrow marble island separated the main room from the kitchen. In the far corner, a queen-size bed was piled with white bedding, and there was a big window seat at the end of the room flanked by flowing white curtains. Ornate mirrors that contrasted with all the white simplicity of the rest of the space hung in various spots and made the apartment feel much bigger than it actually was.

"This place is gorgeous," she said, and she meant it. And so not what she would expect from a thirtyish single man, much less one who quoted the Bible at her with one breath and made suggestive banter with the next. What was this guy's *deal*?

"Can't take much of the credit, I'm afraid." He took her coat—which was actually his coat—and hung it in a small antique wardrobe next to the door. "When I bought this place, I hired a designer and told her to make it look like home."

"And where's home?"

"Charleston."

That made sense. The room looked like it belonged in the pages of *Southern Living*.

"Yeah," he went on. "I showed her some pictures of the house I grew up in, which was pretty big, and said, 'Make me that in miniature.'"

"Well, it's amazing."

"She did a good job." He smiled, taking in the small space with obvious affection.

She'd thought, when she'd first met him, that his smile was smug, and maybe that first one had been. But this one, the first real, full-size one she'd seen, was not smug. It was big and guileless—she didn't see a lot of that in her line of work—and charmingly lopsided. The right side turned up more than the left.

"If I squint my eyes, I can almost smell the magnolia trees," he said.

"You're homesick." Gia wanted to be homesick, suddenly. She imagined it as a kind of dull emptiness that was always with you, like a toothache that never got better, one you couldn't stop prodding with your tongue, paradoxically comforting in its persistence. What must it be like to feel so attached to a place that you hired a decorator to recreate it?

"Homesick? *No*."

He'd spoken so sharply, his vehement answer so out of

proportion to the benign statement, that she turned to him. His brow was deeply furrowed, but when he noticed her looking, his features rearranged themselves into a smile that was clearly false. She'd seen the real one a moment ago, and this was not that.

"Not really. Just not a fan of the cold in New York."

She had no idea what had just happened there. Clearly the guy had some baggage, which, fair enough, considering her own little Ibiza flashback.

But they didn't know each other well enough for baggage, nor were they ever going to, even if she slept with him. So, in an attempt to get them back on more comfortable ground, she opted for teasing. "Not one for snowball fights?"

He looked at her for a long time, like he was trying to figure something out. "Not historically," he finally said, opening the armoire again and producing a towel. "I'll try to get through to the airline. Leave me your info, and I'll rebook both of us. You go take a shower and warm up."

A shower.

Normally the suggestion that she take a shower would have been a loaded one. It would have been delivered with a wink or an intense look. Not a vow to perform air-travel-related logistics. She wasn't sure how to proceed here, and that was not a spot she found herself in very often.

He'd grabbed a second towel from the armoire and was using it to dry his hair. Why was his hair so pretty? She would stop dyeing hers forever if she could have that deep, rich, so-brown-it's-almost-black hair.

Well. All right. Usually she didn't have to initiate these things, but it wasn't like she wasn't capable of nudging this situation along a little.

"I can call a friend and find somewhere else to crash..." She let the sentence trail off in order to test the waters.

She waited for the knowing look. For the come-on.

"Are you kidding me?" He shook his head like a dog, his hair falling perfectly back into place, walked over to the window, and pulled back the curtains. It was as white outside as it was inside. "You are not going anywhere, my friend."

There it was. Maybe not the come-on she'd hoped for, but he didn't want her to leave.

She smiled and took the towel.

"I'll take the sofa. Bed's all yours."

The smile slid off her face.

—⁓—

Gia disappeared into his bathroom, and Bennett enjoyed a whole ten seconds of peace, a respite from the unrelenting beauty of the model he'd inherited for the night, before she called out, "Holy crap!"

"What?" He ran to the bathroom door, afraid she'd fallen or something. He still felt like an asshole for that last assault on her during the snowball fight. If her feet were as wet as his—neither of them had been wearing footwear appropriate for this epic a storm—she might have slipped on the tile in the bathroom.

But then he stopped at the door. He couldn't barge in unless she truly needed help. "You okay in there?"

The door opened a crack. It was a large enough crack to make evident that she was wearing only a towel.

And that she hadn't fallen or otherwise been the victim of a bathroom tragedy, so he took a deep breath and a step back.

"I just pulled back your shower curtain to reveal the most *amazing* bathtub. Can I take a bath instead of a shower?"

"Of course," he said, because that was the correct answer. He did have a pretty amazing bathtub—it was a giant claw-foot soaker—but Jesus Christ, Gia stretched out inside it naked? That was not a visual he needed right now. "Take your time. I'm sure I'll be on hold with the airline for a while—if I can even get through."

And I'll need some time to get the image of you in my bathtub out of my mind.

"Thanks."

Was it his imagination, or did she open the door a bit wider before she closed it? Hold it open for a beat too long and sort of...smolder at him?

No. No. That had to be a trick of his slow-moving, cold-addled brain.

Thirty minutes later, he was stretched out on the sofa listening over and over again to a recording assuring him the airline cared about his call, when she emerged.

There was a billow of steam from the bathroom, and it was almost like when you were at a play and they used that liquid nitrogen to signify that Something Serious was happening. Like Gia was actually the Ghost of Christmas Yet To Come or something.

But that was ridiculous. Bennett had been haunted by a lot of shit, but he'd done his time with his ghosts, had already undergone his own personal Ebenezer Scrooge–esque reckoning. Hell, he was already feeding the Tiny Tims of this godforsaken city.

Gia was wearing what probably passed for pajamas in her universe: baby blue shorts with white lace trim and a fitted spaghetti-strapped tank top made of the same soft-looking material.

And the shorts were *short*. They didn't extend much beyond the tops of her thighs. Or maybe it was just that her

legs were long. Ridiculously long. Long, perfect expanses
of flawless skin.

Her hair was damp; little tendrils curled around her face,
which was bare of makeup. Seeing her like this made him realize how much she must have been wearing before. It was like
a mask had come off. And holy shit, did she have *freckles*?

She did. Just a smattering, but he never would have
known. Those secret freckles…damn. They got to him.

He sat up, moving his legs from where they'd been
stretched out on the sofa. It wasn't an invitation, more that
her appearance had moved him to sit up straight, to come
to attention. But she seemed to take it as one, sitting on the
sofa rather than the armchair angled next to it.

He set the phone to speaker mode and laid it on the
coffee table. "I'm losing hope here. We might need to give
up until tomorrow." He started to rise, intending to make
up the sofa for himself, but she stopped him with a foot.
She'd swung her legs onto the sofa, and now she pressed
the ball of one foot down on the top of the center of his
thigh, as if she wanted to prevent him from getting up. Her
toes, like her ears, were small and perfectly shaped. They
were painted with bright orange polish the exact color of the
middle stripe on a piece of candy corn. He had the strange,
startling urge to put one of those toes in his mouth, almost
as if it *were* a piece of candy.

"*Thank you*," she said, her tone urgent enough that it
drew his gaze from her foot. "I don't know what I would
have done if I hadn't run into you tonight."

That was an outright lie. She'd told him on the train
in from Jersey, after her calls to hotels hadn't yielded a
room—and again just now—that she had colleagues she
could stay with. And anyway, Gia was about as far from the
damsel-in-distress type as it was possible to be.

"I'm pretty sure you would have landed on your feet." The phrase brought his attention back to her literal foot, still resting on his leg.

The foot that started moving upward toward his rapidly hardening dick.

The overture felt half-surprising, half-inevitable.

And oh God, it had been such a long time. He swallowed a groan.

The foot inched up a little bit more. Shit. He was wearing flannel pajama bottoms—he hadn't been kidding about hating the cold—so she'd be able to see the effect she was having on him. He sneaked a glance at her face, and yep, she was riveted by the tenting in his pants. A little smile played at the corner of her lips as she stared at his lap with unbroken concentration, like she was a Jedi master with the power to make men pop woodies with her mind.

But whatever. It wasn't a crime to get turned on. It was, in fact, the logical response to what was happening. He was a mortal man, and Gia was unnaturally beautiful.

It was what he did with that attraction that mattered. That dictated the *kind* of man he was.

He let his hand fall and wrapped his fingers around her ankle. She must have initially thought that he meant it as a sexy gesture, because she pointed her foot and curled her toes and let loose a breathy sigh.

Fuck. That *sound*.

Worse, he was even beginning to *like* her, with her quirky jokes and her old-school camera.

Bennett reminded himself that he was, above all things, disciplined. Discipline was what you needed in a kitchen, and it was what you needed in life. Everything he had today, the life that he'd created for himself out of nothing, was the result of it.

So, even as every nerve ending in his body screamed bloody murder at him, he gently lifted her foot and moved it aside. Off his body. Stood and angled himself away from her as he opened the coffee table trunk that housed the extra bedding. Tried to be casual. Better that than to make a big "it's not you; it's me" speech.

"I changed the sheets on the bed while you were in the bath, so it's all ready for you." He waited a beat, preparing to tear down her argument if she tried to insist that she could sleep on the couch. Or, worse, if she tried to push things further. He didn't want to embarrass her, but he would if he had to.

But all she said was, "You're going to sleep on the sofa?" and it wasn't a suggestive question. She'd gotten his message.

"I do half the time anyway. I usually fall asleep watching TV."

After a beat she said, "Okay."

Her voice was small and sounded almost defeated, but he had to make that not his problem.

All right then. He forced himself to move like a normal person and not a sex-starved robot as he tucked a sheet over the sofa cushions. Forced himself not to watch her pulling back the covers on his bed and sliding under them.

"I'm going to hit the shower," he said when he was done making up the sofa. He'd changed into dry pj bottoms and a T-shirt while she was in the bath, but his hair was still wet from the snowball fight, he was freezing, and, frankly, he was going to have to beat off if he was going to survive this night.

⌒◯

Gia was going to be an insufferable bitch tomorrow. She'd held herself back from lashing out at Bennett earlier, but as she slid under the covers of his bed, a cocktail of shame and lust whished through her veins, making her body practically vibrate. By tomorrow the lust would have faded, leaving only the stinging humiliation of rejection, and that could not be tolerated. She would have to cover it with something else, something less weak.

God. He hadn't even said anything to cushion the blow. No *You're really pretty but I actually have a girlfriend/am a devout Catholic/am secretly gay*.

No, he had just calmly removed her foot from his leg. The worst part was, she'd thought at first that his touch heralded a different sort of intent. That initial contact as he'd banded his hand around her ankle had seemed so possessive, so heated.

She wanted there to be a reason for the rejection, was the thing. She wanted to know *why* he didn't want to sleep with her.

Maybe he didn't find her attractive.

If that was the case, she had nothing else to offer him.

Which stung like hell.

But sometimes the truth hurt.

I surrender.

Bennett's line from earlier popped back into her head, reminding her of memories she'd rather forget.

It had just been a line, probably one Lukas had used a dozen times before her—and after her.

But she had fallen for it without reservation. She knew his type now. Model collector. A certain kind of guy who frequented spots where models hung out. Often, as had been the case with Lukas, they were part of a posse attached to an actual famous dude.

The worst part of it all, the shame attached to the memory, was how quickly and enthusiastically she had remade herself for him. She had changed her hair for him—dyeing it a yellow blond because "Blondes have more fun, right, Gia?" She had turned down a job, too, at a critical point in her career, in order to stay on for a month and party with him and his friends. He'd badgered her about it so much, and she'd mistaken that manipulation for love. She'd thought they were on the verge of something real. How stupid she'd been. She could only console herself that she hadn't *told* him she'd fallen in love with him.

The heartbreak had faded relatively quickly, but the shame stuck with her.

She usually tried not to think about it—she'd gotten quite good at not thinking about it, actually.

But her defenses were down today. The shitty shoot, the battle with the gate agents, Bennett's rejection. This accumulation of little cuts was the only reason she could think of that her mind kept hamster-wheeling itself back to that day on the beach.

They'd had a water fight—not unlike the snowball fight from earlier. Fun and sun and happiness and *surrender*.

And then, when she'd come back from the bathroom much later in the day, tiptoeing up behind him with a bucket of water, intending to get him, what she heard him saying to another of his B-list posse-mates was like a bucket of cold water dousing her.

Gia is *a hot piece of ass, isn't she? But you know who's hotter? Sheena Shelly. We've been messaging, and I think I can get with her. She's going to be one of the Victoria's Secret models this year.*

Sheena Shelly was another model on the shoot. A seventeen-year-old who'd already walked in two Paris

Fashion Weeks. The comment hurt, and not just because it broke her heart. It was the first time she'd felt genuinely self-conscious about her body, the first time she'd been upstaged by a younger model.

Frozen, Gia stood there and watched Lukas get his phone out and show his friend a string of sexts between him and Sheena.

The only good thing about that day was that she had dumped her bucket of water on him—and his phone—before walking away forever.

Actually, that wasn't the only good thing. That had also been the day she'd vowed never to let herself get collected again.

She'd stuck to that vow, and it had served her well. If anyone did any collecting these days, it was Gia.

The shower stopped, the squeak of the pipes as the water turned off suddenly yanking her out of memory lane. She listened to the sounds of Bennett moving around in the bathroom and reminded herself that the world was full of men. Florida would be full of men. There was going to be one at this wedding who wasn't already part of their tangled web of friends. And what was Gia's motto, forged that very day in the Ibiza sunshine? *One man is as good as another.*

She was already facing away from the main room when Bennett came out of the bathroom, but she closed her eyes just in case.

She didn't hear the airline's recording anymore. Maybe he'd given up for the night. Maybe he'd taken the phone off speaker and had it to his ear. She wasn't going to look. Regardless, another day was not going to go by without a plan to get her ass to Florida, with or without the best man.

Preferably without.

But enough brooding. She needed to remember what

was important, and it certainly wasn't Bennett Buchanan, or even her wounded pride. No. Gia's focus for the next week was that Wendy's wedding go off without a hitch. Wendy was the third of their friend group of four to get married in as many years. Gia was the last woman standing. Before Wendy had been Elise and Jane. Elise's and Jane's weddings had both been sites of some serious bridesmaid drama. Not among themselves—they weren't *Mean Girls* types. No, she was talking about Man Drama. Because her best friends, God bless them, had never quite been able to get on board with Gia's motto.

But that was okay. Just because love wasn't in the cards for Gia didn't mean she didn't want her friends to be happy. Gia might not have a ton going for her, but no one would ever say she wasn't a good friend. She valued her girls more than anything. Sometimes it felt like even though Gia's face and body were plastered all over the world in ads and editorial spreads, the girls were the only ones who really *knew* her.

So *nothing* was going to mess with Wendy's wedding. Gia was going to do everything in her power—and possibly some stuff not in her power—to make sure that Wendy had the drama-free wedding of her dreams.

There was some rustling as Bennett settled on the sofa. The sound of blankets being arranged and him shifting around. She'd wanted to protest earlier, when he'd announced his intention for her to sleep in his bed. It didn't seem right that she, the interloper, should get to sleep in his big comfy bed while he contorted his long body to fit onto the sofa. But she hadn't trusted her voice at that moment, and acquiescing had been the path of least resistance.

He flicked off the light next to the sofa, and the room went dark.

And silent. So totally, creepily silent. Maybe it was the snow blanketing everything. Maybe it was being so far off the beaten Manhattan path. Either way, it made Gia feel like she was in a mausoleum. Like she'd died but her stupid heart hadn't gotten the memo and kept thundering along in the charged darkness.

It was weird to be lying in the same room with a man but not *with* him. To be in a bed in close proximity to a man who had no interest in her.

When was the last time that had happened?

Never. It had never happened.

Her cell service was still out. She wanted to ask Bennett if he had Wi-Fi here, so she could text Elise—but she didn't trust her voice not to betray her. The insufferable bitch would come out tomorrow, but as of now, she hadn't quite arrived.

Instead she pulled the covers up over her head and typed a long text to her best friend, even though there was no way to get it to her.

Chapter Three

FIVE DAYS BEFORE THE WEDDING

Gia Gallo was not a morning person. And that was an understatement.

Bennett glanced at his watch for what felt like the hundredth time as he waited for her to come out of the bathroom. He'd given a moment's thought to telling her he'd meet her at the restaurant, but it had snowed all night and it didn't appear that the sidewalks were shoveled yet. He wasn't enough of a dick to leave her to mush through all that alone.

But Jesus Christ, she had been snippy this morning as they'd settled on a plan: go to the restaurant for breakfast and keep trying to call the airline. If they hadn't gotten through by mid-morning, they'd go back to the airport and try to see an agent in person. Her cell service had been restored, so she'd spent the entire conversation madly texting. Gone was the joking, almost-companionable woman he'd dined with last night. Or, for that matter, the silly, laughing woman who'd started a snowball fight with him.

This morning, she reminded him of the way she'd been at the airport.

She was probably one of those people who needed a few gallons of coffee before they could function.

Or, more likely, last night had been an aberration and she actually *was* an intolerable shrew.

When she finally came out of the bathroom, she looked completely different than she had when she'd gone in, which only added to his sense that any softness he'd seen in her last night had been an anomaly. There was no sign of the fresh-faced, freckled beauty with the sleep-mussed hair. She had been replaced by Gia Gallo: Model. It was weird, because when he tried to delineate it, it wasn't like there was that much objectively different. She wasn't wearing a lot of makeup, or at least she'd thoroughly mastered the natural look that was not actually natural at all. Her hair, which had been made curly from air-drying after her bath last night, had been scraped back into a severe bun almost on the top of her head. She was wearing jeans and a loose, short-sleeved gray T-shirt that wasn't nearly warm enough.

None of those things should have been enough to change her entire look, her very essence, but somehow she had completely transformed herself. It was like she was wearing a hyperrealistic mask. Or, again, maybe he had it backward. This was the real her, and the softer, more vulnerable woman who had seemed, for one astonishing moment, to want him was the aberration.

Then he noticed she was still wearing the tiny lady-bug earrings. It was the one accessory that spanned both versions of her.

"Ready to go," she said flatly.

"Great." He rummaged around in the armoire for something warmer for her to wear. It had temporarily stopped snowing, but the forecast said it was only a lull, and it was still freezing out there. He emerged with his old beat-up leather jacket. He hadn't worn the thing for years. Fourteen to be precise. He wasn't even sure why he held on to it. Everything else from that period, and certainly from that specific night, he'd gotten rid of. Hadn't wanted any of it—wished it had gone up in flames along with the car.

Except the jacket. He hadn't been able to make himself throw it out, even though he never wore it. It was like he needed one souvenir to torture himself with, to remind him of who he used to be.

She fingered the soft, distressed leather but made no move to actually don the jacket.

"I don't keep a lot of shit around here, so it's all I have to offer you that even remotely passes for a winter coat, unless you want to wear that sucker again." He nodded at the parka hanging over one of the stools at his kitchen island. He didn't know what he'd do if she wanted the parka. That would leave him with the leather jacket, and that was not acceptable.

"I packed for Florida," she said.

Which explained the short-sleeved shirt. And the tiny pajamas.

But she said it self-righteously, defensively, like he had accused her of something a lot more severe than being caught unaware by a storm.

She put on the jacket. It was too big in the chest, but she was so tall that it fit otherwise.

It looked good on her. Well, anything would look good on her. This looked...*really* good.

They made the short trudge to the restaurant in silence, Gia with her phone to her ear, presumably on hold with the airport. It took a lot longer than it should have thanks to all the snow. It was hard to imagine they'd get out of town today.

"What time do you open?" she asked as he cleared enough snow from the front door to allow him to swing it open.

"Eleven normally, but we're closed on Mondays."

There was a homeless guy huddled on the sidewalk outside. Bennett dug out his wallet and handed him a ten-dollar bill. "The back door to this place is really snowed in. If you want to help me clear it, I'm good for breakfast and coffee."

"Thanks, man. I appreciate it."

"I'll meet you out back in ten. There's a shovel out there."

Feeling Gia's eyes on him, he glanced at her as he unlocked the door. Her head was cocked like she was confused. Then she switched her gaze to watching the homeless man, who was plodding away, presumably heading for the alley behind the restaurant.

"What?" he said.

She turned back to him, still with that quizzical look. "That was really nice." When he didn't answer right away— he was uncomfortable being praised for meeting minimum standards of human decency—she added, "I mean, he doesn't have to be out here. There are all kinds of emergency shelters open in weather like this. You gave him ten bucks. Most people would not be that generous."

Bennett shrugged and gestured for her to precede him inside. "I'm not sure *nice* is the word."

"What's the word then?"

"*Responsible*," he said without hesitating.

"What does that mean?"

"It means that people should take care of each other. Take care *with* each other. I don't ever want to be the kind of person who puts my own convenience ahead of other people's well-being." *Or at least I don't want to be that kind of person ever again.*

He was aware that he probably sounded like some kind of goody two-shoes, but he didn't care. It was his truth—his hard-won truth. And Gia was not going to be a permanent fixture in his life, so he didn't care what she thought of him.

As they made their way through the dark restaurant, he snagged a bar stool, and once inside the kitchen, he set it up at a metal worktable that had a bit of an overhang.

"Oh! Hello!" Her eyes lit up as she sat. "I was on one of yesterday's canceled flights, and I'd like to rebook, please."

She'd gotten through. Good. It wasn't urgent, in theory. They had plenty of time. But he was starting to feel kind of claustrophobic being cooped up with her. Gia had a way of taking up way more space than her slender frame should have been capable of occupying. At least she was being polite as she explained their situation to the agent on the phone, so maybe she would manage to get them on a flight.

"Thursday!" she shrieked. "Thursday is way too late!"

So much for polite.

She held the phone away from her ear for a moment and said to him, in an only slightly lower tone, "Nothing's going today. They say the next flight with room is on *Thursday*."

"Yeah. I got that." He rolled his eyes, and he didn't even try to hide it. He grabbed a French press, dumped some of the restaurant's prepared coffee mixture into it, and set a kettle to boiling.

She rolled her eyes back as she returned to the phone. "Thursday is not acceptable."

Thursday, while not ideal on the whole "get the hell out of this winter nightmare" front, seemed reasonable enough, given that the wedding wasn't until Saturday.

"What about bumping someone?"

Jesus Christ. Was she actually suggesting the airline bump a booked passenger in favor of her?

"No, I am not transporting organs," she snapped.

Yup. She was suggesting that.

Of course she was.

"Listen." Her voice had taken on a conspiratorial quality as she changed tactics. "I'm a bridesmaid, and I have to get to a wedding. I have the bride's dress with me. She needs to get it sooner than Thursday. So it *is* kind of an emergency."

He cringed as he slowly lowered the plunger in the coffee press, embarrassed on her behalf.

"Fine," she snapped. "I'll just be taking my business to your competitors, then."

She jabbed an angry finger at the phone to disconnect the call, and he poured her a cup of coffee.

"Cream? Sugar?"

"Black."

Of course. Just like her heart.

He moved to the fridge to get the jug of sweet tea— the restaurant served it, but they also kept a personal jug for him back here.

"Oh my God."

He smiled. He couldn't help it. They made amazing coffee, if he did say so himself—and he wasn't much of a coffee drinker to begin with.

And, damn, he loved how every time she put something he'd made into her mouth, her response was "Oh my God."

"What is in this coffee?" she demanded, and leave it to Gia to be angry over being fed something delicious.

"It's got chicory in it, some cinnamon—New Orleans style." He decided to play dumb. She hadn't actually said she liked it, after all. "I can make you some regular coffee if you don't like it."

"Are you kidding me? This is the best coffee I've ever had. I might have to take a picture of this coffee."

He shouldn't need her praise. He *didn't* need her praise. But his body must not have gotten that message, because her words heated him from the inside.

He sipped his tea to try to cool himself off. "Aww, don't do that. It's only eight in the morning. Don't waste today's photo on coffee."

She'd grabbed her bag, but she must have agreed with him, because she set it back down. "Why are you drinking iced tea?"

"I'm not much of a coffee drinker. I sometimes have a cup after a meal, but that's about it."

"But it's freezing outside."

He shrugged. Weather didn't really factor into it for him—it wasn't a day unless he'd had a good half gallon of sweet tea.

"There's not enough caffeine in tea."

"That's why I made you this." He slid the French press toward her. "It's all yours. You can slit open a vein and mainline it for all I care."

She snorted. "I'm going to call another airline."

"Let me ask you something." He held his palms toward her like she was a spooked horse he was trying to tame. She raised her eyebrows at him impatiently from behind the rim of her mug. "Just for the sake of argument. The wedding is Saturday. There's some kind of dinner on Friday. I know it's a disappointment to be here in snowmageddon instead of on the beach, but realistically, what's wrong with Thursday?"

"I. Have. The. Dress." Gia spoke slowly, like she was talking to a child, and a simple one at that.

"Which is for the wedding on *Saturday*," Bennett replied, deploying the same tone.

"Wendy has a tailor lined up to do a final fitting on Wednesday at four."

"But I thought she had it tailored here?" Bennett had hung out with Wendy and Noah when they'd dropped in to New York for ring shopping and dress fitting. Wasn't that the whole reason those objects were here now and in need of transport to the wedding?

Gia sighed, and some of the fight left her. "She came to New York to have some work done on the dress. She's wearing her mom's dress, but she wanted to have the sleeves changed, which isn't a minor operation. She went to a bridal salon that I recommended. That I got her into, because you have to know someone for this place. In fact, I'm the one who insisted she get the dress altered here rather than in Toronto. These people are the best in the world, I said. So she had the work done here, and left me with the job of picking up the dress and delivering it."

Okay, so she felt responsible. Not that that excused her rudeness. But at least it contextualized it.

"Anyway, you don't just get one fitting on a dress done. You need tweaks at the end." She performed an exaggerated sniff.

"Excuse me for not knowing how wedding dress fittings work," he snarked, hating that she could bait him sufficiently that he'd rise to it. With Gia there seemed to be a disconnect between the things she made him say and his rational mind. He had a lot invested in there *not* being a disconnect. He'd worked hard to ensure that his rational mind ruled over impulse. But that sniff had set him right off. It reminded him of his mother. It took a pretty good dose of arrogance to just assume that everyone knew the ins and outs of the high-fashion world—or, in his mother's case, of old-money southern etiquette.

He was also pretty sure Gia was making this into a much bigger deal than it needed to be. Wendy wasn't the kind of person who was going to freak out over circumstances that were beyond their control, and surely if a tailor could make "tweaks" on Wednesday, he or she could just as easily do it on Thursday or Friday. But Gia clearly felt responsible. Irrationally so, maybe, but, to be fair, he understood the suffocating weight of responsibility.

Breakfast. That was what they needed. An infusion of calories might make them both less cranky. "What can I make you for breakfast?"

She paused in poking away at her phone. "Can you do a soft-boiled egg?"

"I can. I can also make you an omelet, eggs Benedict with or without our famous crab cakes, the best croque-monsieur you ever had. And of course I can do boudin in various incarnations. You name it."

"Just the egg, please."

"Waffles," he went on, realizing that he'd forgotten to list the restaurant's sweet brunch items. "No beignets as it's Monday, but I can do cinnamon sugar French toast in a sort of beignet style."

"I'm good with an egg, thanks."

"*An* egg. As in one egg?" She had an award-winning chef—hey, Bennett didn't do false modesty—at her fingertips, and she wanted a single egg?

Well, whatever. Time for him to calm the fuck down. It wasn't like he had any investment in what she consumed.

"Yes, thanks."

He got out a pot, filled it, and set it to boil. Then he paid a visit to the refrigerator to find something for himself. He would have made her anything to order, but for himself, he'd eat whatever needed to get used up. Today that was . . .

"Jesus Christ."

"What? What's wrong?"

Gia's tone was alarmed, which he felt bad about, so he tried to modulate his tone as he answered. "Oysters."

"Oysters?"

"Yup." He pulled out the tray. At least the mollusks had been properly stored—they were resting on damp newspaper and covered with moist towels. "The idiots who closed up last night should have eaten them, or taken them home. They won't keep until tomorrow." He prodded one to make sure it was still tightly closed and therefore alive and edible.

"Curse those losers for leaving you a tray of oysters," Gia teased.

"They didn't know I'd be here. As far as they know, I'm en route to Florida."

She sighed plaintively. "One can dream."

He got out a shucking knife. "I have this thing about food waste. It makes me insane, basically." He picked up one of the oysters and slid the blade between the shells. "Some of it is inevitable—it still makes me insane, mind you, even when it's inevitable—but this was just outright stupidity. I *hate* throwing food away."

"My dad did, too. He used to have this thing he called the clean plate club. He never made you take anything, but if you took it—if you put it on your plate—you weren't leaving until it went in your belly."

"Ah, I know this club. My nana was the same. I guess I grew up to be a card-carrying member."

"My mom used to be the opposite, though." Gia stared into space like she was remembering, but it must not have been a nice memory, because her mouth was pinched. "She was obsessed with dieting. She'd take food off my plate when my dad wasn't looking, and wrap it in napkins and throw it away. She was like the anti–clean plate club, I guess."

That was fucked up. Bennett paused in his shucking and eyed her. "I'll pop your egg in and come back to this."

"No way! Eggs are for plebes. I'm having oysters for breakfast."

He grinned and resumed shucking.

"But you should probably send something outside to the homeless guy."

"Oh, shit." He'd completely forgotten about that. What had he just been thinking about Gia taking up all the space in a room? He poured a to-go cup of coffee and set about microwaving some leftover jambalaya he found in the fridge. "Excuse me for a sec."

He went outside—the guy had cleared the alley so the back door opened easily. He held out the coffee and food. "Thanks, man. You're welcome to come in to eat this— get warmed up."

The man declined, so Bennett told him about pay-what-you-can-night and sent him on his way.

"I've been trying to figure out a way to repurpose leftovers," he said when he came back inside, returning to the topic of food waste as he resumed shucking oysters. "Food banks mostly take nonperishable stuff, but we don't end up with much extra in the non-perishable department because we order only what we need. I mostly have the perishables down to a science, too, and honestly, the dumpster-diving crowd gets the rest, which sounds gross, but there's a difference between produce that's high-enough quality to serve here and produce that's actually gone bad—a good few days' difference. It's the leftovers that dog me. You wouldn't believe how much cooked food gets thrown away, either because we have a slow night and make too much or because people don't finish their plates and don't want doggie bags." Which was another thing that drove him crazy. Who came to a nice place like his, spent money on dinner, and then declined to take the leftovers home? That was the problem with this fine dining bullshit; people were too hoity-toity for their own good. He would take pay-what-you-can night any day. That crowd always joined the goddamned clean plate club. "I wish there was a way to match up hungry people with leftovers."

"You know what you could do..." Gia's brow furrowed like she was thinking hard. "Plug in a refrigerator outside—out back. Stick the leftovers in there. I read about something like this once when I was working in London. It became kind of a thing. Other people—not even people associated with the restaurant—would leave fresh food in there, too. Anyone who needed it could come and take it."

Bennett stopped shucking. He was dumbfounded. Because that was... simple. Effective. "Brilliant," he declared.

"You would probably have to do battle with city inspectors if they found out," Gia went on. "But call it a community refrigerator."

Exactly. His limbs buzzed with excitement. He couldn't yet afford his fully nonprofit restaurant—where every night was pay-what-you-can night—but a community refrigerator was a pretty good stepping stone. He even had a refrigerator in the kitchen that was underused; with a little reorganization, it could easily be moved outside.

"You'd get some good press," Gia went on. "I could help with that, if you like. Then the city becomes the big bad wolf who wants to throw away food and starve homeless people and stifle innovation and all that."

He slid a plate of shucked oysters to the middle of the table between them, then moved to a fridge to grab the trio of dipping sauces they served with oysters. "You are a genius."

She shrugged but also flushed a little. "Nah. That article just stuck with me for some reason."

"Well, thank you." Gia might be hard to take sometimes, but she had just solved one of his most enduring, nagging problems. He decanted the sauces into three little dishes and gestured to them in turn. "Horseradish, traditional mignonette, and lemon dill."

Gia picked up an oyster, drizzled some of the lemon sauce—his favorite—on it, made an anticipatory noise that was half sigh, half moan, tilted her head back, and slurped it up.

God help him.

Oysters were supposedly aphrodisiacs. Bennett had never found them to be personally, but customers who ordered them often asked about the concept. He always answered that the scientific explanation was that they were loaded with amino acids that increased sex hormone production. And depending on how uptight his customers looked, he might add a joking wink-wink throwaway line about the oysters' resemblance to a certain part of the female anatomy.

But maybe he'd had it all wrong. Maybe the aphrodisiac power of oysters was in watching the right sort of person eat them.

Gia lifted her head, but her eyes remained closed. Would she fall back on her post-tasting refrain?

"Oh my God."

Yes. He was still batting a thousand. Not that he'd cooked the oyster or done anything to prepare it other than contract with the best supplier in the city and then throw together a simple sauce, but he'd take the credit anyway.

Gia sighed—a big, heavy, contented one—and picked

up another oyster. She was in her own world, not aware of him at all, so he was free to watch her graceful neck extend as she tipped her head back again. God, it was as bad as watching her eat the boudin balls, though this time she wasn't doing it on purpose. Worse, maybe, because of the barely-there, delicate slurping noises she made as she transferred the oysters from their shells to her mouth.

She worked her way through half a dozen while he watched, torturing himself.

Then, as if she were coming out of a trance, she shook her head and looked down at the plate, then up at him.

"I'm sorry! I'm hogging them all!" She slid the plate toward him, but he held his hands up.

"Nah, that's okay. They kind of lose their appeal when you have them around all the time." Which wasn't actually true, but the pleasure of eating oysters was nothing compared to the pleasure of watching Gia eat oysters. "They're all yours."

A slow smile unfurled as she pulled the plate back.

⌒◌

Triumph.

Gia hung up the phone and did a little victory wiggle-dance on her stool.

"Well?" Bennett looked up from where he was doing prep work for the next day with a few members of his staff.

"We can fly out of Baltimore tonight. The storm hit from Philly northward, so there are no flight disruptions there. I got us on a seven o'clock flight this evening, and the trains are still running out of Penn, so we're set."

He flashed her a smile that…kind of took her breath away. There was just something about its crookedness co-existing with its intensity that got to her.

Which was dumb. He was just happy they had a plan to get out of town. "What time's the train?"

"Three thirty." She checked the time on her phone. "Which means we're suddenly awash in time." She was snowed in in New York City for the next several hours. What did she want to do?

She only had to think about it for five seconds. Normally she wouldn't even have needed to devote five, but she did spare a passing thought for the possible consequences if she messed up. But Wendy seriously would not care if Gia showed up bald, as long as she brought the dress. It was just an informal beach wedding in front of a handful of friends.

And anyway, Gia was an expert. She could always fix it later.

There were also the endless expanses of white in Bennett's apartment, but, once again, she was an expert.

"Any chance I can go back to your place and kick back a little now that we've got the travel sorted?" she asked Bennett.

"Sure." He flipped her the keys. "You need me to come with you?"

"Nope," she said. "But I do need you to tell me where the closest CVS is."

An hour later, she had rinsed away all evidence of her efforts and was eyeing her handiwork critically in the mirror. It looked good. She'd achieved an even application, and her hairline wasn't dyed too badly.

Suck it, Lukas. Blondes do *not* have more fun.

Unless *she* decided to be blond. She *always* had fun with her hair, no matter what color it was. Even though her first home dye job had been Lukas's doing, today she changed up her hair because it was a creative outlet. A kind of liberation. It meant she wasn't on a job. It meant she could be whoever she wanted to be.

She smiled at her reflection. And today she was a badass on the way to a wedding.

~~⌒~~

When Bennett got home a little after one o'clock bearing lunch and planning to get his stuff together for the trip, Gia had blue hair.

"Wow," he said as she beamed at him and performed a twirl. He could only surmise that she'd done this to her hair on purpose.

"Do you like it?"

There was only one answer here, given her obvious excitement, and that was, "Yes."

It wasn't bad. Per se. It was a sort of wash of color over her regular honey brown. The result was a kind of a pastel tint. There was something appealingly badass about it.

But it was *blue*.

Where he came from, only old ladies had blue hair.

To be fair, women Gia's age from his social circles in Charleston walked around with shellacked helmets of hair that made them look like their mothers ahead of their time, and this was certainly better than that.

"I don't have a job booked for at least the next month," she said, as if this explained anything. He must have looked confused, because she added, "I can't change anything dramatic about my appearance before a job, and I *love* dyeing my hair."

"You look like it's 1977, and you're off to a Ramones concert."

He'd meant that only as a statement of fact, but she

must have taken it as a compliment. She flipped her hair and grinned.

"I brought lunch." He unloaded takeout containers from his bag and set one in front of her. "It's only grilled cheese—Monday staff lunches are always simple—but these are made from the best gouda in the city."

"Oh, I'm not hungry."

How could she not be hungry? She'd eaten a dozen oysters five hours ago, and as delicious at they were, oysters weren't exactly caloric powerhouses. Maybe she'd snacked while dyeing her hair.

Whatever; not his problem. He would wrap it up, and she could eat it later.

"Well, it's a good thing you didn't waste your photo on the coffee this morning," he said between bites of his own sandwich. "Blue hair is much more photo-worthy than coffee."

"Oh, I never take pictures of myself."

"You document your life, but you're never in the pictures?" That seemed kind of odd.

"I pose for pictures for a living. I don't need to do it in my spare time, too."

Put like that, he could see her logic. And to meet someone not obsessed with selfies was kind of refreshing.

She got her camera out and opened it. "So I think I'll just snap a shot of you in this gorgeous apartment."

He was in the middle of a particularly gooey bite of sandwich, so it took him a moment to answer. "Nah, you can do better than me and melted cheese."

"That's true," she said, but she winked at him, and her tone was warmer than it had been earlier.

Man. It was going to be a long day. Gia Gallo was one complicated creature, and they had an epic journey ahead of them.

Chapter Four

*O*nce Bennett and Miss Blue Hair had settled in on their train to Baltimore, Bennett let out a big sigh. They were finally on their way.

He didn't like to leave the restaurant. But damn, now that he was away from it, it was...almost nice? Bennett loved cooking. Feeding people was such a powerful, elemental thing: transforming ingredients in the best possible way in order to nourish people. To make them happy, maybe, too, if he was lucky. But the business side of things he could do without. Payroll, insurance, inventory. He understood that all that shit was necessary, that he wouldn't have a restaurant without it. But honestly, he hated it. He hadn't even really realized how much until he was faced with the prospect of a week away from it.

Maybe he should give more serious thought to hiring a manager. He'd always resisted the idea, figuring that because he was so territorial, so obsessed with doing things his way, he'd be looking over the shoulder of anyone he hired anyway. So he just did everything himself. Lived and breathed Boudin. He had literally never taken more than two consecutive days off in the six years it had been open—and those had always included a Monday, when they were closed anyway. A week was unprecedented.

But if there was anyone he'd take a vacation for, it was Noah. The two of them weren't into displays of devotion, but they'd had a pretty serious bromance going there before Noah left town. Bennett was aware that he kept people at a distance since the accident. Even the girlfriends he'd had, he could see, in retrospect, he had somehow failed to fully let into his heart. But Noah had easily become a friend, probably out of sheer proximity. They lived in the same building, and Noah used to come to Boudin almost every day after work. He was a night owl, so they'd often go out after Bennett closed the restaurant, Noah for a beer and Bennett for an iced tea.

Plus Noah was just a good guy. They had a lot in common. They both worked a ton. Neither of them was into the party scene. And they both had almost singular priorities. His was the restaurant; Noah's had been the well-being of his sister and mother, whom he'd supported since he was a teenager and his dad died.

Shit, he missed Noah. It was hard to stomach the fact that he was never coming back to New York. Perhaps some trips to Toronto were in order. Now that Bennett was embarking on this whole strange "take a vacation" thing, maybe he could do it again?

"Hey," he said to Gia, who was staring out the window. "What's the weather like in Toronto?"

"Oh, you know, it's Canada," she said mildly. "We all live in igloos."

He suppressed a grin. "That can't be true, because I source some award-winning Riesling from the Niagara region of Canada, and I'm pretty sure igloos and climates that can support vineyards don't coexist. So there must be *some* part of that country that isn't freezing."

"Toronto's not that different than New York, actually," she said. "Hot and humid in the summer. Some snow in the winter, but also some rain and slush. When you get outside of the city, though, you get some really good snow."

"*Good snow*," he said, teasing her. "I'm not sure I understand those two words together."

"See? You do miss Charleston!"

His impulse was to say no, but maybe she was right. "I miss some parts of Charleston," he conceded. "The weather, for sure. I can't wait to hit the beach in Florida."

"Ugh." She wrinkled her nose.

"Ugh? Who says ugh about a beach? Beaches, like, calm your soul and shit."

"And get sand in your unmentionable areas. I've done enough posing on beaches to make me immune to them. Give me a forest for soul-calming purposes any day. I've been looking into this St. Petersburg place." She got out her phone, punched at it for a second, and handed it to him. She had called up a web page for a place called Boyd Hill Nature Preserve. "I'm a big hiker, but I've never spent any time in southern forests, so it's gonna be all cool and creepy. You guys have some weird-ass trees."

"The South *does* have some weird-ass trees. In my house growing up, our yard had a bunch of live oaks with moss hanging from them. You get used to them, but objectively speaking, they're kind of eerie."

"You miss those trees," she said.

"Yes." He did miss those trees. He hadn't thought about

them in years, but he did. He used to climb up into them when he was a kid, with a bagful of his nana's famous pecan shortbread.

"But not your family?"

He missed Nana. But she was dead. Had been since he was ten, way before his life went off the rails, which he was glad about. She'd never had to see him at his worst. "No," he said firmly. "I don't miss them."

"So you miss the weather and the trees." Gia's tone was skeptical, like that wasn't enough. Like he was withholding some portion of the truth. And she was right.

"I got my start in the restaurant business in Charleston, from this legendary local guy named Marc Lalande. He taught me everything I know. I miss him, and his restaurant."

He *did* miss Lalande. A lot. He had been more than a mentor. He had been the father Bennett needed when he broke with his parents. He had taught Bennett how to cook, but also how to be in the world. How to be a decent man.

"How long since you've been back?" Gia asked.

"I've actually only been back once since I left, which was fourteen years ago." That trip had not been pleasant. It had been too hard, it turned out, to suddenly be back in the land of his misspent youth. It was irrational, but he'd spent the visit constantly looking over his shoulder, alternately hoping and dreading that he might run into his parents.

"Why?"

He shrugged. "You know that saying, 'You can't go home again'?"

She looked at him for a long time, her amber eyes seeming to bore into his soul, but then suddenly she turned and pointed out the window. "What do you think? Picture-worthy? In a there's-beauty-in-decay kind of way?"

He appreciated that she had changed the topic—and he

was pretty sure she'd done so because she understood their conversation was probing too close to old wounds.

Wounds that maybe weren't as scarred over as he'd thought.

He leaned over her a bit to get a better look at the landscape. They were passing an abandoned gas station in snow-covered, decaying Trenton, Pennsylvania. "Nah. I personally think you should wait until we're on the plane."

"Or even *off* the plane." She nodded decisively. "Yeah. Today's picture will be of Florida."

That sounded just fine to him. Enough with winter for a while. Enough with morose thoughts of the past. He was *ready* for Florida.

———∽———

"Ladies and gentlemen, those of you in the gate area awaiting news of flight 2672 to Tampa, I'm sorry to inform you that it has been canceled."

Gia thought for a moment she might cry.

The answer to that impulse was to move. To distract herself.

She tried to get up as the gate agent droned on about the storm that had hit New York taking an unexpected dip south but found herself stymied by a large, heavy arm settling over her shoulders.

"Hey, it's okay. It's only Monday. We'll get there."

She geared up to specify that it was Monday *night*, that the storm was rolling in, apparently bent on stalking them, and that there was no cause for such calm optimism. But as she opened her mouth, it was like instead of expelling words from that orifice, her body got confused and sent a tear out of her left eyeball.

It was a fast-moving one that took her by surprise. She swiped at it angrily, but it did no good; he'd seen it.

"Oh, come on now, sweetheart, don't cry."

"Don't call me sweetheart." The clapback was automatic, and it had the effect of bringing her back to herself, her teary fragility hardening into something more familiar. She twisted away from his arm and stood.

His optimism was replaced by something, too, something stonier and less kind. "So help me, Gia, if you're on your way over there to rip that gate agent a new one, you're on your own from here."

The sudden switch was jarring. She had indeed been getting up to speak to the agent, but she must have still been weak enough, unshielded enough, that his threat reached some part of her that was still vulnerable.

"I'm going to the bathroom," she snapped instead and turned on her heel.

A few minutes later, after texting Wendy about the delay, she stood staring at herself in the mirror.

Why was she acting like this? None of this was Bennett's fault. And he'd been right—it wasn't the gate agent's fault, either.

She jumped when her phone dinged with Wendy's return text.

Seriously do not worry about it. The tailor says she will fast-track the dress whenever you get here. I've shown her pictures, and she says any work will be minor. So relax. I'm sure she can even do it Saturday morning if need be. Enjoy being snowed in with Bennett.

Then there was a string of eggplant emoji. Gia rolled her eyes.

Not sure Bennett's my type.

Which meant *I'm not sure I'm Bennett's type*, but she wasn't going to cop to that. Anyway, she took Wendy's larger point. Gia was known for what her friends called her manizing ways, and she was unapologetic about it. She worked hard, and she didn't do drugs or pop pills like so many models did. A girl had to blow off steam somehow, and, well, it had been a while. That was probably half the reason she was being so uncharacteristically emotional. She grinned and fired off another text.

But that's okay, because you know what I always say.

Wendy's return text quoting Gia's motto came promptly.

One man is as good as another.

Gia could practically hear Wendy's signature cackle. Then her friend sent a more serious text.

I'm sorry I kind of betrayed the cause.

After Elise and Jane fell victim to the wedding bug, Wendy and Gia had enjoyed a brief period of solidarity as the single ladies in the group, and Wendy had, like Gia, always been realistic about romance.

Or she used to be.

Nah. There's no cause. I'm just glad you're happy. Noah's great, and you deserve each other. And I'm going to get this goddamned dress to you if it's the last thing I do.

After pressing send, she thought back to her motto. There was a groomsman she didn't know down there, probably lolling on the beach right now.

Remind me who else is in this wedding party?

Wendy must have gotten her drift, because she sent an eye-rolling emoji and then:

Well, you know, Cameron. So that's not going to work out for you.

Gia actually did roll her eyes. Cameron was Jane's husband, which made him Noah's brother-in-law. He was also brother to Jay, Elise's husband, which made him Elise's brother-in-law, too. Her friends and their tangled web.

Who else is in this wedding party that isn't married to one of my best friends? You might have betrayed the cause, but have some sympathy for the last woman standing. The last woman standing who hasn't gotten laid in a long time. Who's the extra guy again? What's his story?

He's a friend of Noah's from law school, but I don't think he's really your type.

Why not?

Kinda prickly. A bit domineering.

Gia's face heated. She thought about Bennett at work in

his restaurant last night. She could use exactly those terms to describe him, and that certainly hadn't stopped her.

What's his name?

Tobias.

Full name?

Tobias Almanza. And you know, he lives in England, so you could hit him up when you're in Europe working. A man in every port sort of thing. LOL. But maybe that would violate the rule. Is there a distance exception to your whole one-and-done, two-and-through thing?

Gia didn't actually have a rule. Well, okay, she *did* kind of have a rule, but she hadn't given it that stupid name. Her friends had come up with that. She stood by the principle, though. Since she wasn't looking for a long-term thing, she would just as soon not be with a guy who was going to fetishize her for her looks or get all weird and swaggery about dating a model. The circles she had to run in were full of men who liked to collect models, and in the post-Lukas era, she'd die a million fiery deaths before she'd be collected. Even the odd less-gross man who didn't start out that way ended up starstruck, ended up subtly showing her off. Insisting they go to a certain restaurant whether she wanted to or not—that kind of thing. It was a subtle form of control, but no less insidious for its subtlety. Sometimes, to entertain herself, she would test guys. A couple months ago, for example, after a fun hookup with a stock trader, he'd asked her out. She'd shown up for the date wearing sweatpants and no makeup—which she'd actually done because she *liked* him.

They'd been going to some stupid finance-industry party. Watching Mr. Wall Street stammer his way through suggesting that she was underdressed—and then, when she didn't take the "hint," suddenly develop a "migraine" that prevented them from going to the party—had been amusing but also reinforced her stance on things. Had cured her of any lingering crush—forcing a guy to show his hand generally had that effect.

Whenever she felt herself getting too fond of a particular guy, she set up these kinds of tests.

They always failed.

So Gia's modus operandi was to shamelessly use her beauty to snag a guy, but then, before he could get too fixated on that same beauty, to cut him loose. It might sound a little mercenary, but it got her needs met.

One-and-done, two-and-through usually meant once. But if the guy totally rocked her world, she wasn't averse to a repeat performance. Any more than that generally made things messy, and disentanglement became an issue. The third time was *not* the charm for Gia—the third time was a time too many.

And since she was a perpetual globe-trotter, it was a system that worked for her. So, no, Tobias Almanza was not going to be her man in London, as Wendy was suggesting, but she was not opposed to making friends with him in Florida once.

Or twice.

She googled him. The name was unique enough that she got only a few hits. She clicked on his LinkedIn. Hello! Even from the formal corporate portrait, she could tell that Tobias Almanza would do just fine.

And the odds were that Tobias Almanza, unlike Bennett

Buchanan, would not be immune to her looks. She'd be on firmer footing.

She just had to *get* there.

She lifted her chin, assessed her appearance in the mirror, and found it up to snuff. With a fluff of her badass blue hair, she headed back out to deal with that problem.

"Hey."

Gia shrieked and jumped. Bennett was standing right outside the ladies' room. Her face got hot. She felt, irrationally, like he'd been privy to her text conversation with Wendy, but that was ridiculous. Unless he was a hacker in addition to a chef, her secrets were safe.

"Let's drive," he said.

"What?"

"Forget flying. Let's just hit the road."

"What?" she said again. She'd been prepared to do battle—nicely; maybe a little more nicely than she would have without an audience—again with the airline. It had never occurred to her that they could just take matters into their own hands. She spent so much of her time in cities like New York and Paris that she sometimes forgot that driving was a viable option in the regular world.

"Hear me out," Bennett said. "I spoke to an agent. They can book us on a flight out tomorrow evening, but the storm is just starting here; there's no guarantee that flight will actually depart. Florida seems far, but actually, St. Pete's is only a seventeen-hour drive from here—maybe a bit longer with bad weather. If we hit the road now with a goal of getting a couple hours under our belt, we can clear D.C.—hopefully ahead of the storm that's coming—find a place to stay, and then make a big push tomorrow. Even if we have to stay one more night on the road, we can still make it by Wednesday morning, easy."

Gia blinked, astonished by this plan. "That is—"

He must have thought she was going to protest, because he cut her off. "Look. The way I see it, we can either cool our heels for twenty-four hours and have no idea if the flight we're waiting for will work out, or we can rent a car and head south. Take matters into our own hands."

"—the best idea I've heard in a long time."

It was Bennett's turn to blink. He hadn't been prepared for her to acquiesce so easily.

"We've been talking and talking about this damn problem," she said. "I hate talking. Give me a man of action any day."

A smile blossomed, and he held out an arm like he actually *was* the star of a Reese Witherspoon rom-com. "Then we're off to the rental counters."

⌒

They weren't the only ones who'd decided to take matters into their own hands, judging by the lines at the car rental places. Bennett and Gia had split up—after exchanging phone numbers, each went to stand in a different line, hoping that should one company prove not fruitful, they'd have another option.

Bennett's phone buzzed.

They only have a Mini Cooper here.

He thought back to the big white blob he'd seen bearing down on them when he checked the weather before hatching this plan.

I was kind of hoping for something a little more...robust.

No kidding. Also...is this a bad time to tell you that I just realized my driver's license is going to expire the day after tomorrow? They won't rent it to me.

He eyed the counter ahead of him. There were two people in line before it was his turn. Taking a page from Gia's playbook, he elbowed his way up to the desk. Not to get all demanding, though; just to hear what was going on.

What was going on was an argument about how early *tomorrow* a car could be procured.

Mini Cooper it is. I and my valid driver's license will be right there.

"You didn't tell me it was a *convertible*," Bennett said fifteen minutes later as a pimply-faced kid tried to hand him the keys to a what seemed more like a toy car than an actual one.

"That's because *they* didn't tell *me* it was a convertible." Gia's eyes were wide as she took in the tiny turquoise insult to real cars everywhere.

"You don't have to put the top down," said the kid, and Bennett rolled his eyes as he prevented himself from saying, "No duh."

"You still want it?"

"Yes," Gia said. "We want it."

What had he been thinking, to suggest they try to outrun a storm? He tried not to panic. He really did.

But he must not have been doing a very good job, because a few minutes after they had driven off the lot and into the flurries, she said, softly, "Hey." He glanced at her quickly but then back at the road, such as it was—

all he could do was follow in the tire tracks ahead of him because the actual boundaries of the road were obscured by blowing snow.

"If it's too much, we can find a place to stop and try again tomorrow. At least we got a car. That's progress."

He shook his head. "If the storm is moving west and we're going south, it has to be only a matter of time before we're clear of it, no?"

Logic. That was the logical interpretation of their situation. Yes, the conditions weren't great, but if he went slowly and was careful, they'd be fine.

They'd turned the radio on in the hopes of finding a traffic report, but since the road was mostly deserted, he reached over and switched it off, wanting to eliminate all distractions. But taking one hand off the steering wheel called his attention to how badly he was white-knuckling it.

"Wendy told me she can get the dress fitting pushed back, so we really don't have to—"

"I'm fine, okay?" he snapped and immediately regretted it, because she didn't deserve that tone from him. That's how he talked to his staff, and only when they were being idiots.

She sucked in a breath and looked away from him, out the window into the white.

Shit. He sighed and unclenched his jaw.

"I was in a horrible car accident when I was seventeen." He had no fucking idea why he was telling her this. It wasn't like he owed her an explanation. *Anyone* would be on edge driving in these conditions. "The woman in the other car almost died."

"Ohhh," she said slowly, turning back to look at him. "Were you driving?"

"No. My girlfriend was. But only because we'd decided she was less shit-faced than I was."

Her eyes were wide. He had shocked her with his candor. "Oh God. Bennett, I'm so sorry. What happened?"

"I watched the paramedics work on her for what seemed like an hour. She coded. It was just like in the movies." He hadn't been too high to panic. He still remembered the terrible sinking feeling in his gut, the metallic taste in his mouth. It had been one of those crystalline moments when you're in it but also watching it happen from outside, aware that everything is about to change. "They eventually loaded her into the ambulance without having stabilized her. I found out later that she'd made it." And when he'd had to face her in court, all he could see was her lying on the pavement, the life seeming to bleed out of her before his eyes.

"And what happened after that?" Gia asked softly.

"My parents—I come from serious old southern money— hired a gold-plated defense team, and I got off entirely. My girlfriend—Grace—was not so lucky. She went to juvie for a year." His stomach churned as he let the memories in. "I tried to get everyone to understand that it was just as much my fault as hers—she was behind the wheel, but in terms of everything that put us into that car, we were equally culpable. Hell, I was *more* culpable. I was high as a kite on coke, whereas she'd just smoked a joint and had a couple shots."

The shame was as heavy as ever, pressing on his windpipe. It made no sense, but he almost felt worse about the way he'd used Grace than about almost killing someone.

He glanced at Gia again. She was listening attentively and didn't appear to be in any rush to interrupt him with false comfort like others usually did when they heard his tale of woe. And, strangely, that made Bennett relax a little—both mentally and in terms of the pressure on his throat—so he kept going.

"The lawyers spun it out like I was this golden boy, son of the South with huge potential that would be derailed if I went to jail, when really I was just an entitled addict. All my parents' powerful friends, including a US senator and an NCAA Division I basketball coach, wrote character references." God, just saying the words, even after all these years, made his tongue turn bitter. "It was utter *bullshit*. I was so fucking pissed. But I was also scared. And no one would listen to me. You know how you hear the term *white privilege*? Or *male privilege*?"

"Yes."

"It was that. Both of those things. A woman almost died because I thought I was too fucking invincible to call a taxi, and I paid *no* price for it."

"But Grace didn't get off?" Gia asked the question like she could see inside his head.

"Since she was driving, there was no way she was going to get off entirely, but they got her sentence way down." He couldn't help letting loose a snort of disgust at himself. "So she drives in my place because I'm way more fucked up than she is. I get off, and she goes to prison." He had almost killed one woman, and sent another to prison.

Gia whistled. "That's got to be tough."

It was, but it wasn't anything that was worthy of pity. Even though he had lived with the guilt every single day since, it was no less than what he deserved. So he merely shrugged.

"So what did you do?"

He thought about not answering, about changing the subject, but hell, why stop now?

"My parents shipped me off to the best rehab money could buy. I spent three months detoxing and talking about my feelings and shit."

"Did it work?"

"It did." No thanks to his parents—though they had at least paid the bill.

"And then everything was fine?"

He usually didn't talk about his past. In his New York life, Noah was the only one who knew about it. But it was turning out to be strangely easy to talk to Gia. Therapeutic, almost. "Nope. My parents refused to come to any of the parts of my therapy they were supposed to be involved in. There were these family counseling sessions where we were supposed to talk about our relationship and about supporting my future—helping me steer clear of drugs."

"That's harsh. Why send your kid to rehab and then not actually do what you need to do to make it work?"

"They wanted to just throw money at the problem to make it go away. That's pretty much how they handled anything even remotely unpleasant. They were obsessed with appearances—especially my mother. There was *no way* she'd lower herself to sit in a group therapy session and potentially talk about her own culpability in what had happened. Nope; in their eyes they'd written the check, and that was it."

"But what about when you got out? Didn't they want to set you up for success?"

"They didn't want me to come home afterwards. It was the summer after my senior year, and their plan was they'd ship me straight from rehab to Chapel Hill, where they wanted me to go to college—which, I hasten to add, I'd only gotten into because my grandfather and father went there and gave them a shit ton of money over the years." He snorted. "Let's just say that, drugs aside, I wasn't a model student in high school, but there's a building at Chapel Hill with my family's name on it. So my parents got me off the hook legally, paid a small fortune to clean me up, and then they told me I had to go to college to 'uphold the family name' or they would disown me."

"So did you go? I guess you pretty much had no other choice."

"I didn't go." He paused, remembering the fights they'd had when he'd called them from rehab, trying to reason with them. "Not only did I have no desire to go, I was seriously worried about relapsing there. I wouldn't know anyone. There would be booze everywhere, and probably drugs, too. I would be in over my head academically and therefore stressed out. I wanted to move home, get a menial job, and focus on staying clean. At least for the short term."

"Wow. You know, it manifested differently, but my mother was also obsessed with appearances. It must have been hard to move home and deal with that in a time when what you needed was unconditional support."

He didn't miss the remark about her mother and made a mental note to try to find out more about it later, but for now he was oddly committed to seeing his story through. Gia had somehow opened him right up like one of those oysters she'd eaten this morning. "It probably would have been hard, but I didn't get to test that theory, because they didn't let me come home. Having a recovering addict at home was not part of my mother's vision for her life. They said it was Chapel Hill or nothing."

"Like *nothing* nothing? Like, they disowned you?"

"Yep."

"But where did you *live*?" she asked urgently.

He was kind of touched by how invested she was in his story. Her concern seemed so at odds with the entitled, princessy attitude she so often projected. And also at odds with anything he deserved.

He shrugged. "Around. Couch surfed. The problem was

my old friends weren't good for me to be around. They were still partying every night." He paused, wondering if he should tell her the rest. "I lived on the streets for a while at the end there."

"Wow."

He had shocked her. It *was* shocking, if you only knew him in his current incarnation. But, gratifyingly, her shock wasn't tinged with lots of the stuff he often got when he told his story: disgust, pity, judgment.

"So that's why..." She trailed off, and he suspected she was thinking of their encounter with the homeless man outside his restaurant that morning.

"Yes," he said quietly, wondering how he could take some of the heaviness out of this conversation. He didn't regret telling her, but now that he was done with his tale of woe, he kind of wanted to move on.

What she said next accomplished the task for him. "How did you get from all that to having the best balls in Manhattan?"

He laughed, a big, genuine one.

"I was literally plucked from the street by Marc Lalande. He was a chef."

"This was the guy you were talking about on the train!"

"Yeah." After they'd spoken briefly about Charleston, Bennett had spent the rest of their train journey brooding over his old mentor. "He caught me eating out of the dumpster behind his place. He took me inside. More like forced me inside, actually—I was wary of everyone at that point in my life. He gave me dinner, but then he made me wash dishes afterward."

"Ah! All the pieces fall into place. Saved by a chef with a heart of gold."

"He would hate to be characterized that way—he was a

right bastard most of the time—but he did have a soft spot for downtrodden losers. It came from being raised in the church—his uncle was a Catholic priest, and he'd done the whole altar boy thing. And he *did* save me." Part of Bennett hated admitting that he'd ever been the kind of person who needed saving, but he absolutely had.

"So, cue the movie montage in which he gradually turns you into an upstanding citizen?"

He laughed again. He'd seen flashes of Gia's sense of humor last night, and it was coming out again today. She seemed to know instinctively that a little humor to leaven his story was exactly what the situation called for. "Pretty much. He was the first adult I met who didn't give a shit about my background, and so, paradoxically, I wanted to impress him. He fed me a few nights in a row, made me wash dishes, and then told me if I showed up every day and stayed clean, he'd give me a permanent job. So I showed up and stayed clean. He taught me how to get control of myself and my world."

"You make it sound so easy."

"It was, in a weird sort of way. I mean, it *wasn't*." He shuddered, thinking back to those nights alone, first in the restaurant office where Lalande let him sleep in the early going, and then in the crappy single room he'd rented in a grungy boardinghouse. When he'd been on the streets, he'd gone to meeting after meeting—usually several in one day—and had spent the rest of the time hanging out with his sponsor, who was a mechanic and let him lurk in the garage where he worked. The restaurant job was progress, but it had also meant less time for meetings. He'd spent his first paycheck on a phone so he could call his sponsor when, after a long shift at the restaurant, he felt like he was going to die of craving.

"It was the right opportunity at the right time for the right reasons," he said, making sense of it for himself even as he explained it to Gia. "I think some part of me knew I was headed for an early grave if I didn't stay off drugs. And the chance to actually make something of myself, without the assistance of all these opportunities I hadn't earned, appealed to some part of me that wasn't totally jaded. It was the first job offer I'd ever had that hadn't come from my parents' connections—and at the same time it felt like my last chance.

"And honestly, I loved being in the kitchen. The collective mania of the dinner rush, the satisfaction of performing an action and seeing a concrete outcome, whether that be a bunch of clean dishes or a plate of shrimp."

He smiled at those particular memories. He'd known right away, that first night in Lalande's kitchen as a proper staff member—a lowly dishwasher—that all the pain of staying clean was going to be worth it. And he had vowed to work every day of the rest of his life to deserve the second chance he'd been given.

"I worked my way up over the course of a few years from dishwasher to Lalande's sous-chef. Then he made me leave—kicked me out of the nest, so to speak. Sent me to a Michelin-starred place in New Orleans. I didn't love it, but I learned a ton there—about technique but also about how *not* to run a kitchen. The place was a mess behind the scenes. But it turned out I loved Cajun cuisine—Lalande's had been straight-up classical French. So after two years in New Orleans, I was bristling to start my own place."

"So you came to New York?"

He shrugged. "I was done with the South."

"Yet you ordered your interior designer to recreate it inside your apartment."

He quirked a grin. "What can I say? I'm a man of contradictions."

"All the best people are."

Why did that feel like the biggest compliment anyone had ever given him? The shame that had been unspooling in his gut earlier, as he had told her about the accident, was gone, leaving behind a not-unpleasant emptiness.

Silence settled, but despite the fact that he'd just massively spilled his guts, it wasn't uncomfortable.

A few moments later, she broke it by saying, softly, "Thank you for doing this."

"No problem. I think we're through the worst of the storm." Their conversation had distracted him, and now the visibility was better and the snow was tapering off.

"No, I mean the whole thing—the idea of driving. Putting me up last night. Putting up *with me* last night."

He thought of that foot. On his thigh. And damn him, he started to feel like maybe he'd made a mistake in rebuffing her. But no. If a man crumbled every time he encountered serious temptation, what did that say about him? And he had spent his entire adult life controlling his cravings. "Since we seem to be through the worst of it, how about pulling up a map and seeing if you can figure out a place to stop for the night?"

She smiled. "Sure thing."

"I'm starving." Now that the fear had passed, he realized just how hungry he was. And if it was true for him, it had to be doubly so for her. Even if she had snacked that morning, post-oysters, they'd spent the rest of the day with each other, and as far as he knew, she'd eaten nothing. "You must be, too."

The smile slid off her face, and she paused in perusing her phone and looked out the window for a moment. "I am," she finally said. "I am starving."

Chapter Five

They ended up checking into adjoining rooms at a Best Western in a little town about halfway between D.C. and Richmond, Virginia. Then Bennett left, promising to return with dinner.

Gia took a quick shower, then wiped a circle into the fogged-up bathroom mirror and stared at herself, just as she had done in the bathroom at the airport in Baltimore. Just as she had done in most bathrooms for the past year.

She sucked in her cheeks. Lifted her chin. Examined her angles.

Her stomach twisted in on itself.

She was so hungry.

Gia had a problem with food, and she knew it. Half the reason she knew it was that she spent a lot of time trying to convince people she *didn't* have a problem with food.

She told *herself* it was a little problem. A temporary fix. On par with "I'm going past the speed limit because I'm late for an important event but otherwise I'm a good and responsible driver."

But she was starting to fear that she was lying, even to herself.

She was going to have to get a hold on herself for this wedding, though, because Wendy was onto her. She'd made a few pointed remarks about Gia's eating behaviors, and she hadn't been wrong.

It was just that everything was different than it used to be. Not so long ago, Gia could eat whatever she wanted with no consequences. She would joke about her volcanic metabolism as she shoveled French fries into her mouth.

Then something happened. Age. Or so she assumed, as she'd gotten her thyroid checked and all that.

In her moments of rationality, she would tell herself that modeling wasn't ever going to be a career you did forever. She was already on the older end of things. Unless she wanted to move to catalogs, she didn't have that many more years ahead of her, no matter the circumference of her waist.

But she wanted to be the one who decided that. She wanted to say, one day, "I'm done," and have it be her choice. And—this was the key point—when she made that choice, she would have something lined up to move on to. Because even though she could easily afford it, she didn't want to just *retire*. Gia had been hustling her whole life, since her mother had entered her in her first pageant. She didn't know how to *not* hustle.

The problem was, she was deluding herself. There was nothing to move on to. She had no skills to speak of. She'd dropped out after her first year of university. Even before that, she'd never been good at anything—she didn't play sports, or chess. She didn't have a passion for politics or movies or anything like that. She'd had a moment there when she'd been in Girl Scouts for a year, and she'd loved it. Going for badges, learning how to do stuff. Selling cookies—she'd sold the most in her troop by far because she'd had the idea to set up a table outside an old-folks home. But then her mom had made her quit in favor of circus school, saying that Girl Scouts was taking too much time away from preparing for and competing in pageants.

Circus school.

Her mom had been convinced that it would help her clinch the talent portion of pageants, that it was something more memorable than dancing or playing an instrument. She'd been right, of course. There was nothing like a twelve-year-old walking on a wire strung eight feet off the floor to snag the judges' attention.

But short of running off to join the circus, Gia couldn't *do* anything. She had nothing of worth except her face. The size and shape of her body. Her physical shell. That phrase, *more than a pretty face*? It didn't apply to her. It sounded harsh, but Gia didn't believe in self-delusion.

She was kidding herself if she thought she could have a second career.

So then what was she left with, having reasoned herself full circle? Trying to hang on to the one she did have as long as she could. Trying to make sure episodes like that of two days ago—when she hadn't been able to fit into the size two they'd earmarked for her and had to switch dresses with Lily Alexander, who'd had to have the size two pinned— didn't become a thing. Because that kind of news traveled. She had an unplayed voice mail from her agent, in fact, that was probably on this very topic.

And so she was left with the one variable she could control: what went into her mouth.

But she wasn't even being smart about *that*. She wasn't

uneducated about this stuff. The way to slim down wasn't to consume twelve oysters all day—that would only put her body into starvation mode and make it harder to lose weight.

So. Okay. Bennett would bring back dinner. She would eat it. Then she would go to Florida, and she would eat there, too. Get herself back on track with actual healthy, careful eating, not just mindless calorie deprivation.

She could do this.

A knock on the adjoining door startled her. She scrambled to get into her pajamas. Her skin was fully dry. How long had she been standing there in her towel, brooding?

"Good evening," he drawled when she opened the door. He held two pizza boxes and a bottle of wine. His eyes raked down her body, as they had last night. She would have thought the assessment was heated, but that must not be right, given his reaction to her previous advances.

She stepped aside to let him in.

"Weather looks good for tomorrow." He set everything down on the small desk in a corner of the room. She brought over two glasses, and he grinned and twisted the cap off a bottle of red. "Best I could do under the circumstances," he said apologetically. "I figured no corkscrews at the Best Western, and I bought this at a place called Liquor-n-Gas."

"I'm not picky." She held out her glass and pondered the fact that she had given him no reason to actually believe that claim. A significant portion of their time together had involved him witnessing her going postal on airline officials.

He sloshed some wine into her glass, but when she held out the second one, he shook his head. "I don't drink. I just thought you might want a glass of wine after this day."

Oh, of course. He'd referenced drugs in the story he'd

told her about his past, but it made sense that he didn't drink, either. He was looking at her funny, though.

"What?" she said.

"Usually when I tell people that, they try to argue with me. How can you work in the restaurant industry and not drink? How can you have a credible wine list if you don't know what any of it tastes like?"

"Makes total sense to me." She lifted her glass to clink against his bottle of tea. "You just need to come up with some snappy comeback about how you used to be a meth-head."

He laughed, which gratified her, and she tipped her head back and drank, ordering herself not to think about how stupid it was to drink your calories.

She opened the pizza box. "This smells amazing." It smelled so good her hands started to shake.

"Yeah, I've learned that when you're in Nowhereville, USA, in search of food, your best bet is to find a local mom-and-pop pizza place and ask them for their best pie. This guy"—he pointed to the box, which read "Mister Tony's"—"turns out to have an actual Neapolitan granny. He's mostly churning out New York style, but I flattered him into doing us up a pizza Margherita that he makes for staff meals. Of course, the dough won't be right."

"Of course not." Gia tried not to smile. Bennett was pretty cute when he was geeking out over food.

"You have to ferment the dough for a true Neapolitan pizza..." He trailed off, belatedly realizing she was teasing him.

"And what's in here?" She opened the second box to reveal two enormous slabs of bread, each slathered with not only way more cheese than was on the pizza, but easily more cheese than she'd eaten in the past year. "You didn't have enough cheese on bread today at lunch?"

"There's no such thing as too much cheese on bread. And this version of it is Mister Tony's bestselling Wall of Cheesy Garlic Bread—that's its actual name."

"What happened to Mr. Fancy Chef, 'of course the dough won't be right because it's not properly fermented'?" Gia teased.

"I may be a 'fancy chef,' but I have a healthy respect for the marketplace. And Mister Tony says he sells two hundred orders of the Wall of Cheesy Garlic Bread a night—and this is not a big town. How could I possibly resist that?"

"You can probably write it off as market research. Anyway, are we going to talk about this food or actually eat it?"

They were going to eat it. She was going to eat it. She was.

She drained her glass of cheap wine first, because apparently she was the kind of person who needed Dutch courage to eat Neapolitan pizza.

But then, oh, but then.

She could taste every flavor—the mozzarella, the tomato, the basil, even the olive oil. It was delicious. Not otherworldly amazing like the food Bennett had fed her last night, but super tasty. A couple more bites, and she felt the life flooding back into her shaky limbs. Or maybe that was just the wine on an empty stomach. Either way, she felt *good*.

Mostly good. She took stock of her entire body. The shower had helped, but she was still stiff from the train trip followed by the long car ride. One knee in particular was sore. It had been dogging her since the contortions they'd made her undergo on that last shoot. So she picked up the entire box of pizza and went to stretch out on the bed, only belatedly realizing that Bennett was just watching her eat, that he hadn't had any himself.

"Oh, I'm sorry!" She started to get up and move back

toward the table. "I'm hogging it all." What was the matter with her? She'd done that with the oysters, too.

He held up a hand to signal that she should stay, and came around and stretched out on the other side of the bed. It wasn't a come-on. He'd made his feelings on that topic quite clear. It was more a companionable familiarity.

Which was...nice, even as it made her wary. Gia didn't really do companionable familiarity with anyone except her girls.

"Yeah," he said after his first bite. "Not the best pizza you'll ever eat, but totally enjoyable for a random small-town effort."

"Hey, don't knock small towns," Gia said, but then she let loose a big yawn. The long day and the wine had conspired to make her sleepy.

"You're a small-town girl?"

"I know it's hard to believe, given my obvious veneer of big-city sophistication." He snorted. It was so satisfying to be able to amuse someone like Bennett Buchanan. And he had *such* a nice smile. "But yes. I'm from outside a small town called Belleville, Ontario. It's northeast of Toronto. Farm country."

"Your parents were farmers?" Bennett turned toward her, the chef in him obviously interested. "What did they farm?"

"Down, boy. It was farm country, but no. My dad was the principal at the local high school. My mom was a teacher there until they had kids. I was the baby, and she never went back after me."

"Too busy taking food off her kids' plates?"

Normally that remark would have rankled, but for some reason Gia didn't mind it from him right now—possibly because of all the heavy stuff he had told her about his youth. In fact, she was kind of gratified by the annoyed tone he'd used. It was nice, if odd, to have a champion who wasn't one of her best friends. They just reflexively fell into that role. Bennett, on the other hand, felt more impartial; he didn't owe her anything.

"Just me." She thought back to those fraught family dinners. "She never did it to my brother. But yeah, domestic stuff sort of expanded to fill the time available, so she did tend to fixate. She had me in the child beauty pageant circuit."

He rolled his eyes.

"Yeah," Gia said. "It was actually . . . pretty awful."

She had never said that out loud to anyone before. She felt guilty verbalizing that thought, because there was a clear path between all her pageant experience and her modeling career. It had taught her a lot about poise and how to carry herself. It had taught her how to shrug off ruthless assessments of her appearance, how to listen to people criticize her for traits she had no control over.

And she'd been good at it. She'd won most of them. And that had been . . . well, not fun. Grimly satisfying? Maybe that was the right phrase.

"You said in the car that your mother was obsessed with appearances."

"I'm not sure if the pageant thing was the cause of that or an effect. But yeah." He was looking at her intensely, like he was waiting for her to keep talking, but what else was there? *Yeah, it really sucks when your mom makes you start plucking your eyebrows when you're five?*

When she didn't say anything more, his expression changed from intense to thoughtful. "The thing about being obsessed with appearances is, on the one hand, it's shallow. It's about how people will respond to the way things look. It's superficial."

She nodded since he seemed to be awaiting her

agreement. She wasn't sure where he was going with this, but he wasn't wrong.

"So how come, if it's all about the surface of things, it hurts so much?"

Gia sucked in a breath. It was like he had punched her. But it was a truth punch.

He must have sensed that she was bowled over, because he smiled, pointed at her, and said, "You don't have to answer that. It's more of a rhetorical question." Then he held up the remote. "You mind?"

She shook her head, grateful for the reprieve but still amazed at the accuracy of his observation. She sank a little farther back into her fluffy nest of pillows, ate some more pizza, and drank some more wine. They watched the news in companionable silence, making amused eye contact when a reporter interviewed stranded travelers at Newark Airport.

She felt... good. Reassured in the knowledge that they'd outrun the storm and were well on their way to the wedding. Satiated. Sleepy. Calm.

It was weird.

After the news was over, Gia took control of the remote and settled on the Food Network, which was playing a restaurant makeover show.

"I can't watch this," Bennett kept saying, rolling his eyes over the changes the makeover team was proposing. "That there is a perfectly fine restaurant. Not everything needs to be high end. They're going to ruin it."

Gia pointedly didn't change the channel, enjoying his indignant commentary on the transformation. And, though things had gotten kind of serious earlier with the talk about appearance-obsessed mothers—not to mention his big confession in the car—it felt like they'd come through all that and emerged into something... lighter. Easier.

"Honestly, they deserve what they get," he said as the TV restaurant proprietors oohed and aahed at the big reveal. "No one wants to eat pho on silk-covered banquettes. You can't slosh broth on silk-covered banquettes. They're going to lose their existing customers, and they sure as hell aren't going to gain any new ones."

"What those people should do if they want to expand is get a food truck," Gia said. "They're in Ann Arbor, right? That's a college town. Keep the prices low, park near the university. They can call it Pho on the Go or something cute like that."

He rotated his head to look at her. They had both slid down on the bed a bit after eating—Bennett seemed to be victim to the same food coma that had hit Gia.

"That's *exactly* what they should do."

She started, surprised at the praise.

He narrowed his eyes. "You should be a restaurant consultant."

"Huh?"

"After you left the restaurant this morning, some of the guys and I dragged a refrigerator outside and plugged it in. They're going to stick tonight's leftovers in there."

Oh, right. "Well, who knows if it will work?"

"It'll work."

Gia tried to think of the last time someone had expressed such firm confidence in her. It had been the girls, probably—last time they'd all seen each other, she had confessed some trepidation over the *Vogue* shoot, and they had given her a pep talk. It was nice to hear someone else expressing faith in her, though, especially someone like Bennett. Bennett didn't seem like the kind of guy who did false praise.

"Oh no! No!" he shouted at the TV. She'd tuned out, but someone was making some kind of chocolate mousse thing.

"You can't serve that with pho!" He turned to her, mock alarm in his eyes. "These people are *monsters*."

She cracked up. She wished she had a remote control for reality. Because she wanted to pause this entire moment, this feeling of camaraderie. The simple happiness of a joke, a full belly, and progress toward a shared mission.

But wait. She could capture it, if not pause it. She scrambled off the bed, got her camera from her bag, then returned.

"Since there won't be any Florida shots today, can I take your picture? I want to get you with the TV and"— she shoved the pizza box toward him—"dinner. The Mister Tony's logo, specifically."

He turned around so the TV would be in the background of the shot, but then he patted the spot beside him. "Only if you're in it, too."

"I told you I don't do selfies."

"But whatever you're trying to capture about this moment, you're part of it."

"Bennett, I get my picture taken all day long."

"Okay, okay. Compromise." He grabbed one of her feet— she'd been sitting cross-legged—and tugged. He seemed to want her to extend her leg.

Warily, she did. Then he tapped the other shin, so she unfolded that leg, too.

He was sort of…arranging her. Taking her feet onto his lap.

His hands were warm and strong. Tingles danced from her toes to her center, like someone was pricking the entire length of her leg with thousands of tiny acupuncture needles.

Once he'd composed her to his liking, Bennett contorted himself, bending over her feet but also propping the pizza box up. "Am I blocking the TV too much?"

Ah, he was making a picture with all the things she'd said she wanted in it—plus her feet. Smiling that lopsided smile that did things to her. Intensified the tingles.

When she didn't answer right away, he said, "Come on. It's not a selfie if it's just your feet in the shot."

She shook her head indulgently. "Okay." She paused as she looked through the viewfinder. Her orange-painted toes next to his calloused hands made for a strangely compelling image. The way he was lightly holding her ankles suggested familiarity. She thought of those hands at work—shucking oysters, handing a cup of coffee to a homeless man, gripping the steering wheel as he drove in the storm. And now they were on her ankles as if that's where they were *supposed* to be at the end of a hard day.

She wasn't really thinking when she shifted to get a picture of just her lower legs and his hands.

As soon as the camera spat out the photo, she realized her mistake. If she'd been using her phone, she could have surreptitiously taken a bunch more images with the TV and the pizza in them, or she could have stealth-deleted the original shot.

But there was no hiding this. She didn't even try to get it away from him as he twisted to grab the photo and stared at the blurry blob that would sharpen into her suspect image.

She leaned back against the headboard and looked out the window at the storm, waiting to get busted. She would tell him it was a last-minute artistic choice. It *was*. It didn't have to mean anything. He certainly wouldn't read anything more into it.

Or maybe he would, because, suddenly, he was *kissing* her. Because she'd been staring out the window, she hadn't seen it coming.

And to be fair, he hadn't given her any warning. It wasn't

the kind of gentle, incremental kiss Reese Witherspoon's rom-com love interest would've planted on her. There was no lead-in; no tucking of stray hair behind her ears, no endearingly earnest speech, not even any eye contact. It was at once smaller and hotter. He just appeared in her space and covered her mouth with his, pressing his thumbs into her cheekbones as his tongue swept into her mouth. He tasted like pizza, of course, but also, underneath that, like tea.

She felt immediately like they'd been kissing for an hour. It wasn't that she was suddenly, violently awakened. She didn't feel a spike of need. It was more that the need inside her had expanded, like a thing that was too large for her body to contain, so it started spilling out the edges of her skin.

She moaned and opened her mouth wider for him. The need continued to expand even as, paradoxically, it coalesced between her legs.

They were lying side by side now, having slid down the headboard a bit as they kissed, so she swung her top leg over his hip, and one of his hands left her face and clamped down on her thigh, wrapping it around his waist as much as was possible given their position.

He was hard against her belly, so fantastically hard.

This was such a *shock*, but it also felt inevitable. As if that hand *had* belonged possessively on her ankle.

And now it belonged on her thigh.

"Fuck," he muttered against her lips, as the hand, once it had her leg where he wanted it, traveled back up her thigh, grabbed an ass cheek, and squeezed—hard. "Fuuuck." That was followed by an indistinct sound that was a cross between yet another *fuck* and a growl.

His lips had left hers as he let fly that string of curses, and she took advantage of the freedom and pressed her lips against his jawline. Darted her tongue out and licked it, loving the drag of his stubble against the sensitive flesh of her tongue.

The repositioning shifted her, moved her down his body, and it had the effect of lining his cock up against her center.

"Oh my God!" The sudden pressure was so exquisite, it was almost her undoing.

It usually took Gia a while to come. She was good at it. She wasn't afraid of some nonverbal guiding—and when that didn't work, she outright instructed her lovers in the fine art of making it happen. But it didn't *just* happen, was the point. She had to concentrate. She needed a specific kind of not-too-hard pressure.

"Oh my God!" she said again, writhing against him, astonished at her still-expanding need. Was there no end to how good this man could make her feel?

"Fuck," he said again, but this time it was different. It wasn't an expression of lust anymore, but one of genuine regret. Maybe even...disgust?

"I can't do this," he said, and just like that, her need stopped expanding. He pulled away, leaving her confused. Stuck. Turned on but abandoned.

But then he was back, or at least his fingers were. "I'm sorry," he said as he shoved his hand down her pajama bottoms, his fingers skimming over her heat.

"Sorry?" she echoed. That wasn't helping with the confusion.

"Shhh," he soothed, his fingers starting to make circles. He watched her intently, kneeling over her but not touching any part of her body with any part of his, other than those fingers.

She wanted to object, to demand that he explain what the hell was going on, but— "Oh!" Her hips bucked against his hand. Still watching her like she was about to reveal the answer to an ancient mystery, he retuned his touch, working with the rolling of her hips and tightening the circles he was making over and around her clit.

The impending orgasm was climbing so high inside her. All that expanding desire from earlier had made so much room in her body. Pleasure kept expanding into that space, up and up and up. Out, too. In all directions at once. She held her breath. It was almost painful. She needed it to stop, even as she never wanted it to.

"That's it," he crooned. "That's it. Come for me, Gia. Be a good girl and come for me."

And she did—gasping as her body exploded, even as part of her hated how easily he could control her response.

He left his hand on her through a long series of aftershocks, still watching her intently.

Eventually, the attention shaded into a scrutiny that felt more invasive than she was comfortable with. It was starting to feel like he could actually see *inside* her.

"What was that?" she demanded as she scrambled away from him and sat up. Her instinct was to cover herself, but of course she wasn't naked. How was it possible she'd just had the most intense orgasm of her life while fully clothed? And more to the point, why had he jumped ship halfway through?

"I'm sorry." He raked a hand through his hair, and his face twisted into a grimace. "I got carried away. I forgot myself."

"You *forgot* yourself?" What did *that* mean?

"I don't do casual. That should not have happened."

"You don't do *casual*?" She had been reduced to repeating his sentences back to him, but in her defense, that was because nothing he was saying made any sense.

"Yeah, I don't sleep around."

Oh my God. The Bible verse he'd quoted at her yester-day. His devotion to pay-what-you-can night and the way he'd helped that homeless man. And he'd mentioned that his chef-mentor was Catholic. It all made sense now. He'd probably found Jesus as part of his recovery. Well, at least there was a reason he'd rejected her last night. "You're some kind of religious nut."

That made him smile, which in turn made her realize how serious his face had been previously, while he'd been getting her off.

"No. I was raised Southern Baptist, but I haven't set foot in a church or opened a Bible since I left home. It's just that casual sex is not…something I allow myself to indulge in."

She scrambled under the covers, suddenly feeling too ex-posed, which was ridiculous because she wasn't naked, and anyway, he'd had his hand down her shorts just moments ago. "But not because the Bible tells you it's a sin." She was still struggling to make sense of all this.

Another smile, but it was a wistful one. "No. It's more a matter of personal ethics. I keep sex confined to serious relationships. Or at least relationships that seem like they have the potential to become serious."

"What are you saying? You want me to *date* you?" Be-cause that was not happening. No matter that they'd reached a kind of truce earlier, or that she'd been getting stupidly moony over his hand on her ankle. Just like Bennett appar-ently didn't do casual, Gia didn't do anything *but* casual.

The smile slid off his face. "That's not what I said."

Oh. *Oh.* It had not occurred to her both things could be true: Bennett didn't want to have sex with her *and* he didn't want to date her. Her face blazed. "So if I was such a big fucking mistake, what the hell was that?" Enough with the confusion. She was moving on to anger.

"You're not a mistake. *I* made a mistake. It's not the same thing. It's not your fault I'm like this. And I believe in finishing what I start."

She dropped her gaze to his jeans. There was still a telltale bulge there. "So what are you going to do now? Go back to your room and beat off, and somehow you're magically absolved from having had casual sex? As long as you didn't stick your dick in me, it's all good?"

Was she being too mean? He was clearly already upset with himself. But God, why was it that her encounters with Bennett the last two nights—him rejecting her and him giving her a bone-shattering orgasm—had *both* resulted in her humiliation? How could such polar opposite inputs lead to the same awful outcome?

"I'm not saying it makes sense from the outside," he said quietly. "Things don't have to make sense for them to work." When Gia's only response was an eye roll, he said, "I think I should go now. I'm happy to talk more tomorrow if you like. Should we make it an early start? Say six?"

She made a vague gesture of agreement and watched him leave, the click of the door behind him like thunder in her ears.

⸻

She hadn't said, "Oh my God" when she first bit into the pizza. That was the only way he could make sense of what was happening to him.

Bennett turned on the shower and hesitated over what temperature to make the water. The obvious answer was arctic cold. But, realistically, he knew it wouldn't make any difference. The coldest water in the world wouldn't douse the fire she'd stirred up in him. So he turned the heat up, got in, and took himself in hand.

Every time Gia had eaten something Bennett had served her in his restaurant, she'd let loose an "Oh my God" tinged with equal parts surprise and carnality. Every single time: the boudin balls, the wine he'd selected, the coffee, the oysters. Even the beets in his salad. Her eyes had widened, and her jaw had relaxed. It was like her body was having an involuntary response that her mind could only react to by saying, "Oh my God."

Earlier tonight, she'd clearly enjoyed Mister Tony's pizza. Mister Tony's pizza had been, objectively, very good. But there had been no "Oh my God." No eyes rolling back in pleasure. No greed-tinged sighs.

It all probably would have been fine—he was practiced at keeping his impulses in check—but damn her, she *also* kept offering up these perfect, simple solutions to restaurant problems, both his and those of the poor victims of that stupid restaurant makeover show.

And then her feet were on his lap. Her perfect candy-corn toes that made him want to put his mouth all over her.

He would have restrained himself, but that *photo*. That had been his undoing. As it had come into resolution, he'd stared at it in disbelief, pretty sure her decision to focus in tightly on his hands on her legs meant that whatever it was between them tonight, she'd felt it, too.

And then he'd started wondering, as he kept staring at the picture, waiting for the orange of her toenail polish to darken to its final shade, if there were other contexts in which she would say, "Oh my God!" like that.

It turned out there were.

Jesus fucking Christ, he'd never seen a woman come like

that. He flattered himself a decent lover. He didn't do casual, not as an adult, but he'd had his share of girlfriends, and none of them had had any complaints in that department.

But Gia. The way she just…lost herself. Surrendered to sensation.

It kind of reminded him of their snowball fight.

It was the flip side of the version of her who had freaked out at the airline employees. Good Gia and Bad Gia were equally adamant. Whether it was irrational anger or silly joy—or the peak of sexual pleasure—he was starting to understand that Gia, when she was in, was all in.

The warm water pounded down on him, and it only took a few strokes before he put himself out of his misery.

He knew, though, that the reprieve was temporary.

It was going to be a long drive tomorrow.

Chapter Six

FOUR DAYS BEFORE THE WEDDING

*B*ennett didn't do casual, but Gia didn't do *serious*, and *this* was why. Because serious meant you were *stuck* with the person—you couldn't just flee—no matter how awkward the morning after was.

And this one was awkward. Painfully so.

After they threw their bags into the car in the predawn dark and Bennett, ever the chivalrous southern gentleman, held the passenger door for her, Gia reminded herself of her motto: *One man is as good as another.*

The only way that wasn't true was when you started to hang on to them, when they became differentiate-able.

And that way lay ruin.

As soon as she got into the car, she picked up her phone and texted Wendy.

So hi how are you also I fooled around with the best man last night SORRY

Normally a text like that would have been directed at Elise, who was Gia's bestie among besties. They'd met during Gia's one year at university—Elise, three years older, had been Gia's resident assistant. They'd fallen instantly into friendship, even as Elise had earned her stripes advising Gia as she considered dropping out to model.

So normally Elise would be the recipient of any relevant "I need to deconstruct this sex" texts.

Not that very many of them were relevant—it wasn't often that Gia needed to dissect the emotional aftermath of a sexual encounter. But Elise, all settled and married and knocked up, liked to live through Gia, so Gia sometimes amused herself by telling Elise about her best and worst experiences.

But in this case, she figured that since Wendy was marrying Bennett's best friend, she should probably fess up—in case news of last night got back to her through her husband-to-be.

Gia was surprised the reply came right away given that it was six in the morning and Wendy was on vacation. But that was Wendy for you. She probably got up early to work in secret.

LOL. Don't be sorry. I bet that was...intense.

That's one word for it.

I thought you said he wasn't your type.

Well...

Will Mr. Buchanan be granted a repeat performance? A two-before-you're-through?

The answer to Wendy's question—the horrible truth—

was that although Gia *would* grant Bennett a repeat performance, *he* wasn't going to grant *her* one. That was uncharted territory, and more than she wanted to admit, even to Wendy. So she went with a vague reply.

I don't think so. He's in the one-and-done camp.

Poor guy. At least he tasted glory the one time.

Haha. Anyway, we're on the road now—just coming up on Richmond, Virginia. If all goes well, we'll be there super late tonight.

Don't push yourselves. There's no hurry re the dress. I canceled the Wednesday appointment, and the tailor confirmed she can do it pretty much anytime the rest of the week. You guys must be exhausted. Spend another night on the road. And consider granting Bennett a repeat, because I have confirmed that Tobias Almanza is a no go.

Why?

So I thought initially he was kind of prickly and stuffy, but, damn, get some booze into him and he turns into Hector. Remember Hector from Jane's wedding?

How could I not? *searches for vomit emoji*

Wendy was referring to one of the groomsmen in Jane and Cameron's wedding. At the bachelor and bachelorette extravaganzas in Vegas, everyone—except Wendy—had tried to pair Gia off with Hector, the only other single member of the wedding party. But Hector had been a gross player. *One man is as good as another* didn't literally mean any man. It meant *One desirable, respectful man is as good as another.* Gia had standards. She had choices.

She glanced at Bennett.

She *usually* had choices.

Why can't this Tobias dude be an old-school British gent? Or, wait, Idris Elba. He's British, right? I'll take Idris Elba please.

Oh, girl, he is so far from Idris Elba, I can't even.

Why do all of your husbands have such bad taste in friends?

Probably because they're so amazingly excellent at picking wives. No good judgment left to pick decent friends.

Touché.

This was the part where a lot of people would text something meant to be comforting, something along the lines of *Don't worry, someday your prince will come.* Wendy didn't go in for that bullshit, though. She knew Gia was not waiting on a prince. So she just sent Gia a selfie of her and the other girls goofing off on the beach along with:

We can't wait to see you. It's not the same without you. And lest you think I'm a self-obsessed bride,

I would like to inform you, soon-to-be BIRTHDAY GIRL, that we have PLANS for you.

Now there was a declaration of love that meant more than anything any man could say.

It wasn't that Gia was antilove, in theory. It worked for other people. She'd seen it happen to all three of the girls, and she was truly happy for them.

It just didn't work for *her*. She'd come close once, with Lukas, and she'd gotten burned. But in retrospect, that hadn't been love. It had been a one-sided infatuation with an asshole who'd tried to make her into his fantasy woman. Thank God all she'd really let him control was her hair color. And as she'd later learned, it was easy enough—and downright fun—to change back to whatever the hell color she wanted it to be that day.

No, that had been her one foray into "love," aka letting a man control her.

And it wasn't as if, in the years since, she'd had to walk around protecting her heart, actively trying to *avoid* falling in love. It hadn't come up. She'd never been tempted—not once. When she got the niggling sense that she might be getting overly fond of a guy, she set up a test, he failed it, and that was that. She'd never had any problem moving on.

So she'd been left to conclude that she was not made for love.

Not romantic love anyway—she was fiercely devoted to her friends, even if they were falling like dominoes.

"Do you want to drive through somewhere for coffee?" Bennett asked, halting her little foray into self-analysis as he pulled away from the hotel.

"God, yes." The vision of a huge steaming cup of coffee made her forget for a moment that she was mad at him. Also, thinking about coffee was a lot more pleasant than thinking about Lukas.

"Or we could stop for breakfast, if cold Wall of Cheesy Garlic Bread isn't your thing at six a.m." He nodded at the pizza box he'd placed between them.

She demurred on breakfast, so they pulled into a drive-through. Once she had her coffee and he an iced tea that he'd added several packets of sugar to—he was so *weird*—and they'd gotten on the highway, he cleared his throat.

"So, ah, I just wanted to say again that I'm sorry about last night. It won't happen again."

"Well, that's too bad," she shot back before she could think better of it. But *damn*, that orgasm. She could talk herself in circles inside her head, but the truth was she would gladly grant Bennett a repeat performance for another one of those.

He smiled, and she decided to press her luck, because she really was curious—and she'd chilled out since yelling at him last night. He didn't want her—so what? One man was as good as another, right? "But tell me, this rule of yours about not having casual sex. Doesn't that make for some serious...dry spells?"

He laughed. "It does make for dry spells. My last girlfriend was"—his eyes narrowed, and she could tell he surprised himself with the answer he calculated—"was almost a year ago."

"You haven't had sex for *a year*?" She tried not to sound gobsmacked, but honestly, sex, as long as it was of the safe variety, was one of the world's few guilt-free pleasures, and she just didn't see why someone who wasn't denying himself for religious reasons would abstain.

"Don't you find, though, that sex is so much better when you're actually involved with the person?" he asked, deflecting her actual question.

"I do not."

"Well, okay, maybe your sample is tainted. Have you only dated losers?"

"I haven't dated anyone. Not in a relationship, 'we're going steady' kind of way."

Except that one time—or so she'd thought. But she didn't count Lukas.

It was Bennett's turn to be gobsmacked. "What? How old are you? And how is that possible?"

"I'm twenty-nine." She was going to turn thirty tomorrow, in fact, but she didn't add that qualification. She was still twenty-nine, and she was sticking to it, thank you very much. She moved on to answering his final question. "And that is possible because love is a state of being to which I'm immune."

"So no love. No romance. Just sex."

"That's right." She chuckled. "In fact, the surest way for a guy to get rid of me is for him to declare his devotion." He blinked rapidly, taking in her answers, so she took advantage of his silence and asked one of her own. "How old are you?"

"Thirty-one."

"Okay, so how many people have you slept with?"

"Twenty-five."

She choked on her coffee, earning her a concerned glance, which she waved off. When she'd recovered herself, she said, "You only have sex within the confines of serious relationships, but you've slept with *twenty-five people*? Math was never my strong suit, but how does that add up?"

He chuckled. "I only have sex within the confines of a serious relationship *now*. Before..." He hesitated. "Before the accident, I was a total man-whore."

She'd been about to laugh at that phrase, but the change in his face had her swallowing it. The way his brow knit suggested he was revisiting a painful memory. He seemed like he was on the verge of spitting something out. Like he wanted to speak but couldn't quite make himself.

"What is it?" she asked gently.

"The girlfriend who was driving the night of the accident? The one I told you about?"

"Yes?"

"I didn't love her."

Oh, Bennett. He was so hard on himself. "Does anybody really love their high-school girlfriends or boyfriends? It's always just puppy love at that age, isn't it?"

"No. I mean, I *never* loved her. Not even in that puppy-love kind of way. I never even liked her, really. She was mean and not that smart, which isn't a very attractive combination." He pressed his lips together in a grim line for a quick moment before saying, "I was just using her because her brother was a dealer. She was an easy and quick path to drugs."

Ah. Bennett was like a rare, complicated flower blooming in many phases. She understood him so much better now. She also understood how hard this burden was for modern-day, morally upstanding Bennett to live with. Before she could come up with anything comforting to say, he added, his tone dripping with disgust at himself, "Of course none of that prevented me from sleeping with her—at least when I wasn't too stoned for my dick to work."

Feeling like anything she might say would only sound hollow, she laid her hand on his forearm.

He glanced over at her. "I wanted to tell you so you understand that last night really wasn't about you."

She believed him, and as much as she wanted to be impervious to his opinion of her, it was a weight off her shoulders. They looked at each other for a moment—it was just a moment, as he had to keep his attention on the road—but it was a look that said things were okay between them.

And if that was the case, she was going to attempt to

lighten the mood with a little humor. As with last night's "driving plus confessions" session, she sensed he would appreciate it, that something had been achieved by the confession but that he didn't want to wallow in it.

"So. About these twenty-five belt notches. How many are from your wild youth, and how many were girlfriends you were gaga for?"

He flashed the lopsided smile. "Twenty-one to four."

It tickled Gia that he'd kept track of his preaccident conquests. The way he talked about his degenerate youth, he didn't seem like the kind of guy who would have bothered keeping track.

"And I wouldn't say I was gaga for my girlfriends."

"Huh?"

"I tried to be."

"What does that mean?"

"Well, I *liked* them. I grew to love them, in a way."

"So you don't have to be in love with someone to have sex with them?" She was asking not to bust his chops, but because she was truly interested. He seemed to have such high expectations of himself, yet they didn't map onto the societal binaries that usually governed sex and love. He was so confusing, but also so stupidly compelling.

"I wish it could be that way, but no. It's more like..." He shook his head. "It's hard to explain."

Her stomach growled. Her first impulse was to ignore it, but she forced herself to open the box of garlic bread, pull off a wad of cheese, and put it in her mouth. "Try."

"I don't have to be in love with them, but I have to be *with* them, you know?"

"I don't know." This was actually kind of satisfying, teasing out these insights. Maybe post-modeling, Gia should study to become a shrink. Too bad she wasn't smart enough.

"They have to matter to me," he said, speaking slowly, like he was articulating his position for the first time. "I have to be all in." Then he shook his head. "No, it's more than that. It's more like I have to know that I'm not going to leave."

Gia's mouth fell open. The weird-ass flower just kept on blooming. "Like *ever*? How is that even possible? Do you have a crystal ball?"

"No, but I have self-discipline."

"So numbers twenty-one through twenty-five left you."

"They did. Or I could tell that they wanted to and would be better off without me, so I did it preemptively."

"You dumped them to save them from you."

"You're twisting what I'm saying."

"You're atoning."

That was it. That interpretation made everything about him, from pay-what-you-can night to the community re-frigerator to his rejection of her despite his obvious arousal, make sense. He felt responsible both for the woman who'd almost died in the accident and for the girlfriend he'd never loved who'd gotten tangled up in the tragedy. Because he used her and she got hurt. He was trying to make sure nothing like it ever happened again. Gia smiled, satisfied to have cracked the mystery that was Bennett Buchanan.

"What?" His voice had taken on the annoyed tone he used with his kitchen staff.

"You're atoning for your past. You feel guilty, and now you're overcorrecting."

He shook his head. "I'm not atoning. I'm just careful. I'm done using people. I'm done taking them for granted. I'm done putting my fleeting desires above the well-being of others."

"That's all fine, admirable even, but don't you think it's

possible to have casual sex with someone without using them? Or maybe using them the same way and to the same degree they're using you? An equal exchange." She was going to say more, about how people used each other all the time, and not just for sex—that it was the way of the world, and that the mature thing to do was to be up-front about it. But she realized that it might sound like she was trying to argue her way back into his bed. And though of course she would freely admit that she wouldn't mind finding herself there—*one* more time—it wasn't going to be after she'd had to convince him.

"Anyway," he said, "the point here is that I have better data than you do. I've had it both ways, and I can report with absolute confidence that sex is better with a long-term partner."

"So you're saying that sex is better when it's overlaid with all the insecurities and indignities that come with a long-term relationship?"

She was kidding, sort of.

"No. It's better when you *know* someone. When you're invested in making them feel good. When you know what works."

She wanted to point out that he hadn't seemed to have any trouble figuring out what worked last night, but again, the point here was to avoid sounding desperate, so instead she just rolled her eyes. It was a good-natured roll, though, which was kind of remarkable given that she'd expected this day to be humiliating and painful. It was turning out to be neither of those.

Strangely, knowing that Bennett was doing some big, pointless atonement thing lifted her spirits considerably. He was torturing himself and trying to twist his behavior into some kind of pattern he thought was essential. Which meant his weirdness truly had not been about her. He had been telling the truth when he said the rejection wasn't personal. And he *had* wanted her—she'd seen and felt the evidence.

He just wouldn't let himself have her.

Which, now that it was put in the correct context, was...interesting.

It almost felt like a challenge.

⸻

As the morning wore on, the sky lightened, and so did Bennett's mood. Part of it was the catharsis of confession. But part of it, he suspected, was his confessor. Gia. She'd done another of her presto-change-os, going from cranky and borderline intolerable to kind and compassionate to funny and downright friendly.

It was disarming, but also contagious.

"What the heck is this 'South of the Border' thing I keep seeing signs for?" Gia asked several hours later, after they'd traversed most of North Carolina.

"It's a run-down amusement park," he said, "and I say we pull off and see what they serve for lunch at run-down amusement parks."

"Sure. You must be tired of driving. Why don't you let me take a shift? I've got one more day of legal driving."

"Yeah, but you're not on the rental agreement."

"Wow, you really are a goody two-shoes."

"Anyway, it's no problem," he said, and he meant it. Driving wasn't something he did much anymore, not since he'd moved to New York, but he enjoyed it—when he wasn't in conditions that made him fear crashing. It was meditative. It let him get out of his own head. Normally. Maybe not at this exact moment. Because that shit Gia had said about him atoning? That was *definitely* lodged in his head.

He pulled off. "So there's this creepy Pedroland thing I remember visiting as a kid. It's definitely seen better days. So probably this is the part where a deranged clown murders us."

"Hey, I went to circus school. I can totally take down a deranged clown."

"You went to *circus school*?" Had he heard that right?

She laughed. "Yeah. I can juggle and everything."

Damn. Juggling was not, inherently, an attractive activity. And yet...

"Yeah, I hated it, but it was part of my mom's pageant domination plan."

"Are you close with your mom today?" He wasn't sure why he was asking. The answer had absolutely no bearing on his life. It was just that he was getting a picture of Gia's mom, and it was making him...cranky.

She tilted her head, seeming to give the question serious consideration. "We get along fine, but we're not close. I think she takes credit for my modeling career—which is fair. But it's like now that she has no project, nothing to groom me for, there's...nothing left to base our relationship on."

He opened his mouth to say more, to ask about her dad, because he found himself desperately hoping that her dad somehow made up for her mother's remoteness. But then he shut it. He didn't know these people. After the wedding, he'd never see Gia again.

They strolled in silence for a few moments until she pointed at a mini-golf course and said, "Hey! Let's play!"

"Shouldn't we just eat and get on the road?" Her mood had done a one-eighty since early this morning, but they did still need to get that dress to Florida.

"Nah, it's okay. Wendy moved the tailoring appointment, so the pressure's off. We don't need to arrive today."

It was hard to deny Gia anything when she was like this. And he didn't want to, really. After witnessing that orgasm last night, he was afraid he would pretty much do anything she asked him to do. Well, almost anything. And mini-golf was easy, relatively speaking. There were no moral gray areas in mini-golf.

She turned out to be really bad at it.

"Have you never done this?" he asked incredulously as she finally sank the ball in the first hole, seventeen strokes to his four.

"Only once, and I think I was about seven. Also, I'm not known for my athletic ability. Muscles are frowned upon in my line of work."

"It's mini-golf. No athletic ability or muscles required."

She responded by sticking her tongue out at him.

By the third hole, he couldn't stand it anymore. "Let me help you."

He tried to correct her form verbally, and by modeling the correct stance, but it wasn't doing much. So, God help him, he did that thing where he stood behind her so they could both hold her club.

Because that was *such* a good idea.

Gia was tall—they were pretty much the same height—but slim, with narrow hips and shoulders, so their bodies fit together perfectly for this task. Everything lined up—her legs against his, her back against his chest, but his broader build left room for him to wrap his arms around her.

When he finished aligning them by placing his hands over hers on the club, she let loose a little breathy sigh of contentment, and her shoulders fell as her body relaxed.

It was contagious. It felt strangely good to be holding her like this. Also strangely intimate, which was ridiculous because last night they'd made out like feral teenagers and then he'd made her come. So getting all weirded out over standing with his arms around her made no sense.

He was starting to understand, though, that logic didn't really apply where Gia Gallo was concerned.

There was no way to back out now, so he spoke in her ear. "Keep your elbows straight but not locked, swing, and…" They hit the ball together and watched as it took off down the green and landed respectably close to the hole. "There you go."

It was *way* more difficult than it should have been to let go of her.

But once he did, he took his turn, and then they moved toward the hole for the putt.

"Help me again." She set up her putt but looked entreatingly at him over her shoulder.

Well, shit. He'd created this monster.

So he did as she asked, lining up their bodies, then setting up her shot. He tried not to be too obvious about burying his nose in her hair. It smelled like mint and rosemary.

The ball went in, and she wiggled with happiness.

He'd been trying to keep the contact between their lower bodies to a minimum during the shot, but so much for that. She bounced around and her ass dragged back and forth over his cock, which had definitely taken note.

Strangely, he wasn't as embarrassed as he would have expected to be. She knew his deal—that he was attracted to her but wasn't prepared to act on it. She might think his deal was insane, but she knew it. There was something freeing about having all his hang-ups out in the open.

So to speak.

"Oops." She pulled away from him and let her gaze rake down his body. "Sorry. I think that counted as 'casual.'"

And she was going to harass him about it, the little minx.

He didn't hate it.

Chapter Seven

After lunch, Bennett started yawning like crazy, and Gia wrested the keys from him on their way back to the car. She'd slept like a baby last night after that spectacular orgasm, but she wondered if Bennett had had a sleepless night, all wound up and filled with lust and guilt. "One last day of legal driving," she insisted, promising that she'd do this one shift with the utmost caution, staying under the speed limit and not straying from the highway.

They passed a tourist information stand filled with brochures, and she noticed one for Charleston. She snagged it. "Hey, we're pretty close. It's not that far off I-95. You want to stop?"

He didn't say anything right away, which made her doubt the sincerity of his eventual "No."

"You sure?"

"We don't have time."

Which wasn't exactly a heartfelt refusal.

"We don't have to stay long. We can just pop in and see your friend Marc."

"No, no. Stopping in Charleston is . . . not a good idea."

That pause, though, had suggested he didn't mean what he said. That he might, in fact, mean the *opposite* of what he said.

Anyway, it was a moot point, because he conked out almost immediately—she'd been right about his exhaustion.

She took a certain kind of pleasure in driving as he slept. It felt like she was doing something useful. Directly contributing to solving a concrete problem: getting their asses to the wedding. She'd felt the same way when he'd reported that he'd implemented her community refrigerator idea. It wasn't that Gia didn't think fashion had any value. It absolutely did. It brought people joy—and jobs. It made the world beautiful and was an avenue of self-expression that was available to all, whether you were shopping the ateliers of Paris or Goodwill. But lately she was starting to wonder, as she strutted or posed, what the point of it all was, or at least her involvement in it.

But again, she always came back to the same question: What the hell else could she do?

Enough with the brooding. She glanced at her passenger. He was awfully cute as he slept. He looked both older and younger, which should have been impossible. Free to observe his face at rest, she noticed the beginnings of crow's-feet, and the sun glancing off his stubble revealed a few silver hairs. But at the same time, slumber lent him a vulnerability such that she fancied she could see the younger, troubled Bennett inside the modern-day, capable man.

She drove for more than an hour while he slept. Then she started seeing signs for Charleston.

She thought about that hesitation, when he'd said he

didn't want to stop. She thought about him saying, on the train, that he didn't miss his hometown. He'd been lying, she was pretty sure. There had been something in his eyes, something wistful and yearning, when he'd talked about Chef Lalande.

And honestly, as much as she'd been the one cracking the whip to get them to Florida, she suddenly wanted to put the brakes on. To slow them down. Just a little. Wendy had put off the tailoring appointment, so what could a little detour hurt?

Without letting herself analyze her impulsive decision too much, she exited the highway for I-26, which would take them to Charleston. She took advantage of a slowdown in a construction zone to search her map app for the restaurant, keeping one eye on the road so she wouldn't get her "not on the rental agreement" ass into trouble.

When she cut the engine in front of the restaurant, he woke up. Keeping up the adorable thing, he shook his head and was all sleep addled and confused at first.

"Oh, man, sorry, I really passed out there. Let me stretch my legs for a minute, then we can swap and..."

He inhaled sharply and leaned forward in his seat, closer to the windshield, as if that extra few inches would clarify what he was seeing.

"What did you do?" he whispered, and Gia had a moment of panic.

"I'm sorry. Was this a bad idea?" She had only wanted to please him. To give him what she thought he secretly wanted.

Well, that, and, stupid girl that she was, she had wanted to prolong their road trip.

But she suddenly grasped what a breathtakingly pre-sumptuous overreach this had been. Yes, he'd told her some shit about his past, but that didn't mean she *knew* him. He had *told* her he didn't want to stop, and she'd ignored his wishes and brought him here anyway—while he *slept*. "We can just leave," she said quickly. She started to insert the key into the ignition, but he grabbed her hand to prevent her.

He didn't let go of her hand, but squeezed it—hard. "Thank you." His voice was raspy, and Gia's throat tightened, even as relief flooded her.

"Come on." He let go of her hand, but, oddly, grabbed it again when they got out of the car.

"Welcome to Marc's." A woman smiled them from the hostess stand. "Do you have a— *Bennett*? Bennett Buchanan?"

"Fanny." Bennett dropped Gia's hand and wrapped the older woman in his arms.

When they separated, Fanny had tears in her eyes. Then she started swatting Bennett and peppering him with questions. What was he doing here? Why hadn't he called? When was he coming home from that god-awful Yankee city?

Bennett didn't appear to be crying like Fanny did, but he did noticeably swallow a few times while she interrogated him. "I was in the neighborhood." He winked at Gia. Then he turned to take in the room. He was trying to hide it, but he was clearly overcome with emotion. "Looks exactly the same," he proclaimed, his voice thick.

The restaurant was a classic French bistro with exposed brick walls, ornate chandeliers, white-clothed café tables, and specials written on a chalkboard.

Bennett was craning his neck now, like he was looking for something in particular.

"Go on." Fanny hitched her head to the back of the

space. "He'll be so happy to see you. Might get him out of his mood—the mushroom supplier's delivery today did not meet his expectations, and he's right pissed about it."

Bennett cleared his throat. "Don't mess with the cream of mushroom soup."

"I can get your friend something to drink. Maybe you'd like to introduce us? Or do you not do manners in New York?"

Bennett chuckled and performed introductions.

Gia made to follow Fanny, intending to leave Bennett to his reunion with his mentor, but he grabbed her hand again—what was the deal with all this hand-holding?

"Nope," he said to Fanny. "She's coming with me."

As he approached the door to the kitchen, Bennett's heart pounded like he was about to step out on stage in front of a million people.

Gia's hand was the only thing keeping him from totally losing his shit.

Gia. He clutched her hand like it was a lifeline, but he couldn't look at her, or he *would* lose his shit.

The way she had just *known* that he needed to come here. That passing by so close to Charleston without stopping was killing him. But *also* that he was afraid. Not that he was afraid of Marc, or the restaurant, but that being back in Charleston at all was such an emotional minefield that it just needed to *happen* to him.

And she had made it happen.

She had a way of doing that. Of wresting control over a situation and making the world bend to her will. He admired the hell out of it. He might not agree with her will all the time—her stance on relationships, for example—but she was so very *effective*.

Which was maybe not the right, or the only, word a man should use to describe Gia Gallo, but his brain wasn't working well enough right now to come up with anything other than that. He was just so...overcome to have woken up and found himself outside Marc's. The place where he got his life back. His home—way more than the actual house he grew up in had ever been. But also the place that was full of so much unresolved shit.

He had invited his parents here once. It had been about a year into his tenure at the restaurant. He'd been promoted from dishwasher to line cook, but Marc had been taking him aside, giving him special lessons. Making him dice one thousand onions until he got it right. But also asking for his input on menu planning. The cravings were becoming more manageable, and he was starting to imagine a future in which this was his career and in which drugs didn't occupy his every waking thought.

Marc, who knew his whole sob story, had suggested he extend an olive branch. Invite his parents to the restaurant. Cook them a special meal. Which he had spent weeks planning with Marc's help.

And then his mother had balked. Had freaked out when they pulled up because she'd never been to this part of Charleston before and there was a halfway house down the street. She'd refused to get out of the car. And therefore so had his father.

And that had been that.

The last time he'd seen his parents. And he hadn't even interacted with them. He had merely overheard it all go down from inside the restaurant door, peeking out so he could see them, but they couldn't see him.

But they weren't here now.

Marc was here, though, just behind that door.

Realizing that he was probably exerting way too much pressure on Gia's hand, he paused and tried to take a deep breath. It didn't work. Everything in his chest was tight. *Shit.* If he had to make a list of people he didn't want to see him cry, Chef Lalande and Gia would be right up there. He did, however, force himself to gentle his grip.

She wasn't having it. She squeezed tighter to compensate. Because she knew. Somehow, she knew.

The gesture loosened something in his chest, and suddenly there was enough space for the deep breath he'd been trying for. The Gia effect.

He pushed through the door.

There it was. Just like the front, the kitchen was the same as it had always been. It was midafternoon, so it wasn't busy, but there was the din of dishes being washed. The hacking noise of a chicken being cut up. The heat, despite the chugging of the air conditioner. The smell of melted chocolate—the pastry chef would be getting tonight's dessert ready around this time.

"Close the goddamned door!"

Chef's voice, as ornery as ever. Bennett realized with a start that he sounded the same way at Boudin. He had not yet mastered Marc's ability to see what was going on behind him, though. His mentor was crouched over a worktable with his back to the door, and there should have been no way for him to know the door was open. He could probably sense changes in the air currents or something—he had always had a sort of Jedi master thing going.

Bennett hadn't moved fast enough to do Chef's bidding, so Marc turned, and he was pissed.

"What part of *close the goddamned*—"

The great Marc Lalande, struck dumb. Bennett had never thought to see it happen.

But his amusement was brief. It was almost like he and Chef *were* Jedis, communicating without speaking. He saw nothing on his mentor's face, but he knew that by standing there *not* speaking, which was not something Marc did, he was saying volumes. There was so much between them, so many emotions, that it was impossible to label them individually, much less put a name to the complex soup that resulted when you mixed them all together.

Somebody had to say something, though, so Bennett did. "This is my friend Gia. I was thinking maybe we could make her a snack?"

—◠

"Oh my God," Gia said twenty minutes later as she bit into a French fry. But calling it a "fry" didn't do justice to the salty creation that was perfectly crunchy on the outside yet perfectly fluffy on the inside. And dipped in a truffle aioli that was so good it could probably be used to broker world peace? "Oh my God," she said again, after her second fry. She couldn't think of anything else to say.

Suddenly aware that Bennett was looking at her funny, she paused in dipping French fry number three. "What?"

He ducked his head and smiled to himself like he'd been busted enjoying a secret pleasure. "Nothing."

"How can a potato taste this good?" she demanded. It was irrational, but sometimes Bennett's food almost made her angry. It shouldn't be possible for a mere mortal to continually produce food this amazing and to do it so casually, like it was nothing.

She needed to take a vacation from work more often.

She was several days away from her last job, and she had at least a month until the next one, depending on when she started booking again. She really needed to listen to that voice mail from her agent—but she kept putting it off because she was starting to feel her "little problem" loosen its hold on her a bit.

And she was glad about that, because it suggested that maybe her "little problem" was just circumstantial.

Which begged the question of what she planned to do about changing her circumstances.

She ate another fry.

"The raw frites are soaked in an ice bath," said Chef Lalande, answering what she'd meant as a rhetorical question.

"Obviously," Bennett said.

Lalande shrugged. "People cut corners these days."

"But not him." She jerked a thumb at Bennett.

"No," said Lalande, though Gia hadn't meant it as a question so much as a statement of fact. Bennett was not the sort of man who took the easy way out—of anything. Which, on the one hand, meant he was still punishing himself for something that had happened nearly fifteen years ago.

But on the other, it made for freaking fantastic fries.

Not to mention orgasms.

Not that she would ever get another one of those.

She sighed and ate another fry.

"Then they're double fried," Lalande continued, still lecturing her on the heavenly fries. "But I have to tell you, no one has ever done frites as well as this guy, including me."

Bennett blushed. He actually *blushed*. Clearly his mentor's approval meant everything to him. The two men had shared an intense and almost silent reunion, the emotional undercurrents of which she hadn't been able to read, other than to note that they were strong.

"So how long have you two been together?" Chef asked.

Gia corrected him. "Oh, we're not a couple."

They had explained their unexpected arrival, telling Chef about the wedding and the canceled flights, but now that she thought about it, they'd been holding hands when they came into the kitchen, so his conclusion had been logical.

Lalande looked between them, his eyes darting back and forth a few times. "Okay."

He didn't believe them. Her impulse was to double down on the correction, to make sure he knew that they weren't together because she didn't do that. But what did it matter? They were just passing through. It wasn't like she'd ever see Chef Lalande again.

As she ate, Bennett and Lalande caught up, talking about people they knew and about the restaurant's summer menu.

"So how's it going with the community restaurant thing?" Lalande asked Bennett.

"I was at the last pay-what-you-can night, and it went great," Gia said.

"I thought you were going to do the pay-what-you-can thing all the time by this point," Lalande said. "Wasn't that the plan?"

"That was the plan," Bennett said. "I just don't have the money together yet."

"What?" Gia asked.

The men continued to ignore her. "If you wait until you can fund it yourself, you'll be waiting forever," Lalande said. "You're going to have to get some donations. Shouldn't be that hard. There's a lot of money rolling around New York City."

"I don't want to be beholden to some board of society

matrons who fancy themselves foodies." Bennett's voice dripped with disdain.

"It's not like you're going to be beholden to them," Lalande said. "I mean, yes, you'll have to kiss their asses a bit, but you don't have to let them in your kitchen." The older man shuddered like the very thought repelled him.

"Will someone please explain to me what is going on?" Gia said.

"Sorry," Bennett said. "I want to get out of the mainstream restaurant business. I'd like for Boudin to be a full-time community restaurant. That's always been the plan. You were there for the last pay-what-you-can night. I want it to be like that all the time. If you can't pay, you can work. If you can't do either, you still eat. And we'll have partnerships with farms, but I also want to eventually be able to amass some land in the city to plant a big garden that people can help with, too. The idea is to bring good food to people, regardless of their ability to pay, and to involve them in every aspect of it, from growing to preparing to serving. So the whole thing is a community effort—people taking care of each other through the hub of this restaurant."

"Doesn't Bon Jovi have a place kind of like that in Jersey?" Gia asked.

"Yep. Except I don't have Bon Jovi's money or fame. The restaurant in its current incarnation is going really well, and I've been saving aggressively, but I don't have enough to get it going. Basically, I need an endowment that generates enough interest for me to operate the place."

"And he refuses to prostrate himself before Manhattan's wealthy and powerful." Lalande rolled his eyes, but there was affection in his expression. "I mean, I get it. He's a control freak. I am, too. But there's basically money growing on trees there for the taking."

"I don't want to turn it into some pet project for rich people," Bennett said to Lalande. He turned to Gia and explained, "The point is, it's a *community* restaurant. The community sustains it. I'm not sure exactly how much I'll need to subsidize it. I'm trying to be conservative in my estimates, but I'm thinking the reputation of the place is such that I might be able to attract a fair number of customers who will pay full price."

"Or more." Gia thought of the wealth rolling around the high-fashion industry. She'd seen people pay much more than Bennett was asking for food that wasn't nearly as good. "What if you didn't even put prices on the menu or the bills? So there is no 'full price.' It's literally pay what you can, or what you think it's worth, without there being a preconceived value attached to the food. That way there's no shame in not being able to meet a benchmark. And the flip side is that I bet a lot of people would overpay. Your food is amazing, and Chef Lalande is right, there's a lot of wealth in Manhattan. Certain kinds of people are used to paying more for food that isn't as good as yours, and…"

She trailed off, realizing that both men were looking at her oddly, Bennett with his eyes wide and Lalande with a smirk.

"That's a brilliant idea." Bennett seemed stunned by what he'd just heard. "I have a business plan done, but the cash flow model depends on the food all being a certain price. But if some people would overpay…"

He stared into space, and Gia suspected he was redoing his models in his head.

"Agreed." Lalande dipped his head at Gia with what looked like…respect? Damn, that was gratifying. "But your essential problem remains. You're still going to need a wad of cash to get started and to backfill lean times. A cushion, given that there's not a lot of precedent for the model you're talking about. There are a lot of unknowns."

"Right." Bennett shook his head. "Right. I'm working on it."

"If you won't solicit donations, how about a silent investor?" Lalande asked. "You just need to find someone who expects a negative return and won't meddle. Ha! Good luck with that."

Holy shit. The idea arrived fully formed in Gia's head. She could give Bennett the money. She had more money than she needed and was itching to do something useful with it. Something like that would be the perfect next career move for her. Except for the "no meddling" part. She wanted not just to shovel cash at a good cause—there were plenty of those around—but to actually *do* something. To occupy her days doing something meaningful.

Anyway, it was moot. Bennett wasn't going to take her money for a business venture. He certainly wasn't going to let someone with no experience and no skills actually be *involved*, and she couldn't blame him.

But it was an interesting idea she might give some thought to later. She liked restaurants—hence her Food Network habit. And she'd really enjoyed the behind-the-scenes glimpses she'd gotten both here and at Boudin.

"Well, I guess we should hit the road if we want to make it to Florida tonight," Bennett said, pushing back from the table.

"Maybe make one more stop before you do?" Lalande said to Bennett, and she saw something pass between the two men. When Bennett didn't say anything, Lalande added, "You're building this up in your mind to be way bigger than it has to be. What's the worst that can happen? They slam the door in your face? Then you're no worse off than you are right now."

"Oh, trust me. I'd be a lot worse off." But Bennett smiled as he spoke.

Lalande made a shooing motion, blew her a kiss, and they were on their way.

—⎯◌⏑

"Where to?" Gia asked when they were back in the car. She'd gotten in the driver's seat, and Bennett had not protested. It was easier to keep going with the flow. To keep letting Gia take care of him. Scary, but also easy. Which were not two things that should have gone together, but as he was learning, Gia was capable of inspiring all sorts of wonky, mixed-up emotions.

"Florida," he said, but his voice sounded like he'd sucked in some helium and was auditioning for the next Alvin and the Chipmunks movie.

"Say it like you mean it," she teased. She started the car but did not put it in gear.

"Lalande has always been after me to reconcile with my parents." Which he realized was not an answer to her "Where to?" question.

Except it must have been enough of one, because she nodded determinedly and said, "Your parents' place it is." Her lip curled. "But don't expect me to like them."

"Hang on," he said.

She ignored him. "Reconciliation. I get it. I mean, I get it on paper, but these are the people who turned their backs on you when you needed them the most. These are the people who refused to make even minimal gestures to help you at critical moments. So to my mind"—she wrinkled her nose—"fuck them." Then she smiled. "But I'm more of a bitch than most people, so you just tell me where to go. And after this is over, however it turns out, I'll buy you the biggest sweet tea you've ever laid eyes on."

He blinked, surprised by the outburst but also incredibly touched by it. Gia played the role of the jaded hard-ass who didn't get attached, but underneath all that was a compassionate woman who felt a lot. He wondered suddenly if she felt too much—maybe that was why she was the way she was.

Also, was he really going to do this?

"The thing is," he said, struggling to explain, "Lalande usually turns out to be right about everything. He was the only person who ever believed I could amount to anything without my parents' money. And he always used to say, if you're avoiding doing something, that's a sign that you should actually do that thing."

Gia's eyes widened.

Wait. Had those amber eyes just filmed over with tears? "What's wrong?"

She shook her head rapidly, and suddenly she looked fine. "Nothing. I was just thinking that is actually some pretty spot-on advice."

"Yeah, that's the thing about Chef. He's always right, in a 'wisdom of the ages' kind of way." He sighed. "It's annoying."

"What do you think will happen when you just show up?" Gia asked.

"I have no idea." Which wasn't precisely true. He'd imagined the scenario a bunch of times. Rehearsed several outcomes. They just weren't good ones.

"Well"—she grinned at him and started driving—"there's only one way to find out."

Chapter Eight

$\mathcal{G}$ia started to have second thoughts as she followed Bennett's directions and turned onto a drive marked PRIVATE. The "yard"—that was what he'd called it—was lined with those big trees he'd been talking about on the train. They had that weird white moss dangling from them. She'd never seen one in person, but they screamed "southern gothic." Also...

"This is not a yard, Bennett."

He smirked.

"This is a freaking *estate*."

"My parents have shitloads of money."

She had to hand it to him—not many people would have had the guts to walk away from this kind of money. And money was exactly what he'd just been saying he needed, for his community restaurant. That kind of principled stand was...strangely hot.

After a minute of driving, they emerged from the trees in front of a giant white house studded with black shutters. The entire front of the house—all three of its stories—was covered with porches. The front lawn featured a breathtaking series of terraced gardens. It looked like something out of *Gone With the Wind*.

Yep. Second thoughts were taking root with a vengeance, digging their tentacles into her like the moss on those spooky trees.

Back at the restaurant, she'd totally bought into Lalande's argument as recounted by Bennett. More than that, the idea that things you didn't want to face were the exact things you *should* face? The notion had taken her breath away. Brought tears to her eyes.

She needed to keep eating, regardless of the career consequences.

It had gotten easier. She hadn't even hesitated—much—when Bennett had presented her with the fries he'd made in Lalande's kitchen. She'd known they would be exquisite, like everything else he'd fed her.

But it was more than that. It sounded utterly absurd, but somehow, being with Bennett made some of her usual anxieties feel further away. They were still there, hovering, but they didn't have quite the same hold on her that they'd had even a few days ago. It didn't feel like they were *inside* her anymore.

It probably wasn't Bennett per se, though. Or not only Bennett. It was being so firmly out of her usual routine. Not being faced with casting calls and sample sizes too small for her ass. She hadn't even listened to that voice mail from her agent yet. Being in between jobs, having a month of cushioning, was turning out to be strangely liberating.

So, yes, she had seen the wisdom in Bennett's impulsively coming here. She wanted him to experience some of that liberation, too.

She'd thought.

She wasn't so sure now. This place was intimidating as hell.

"Wow." She cut the engine. "I seriously can't believe you grew up here."

He was silent, almost as if he hadn't heard her, his mouth a grim line and a muscle in his jaw twitching.

She waited a few beats, but when he made no move and didn't speak, she tried again. "You don't have to do this, you know. You don't even have to tell Chef Lalande that you didn't do it. He doesn't know you're here, so he'll never know you bailed."

He started nodding then, very slightly, but repeatedly. "But I will."

"Okay then. I'll wait here, getaway car at the ready?"

That got his full attention. He turned in his seat, his eyes boring into her face in a way that would have felt sexual in another context. He was looking at her like she was a delicious dessert, or a life raft.

"Would you come with me?" he asked softly, and then the intensity of his regard evaporated, replaced by a sheepish grin.

"Of course." She was disproportionately thrilled that he'd asked. The idea that her presence might provide some measure of support or comfort was almost enough to bring back those tears that had been threatening.

"I have no idea how this is going to go down," he said. "It might be ugly."

"Pshaw." She waved a hand dismissively. "I work in fashion. I'm well versed in ugly. I *know* ugly, my friend."

He cocked his head, and his stare turned quizzical.

"What?" she said.

"I think I know what you mean, but it's just a funny thing to hear you say, because you're the most beautiful person I've ever met."

⟶ ⌒

They might not even be home, Bennett told himself as he levered his body out of the tiny car. They'd had him later in life, so they would be into their sixties by now, but even so, he'd be surprised if his father was retired. And his mother used to have DAR meetings on Tuesday afternoons—how the hell did he remember that?

Anyway, it wasn't like he was off the hook if they weren't home. He couldn't come this far and not follow through. If no one answered the door, they'd have to wait. It would just be—

Gia grabbed his hand, interrupting the tumble of his manic thoughts, and the fact that it was her taking his hand and not the reverse gave him a weird injection of confidence. Like if Gia was on his team, it was going to be okay, even if things went to shit.

"Let's do this," she said.

He nodded, led her up the steps to the porch, and rang the doorbell.

If he'd been harboring any hope of putting this off, or perhaps a wish that the door would be answered by Mrs. Johnson, the longtime housekeeper, they were dashed when he heard footsteps clacking across the tile entryway.

He'd forgotten that noise, but it was immediately familiar, as close to him as if he'd never left. His mother always wore high heels, even at home.

She swung open the door, talking as she did so. "I told you that the peonies aren't—"

She froze. Blinked rapidly.

She was so old. Life had lurched ahead without him. Of course it had. Not that her face betrayed her sixty-five years—his mother would never allow that to happen. It was more the reverse—she was too taut, her skin too smooth and stretched too tightly over the bone. She'd always been slim, but she was tiny now, like a little shrunken bird.

But the Chanel suit was the same. And the shoes.

Gia squeezed his hand.

"Hi, Mom," he croaked.

"Bennett," she said, like he was merely here for a routine visit. Like it hadn't been fourteen years since they'd seen each other. She was no longer blinking, just looking at him with her eyebrows raised questioningly.

Gia squeezed harder.

"I've come to..." What? *Apologize* was not the right word, though he supposed some *I'm sorry*s were due on both sides. *Make peace* didn't seem right, either, because that implied that they'd been at war, and they hadn't. All there had been between them for the past fourteen years was silence. An absence. A hole.

"You need money," his mother said, and he sensed Gia stiffen beside him.

"No," he shot back, trying not to betray the hurt his mother's assumption brought to the surface.

"Mrs. Buchanan." Gia extended her hand—thankfully, Bennett was holding her left hand, which left her right free to offer to his mother in the form of a handshake. Bennett didn't think he could do the rest of this without Gia's hand in his. It was small but powerful. "My name is Gia Gallo. I'm a friend of Bennett's. We're road-tripping to Florida for a wedding, and we thought we'd stop in."

That all sounded...reasonable.

His mother hadn't taken Gia's hand. She merely let her gaze flicker up and down Gia's body. It stopped on the blue hair, which Bennett realized with a start he'd gotten used to. But yeah, blue hair would not be in his mother's wheelhouse.

None of it seemed to faze Gia. She just smiled brightly, though Bennett recognized it as false—and was somewhat startled to realize he knew her well enough to make that judgment.

His mother stepped back and gestured them inside without a word.

The smell of hydrangeas hit Bennett as they moved into the entryway. His mother always kept a large vase of them on the marble table in the center of the grand foyer, and the sense memory bore down on him with a force that mere flowers should not have been capable of.

"Shall we sit in the garden?" his mother asked, as if this were an unremarkable social call.

"That would be lovely," Gia said, when Bennett took a little too long to answer.

Before he knew it, his mother had called for refreshments, and a housekeeper he did not recognize had brought a pitcher of tea to the veranda out back.

He watched Gia screw up her face when she took a sip of the tea. It was extremely sweet, and if you hadn't grown up on it, he could see how it would be distasteful. That little nose scrunch was another gesture he recognized as distinctly hers.

"Where's Dad?" he asked.

"Probably in his library," his mother answered.

Jesus fucking Christ. Bennett had assumed his father was at work. Because, really? He appears on the doorstep after fourteen years, and his father is in the house and his mother doesn't even bother summoning him? Weren't southerners supposed to be warm?

Had his mother *ever* been warm?

Gia took another sip of her tea, and this time it was followed by a little cough. She was trying not to be rude, but she hated it. *Warm* was not a word he initially would have used to describe Gia. Certainly not when she was flipping out at the airport or bristling over the lack of Wi-Fi at the restaurant. But there was something that ran deeper with Gia. Something subtler and stronger and less cloying. It *was* a kind of warmth, or maybe *loyalty* was the better word, but you had to *earn* it, which made it all the sweeter.

He cleared his throat. "Do you think you could go get him?" Because, shit, were they just going to sit here and stare at each other like they were statues in the Museum of Southern Gentility?

After a tense moment of silence, his mother nodded, rose, and clacked out of the room.

He reached over, picked up Gia's tea, and drained it.

"Oh, thank God. I didn't want to be rude, but..." She made a face.

"I know." And his mother's tea was much sweeter than his—he'd downscaled the sugar in his over the years. "It's an acquired taste. They pretty much hook you up to an IV of it from childhood here."

"Also..." Even though they were alone, Gia turned her head toward him as if she meant her expression exclusively for him. She made an exaggerated face of incredulous disbelief.

He wasn't sure if she was referring to the over-the-top

grandeur of the house or the low-key freeze-out his mother was performing, but either way, his response was the same. "I know."

She pursed her lips and performed a tense sigh. The idea that a third party, an impartial observer, was offering up some solidarity was buoying. He could do this. He still had no earthly idea what he was going to say, but he knew now that his goal was to make his parents less…a thing. Like turning on the light and realizing that the monster lurking in the corner was just a pile of clothing.

Didn't mean he wasn't nervous as hell, but he was ready to unmask the monster.

"Bennett?"

His father appeared at the door, alone. He looked older, and unlike with Bennett's mother, it had been a more straightforward sort of aging. His face was creased with deep lines that hadn't been there before. He was much thinner— almost gaunt. His father had become an old man.

"Bennett," he said again, and his voice wavered this second time.

Bennett stood.

And eff him if his father didn't walk over and embrace him.

Bennett was stuck there for a moment, paralyzed. His father had *never* been a hugger.

Tentatively, almost as if some part of him expected the gesture to turn into a prank, he let himself hug his father back.

His father tightened his grasp, holding on to Bennett with a strength that was belied by his outward fragility.

This was *not* the reaction he'd expected from his father. Not that he'd expected it from his mother, either, but his father had always been the less involved parent. He would show up at Bennett's baseball games, but only when his mother made a point of having his secretary put them in his schedule. His father had always followed his mother's lead—going where she said to go, wearing what she said to wear.

Not getting out of the car that night at Lalande's when she said not to.

Bennett had to clear his throat when they separated. "I thought you'd be at work."

"The old ticker gave out." He sat down. "Quadruple bypass six months ago. Meyer made me retire. Didn't believe me when I vowed to scale way back."

Bennett laughed. He could picture it. Dr. Meyer had been the family physician since before Bennett was born— he had delivered Bennett, in fact. "Dr. Meyer was always a smart guy."

The news was jarring, though. As much as he'd thought he'd been content to cut all ties with his parents, it was alarming to learn that his father could have died, and Bennett never would have known. His throat thickened.

"Dad, I—"

His mother reappeared with the housekeeper in tow. The woman, who was not wearing a uniform as Mrs. Johnson had during Bennett's youth, set a tray of lemon bars down on the table. When his father reached for one, she swatted his hand away. Bennett sucked in a breath. Mrs. Johnson would never have said a word to Bennett's father, much less touched him.

"Those are not for you, Brian." She handed over a small bowl of what looked like popcorn seasoned with some kind of spice.

His dad rolled his eyes. "Rae Lynn is determined to keep the grim reaper at bay."

His father would never have called Mrs. Johnson by her

first name. Bennett didn't even know what it was. But the housekeeper calling his father Brian? Well, shit. Bennett about had to call for some smelling salts.

"Well, someone has to do it," Rae Lynn snapped, but there was affection in her sass, as there had been in his father's complaint.

Which was...utterly unprecedented.

"Where are my manners?" His father introduced Bennett to Rae Lynn. That, in turn, prompted Bennett to introduce Gia.

Once that was done and Rae Lynn had retreated, there was nothing left to do but find some goddamned words to say. To deliver his nonapology, closure, whatever speech.

"I'm sorry I didn't call first. I—"

"We're sorry," his father said, which caused his mother to stiffen and Bennett to stifle a gasp.

"That's not..." He'd been going to say, "That's not necessary," but actually...maybe it was.

"We handled things poorly back then." He glanced at Bennett's mother, whose face betrayed nothing. "*I* handled things poorly."

"Your father's brush with death has made him emotional," his mother said tersely, the slight wrinkling of her nose as she spoke communicating her opinion on the display of emotion currently underway.

"Maybe so," said his father. "But the fact remains that I never intended, or wanted, not to see my own child for so many years." He turned to Bennett. "We should have gone to therapy with you. We shouldn't have forced Chapel Hill. Most of all, we should have let you come home. I'm so sorry we didn't."

"So in retrospect, you wanted to have an addict in the house?" his mother said incredulously.

"No," his father said. "In retrospect, I wanted to have a *son* in the house."

Bennett had to swallow a few times before speaking. "It worked out okay. I found my feet. And..." He had to meet his father halfway here. "I'm sorry." The words were coming out easily now, almost of their own accord. "I'm sorry I caused you so much grief."

His throat was impossibly heavy, but the rest of his body felt like it was floating to the surface of a lake after years of being submerged.

When nobody spoke, Gia said, "Did you know that Bennett owns a Cajun restaurant in Manhattan?" Her voice sounded strange amid the conversational swirls of all these Buchanans. It was high and girlish and lacked the southern drawl so apparent in everyone else's voice. It wasn't a bad strange, though, not at all. It was a familiar, soothing balm.

And he found he wanted his parents to know of his success.

His parents answered Gia's question at the same time. His mom said, "No," and his dad said, "Yes."

Then his dad turned to his mom and said, "Oh, come on, Rhonda. Tell me you haven't googled him."

His mother said nothing, just continued to look like she was sucking a lemon.

His father's eyes had grown suspiciously watery. "I thought so many times about sending a letter to the restaurant. I wrote a few—pretty much every year around Christmas." He paused and cleared his throat. "But then I would tear them up. I wasn't sure you would want to hear from me. I wondered if sending a letter would be selfish. Would open wounds that I hoped had healed over for you." He blew out a breath. "But now that you're here, I can see that was another misstep. Another thing to be sorry for."

Bennett wanted to say it was okay, to offer some

absolution—he had felt the same way, hesitating over emails drafted but not sent many times over the years—but he found he couldn't speak.

"The restaurant is a big success." Gia, bless her, was filling the awkward silence that had settled. "The food is out of this world."

"I'm sure it is." His father smiled with something that looked like...pride?

"And how did you get into...cooking?" his mother asked, emphasizing the word *cooking* like it was distasteful. And for her, it would be. Bennett was supposed to become a southern gentleman lawyer, join his father's practice, which had been founded by his great-grandfather. In his mother's view, he might as well have become a garbage collector.

But to his surprise, he didn't bristle at the veiled criticism. He found he didn't care what his mother thought of him. Well, that wasn't true, exactly, but he understood that he couldn't *control* what she thought of him. And that, in turn, meant she'd lost her power over him. That he was a disappointment to her was unfortunate, but it didn't matter, materially, to his life. The apology from his father had been more than enough.

"It's a long story," he said, casting his mind back to the night Marc caught him behind the restaurant.

"Maybe you'll tell it to us over dinner?" his father asked, and it was impossible to miss the hope infused in his voice.

It was hard to imagine telling his father the story. Because it wouldn't just be the story of how he got into cooking, but the story of his life. He struggled with how to answer.

"They're saying thunderstorms beginning in a few hours," his father went on. "You'd be welcome to stay the night." He looked between Bennett and Gia. "Both of you."

The olive branch his father had extended was both welcome and astonishing. But it was also...too much. He needed time to adjust to this new reality. To absorb the fact of this incredible détente. He didn't want to be rude, but suddenly he had to get out of here.

But how to look at his father and refuse, after the man had reached so far over the chasm that separated them?

"Your invitation is so kind," Gia said smoothly, "but I'm afraid we're on a bit of a schedule. We're on our way to a wedding in Florida. We were supposed to be there two days ago. I'm sure you heard about the big storm that hit the eastern seaboard?" His father nodded. "Our flights were canceled, so this whole road trip is a bit of a race against the clock. So I think we really need to get some miles under our belt, especially if a rainstorm is going to hit."

His father nodded, resigned. "Well, I'm grateful that you made the detour to see us."

"I'm glad we did, too," Gia said. "Perhaps we can plan for dinner at Bennett's place in New York?"

Yes. Exactly. Telling his father the story of his life in the confines of Boudin was something Bennett *could* imagine. He'd be able to *show* his father his success, to let the restaurant speak for itself. Leave it to Gia to arrange the perfect scenario, one that didn't make him want to panic. He almost laughed at how spot-on she was—she knew what he needed before he did.

"Yes," his father said. "Name the date, and we'll be there."

Bennett's mother remained silent. Bennett wasn't sure "they" would be there, but that would be okay.

"So why don't you all exchange numbers, and Bennett can be in touch about getting together in New York?" Gia said, and God bless her, she was doing an A-plus job of moving them along.

His father produced a phone from his blazer pocket. "And I'll look forward to getting to know you better, too, Gia. I'm so glad Bennett has found someone like you."

Bennett was about to issue the "we're just friends" correction, but Gia grabbed his hand. Ah, the feel of her hand. It was soothing even though he wouldn't have thought he needed soothing now that the visit was almost over and had gone better than he had expected. She beamed at him and said, "I'm the lucky one."

What?

"Are you married?" his mother asked, and Bennett didn't miss her glance down to their joined hands.

"No," Gia said. "We actually haven't known each other that long."

"Well," said Bennett's father, "sometimes you just know."

"Sometimes you do." Gia's eyes twinkled. Ah, now she was playing him. But he couldn't find it in him to be annoyed. To be anything other than profoundly grateful to her, in fact. And if there was a little part of him that wished what she was implying were true—that they were really together? Well, that was neither here nor there.

"I insist you have a lemon bar before you go." His mother pushed the tray toward them. When neither of them reached for one, she added, "What will Rae Lynn think if no one eats one?"

Gia smiled—it was a fake one—and picked up a bar. Bennett followed suit. The old housekeeper's lemon bars had been pretty damn good, and if these were from the same recipe, it would be no hardship to eat one before they left.

"Delicious," he said, and it was the truth. A nice mixture of tart and sweet, a good flaky crust.

Gia took a small bite of hers. He braced himself for a moment. Would she let loose an "Oh my God"?

She chewed and swallowed and remained silent.
He gloated inwardly.

—⁀ᗡ—

Gia wanted to run to the car. The only thing that stopped
her was the presence of Bennett's parents on the porch
watching them take their leave. So she forced herself to
smile and walk slowly, telling herself she was practicing
her bridesmaid walk.

"You didn't want to stay, did you?" she whispered. She
was almost certain the answer was no, but she had to check.
"Because we can easily do that." Even if they waited until
tomorrow to leave, they'd still arrive with time to spare,
given that Wendy had moved the tailoring appointment.

Bennett placed his arm around her shoulders as they
walked, presumably to shield their conversation from his
parents, but oh, it felt good.

"Hell no."

That was a relief. She would stay if he wanted to, but
she'd had about enough of this stifling southern gothic
soap opera.

"Let me drive," she murmured as they approached the car.

"I'm fine now."

"I want to do it." She wasn't sure why she was so
adamant. It was probably a bad look, in the eyes of these
traditional southern people, for the woman to drive. It likely
emasculated Bennett or some shit. But then, they were getting into a tiny turquoise toy car, so what did it matter?

She just really wanted to drive. To be the agent that
hightailed them out of here. She sort of felt like she'd gotten
Bennett into this, and she wanted to get him out of it.

He gave her the keys without any further protest, which

surprised her a little. So many guys made driving into this big symbolic thing that was somehow tied up in their masculinity. She would like to think it meant he trusted her, but he probably just wanted to get out of here without a big argument.

"Bye!" she called, pasting on a smile and waving to the Buchanans.

They got in the car, and she punched it, spraying gravel behind them as she took off through the creepy tree archway.

But then, just as they'd cleared the trees, she thought about how their creepiness was kind of cool. And the car was out of sight of the house now. So she stopped, reached into the back seat for her bag, and produced her camera. Bennett watched in silence as she hopped out of the car, aimed the camera at the oaks, and took a picture.

They didn't speak, as if by mutual agreement, when she got back in. She merely handed him the photo and hit the gas again. He held it, waving it idly to speed the developing process, like they did this every day. She waited until they were fully clear of the property and she was accelerating up the road before glancing over at him. He must have felt her attention, because he turned to look at her, too.

She wasn't sure how to interpret what had happened back there, other than to know that it had exhausted her. Which was absurd, because the whole thing had been twenty minutes, and it hadn't been her family. Still, the combination of Bennett's mother's iciness and the heavy, unnamable emotions emanating from Bennett and his father had made for a potent, exhausting twenty minutes. It had been difficult to read the subtle undercurrents at work, to help Bennett, which had been her aim, without overstepping.

She raised her eyebrows questioningly.

"I don't know," he said, somehow intuiting that her unspoken query had been something along the lines of *What the hell just happened there?* "I can't even…"

She nodded. She got it. He would probably have to process all that had happened for a good long while.

"But thank you." The emotion was back in his voice. She wasn't sure what he was referring to, but again, he answered her unasked question. "For getting us out of there when I didn't know how." He blew out a breath and let his head fall back against the headrest. "For bringing me to Charleston to begin with." Then he lifted his head and she felt his attention back on her, though she kept her eyes on the road. "For being with me. I know this whole detour has been… intense."

"No problem. I'm the one who kidnapped you while you were sleeping and brought you here. And sorry I sort of pretended to be your girlfriend. It just seemed…" What? The truth was that she'd wanted to make him look good in front of his parents, and she had suspected they—or at least his mother—were the sort of people who would put stock in a settled, monogamous relationship. She'd wanted them to think of Bennett as the sort of person who inspired loyalty and trust. Which he was. He would make a great boyfriend—for the sort of woman who did relationships. "Like the path of least resistance," she finished lamely.

"So now that you're my fake girlfriend, you're going to have to come to New York for this hypothetical dinner, or else fake dump me beforehand."

She chuckled. "Maybe you'll fake break up with me first."

"Unlikely."

"How do you figure that?" She was suddenly a little too interested in his opinion on the demise of their fictional relationship.

"Of the two of us, you're *definitely* the one who's a flight risk."

She shrugged and tried not to smile. She couldn't argue with that assessment.

The sky had grayed over while they were inside Bennett's parents' place, and now the first drops of rain were starting. She flipped on the wipers and merged onto the highway, still feeling the urge to get them the hell out of Dodge.

They drove in silence for a good hour through the rain. There was still enough light to see by, though, and the rain wasn't heavy, so there was no reason for her to be ruffled, but the farther they got from Charleston, the more unsettled Gia became. The feeling was growing stronger with each passing mile. Something was wrong with her body. It wanted out of the car. Eventually it got so intense that she had to silently lecture herself to keep her limbs still and the pressure of her foot even on the gas pedal. Which made no sense, because at work she often stood still as a statue in wildly uncomfortable poses and surroundings. Stick her on a beach in fifty-five-degree weather with sand in her butt and she would smile through the whole thing. But now, suddenly, she just needed *out*. The impulse she'd had to flee Bennett's parents' house, and then Charleston itself, had been focused, like a laser. Now it was as if there had been an explosion inside her—a crack of thunder to accompany all this rain—and all that concentrated focus had scattered to the wind, leaving her jumpy and unsettled.

Rationally, they should make as much progress as possible this evening, if not push all the way through. Though it seemed like a lifetime had elapsed since they'd left Virginia before dawn, it was only six o'clock. They could make it most of the way, if not all, this evening if they wanted to.

But once they got back on I-95, Gia started seeing signs for hotels. She could feel herself weakening. She was just so *done* with this day. It was like all those scattered pieces of her attention had become magnetized, and the Hilton Garden Inn was her true north.

As they approached the exit they would have to take, there was a giant crack of thunder. Just the cosmic nudge she needed.

She pulled off. "Okay, that's it. We're done."

"Really?"

"Really. I need a drink." She glanced over at him. "And I imagine you probably need several gallons of your sugar water. On me, remember?"

By the time they pulled into the parking lot of the hotel, it had started hailing. She smiled. The universe was with her. There had been no rational reason to stop at six o'clock in the evening—"I'm antsy, and I can't be in the car anymore even though I'm the one who's been obsessing over getting to Florida as fast as possible" was certainly not going to make the grade.

But pea-size hail that was shading into marble-size hail? *That* was a good reason to stop.

"Damn," said Bennett as she pulled into the crowded parking lot. "Good call."

She preened a little, as if she had a meteorological crystal ball and had done this solely to spare them the hail.

He tapped the dashboard. "I'm not sure this sorry excuse for an automobile would have survived this." He twisted around, reached into the back seat, and grabbed the leather jacket he'd lent her—she had thrown it back there this morning. "Don't move." In a flash he was out of the car and had come around to the driver's side. He opened her door and held the jacket over it, holding it with one hand while he used the other to gesture her to his side. "I'll come back for our stuff once we're in the rooms."

She ducked her head, stepped under the makeshift umbrella, and allowed him to tuck her close to his side.

"Ready?" He arranged the jacket over their heads.

"Yep," she said, and they ran.

The parking lot had been almost full, and they'd had to park at the very end, so they had a fair amount of terrain to cover. "Ahhh!" she shrieked as she took too big a step, losing her footing and lurching forward, out from under the protection of the jacket and Bennett's arms. "Ow!" The hail *hurt*.

"Behave," he admonished. "Just for once, okay?"

"I'm trying!" she protested.

A few more janky steps, and they got themselves in sync. They were no longer working against each other, but together, like they were on the same team. It had felt like that at Bennett's parents' house, too, except this time, their foe was not an icy, disdainful mother but *actual* ice falling from the sky, which somehow felt like much less dire a threat.

"This is crazy!" She laughed as they jogged along.

It was like their snowball fight of two nights ago. They were at the mercy of the elements—and these were some crazy-ass elements. But again, instead of being poised to fight each other, they were allied against the hail. Against Bennett's parents. Against the world.

He was laughing, too, as they reached the shelter of the overhang that extended from the hotel's main entrance.

"I don't know why I didn't just drive up!" Gia exclaimed, taking note of other cars idling under the protective covering, presumably while their occupants checked in.

"Because you are not accustomed to roadside motels," Bennett said, and he was right. "You're not accustomed to car culture."

"That's...exactly right." It was still so weird, the way Bennett made these observations about her that were spot-on. It was like he knew stuff about her that she herself didn't consciously know. She made a sheepish face, meant to agree with his assessment.

"It's not a character flaw," he said. "You're used to New York and Paris. You don't just drive up to your target establishment in cities like that."

They'd reached the front desk, and Bennett turned his attention from her to the woman behind it.

"Good evening, ma'am."

That was followed by an exchange about the weather that went on way longer than it would have in New York. Gia bit back a laugh, listening to Bennett's drawl deepen as he flirted with...Gia glanced at the woman's name tag. Oh my God, her name was *actually* Reese.

This was *totally* the beginning of a rom-com. Freak hailstorm brings handsome stranger to the front desk of a roadside hotel. Reese probably had something tethering her to this town—an ailing parent, an unpaid debt that had been run up by her loser ex-husband. Something keeping her here, in need of rescuing.

"Good thing you pulled off here," Reese said. "You gotta go a long way down 95 before you hit any more hotels."

Reese was cute as a button, too. She didn't look like her Hollywood counterpart, but she was clearly a southern belle, with her perfectly coiffed honey-brown hair and her frosty pink lipstick. She was wearing a uniform, but Gia was having no trouble picturing her in a debutante gown. She probably had a tiara behind the desk for when she clocked out.

"Stopping here was a smart move," Reese went on, clearly trying to flatter Bennett.

Gia waited for Bennett to inform Reese that the idea

to stop had actually been hers, but he just flashed Reese a thousand-watt smile and said, "Well, ma'am, given this here hail, we are certainly hoping there's a room at the inn."

"Two rooms," Gia said automatically, which caused Reese's smile to sharpen.

"Actually," Reese said to Bennett, stretching the word out on her tongue, "it's not *ma'am*. It's *miss*." Then she looked between him and Gia like she was trying to make sense of their relationship.

Join the club, Reese.

Gia's legs started feeling jumpy again, like they had in the car, but this time, instead of wanting to get off the highway, they wanted...to move her over so she was standing closer to Bennett? What the hell? And it was all she could do to prevent her hand from joining the party, from floating up and settling on his forearm.

Anyway, it didn't matter. No need for her to piss on her territory, because Bennett didn't do casual. He might charm the pants off Reese, but only metaphorically. Reese was no threat.

No. Wait. That wasn't why it didn't matter. It didn't matter because there was nothing between Gia and Bennett. *God.*

Bennett paused, taking in the "ma'am/miss" correction, which anyone could tell was meant to telegraph to Bennett that Reese was single. And probably also taking in the fact that Gia was kind of invading his personal space. He cleared his throat awkwardly, almost guiltily, which was ridiculous. There was no law against flirting—Bennett was eminently flirt-with-able, and he owed Gia nothing.

"Right. *Miss*," he said to Reese, in a tone that Gia had trouble reading. In the movie, this would be the part where he turned up the wattage on the grin, leaned in close, and made a remark about how it seemed impossible that a woman as pretty and charming as Reese could be single, but he didn't seem to be playing his part.

"I have one room left," Reese said.

Of course. Except the plot was messed up because it should be Bennett and Reese forced to share the last room, right?

"This storm has pushed us to our limit," she added.

And you, Reese, have pushed me to mine.

"One room will be fine." Gia pulled out her credit card, let that renegade hand settle possessively on Bennett's forearm, and smiled blandly at Reese because goddammit, if Bennett was going to refuse to sleep with anyone tonight, it was going to be *Gia*.

Chapter Nine

As they walked down the hallway toward the last room in the hotel, Bennett told himself it didn't matter. They'd slept in the same room two nights ago, at his place, and they'd fooled around pretty extensively last night. Gia had gone from being a stranger to someone who knew all his shit. Like *all* of it—his checkered past, his modern-day hang-ups, his fucked-up family. So sharing a room with her was not a big deal.

"Don't worry," Gia said, apparently reading his mind. "Your virtue is safe with me. I just didn't think we should give up a sure thing, what with the hail out there." She unlocked the door. "And look—two beds, so you're safe."

He chuckled. Right. This would be no problem.

She sighed, reached her hands up over her head, and stretched, sticking her chest out and arching her back. She either wasn't wearing a bra or it was a thin one, and the air conditioner, which was on full blast, was making her nipples hard.

"I'm going to take a shower, okay?" she said over her shoulder as she turned toward the bathroom.

No problem.

She furrowed her brow and turned back to him, clearly waiting for his agreement—she was being polite, making sure he didn't need the bathroom before she went in. But of course she could not see inside his head, where he was chanting *No problem* over and over again. Nope, from her perspective, he was just standing there mutely staring at her.

"No problem." It came out a little too loudly as he attempted to get his mouth to add sound to his previously silent mantra. "I'm going to go back out and get our bags."

"Why don't you call down and ask *Reese* if she can send someone up with the bags?"

"Who?" He had missed something, because he had no idea who she was talking about.

"Your admirer at the front desk."

Right. "Yeah, well, I think this is more of a 'get your own bags' kind of place than you're probably used to. I'll get our stuff, you shower, and then we can go across to the restaurant when you're ready." Which was an Applebee's. How the mighty do fall.

"Nope. I'm done with this day. I know it's ridiculously early, but after this shower, I'm not getting dressed until tomorrow."

Of course she didn't actually mean she was coming out naked. She meant that after the shower, she was getting into her pajamas.

No problem.

He sighed, nodded, and headed back outside. Came back and dropped her bag just outside the bathroom door before leaving again.

When he returned twenty minutes later with some take-out from Applebee's and the bottle of wine from last night, which he'd stashed in the trunk, she was sprawled out on the bed in those goddamned tiny-ass pajamas.

Her eyes remained closed as she spoke. "Shower's all yours. The bathroom door's busted so it doesn't close all the way, but I'm so tired, I'm not opening my eyes until morning." She smiled to herself but kept her eyes closed. "Just pretend I'm not here."

"You can go ahead and open your eyes if you like. I'm pretty sure I'll be okay."

Because that was the rational thing to say.

Rationally, there was *no problem* here.

But in truth, the idea of taking a shower on the other side of that flimsy, half-closed door from her was…kind of a problem. It was one thing to beat off in the adjoining room, another with her *right there*. But he didn't see how he was going to survive this night without taking the edge off. He'd had to do that each of the last two nights.

She opened her eyes but her body remained still. "Oh, good. I mean, I had the best orgasm of my life last night thanks to you, so, really, there's no reason to go all Victorian modesty overkill at this point."

Wait. *What?* His cheeks heated. Jesus fucking Christ, that bomb she casually dropped went straight to his already susceptible dick. Or his ego. Or maybe the two were, at this moment, one and the same.

She sat up. "Sorry. Am I making you uncomfortable?"

"No." He opened the takeout containers and set plastic cutlery and napkins out on the desk. *Not in the way you mean, at least.* "But the best orgasm you ever had? I just find it hard to believe that someone of your, ah…"

"Degree of sluttiness?" she suggested perkily.

"That was *not* what I was going to say."

She shrugged. "Well, what can I say? You're a talented man, Bennett." Then she sighed, a little wistfully, he thought, and dammit, that made his dick even harder.

She extended a hand. "Hand me that bottle."

He twisted off the cap and did as she asked. He was about to fetch her a glass, but she lifted the bottle to her lips, tipped her head back, and took a deep drink. Helpless to look away, he watched her throat undulate as she swallowed.

After several moments, she lifted her head, popped the bottle out of her lips, and wiped her mouth with the back of her hand.

"Anyway." She settled herself back against the headboard with her legs stretched out on the bed in front of her. "You don't have to worry about me. I got your message loud and clear."

"What message?"

She rolled her eyes. "The 'I don't want to sleep with you, Gia' message."

"It's not that I don't *want* to."

She raised her eyebrows playfully. He wanted to lick them. Jesus Christ, he wanted to *lick* her *eyebrows*.

They were just so... perfect. Full and symmetrical and the color of molasses.

He was so fucking screwed.

She scrambled off the bed and went in search of the remote. "I'm teasing you, but I get it. You know I would never force myself on you, right?"

"Uh, right." He tried not to laugh. The image of Gia physically accosting him was too funny. He might be a little out of step with the times in terms of his moral code, but he wasn't a trembling virgin.

"I don't really do repeat performances, anyway." She switched on the TV.

He rolled his eyes. "Right. God forbid you should actually get to know someone or, I don't know, have *two* of the best orgasms you've ever had in your life."

"Are you offering?"

Was he? *Shit.*

She waggled her eyebrows. "If it makes a difference, I'll tell you that two times is my max with the same guy. It's kind of a rule I have."

"A *rule*?" Jesus Christ, she was a complicated woman.

She shrugged. "Keeps me honest."

"What the hell does that mean?"

"I don't want to be anyone's girlfriend. I also don't want to mislead anyone. So I make sure I don't."

"So when you said before that the fastest way to get rid of you was a declaration of love, you weren't kidding."

She laughed. "Exactly. And it doesn't even take love. Mild devotion is enough to make me run for the hills. So I just cut things off before that can happen. It's better for everyone."

"That sounds awfully lonely." Jesus, it sounded terrible. He might not have found "the one," but sex aside, he couldn't imagine having gone his entire life without a real romantic relationship.

She looked at him a long time before speaking. Then, after a lengthy, uncomfortable assessment he feared he'd failed, she dismissed him by picking up the remote. "I'm awake now. I'm gonna try to find a Food Network show that you'll hate."

He shook his head, trying to dislodge thoughts of her "rule"—and her claim that he was responsible for the best orgasm of her life. He grabbed one of the takeout boxes

and sat next to her on the bed rather than going to the
other one. He had the absurd impulse to demonstrate that
he wasn't afraid of her. He could shower later. "You want
some dinner?"

"No thanks," she said as the TV switched to Rachael
Ray, whom, yes, Bennett hated. "Aha! Victory!"

Then the lights went out.

Everything went out: lights, TV, the hum of the air
conditioner.

"Fuck me," Gia said.

I'm trying not to.

—ᴄɔ

"The power went out," Bennett said.

"Yes, thank you. I got that." Gia was being kind of
a bitch, but she didn't care. She was tired, hungry, and
sexually frustrated. Which all would have been okay, or at
least endurable, but she was also a bunch of other confusing
things, the most disconcerting of which was sad. Sad that
she was never going to fool around with Bennett again.
Also strangely disappointed that their epic journey would
be over by this time tomorrow. The idea of being around
Bennett in the bigger group of her friends was…weird.
It felt like sharing something she didn't want to share.
As had been the case with Reese. Which, speaking of,
in addition to tired, hungry, and sexually frustrated, she
was also jealous of a hotel receptionist she was never
going to see again and what. The. Hell. Was *wrong* with
her?

"I'll pop downstairs and see if it's just us or if it's the
whole hotel."

"I'll come, too," she said automatically, her body having

propelled itself out of bed before she finished the sentence, because God forbid Bennett should encounter Reese un-chaperoned.

It was pitch-black in the room, so she held her hands out in front of her and started shuffling in the direction of the door.

She stopped when she hit him.

She expected him to argue, to tell her to stay put while he investigated, or at least to insist that she shouldn't come down to the lobby in her pajamas because that wouldn't be *proper*, but he didn't. He just wrapped her hand in his—which was starting to feel downright normal—and led them out of the room.

The hallways were dim, lit by what appeared to be backup lights, probably powered by a generator.

"Looks like it's at least the whole floor." Bennett didn't drop her hand even though there was enough light to see by in the corridors and stairwell.

They found Reese addressing a group of guests. "As far as we can tell, it's the whole county. The hail took out a bunch of substations." She looked up as Bennett and Gia approached, and her eyes flickered down to their joined hands. *Ha. Take that, "miss."*

"The lobby is being powered by generators, so you're welcome to settle in here."

Bennett turned to Gia, a question in his eyes.

"Nah," she said. "I'm not afraid of the dark."

So they turned around, still holding hands, and headed back to the stairs.

When they reached their room, Bennett dropped her hand. Something inside her sent up a protest, but she quashed it. Once inside, she felt her way over to the window to open the curtains. Not that that helped—the storm was still raging. The hail had stopped, though, replaced by an old-fashioned deluge.

She left the curtain open—there was something oddly enjoyable about being at the mercy of such powerful forces yet being safe inside, tucked away from them—and made her way back to the bed.

"I have almost no battery left on my phone," she observed.

"You want to use mine to text Wendy or anything?" He sat on the other side of the bed and picked up his, his face lit by the blue glow of the screen as it came to life.

"Nah." She noted that he'd come back to her bed rather than claim the other one. "We should save the power on yours in case the blackout becomes a long-term thing."

"We should probably just go to sleep," he said, but he didn't sound like he was really endorsing the idea.

"You tired?"

"Strangely, no. I would have thought that this day would have long since done me in, but I guess I've got a second wind or something."

"Me, too." She'd been tired before, but now she was back to being restless and jumpy.

He got up, moved away from her, then came back. "We can play a game I like to call eating lukewarm chicken wings in the dark."

Gia's stomach growled—audibly, so she couldn't claim she wasn't hungry. Anyway, she'd decided she wasn't going to continue starving herself on this trip—and it seemed like it was actually working. So she reached toward the box, felt her way inside, snagged a wing, and then carefully found and lifted the bottle of wine from the bedside table.

"Chicken wings are weird," she said before gnawing off a bite. It was your basic wing—not that she'd had one for years, but somewhere in her brain, synapses fired and recognized the greasy meat and sweet barbeque sauce as "wing, chicken." "Like, do chickens actually fly? They don't, do they?"

"They can. Short distances—some of them, anyway. But they're bred with a high weight-to-wing ratio these days, so they're not really very well suited to it. But if you chase one with a cleaver, yeah, it will sort of hop-fly away from you."

"You sound like you're speaking from experience. Have you chased a chicken with a cleaver?"

"I have."

Why did she find that hot?

"I got it into my head once that I should have the experience of personally butchering some of the animals we serve in the restaurant, so some of our suppliers let me visit their farms and do the dirty deed."

"Well, aren't you a badass, Chef Buchanan?"

"You wouldn't say that if you'd seen me do it. Let's just say it took me a *long* time to catch that motherfucker. It was not a very manly or dignified effort."

She snort-laughed.

"We have a saying in the South—*madder than a wet hen*. That day taught me *exactly* where that saying came from."

He found her hand in the dark and stuck another chicken wing into it.

She wanted to keep asking him questions. She felt like she could sit here all night asking him questions, in fact. Little ones like what was the spice mixture in his boudin balls and big ones like was he actually going to have his parents to the restaurant?

"Okay, we need a new game," he said. "Would you rather? Would you rather kill a chicken with a cleaver at close range or kill a cow from afar with a dart gun?"

She cracked up. "I would rather play truth or dare."

It had just popped into her head. The dark, the air of confession and closeness—it reminded her of the slumber parties of her youth.

"Truth or dare?" He barked a laugh. "And then we'll braid each other's hair?"

"Yes!" She reached up and took her damp hair out of the bun she'd twisted it into after her shower. The idea of his hands combing through her hair, of his fingers on her scalp, made her stomach clench with something other than hunger. "Come on!" She swatted his shoulder to cover her unease. "I'll go first."

"Okay," he said laughingly. "So how does this work? I ask you a question and you have to tell the truth?"

"Yes, if I choose truth, but if I choose dare, you think up a dare and I have to do it."

"What if you refuse both?"

"I face the wrath of my peers?" She laughed. "It doesn't sound very daunting, does it? But I can assure you that when I was twelve, I would have done anything to make my so-called friends like me—though that was pretty much a lost cause."

He was silent for a long moment before saying, "Okay. Truth or dare?"

"Truth. Dare is gonna be pretty hard around here. We don't have parents' closets to raid or a kitchen from which to concoct disgusting things to eat."

"Why didn't your friends like you when you were twelve?"

Whoa. He didn't mess around, did he?

"You don't have to answer that if you don't want to," he added quickly.

"You're not very good at this, Bennett," she teased, even as she thought seriously about the question. She wasn't sure she knew the answer. If she had, back then at least, she wouldn't have been such an outcast, would she?

"I'm not that likable, generally," she said. But knowing that if she was choosing to answer, he wouldn't accept something that vague, she added, "This is going to sound like a horrible, privileged, clichéd thing to say, but I think they were jealous. Girls are mean. My mom had me on the child beauty pageant circuit, as you know."

"This would be the appearance-obsessed mother?"

"That's the one. And she didn't mess around. She had me painted and plucked and made up to within an inch of my life, so I actually won most of them. But it was a double-edged sword, because the girls in my social circle started to...well, to bully me, basically. As an adult, I can look back and be pretty sure that it was a situation of..." She trailed off, not knowing how to say it without sounding like an asshole. So she put on a fake theatrical voice and trilled, "Don't hate me because I'm beautiful."

He didn't say anything. Which was awkward. So she kept talking. "And around that time, my mom started me in some regional modeling gigs, too, which didn't help. I used to hear them talking about me behind my back. At a sleepover once, I'd gone upstairs to go to the bathroom, and when I was on my way back down, I heard them talking about what a conceited bitch I was. I sat there on the stairwell panicking, trying to think up an excuse to leave, but it was the middle of the night, so I was stuck." She still remembered sitting on the scratchy carpet of the stairs, shivering because it was winter, and wondering how long she could hide out there before they'd start looking for her. "I saw then that I'd been playing it wrong. This group of girls used to ask me questions about modeling all the time. They seemed really interested, so I'd try to entertain them with stories. I was in

and out of school because I had jobs, so I didn't have a lot
of friends. All I'd wanted was for them to like me. But I
guess they saw it as bragging or something."

He still didn't say anything. She couldn't even hear him
breathing, though she could sense his weighty presence next
to her. She sighed. She needed to wrap this up. This was
truth or dare, not psychotherapy. "I don't know. When your
whole point in life is to be good-looking, it's hard to find
people who actually like you for you."

That loosened his tongue. "Your whole point in life is
not to be good-looking."

Whoa. He sounded really peevish.

"It kind of is, though. People pay me to wear clothes, or
makeup, or whatever, and look pretty doing it."

"Yes," he said dismissively, "but that's your *job*. That's
not *you*."

He didn't get it. "So the restaurant. The current one and
the community restaurant you want to open. Those are just
jobs? They're not tied up in who you are as a person?"

"That's different."

"Why? You love food. You want to help people. All those
parts of you get tangled up in your job. They *created* your
job. I'm good-looking. That's my big 'skill'"—she made air
quotes with her fingers even though he couldn't see them.
"So I became a model. There's no shame in that."

"Of course there's no shame in that." He was still irritated.
"All I'm trying to say is, yes, you're extremely beautiful.
But you're a lot of other things, too. And anyway, I suspect
being a successful model takes more than just beauty."

There was something about the dismissive way he ac-
knowledged her beauty, like it was a fact but not, ultimately,
a very important one, that made her shiver even though the
room was getting hot without the air-conditioning running.

"*Anyway*," she said, wanting to end this line of discussion. "The relevant point to this 'truth' is that when beauty is what you're known for, it's hard to make friends. To forge real relationships you can rely on."

"Is that why you only do casual?"

"That, my friend, is another question." He was spot-on, though. The way to avoid being used or fetishized by men for her beauty was to keep them at arm's length: one-and-done; two-and-through. But she didn't want to get into that with him. It was her system, and yes, maybe it was kind of fucked up, but it worked just fine. Hadn't he told her only last night that things didn't have to be rational for them to work? "It's your turn. So, what'll it be? Truth or dare?"

"Truth."

"What do you hope happens with your parents?"

He huffed a self-deprecating laugh. "You don't mess around, do you?"

"Well, I dunno, you've already told me about your dramatic criminal past and about your weird-ass rules of dating, and no one was making you say any of *that* stuff, so this seems like a softball of a question, relatively speaking."

He chuckled. "Touché." Then he got up. "I think I'm gonna need to find my tea for this. You want a glass for your wine?"

"Nah. I'll stick with chugging straight from the bottle. Not very dignified, but it seems safer than trying to pour red wine in the dark."

He'd been sitting cross-legged on the bed before, but when he came back with his drink, he mimicked her position, leaning back against the headboard and extending his legs in front of him along the bed. Not that she could see him doing it. She could *feel* it. He was close. There were only a couple of inches between her shoulder and his, between her thigh and his.

He took a long drink before speaking. "I don't even know, really, and that's not just me trying to get out of answering the question. For a long time, I wanted to not care. They weren't in my life for so long, and I always thought if I could just wash my hands of them, that would be ideal, but..."

"You couldn't."

"Basically. I went about my business. It wasn't like it crippled me or anything, but I suppose I always had this unresolved junk hanging in my mind when it came to my parents. For God's sake, it kept me from ever going back to Charleston, and I love Charleston. That's pretty fucked up, isn't it?"

"Eh, I think it's pretty normal. Human beings will go way out of their way to avoid facing uncomfortable truths."

She set down her half-eaten chicken wing.

"So, as for what I actually *want*... Well, you could probably surmise that my father's reaction to my appearance was unexpected, to say the least."

"I did."

"And this idea you floated, of them coming to the restaurant..."

"I'm sorry again about that. I overstepped. It's not my business."

She felt him turn toward her. "No. It's perfect, actually. Because I think the best-case scenario, one I never even dared to imagine, is some kind of meaningful relationship with my father." He laughed in what sounded like disbelief. "If you'd asked me yesterday if that was possible, I would have bet the restaurant against it. But having him come to me, having him see what I've made. He might... I don't know? Get it?"

"He will." Of that she had no doubt. No one could see Bennett at work in his restaurant, eat his food, and not be blown away by his utter mastery. By his unmitigated success.

"And as for my mother?" He snorted. "I guess we all have to have at least one terrible relative, don't we?"

She reached across the few inches of darkness between them, found his arm, then slid her hand down it until she reached his bottle of tea, and clinked her wine bottle against it. "Here's to terrible mothers."

"Yeah, I think I'd like to have a word with yours."

"Ha. It's your turn. Dare me to call her, while your phone still has juice, and you *can* have a word with her." But then, lest he think she was serious, she quickly added, "But you can't, because I pick truth again." There was only enough room in this crazy day for one of them to confront their fucked-up families.

"Okay," he said. "What's the deal with the ladybug earrings?"

She jumped a little. She had not expected an easy question like that. But also, it was kind of weird to be asked about the earrings while they were sitting in the pitch darkness. It wasn't like he could see them at the moment.

"Elise gave them to me. She's the fourth bridesmaid."

"Right. You, Jane, Wendy, and Elise. You four are tight? Or is that another question?"

"Nah, that's just backstory. Yeah, we're..." *Best friends* was the answer, but sometimes those words didn't seem strong enough. Embarrassingly, her throat tightened. She swallowed hard. "They're my people."

"They don't give you the shit that those preteen harpies did?"

She laughed. "No. That's why I love them. And also

probably why I was such a bitch when you met me. It sounds dumb, but I would do *anything* for those girls. So I lost my mind a little about getting the dress to the wedding."

"You're loyal. It's a good thing."

"Well, I'm loyal to *them*. Everyone else can fuck right off."

He chuckled. "So why do they inspire loyalty when no one else does?"

"Because they know me."

"They know *you*. The you that's more than your beauty, you mean."

"Well—"

"So you admit that you have more to offer besides beauty." He spoke with a triumphant, teasing tone as he referred to their previous conversation about her skills—or lack of them.

"I don't admit it." He started to object, but she kept talking. "It's not like I have bad self-esteem, Bennett. I know I'm not book smart. But I *am* self-aware, which, of the two, I'll take any day. I *don't* have any other skills, but I do have feelings. Likes and dislikes. That sort of stuff. Those girls know about all that stuff. That's what I'm talking about."

"But you *do* have—"

"So there's the four of us." She interrupted him because she wasn't getting into this argument again. "But we also kind of sort into pairs of best friends. Wendy and Jane go way back to childhood. They went to university together, where they met Elise. I was younger than them—I was in first year when they were seniors. Elise was my resident assistant. So it was her *job* to like me, which she teasingly reminds me of when I'm being a brat."

"But you became real friends."

"Yep. Right away. I mean, she did her job—she counseled me as required and made me come to excruciating group events where we practiced rolling condoms onto bananas. And she was a great sounding board when I was considering quitting school to really give modeling a go. But from the start, it went beyond that. It was like, with her, I just knew."

"Like love at first sight."

"I wouldn't know about that. Anyway, the earrings: Elise gave them to me when I left school. She used to call me Ladybug, because when I started school, I'd done my hair in this black-to-auburn ombré. It looked horrible."

"Ombré?"

"It's like where one color gradually bleeds into another."

"Like a peach. Kind of red in the middle, near the pit, but it becomes yellow as you move toward the skin."

"That's actually totally right." Leave it to him to come up with a food example. "So that's it. Not much of a story there. What made you ask that question?"

His hand came to her ear, and it sent a bolt of awareness down her neck. A finger traced the outer shell, and then came down to the lobe until it found the earring.

"I don't know." His voice was hot and dark, like the room. "I like them." His hand lingered.

She had to force herself to keep still. She wanted to roll her neck, to shove her head toward him and purr, like a cat begging for a caress. His touch felt so good.

"Dare," he said suddenly, and oh, she was tempted. The setup was perfect to ask for something dirty. That's what you did when you played truth or dare in the dark with boys, right? What would she ask, if she could? The first thing that popped into her mind was *I dare you to put your head between my legs and eat me out until I scream.*

Which…hell. But she wouldn't go there. She wasn't a jerk.

Well, she *was* kind of a jerk a lot of the time, but not of the sexual-predator variety.

She huffed a sigh, half-aroused by her dirty imaginings, half-frustrated by the knowledge that they would never come to be realized.

"What?" he said.

She had to think of something else. She cast around, trying to remember the things they used to make each other do when she was a kid. Usually it involved consuming cayenne pepper. "Um, I dare you to do twenty push-ups."

The hand on her ear disappeared, and she wanted to howl in protest.

"Okaaay." He stretched the word out to signal his skepticism.

She didn't blame him. It wasn't a good dare. Or at least it wasn't a good dare for the dark. If he was going to do push-ups, she wanted to watch him. You know, just to continue torturing herself.

He got off the bed, and she heard him drop to the floor.

"Don't cheat just because I can't see you," she teased.

"I never would." She knew it was true. He was a man of his word.

The dare wasn't entirely unsatisfying because after what she assumed were the first few push-ups, he started huffing and grunting, which was...affecting. She shifted around on the bed, restless. Achy—but she told herself that was from the sedentary driving day. The knee that had been giving her trouble since the *Vogue* shoot still hurt.

"Twenty." He got up, breathing heavily. "Damn, it's getting hot in here without the AC." Then she heard the swish of fabric. Was he taking his shirt off? That would be an entirely reasonable thing to do in this heat, post–twenty push-ups, but...gaaah.

"Dare," she said as he sat, heat radiating off his torso.

He chugged his tea and leaned back against the headboard where he'd been before. "I dare you to tell me something no one else knows about you."

"That's not fair. That's more like a truth."

She sensed rather than saw him shrug. "I dare you to tell me a truth."

The answer popped right into her head. Or maybe not—maybe it was already there, just waiting to be found. She'd certainly been thinking enough about it in the last couple days.

She didn't have to tell him *that* truth, though.

There were any number of things she could say. She could tell him about the time she and another model broke into the pool at the Ritz Paris after hours—Elise knew about that, but it would sound credible as something she'd never told anyone. She could tell him that she was thinking of getting an apartment in Toronto, because she'd lately been overtaken by this weird compulsion to put down roots somewhere.

But there was something about this night that invited confidences. That was ripe for truth. No, that wasn't entirely it. There was something about the particular combination of this night and this man. He'd told her so much, so easily, about his life. Opened himself to her, a person who hadn't been very kind to him initially.

And, astonishingly, despite the darkness, he seemed to see her, to really *see* her, in a way that no one besides the girls did.

And the answer to his question was *right there* in her throat, bubbling up. It wanted to be out in the world. So she opened her mouth to free it. She spoke in the barest of whispers, but she knew he would hear her, because he paid attention to her.

"I have a problem with food."

Chapter Ten

I know," Bennett said. When she didn't say anything else, but rather expelled a loud breath that sounded like it was partway to a sob, his heart broke a little. "Oh, sweetheart." He set down his tea, wrapped his arms around her, and pulled her to his chest. The dark made it easy to make the probably-too-familiar gesture without overthinking it.

"I just...I used to be able to eat whatever I wanted and never gain weight."

She spoke haltingly. He stroked her back and held her, sensing she was working through her thoughts as she verbalized them.

"But not anymore. Now...I don't know."

She sounded disgusted with herself.

"That's normal," he said. "That's just, unfortunately, what happens to your metabolism as you age. It's true for all of us."

"I know," she whispered. "I know that with my mind."

He tightened his arms around her, feeling a little bad about how sweaty he was, but she didn't seem to mind. In fact, she burrowed into him, so her next words were somewhat muffled as she spoke them against his skin.

"I'm stuck. Modeling is my thing. It's what I do. I'm good at it. But I'm getting too fat to keep doing it."

"Okay, you're not fat. That's just objectively not true." He knew she knew that—she *must* know that—but he couldn't let that one slide.

"You know what I mean. I already have a rep in the industry for being difficult."

"What does that mean?"

"I don't take shit."

"What do you mean by shit?"

"Oh, you know, sexual harassment mostly."

Jesus Christ. Something inside him, some sleeping monster he'd had no idea was in there, got to its feet and bared its fangs. With great effort he leashed the monster and forced his tone to be measured so as not to puncture the astonishing intimacy they seemed to have achieved. "That doesn't sound like 'difficult.' That sounds like 'smart.'"

She ignored the correction. "So now I'm difficult *and* fat. On my last job, they had to have me trade dresses with another model because I couldn't fit into the one they'd wanted me in."

He thought back to that first evening at the airport, when she'd been raging and then surprised him by blurting out how hungry she was.

Yeah, this was not okay. He knew, rationally, that he couldn't solve this for her, but there was no way she was going back to that fucked-up world believing that she was somehow not good enough for it. He couldn't say it like that, though. She would only bristle and remind him that he had no claim on her. And she would be right. So instead he tried, "Maybe it's time to do something else."

"But what else? That's the problem."

Suddenly it all made sense. All her talk about not having any skills. Which was not true. She was funny and smart. She'd solved a bunch of his problems, little ones like what to do with all the leftovers at the restaurant and big ones like his freaking *family*.

She probably wouldn't listen to his objections, though. In fact, she was starting to get restless in his arms. She probably regretted her confession, and she was getting antsy now, in search of an escape.

"There's nothing else I *can* do." She pressed against his chest to try to free herself from his hold. "So I just have to work harder to—"

He couldn't stand to hear her run herself down anymore. He also couldn't stand the thought of letting her go, so he did what felt like the most logical thing in the world: he put his mouth on hers in order to *make* her stop talking.

Hell, he still had one more kick at the can before her stupid rule about not sleeping with the same guy more than twice kicked in, and he'd already broken *his* rule, so why not? Because kiss his grits, but all of a sudden he would throw his stupid code, the one that had governed his whole life since he'd left the gutter, out the goddamned window for one more chance with her.

She gave a squeak of surprise, but it was followed by a sigh, and she went limp in his arms and opened her mouth to him so fast that he might have laughed had he not been so incredibly turned on by her surrender.

He groaned and deepened the kiss, sliding his tongue into her mouth. He was rewarded with an answering moan, but then she pushed on his chest again, and he couldn't ignore that.

Regret sliced through him as he loosened his hold on her so she could pull away.

She touched his face, the way a blind person would, and perhaps it was her way of trying to read his expression in the dark. "I thought you didn't do casual."

Relief replaced regret at the idea that she wasn't necessarily calling a halt to the proceedings, just checking up on him and his morals. He grinned under her fingers. "I'm making an exception."

"I'm not going to be your girlfriend." Her hands shook a little as she spoke, though, and he sensed she was weakening.

"I know." He gently pulled her hands down and dipped his head to press a kiss to her throat.

She sighed and threw up another warning. "I'm not going on any dates with you."

"I know," he repeated, finding her waist in the dark and letting his hands settle there.

"So this goes against all your rules."

"I know." It made no sense, but he was going to take Gia however she would have him for as long as she would have him, even if that was only one more time in a pitch-black hotel room. He slid a hand under her tank top and let it come to rest on her taut stomach. He wouldn't go any further until he knew for sure that she was okay with this, though, so he asked the question that would make his intentions crystal clear: "Do you have condoms somewhere in that giant handbag of yours?"

Please let her have condoms.

"Yes." And with a sigh that shaded into a moan, she was finally done objecting.

He slid his hand up over her ribs, then over the gentle

slope of a breast, and she sucked in a sharp breath as he reached the hard nipple at its center. "But first can you—" She moaned again, louder this time, and he *loved* being able to make her do that.

"First can I what?" He tweaked her nipple.

"Oh!"

"I didn't quite catch that," he teased. Suddenly intent on making sure she never managed to articulate whatever it was she'd been planning to say, he let one of his hands slide down her shorts. He burrowed his fingers inside her panties, wishing for enough light to see what kind they were.

"You bastard," she panted, arching her back in a way that suggested she thought he was, in fact, the opposite of a bastard.

"I'm pretty sure that wasn't it." He swirled his fingers lightly, the way he'd figured out she liked last night, when he'd been able to study her face as he got her off. "You were saying you wanted me to do something?" He swirled again. "Something other than this?"

She yelped in frustration and grabbed his face with both hands, as if she was forcing him to look at her even though the dark made it impossible. Then she spoke clearly and confidently, all her problems with speech disappearing completely. "Yes. I want you to go down on me before you put on a condom and fuck me."

Oh, fuck. Jesus Christ. She'd called his bluff. He'd thought he had her at his mercy, but the joke was on him. For a moment, he was afraid he was going to come in his pants like a teenager. But he got control of himself and wasted no time shoving her shorts and underwear off and settling his face between her legs.

"Oh my God!" she cried when his lips made contact with her.

All right; that was better. He liked making her lose her mind like that. He chuckled and burrowed his tongue inside her.

"Oh my God!"

Yep. *Oh my God*—at least when it came from Gia—had officially become his favorite phrase.

He wondered how many more times he could make her say it before the night was done.

Her hands came to his head, and her hips lifted off the bed as he worked her with his tongue. "Be *still*," he admonished as her thrashing made him lose his rhythm. "I'm fixin' to eat you out here, but you have to stay still."

She moaned, a torturous noise that was half pleasure, half frustration, like she wanted to comply but couldn't. So he hooked his arms under her legs, clamped his hands down on her hips, and immobilized her against his face. His intent was to spread her open before him, to have her utterly at his mercy. But once again, he wondered if the joke was on him, because it felt like the reverse was true, like he was a penitent, bowing before a goddess.

"Oh my God, Bennett. I'm going to come."

He paused long enough to chuckle and say, "That's the idea."

"No! It's too soon. Too fast and— Oh! Oh my God!"

Her legs clamped around his head, and she went utterly quiet. The delicate flesh against his mouth fluttered and fluttered. He flattered himself that it lasted a long time, and he tried to prolong it even more by staying with her, helping her ride out the aftershocks.

There was something to be said for this blackout. It had enabled their game of intimate confessions. It made it feel like they were on a break from reality. But now, as Gia went postorgasmically limp, he wished more than anything that he could see her face.

He settled for pressing a kiss on her inner thigh, then disengaging himself from her legs and feeling his way back up to her.

"Everything okay up here?" he asked, grinning stupidly into the darkness, loving the taste of her on his lips.

It took a while for her to answer, and when she did, her voice had lost that bossy, almost-confrontational tone that drove him so bonkers.

"Yep," she said. "Everything's fine."

─ C⅃

Everything was not fine.

Everything *had* been fine—everything had been *spectacular*—until that kiss.

She should calm down. It had just been a quick kiss on her thigh, a mere peck, over in an instant. It didn't mean anything, had been a mindless gesture.

The problem was, it had felt like an *affectionate* kiss. There was no reason, beyond the expression of affection, to deliver that kind of kiss after everyone had gotten what they came for.

Except, of course, everyone had *not* gotten what they came for. Once again, Bennett had left her a pile of helpless mush and had not gotten off himself.

He intended to, though, she was pretty sure. He wouldn't have asked about condoms otherwise.

Okay, so she had to get past the stupid kiss.

Because despite her discomfort, she really, really wanted to find out what Bennett Buchanan was like when he lost control. He was so disciplined, normally; he exercised such mastery over himself and his kitchen—and over her. What would he be like when he stopped doing that?

The weird thing about Bennett was that when she was with him, she could feel things that were contradictory. She could hate that he'd kissed her thigh but still want him more than she'd ever wanted anyone. She could be uncomfortable yet move through that discomfort and not die.

"Give me your phone." She pushed back against his embrace—he'd sort of sprawled over her after her orgasm.

He made a vague noise of displeasure and tried to hold on to her, but she slithered out. "I need the flashlight on it. The condoms are in my makeup bag in the bathroom."

That spurred him into action so fast, she cracked up.

The phone's light cast an eerie glow over the room as she made her way through it, making everyday objects— a TV, a dresser—look weirdly distorted. Distortion: everything that should be familiar made strange. Wasn't that the perfect metaphor for this unlikely night?

Inside the bathroom she found a condom. Then optimistically dug around to find a second one—hey, you never knew. When she was done, she held the light up and looked at her face in the mirror.

The other amazing thing about Bennett?

She had told him her secret, and he was still here.

He still wanted her.

Wanted her so much, in fact, that he was breaking his weird commandment against casual sex in order to have her.

And she was pretty sure her beauty didn't have anything to do with it, judging by the way he had, on more than one occasion, vehemently insisted that she had more to offer than a pretty face.

It was an astonishing thought.

Plus it was pitch black, so he couldn't even see her.

"I'm not sure if it's possible to die of blue balls, but I think we're about to find out!" he shouted from the bedroom.

   She grinned at herself, liking the satisfaction—and
power—she saw in her reflection. When she turned away to
head back to the room, no trace of her previous discomfort
remained.

   She held the flashlight up when she got to the edge of
the bed, dropped the condoms on the nightstand, and said,
"Take off your clothes."

   He snorted. "Bossy, bossy."

   She rolled her eyes. "Please, Mr. Buchanan, sir, would
you consider disrobing?"

   Without a word he did. She kept the flashlight on him.
His shirt was already gone, of course, from his push-ups,
but he lifted his hips and pulled his pants off, snagging
the waistband of his underwear along with them. Then he
leaned back against the headboard in a pose that was, on
the surface of things, casual and lazy. But she could feel the
tension radiating off him.

   And, of course, his dick gave him away. Shameless,
she aimed the phone's light straight at it. It was a nice
one—pleasingly large and with an interesting curve that she
suspected might be capable of rocking her world.

   "Do I pass?"

   "Yes," she whispered, her mouth suddenly dry. She cut
the light and put the phone down with a shaking hand,
plunging them into darkness again.

   Was she *nervous*?

   Okay, hell no. She didn't get nervous when she had sex.
Nervous wasn't in her repertoire.

   So, before she could overthink things, she climbed on top
of him. Straddled him. Lifted her arms as he reached for the
hem of her tank top—he'd taken her shorts off before—and
pulled it over her head.

   Then, emitting a huge sigh, a relieved one like you might

make as you stepped into a warm bath after a long, hard day, he wrapped his arms around her and hugged her.

Hugging was another thing that wasn't really in her repertoire, at least not when it came to sex.

But once she forced herself to relax into his embrace, it was actually kind of awesome. His arms banded around her tightly, enough to make her feel contained. Wanted. Safe. She pasted herself even closer to him, smashing her breasts against his chest and hugging his outer thighs with her inner ones.

It was her turn to sigh, and with this one all the vestiges of her apprehension dissipated.

Another example of Bennett inspiring her to endure initial discomfort for a bigger payoff.

They stayed like that for a long time, breathing together in the dark. Even as it was invigorating and lust-inspiring, it was calming. It made space. Enough space to relax and just be.

Enough space for something weird to happen, something she hadn't seen coming: a wave of emotion. It came over her steady and sure, just like an actual wave, gaining speed as it approached. She couldn't even really identify it, label it anything other than "emotion." Though her first impulse was to turn away from it, to hunker down behind a wall of sandbags, she wondered what would happen if she *didn't* do that. If she let it come.

If she let herself react to it—that was the scariest part. No, letting him *witness* her reacting to it. *That* was the scariest part.

Tears prickled in the corners of her eyes. A deep inhalation she attempted in order to calm herself surprised her by becoming a sob on the exhalation. She let it happen.

Bennett tightened his hold on her. She kept…letting it

happen. She didn't fight the tears that had gathered in the corners of her eyes, just let them spill over. Let her body quiver as she cried. Surrender was unfamiliar but a profound relief.

He had to feel the wetness on his bare shoulder, but he did not remark on it, just kept holding her. She thought of the storms they'd passed through—snow yesterday and hail today. Here was another one.

But somehow, astonishingly, it was okay. She could ride it out.

Eventually her faith was rewarded, and the wave passed. She felt empty in a good way. Like her tears had carved out some of the junk inside her, leaving behind a hollow that was hers to fill as she liked, with intention and care.

Her next deep breath wasn't shaky at all; it was cleansing. As her lungs filled, her chest expanded, reminding her of his proximity, drawing her attention to his hard chest and to her own suddenly sensitized breasts.

She knew he would make no move. He would sit here and hold her forever if she wanted him to, she was pretty sure, but he wouldn't presume to touch her beyond that, not after that episode.

If she wanted anything to happen, it was up to her.

And she wanted something to happen, desperately.

She had been straddling him, but sort of sitting back on his thighs, so while their torsos had been mashed together, their pelvises had not—which suddenly seemed like a lost opportunity. So she wiggled herself up until he was pressed right against her center. Amazingly, her tears had not been a boner killer.

"Gia," he bit out.

"Shhh," she said, though it was funny that it would be *she* whispering soothing reassurances in *his* ear and not the reverse. Before he could say anything else, she lowered her lips to his.

They kissed slowly at first, tongues leisurely exploring. She ground down on him, the slickness of her arousal making her feel powerful. Eventually his hands came down to her ass, helping press her against him, increasing the pressure as he rocked his hips up to meet her.

She gasped as her desire, which had been unfolding in a controlled way, suddenly overwhelmed her. Her head lolled back, and once the seal of their lips was broken, he moved his mouth to her ear, biting down gently on the lobe.

"Oh!" she exclaimed. The dark made every move a surprise. His mouth was one place on her body, and then, with no warning, it was another place. No sooner had she gotten used to him playing with her ear than his mouth moved from her flesh to her earring. She felt more than heard the clack of his teeth against the metal.

"These fucking earrings drive me crazy," he rasped.

"I thought you said they were cute."

"I was trying not to freak you out, but *cute* is not the word. They're ... fuck. I don't know. Evil."

She laughed even as she moaned, which was not a combination that had ever come out of her mouth before. "Evil ladybugs."

He clamped down harder on her ass and bucked his hips up even as his lips moved to her breasts, lavishing them with openmouthed kisses.

"Can you come again?" he asked, and just as when she thought she might explode from all the attention on her breasts, he worked a hand between them and sought out her clit.

"Yes!" she practically shouted. Then, a little abashed, she lowered her voice. "But you'd better put on a condom, or I'm going to continue to outnumber you on the orgasm front."

"Well, if this is our final performance, you outnumbering me sounds like a good idea. In fact, I think my masculine pride demands it."

"No way." She scrambled off him and felt her way to the condoms, handed one to him, and then moved back between his legs. This time she left some room between them, though—enough to bend down and lick his penis. "Time for you to catch up," she said before she took the head into her mouth.

It felt like an imperative, in fact. If he hadn't had sex with a human since his last girlfriend a year ago, he was long overdue. And she was dying to witness his loss of control. To be the cause of it.

And it was working.

"Oh, fuck." His hands flew to her hair. They rested gently there, but she could tell it was an effort—there was so much tension coiled in them. He was still holding back. His body was practically vibrating, every inch of him leashed. She took him deeper.

"Oh, no, you don't." He pushed her gently off him.

She made a mew of disappointment, but then sucked in a breath when she heard the sounds of him sheathing himself.

"Get up here." He clamped a hand on her arm and pulled her back onto his lap. A bolt of lust tore through her as she positioned him at her entrance.

"Yeah," he said. "Yeah, ride me, Gia."

She moaned as she sank down on him, savoring the delicious stretching sensation. When he was all the way in, when they were as close as they could be, another involuntary moan ripped from her throat.

"Does that feel good?" he rasped, wrapping his arms around her like before, except this time he was inside her, and instead of crying, she was moaning.

"Yeah," she breathed, though as good—as *amazing*—as it felt, she didn't want to be still anymore, so she started to move, to lever herself up on to her knees, pulling almost all the way off him and pausing—probably for too long, but she wanted to make him lose his mind—before lowering herself again.

He made a wild, half-unhinged noise, and she loved it.

"Does *that* feel good?" she asked, mirroring his earlier question.

"Fuck yes."

So she did it again, pausing a bit longer at the top of the stroke, just to toy with him, to stretch out the delicious anticipation of the friction yet to come.

And when she slid down, she went harder, deeper, summoning another moan from him in the process. She was unraveling him, and she was pretty sure not many people had ever managed to do that.

On the next thrust, he raked his teeth gently over her collarbone as he growled.

She extended the next pause even more, and he clamped his hands on her ass and bucked off the bed. She resisted, pulling back a little as his hips jerked, maintaining the distance between them so only the tip of his cock was inside her.

"You're *killing* me," he growled.

"What? You don't like this?" she teased, putting on her best coy voice even as it was increasingly difficult to keep up her measured assault.

His answer was an indistinct grunt.

"Well, if you don't like it, you'd better tell me what you *do* want," she breathed, using all her willpower to pull herself fully off him.

It was a bluff, but as soon as she was kneeling above

him, his cock no longer inside her, her body gave a quick, angry spasm, like it was *mad* at her.

"Oh," she bit out, surprised by how *bereft* she felt without him.

But he knew, somehow, or he felt the same, because he surged to his knees and spun them so her back was to the headboard. It was physically awkward for a moment, but then he grabbed her thighs and wrapped them around his waist, and *oh*.

"Is this okay?" he whispered, pausing outside her entrance.

"Yes." It was more than okay. She was pinned between his body and the headboard, her legs wrapped around him, and he was about to lose control. But, ever the gentleman, he was asking permission.

"Yes," she said again. "Go."

And he did. He started pistoning into her, hard and savage and fast.

She tried to grab on to his shoulders, to hold on and brace herself, but he was slick with sweat, as was she, so she let her arms fall limp and surrendered to the sensations. To the sounds of Bennett Buchanan finally, finally losing it.

"Oh, fuck," he said. "Fuck. Gia."

He'd been holding her legs, but he let go of one, and with one hand brushed her hair, which was tangled and matted, away from her face.

"I wish I could see you." He continued the punishing pace of his thrusting. "I don't care what you look like…in a magazine. Or…how much you weigh." It was hard for him to get the words out; his sentences were broken by his efforts.

It was hard for her to hear them, too, because another orgasm was building. But she forced herself to pay attention.

"I bet you've never been as beautiful as you are right

now," he rasped, his rhythm stuttering. "And I wish I could see it."

The lights came on, and the room roared to life.

"Bennett!" she screamed as she came. His face was right there, inches from hers, glistening with sweat. His pupils constricted rapidly in response to the sudden flood of light, but his gaze didn't waver as his final few strokes inside her grew even more wild, uncontrolled.

He came, too, his body jerking but his eyes still not leaving hers.

Gia blinked, the brightness hurting her eyes. She became conscious of the blaring of the TV and the noise of the beleaguered air conditioning unit chugging to life.

Bennett seemed aware of none of these things, even though, at least in terms of the light, he was getting what he'd just wished for. He continued to study her face like he was trying to memorize it.

Then, as if he was coming to some private conclusion, his features relaxed into a smile. "I knew it."

Chapter Eleven

THREE DAYS BEFORE THE WEDDING

When Bennett woke up with a sleeping Gia in his arms, it was dark. Not the dark of before, though. It was a less heavy, predawn dark. He could make out shapes in the room: the bulky dresser, the open door of the closet.

The gentle curves of the woman tangled up with him.

He felt a little like he was at a precipice. Not just the pivot point between night and day, but between…what? Before and after, as stupid as that sounded.

Like everything about him had changed.

Which, again, he tried to tell himself, was ridiculous. He'd had good sex before.

Well, okay, he'd never had precisely the *spectacular* variety that had gone down last night, but it was still only sex. He wasn't a teenager or a doomsday cult member. Even he, who liked his sex to come with a degree of devotion and commitment, knew it didn't have the magical power to change personalities and heal wounds and shit.

But then he started to think about the boundaries of the concept of sex itself.

He had never been one of those dudes who thought that for something to meet the threshold of "sex," a penis had to go into a vagina. No, they'd definitely had some variation on sex two nights ago when he, fully clothed, had gotten Gia off with his hands. She had called him on that very thing, and she'd been right.

But what about last night? Where had it started and stopped? She'd come twice, and he'd had the world's most earth-shattering orgasm, yes. But what about the part in between, when they'd pressed their bodies together and he held her while she cried? Had that been sex? There had certainly been...caring involved. He'd been gutted by her confession, by her pain. In awe of how vulnerable she'd made herself, when that was clearly not something she did very much of.

She must have sensed the relentless churning of his brain, because she stirred. He loosened his hold on her slightly, intending to let her settle before grabbing her again, but she kept moving. "Bennett?" Her voice was muffled by his chest, and she sounded adorably bewildered.

"Shhh. It's not morning yet. Go back to sleep."

He had no idea what version of her he'd get when she fully woke up. Would she be pissy and defensive, like he'd seen her before? Embarrassed about her confession?

Would she sleep with him again? Would he be able to talk her into breaking her stupid "two times only" rule? He'd broken his rule to be with her, so maybe he could convince her to do the same.

She sighed and snuggled against him, and he held her as she drifted off.

So many questions without answers. He did know one

thing with certainty, one unsettling thing. He didn't want this to end.

⟶ ☙

Waking a guy up with a blow job worked better in theory than it did in practice.

The way it was *supposed* to work was that Bennett would be all sleepy and cozy, and she would wrap her lips around his already-firm morning wood and proceed to blow his mind.

Gia had woken up before him, and he was out cold. It was weird, waking up next to him. It wasn't that she hadn't had her share of mornings after. Even though she liked to keep sex casual, she wasn't one of those slam-bam-thank-you-sir types. If she liked the guy enough—and she generally only slept with people she liked—she'd stay over. She wasn't above some postcoital coffee and conversation.

So it wasn't waking up with a guy that was inherently weird; it was waking up with a guy who knew her as well as the girls did. Hell, maybe even better, as impossible as that seemed. She hadn't told the girls about her increasing issues with food, for example.

She had never cried in their arms.

The *really* weird thing was that she wasn't panicking. She wasn't defaulting to her usual defensive postures after someone had witnessed an uncomfortable truth about her. Maybe the difference was that usually when that happened, it was accidental—like Bennett seeing her losing her shit at the airline employees. Last night, she had, of her own volition, revealed an uncomfortable truth. Maybe that made all the difference.

Or maybe it was just Bennett.

Which *did* kind of freak her out. Yet at the same time, she was suffused with gratitude toward him. He had reacted in exactly the right way to her big confession. He'd heard her, but he hadn't talked at her. Hadn't lectured or dismissed. Had simply held her like she was important. And then blown her goddamned mind. Twice.

Awake before him, she had sighed and shifted a little, hoping it might "accidentally" wake him up. In addition to all these confusing emotions, she was horny. That, at least, was familiar. Actionable.

He was out, though. She didn't blame him. What a day they'd had yesterday, dodging storms and confronting demons.

So down she went, under the covers.

But there was theory, and there was practice.

When she took him into her mouth, he jumped about a foot, shouted, "What the fuck?" and almost kicked her in the face.

She cracked up as she tried to extricate herself from his legs and the covers.

As soon as he realized what was happening, he started apologizing. "I'm sorry! Are you okay? Oh my God, I'm such an idiot."

"I'm fine." She couldn't stop laughing. "I was just trying to...wake you up."

"What happened to the two-times rule?" he asked, helping her get free of the tangled sheets.

She plopped onto her back and turned her head to look at him. He was adorably disheveled. And stubbly. And delicious. "Well," she said, casting about for a loophole, "I'm counting the first time as a half, because you didn't come. You didn't even take any clothes off, so..."

"So that means you *don't* get to come if we go at it

again?" He furrowed his brow. "I don't think I can be down with that."

Damn, he was *adorable.* The chivalry just never ended with this guy. It was ingrained in him, probably from some combination of his southern upbringing and his compulsion to atone for the mistakes of his youth. She still thought he needed to let up on the atonement, but in this particular instance it was working to her advantage.

She bit back a grin. "So what you're telling me is you *don't* want me to blow you. Okay." She hopped off the bed, pretty certain of how he would react.

His hand shot out and clamped down on her arm. "Hang on now." Then he pulled her back onto the bed, and they got all tangled up, limbs entwined as he tried to kiss her but couldn't quite reach. "I'm just saying you might need to be a little less stringent with your math."

"Nope," she teased, though she was fully prepared to blur the rules this morning. She squirmed out of his reach even as he kept trying to kiss her, aiming for her prize. He fought her, but only half-heartedly. She was tall, but he was a lot bulkier than she was, and could have her flipped over and pinned on the bed the moment he decided to. Which was kind of hot. But not her goal right now.

When she finally worked her way down his body and got her mouth around him again, he gave up the struggle, falling back flat on the bed with a surrendering groan.

Kneeling between his legs, she stroked him a few times with her mouth, then paid some attention to his balls to see if he liked that. And…yes, he did, judging by the way he sounded like he was being tortured even as he gasped her name.

She loved that, the way he said her name so often when they were having sex. It wasn't that unusual, she supposed, but the *way* he said it. It was like he was surprised and honored and turned on all at once that it was her, specifically *her*, he was with.

As if to punctuate her thought, he said it again. "Gia," The pleading urgency in his tone inspired her to get serious. She went back to his cock and took him in as deeply as she could, letting her senses fill with him. Pouring all those heavy, unnamable emotions into it, reveling in the way he kept gasping her name as his hands stroked her head.

It didn't take long for his hips to start jerking. She let him push her off him but held him with her hand as he climaxed, long ribbons of come painting his chest.

Her hand went to her clit. *Jesus, that was hot.*

He grunted. "You got that right."

Oh, shit, had she said that aloud?

Well, whatever. It wasn't like it was a secret. She kept her hand moving. She couldn't not. She was wound up, and looking at him like that, all spent and sated and immobilized, was only fanning the flames.

"Just...need...a second," he panted, his drawl extra thick as he lifted his head to look at her with what seemed like enormous effort.

"You stay where you are," she instructed, an evil scenario taking root in her imagination.

She usually masturbated lying down, but she arranged herself on her knees so as to maximize his view. She let one hand drift up to cup a breast as the other stayed on her clit.

"Oh fuck," he said.

She smiled. That was another thing he said a lot—when he wasn't gasping her name. She liked it. It was as if there was no intermediate degree of arousal for him when they were together—no *oh damn*, much less any *mmm, that feels good*. He went right to *fuck*, which made her feel like she cranked him up to eleven every time.

Which begged the question of his maybe being…right? Could she have been missing out on some kind of sexual nirvana by never having been with the same person continually?

She shoved the question aside for later, because she wanted her little show to blow his mind, and because she was so turned on herself that thinking was becoming difficult.

She heaved a big sigh. It wasn't manufactured, but Bennett's obvious appreciation of it—he closed his eyes momentarily like she was too much to look at—inspired her to perform a second one, except this time what began as a sigh ended up as a moan.

His gaze was riveted to her fingers, which she moved in the circles that always did it for her.

"You paid attention," she said, nodding down at her fingers. She'd never had a man figure out such a surefire route to her pleasure so quickly, at least not without some coaching.

He smirked. "I have my faults, but I'm a quick learner. You like a medium-pressure swirling kind of motion."

"That's exactly right. Usually I have to…give instructions."

"Not with me. I learn quickly, *and* I remember stuff." He made a move toward her, but she shook her head. Took her hand off herself and held up a censuring finger. When she was satisfied that he was going to stay where he was—she was enjoying the hell out of this little performance—she let her hand slide back down her body. Both of them, this time, in fact. She returned the pads of two fingers to her clit and let a finger from the other hand slide inside.

He made a strangled noise, and she couldn't help letting loose a triumphant laugh.

"What do you think about when you touch yourself?" he asked, his voice low and gravelly.

She smiled. He liked a little bit of dirty talk, didn't he? Also something she filed away for later. Assuming there was a later. Which there might not be.

Which there probably *wouldn't* be.

But there she went thinking again. And "I'm talking myself in circles trying to decide what it might mean if I let myself have sex with you again," was probably not the kind of dirty talk that was going to turn his crank—and that was her aim here: maximum crank turnage.

So she told the truth. "When I'm by myself, I think about someone fucking me from behind. Hitting my G-spot. I have a pretty good vibrator at home. It has a curved head." She glanced down at his dick, which, amazingly, was growing hard again. It was perfectly shaped for such an endeavor. "There's no better orgasm than a G-spot orgasm."

His eyes flared. Then he shocked her by getting up. Bolting into the bathroom.

"Hey!" she protested. But then she heard something. The crinkling of a wrapper.

"Oh," she whispered, her desire receding even though she continued to stroke herself. It was as if her own touch wasn't enough anymore.

When he came out of the bathroom, he was erect and sheathed in a condom.

"G-spot, you say?" His gaze was hot and challenging.

The way she'd arranged herself, she was facing the bathroom, which meant she was now facing him.

They stared at each other in silence for a long moment, a standoff—though she didn't know why, because she was always going to surrender. She just liked playing with him, she supposed. Which she had to grudgingly admit was probably also a benefit of sleeping with the same person on the reg.

Yet another thought for later. For now, she licked her lips and let her eyes rake slowly down his body. It was the first time she'd really seen it, all of it at the same time, in the light of day. His torso was gently sculpted, his chest lightly sprinkled with dark hair that picked up again under his belly button and ran in an orderly line down to that cock that the universe—or God, if you took his quasi-religious view of things—had given the perfect curve.

Then, slowly, so slowly it almost pained her, she turned around. Shot him a glance over her shoulder. And just in case her intent wasn't already crystal clear, she lowered herself to her hands and knees on the bed.

"Gia," he groaned, and then, without preamble, his hands were between her legs, roving around, checking if she was ready. And yes, she was. Just in case the slickness he found there wasn't enough of a signal, she looked over her shoulder again and said, "Please."

"There's no better orgasm than a G-spot orgasm?" He slid right in. "I thought you said the best orgasm you ever had was two nights ago."

She laughed, then gasped as he started to move. "Best non-G-spot orgasm," she panted, even though it wasn't precisely true. It wasn't like she was keeping score, and even though the intensity of the physical sensation of a G-spot orgasm could be, for her, huge, there was something about Bennett that...well, he was kind of in his own category, no matter what type of orgasm he was dispensing. But she wasn't about to tell him all that, so she defaulted to teasing. "Best non-G-spot orgasm I ever had."

He seemed to take it as a challenge, which was what she'd intended. He pressed her down onto her stomach, but not before reaching a hand around and sweeping it around in that now-practiced way of his. Then he draped his whole body over hers, so that every inch of the back of her body was covered by the front of his.

She was wedged between his hand and his body, and it. Was. Glorious.

She moaned, as loudly as she wanted to, and then she did it again, louder. He was rubbing perfectly against that spot inside her that made her lose her goddamned mind. Pleasure hurtled toward her.

"You like that, do you? You like being filled up?"

She nodded frantically.

"I like it, too," he rasped. "I'm so deep inside you, and you're so tight."

Gia tried to push back against the oncoming tide.

"I think you like my cock more than your stupid rules," he said, and she couldn't argue the point.

"You always make me come too fast," she complained, even though complaining was the last thing she should be doing right now. But stupidly, she couldn't just agree with him that yes, she liked his cock more than her "stupid rules."

"Oh," he said, low into her ear, and then he bit down on her earring like he had last night. "Oh, should I stop then?"

"No." She moaned when he started to pull away. "Keep going."

Then he surprised her by dropping the dirty talk. "I don't have that much experience with G-spots. I've only ever found them a handful of times, and it was always with my hand. How will I know if I'm hitting it?"

Correction: he'd dropped the *intentional* dirty talk. His frank, unabashed admission and question turned her on as much as anything between them had. Most guys she knew would never admit ignorance of something like that.

But then, most guys she knew weren't capable of making her feel like this.

"You're hitting it," she assured him, and then she shrieked as he thrust extra hard and then stayed buried in her, grinding around. "I think it's possible your dick was made to hit it."

He let loose a string of *fuck*s as he continued to grind inside her. The hand wedged against her clit couldn't make his usual light circles because she was lying on top of it, but he pumped his whole hand, effectively forcing her to hump his arm while he kept grinding into her, dragging his cock back and forth over her sweet spot.

"Oh my God!" she shouted.

~ॐ

Bennett's last thought before Gia exploded underneath him was that she was right. His dick *was* made for her G-spot. Or made for *her* or some shit like that.

And his last thought before *he* exploded was that this wasn't over.

Fuck her rules. Fuck *his* rules. They could call this whatever she liked that made it okay: casual, a hookup, a booty call.

Because this was not over.

No fucking way.

Chapter Twelve

When Gia got to the Applebee's across the parking lot from the hotel, there was a single egg lying on a plate in the spot across from Bennett.

She'd sent him ahead after their post-sex shower—he had insisted she shower first, but then climbed right in with her, being all sweet and considerate as he washed her hair and as she stood stunned under the spray.

It had been too much. She'd needed a moment, so she'd shooed him away after he got dressed, telling him she needed some privacy to get ready.

And just when she'd worked herself up to face the fact that the fun was over—they'd be in Florida by the end of the day, and more than that, she needed to retreat from him for her own well-being—he'd gone and ordered her a goddamned egg.

"Soft-boiled," he said as she sat down.

Of course it was. What had he said in bed this morning? *I learn quickly*, and *I remember stuff*.

"I hope it's okay. I had to explain it to them. Soft-boiled isn't really in the repertoire at most places in the US." He twisted around to flag down a server and order her a cup of coffee, so he didn't see her blink back tears as she picked up a spoon and cracked open the egg.

That stupid egg was the perfect gesture.

It said not only that he hadn't forgotten that she took her eggs soft-boiled, but that he hadn't forgotten the big confession bomb she'd detonated in his arms last night.

But also that he wasn't going to make a federal case over it, at least not now. It was like he somehow knew that would be the quickest route to her shutting him down. She wouldn't even want to, necessarily, but it would happen automatically, in the daytime with her defenses engaged.

"Thank you," she said when the server set down her coffee. She was looking at Bennett as she spoke, though.

He smiled. "I was thinking about something before you got here, and I have a question for you."

Well, shit. So much for no federal cases. Here they went.

"Does your driver's license expire today because today is your birthday?"

She blinked. She'd forgotten. Well, she hadn't *forgotten* forgotten. She knew when her own birthday was. She had been well aware of it yesterday as she fought him for control of the car keys, arguing that she was still legal to drive for one more day.

She just hadn't remembered it this morning, on account of all those damned orgasms.

She smiled. "It *is* my birthday."

"Ha! I thought so. Don't move!" He pointed a finger at

her like he was robbing her, and she played her role, lifting her hands up into the air.

Then, to her utter astonishment, he reached across the table and slid a birthday candle into her gelatinous egg. Because it wasn't in an egg cup, was just rolling around on her plate, he had to pick it up and hold it in his hand. Then the other hand produced a lighter.

And the tears were back, little motherfuckers, threatening behind her eyes.

To distract herself from the wave of emotion that was hitting, she dug out her camera and said, "Say cheese. It's only seven in the morning, but I can guarantee this is going to be the highlight of the day."

He smiled for the camera, and when she was done she asked, "Where'd you get the candle and lighter?"

He waggled his eyebrows as he lit her candle. "I shamelessly manipulated that front desk woman at the hotel. Maybe you were right—I think she *is* into me."

She stared into the flame, and, paradoxically, it made her remember the darkness of last night, the magical darkness that had made her the opposite of afraid.

"Are you going to sing?" she said, aiming for a teasing note but not quite hitting it.

"I am not going to sing." His eyes danced. "But I am going to wish you a year of…" He trailed off and pursed his lips. He was trying to find the right thing to wish her. "A year of no regrets."

It wasn't the generic "health and happiness" sentiment most people would have expressed. *No regrets.* It was a good wish, if an impossible one.

"How old are you?" he asked.

"Thirty." She rolled her eyes. "It's a big one."

"Ah! Then I wish you a *decade* of no regrets."

"Just a decade?" she teased.

"Point taken. How about you leave all those regrets behind in your twenties? Leave them behind for good."

"Okay," she whispered, and, wishing it could be so easy, she blew out her candle.

—⎰

As Bennett pulled onto I-95, all was right with the world.

Well, of course that wasn't true, not in any real sense. The world still contained hunger and poverty and war and— he glanced at Gia—eating disorders and sexual harassment and women who had no idea what they were worth.

But right here, right now, the cold of a New York winter was a distant memory, he'd been well and recently laid, he had a pretty damned amazing person in the passenger seat next to him, and he was on his way to his best friend's wedding.

"I've missed Noah," he said, apropos of nothing, but wanting to share with Gia how happy he was to be on his way to see him.

"Aww," she said. "Best boyfriends!"

He rolled his eyes, but in a self-deprecating way, because she was right. "I could deal with that endless trip of his, but it kind of guts me to think that he's never coming back to New York."

"Thrown over for Wendy," she teased.

Bennett nodded. "Not that I blame him. Wendy is pretty amazing."

"She is. So are Jane and Elise."

"I've met Jane, of course." Noah's sister had been a frequent visitor to New York over the years. "And yes, she's pretty great, too." Elise was the only one he hadn't met.

Gia's best friend among best friends. Part of him wished he could enlist her to help Gia with the food stuff, but if Gia hadn't told Elise, no way was he going to break her confidence.

He didn't know what to do about that, truth be told, and when he thought of it, it deflated his good mood somewhat. He didn't kid himself that he could "save" her. He wasn't a white knight, and lucky for him she would never tolerate one. All he knew how to do was to...try to take care of her. And the only way he could think to do *that* was by being there. Trying to help in little ways. For example, he'd been stupidly gratified when she'd eaten the egg he'd ordered for her that morning.

"So what's keeping you in New York?"

"What?" The question startled him.

"You hate the cold, your best friend bromance soul mate moved away, it's super expensive there, and you're trying to save money for this community restaurant initiative. There are people down on their luck pretty much every-where, and—"

"I know, but—"

He'd interrupted her, but she interrupted him right back. "And you just made peace with your parents, or at least you're on your way to doing that. You clearly love Charleston. And Chef Lalande is there. Why not move back?"

"I...have no idea." He'd never thought of it, had honestly never considered doing a restaurant anywhere else. New York was where you went when you wanted to go big in the restaurant world.

But did he want to go big?

Not really, right? If he did, he'd be working on earn-ing a Michelin star, not on feeding high-quality food to the hungry.

Fucking hell, maybe she was right. Why *couldn't* he do that anywhere?

Then he thought about how the farther south they got, the more alive he felt.

He glanced at Gia. She was staring at him, eyebrows raised like she'd just yelled checkmate across a chessboard.

Or maybe that aliveness, that ever-increasing stirring in his blood, wasn't the weather; maybe it was the woman next to him.

⎯◦◦

Bennett sure was in a good mood. Gia, on the other hand, was unsettled. The farther south they got, the worse it became. By the time they stopped outside of Jacksonville for lunch, she was pretty much having a low-grade panic attack. Which was absurd, because getting to the wedding had been her singular, driving goal for so long. Now it was within reach, and she was losing her shit?

She tried to break it down as they pulled into a truck stop restaurant for lunch.

First there was the immediate problem of lunch—namely, that she was going to have to eat something.

She and Bennett had been together 24-7 for the past three days. There was no way to brush off a meal the way she usually did. He knew she hadn't "eaten earlier," that she hadn't "had a big breakfast so she wasn't hungry for lunch." Beyond that, even, she had confessed her secret to him.

He *knew*.

She was pretty sure that if she ate something reasonable, he wasn't going to say anything. He was watching, though. He couldn't hide it as he slid her a menu and said, with an air of forced casualness, "Hey, cool, they have a salad bar."

He certainly wasn't saying that for his own benefit—there was no way he was having the salad bar.

So, basically, she had talked herself into a corner. If she didn't want him to make a big deal over lunch, she had to eat.

She wondered if some part of her, some self-preserving part running on pure survivalist instinct, had told him for this very reason. If she'd talked herself into a corner on purpose.

The second part of her unspooling unease was the birthday thing. She was thirty freaking years old. That was hella old for a model with continuing runway and editorial ambitions.

"You know how some models cross over into lifestyle?" she said suddenly.

He furrowed his brow. "Doesn't everyone have a lifestyle?"

He was so cute in his cluelessness. "No, I mean *lifestyle* like they make themselves into brands that sell stuff, like housewares. Cindy Crawford, for example, sells La-Z-Boys."

"Cindy Crawford sells La-Z-Boys?" His confusion deepened, and so did her amusement.

"Yeah, or they sell, like, really expensive T-shirts by posing idly on verandahs with windblown hair and making you think that if you bought that T-shirt, you too could be beautiful and carefree."

He barked a laugh. She hadn't really been kidding, but she smiled at him.

"You want to do that?"

"No." She really didn't. "I've always been adamant that I'm not interested in being a brand. I have no interest in acting, either, like so many models do. I get terrible stage fright, actually."

"Still? Haven't you been at this for years?"

"Every single runway I walk down, I'm sure it's going to be my last because I'm literally going to die."

"Huh."

"So no gooping for me, is my point."

"No *what* for you?"

She let loose a big belly laugh. She adored the way he was trying so hard to listen to her, to follow the conversation, but he was just not tuned into this world. Which was part of what she loved about him.

Liked. *Liked* about him.

"Lots of them don't even go that far," she said, not bothering to explain goop to him, because if she tried, pretty soon they'd be talking about jade eggs and hoo-has. "You don't need your own brand these days. You just build up a huge social media presence, and then companies will get you to do sponsored posts and stuff. Like, oh, look at me, I just happen to be sunning myself here on my yacht with a million bottles of Coppertone casually strewn about."

"That's a job?"

"Well, they pay you for it."

"Do you need the money?"

She shook her head. "No. Anyway, I've avoided social media like the plague. I'm not on any of it."

"The 'no selfie' thing—I knew you were smart."

"I didn't want to be famous, you know? I've worked at the peak of this business, but I'm not known outside it. I don't get stopped on the street. I designed it that way intentionally."

"Like I said: smart."

"Yeah, but maybe not. Maybe I should have thought more long-term."

"Is this about your birthday?"

She shrugged. It was totally about her birthday, but she didn't want to cop to it—which she didn't have to, because the waitress arrived.

"I'll have the salad bar," she said, surrendering her menu and suppressing a sigh. She'd been thinking, recently, that things were getting better on the eating front. But that brief burst of optimism must have been an aberration. You didn't have to be a shrink to see why. It was her birthday, which reminded her about her career dilemma. The more out of control she felt—and in her line of work, turning thirty was enough to make anyone feel out of control—the more she tried to exert control elsewhere. But just because she could recognize this pattern didn't mean she knew how to break it.

Bennett ordered a patty melt and fries, which only proved her previous point: He was watching. He had pointed out the salad bar for her benefit.

The server departed, and they were left staring across the table at each other. She was sorry she'd started this whole conversation. She'd been thinking out loud, but that was a dangerous thing to do in front of He Who Is Always Watching.

"I'm going to hit the salad bar." She stood, but he clamped a hand down on her forearm, preventing her from walking away.

"You can do whatever you want, Gia. If you want to do something else, do it."

Yeah, that "dream big" bullshit was something you told six-year-olds. Not thirty-year-olds with no postsecondary degree and no skills to speak of.

She smiled weakly and pulled out of his grasp.

At the salad bar, she took a deep breath as she surveyed the offerings. It was better looking than she would have expected from a truck stop like this.

She filled her plate with lettuce and fresh veggies. And

she should have some protein. She selected a few slices of chicken breast. Oh, and there was shrimp that didn't look half-bad. Okay. She could do this.

"Finding everything okay?"

There was a man straightening out the dressings section. He wore a tag that said "manager" under his name.

"I am, and I have to say, I was glad to stumble onto this salad bar. It's nice to have some fresh options while road-tripping."

"Yeah, I hear that from people a lot."

"You should advertise it. It's not something you expect at a truck stop, you know? You have those billboards up on I-95, which is what drew us in. My...friend is always in search of nonchain, mom-and-pop places. But I bet if you actually said on there that you had a fresh salad bar, more people would come."

The man was looking at her funny. Okay, fair enough. He didn't need a lecture from her on how to run his business.

"You know what? You're right. I'm not sure why we never thought of that."

Gia blinked, surprised by his enthusiastic response.

"Your lunch is on the house, young lady."

She gloated as she slid back into the booth across from Bennett. "My lunch is free because I'm a business genius!"

"What? Why?"

"I was just chatting with the manager. We were talking about how they should advertise that they have a salad bar. There are lots of truck stops on this interstate, but how many of them have a huge salad bar like this? It's a competitive advantage, but most people, unless they've been here before, wouldn't know it was here. I bet a lot of truckers get sick of the usual fast food."

"I bet you're right," Bennett said quizzically.

"Or, oh! What they should do is measure it. It's really big. Then they can say, 'fifteen feet of fresh salad bar' or something."

Bennett cocked his head. He seemed to be giving the matter more consideration than it deserved. "I wondered what you guys were talking about. You looked really ... animated."

It had seemed like he was going to say something else, but stuck the word *animated* in there at the last minute. But he seemed to be done talking and was looking down at his lap with a weird look on his face.

Okay, well, lunchtime. Suppressing a sigh, she stabbed a beet and put it in her mouth.

"What's the matter?" he said, and she realized she was making a face.

"Nothing. I was just thinking about those beets on the salad you fed me at Boudin. This is nothing like those beets." It was about as far from those beets as Salisbury steak was from filet mignon.

He grinned. "The next time you're in New York, come by, and I'll feed you all the beets you can eat."

And suddenly, with a great big sickening thud, the third item on her little "Why is Gia having a low-grade panic attack?" list rose in her consciousness.

The closer they got to St. Pete's, the closer they were to the end of ... them.

Bennett was, quite reasonably, referencing a time in the future when they would be separated by many miles. When she might "visit" him, and he might make her dinner, like they were old friends.

They had been floating in this weird bubble where it was just them. Gia and Bennett versus the elements, whether those elements were actual storms or metaphorical ones. They'd been operating outside the order and strictures of normal life, beyond the reach of the forces of chaos that usually governed relationships.

And now it was time to give it up. Give *him* up.

She didn't want to.

But hey, she was pretty good at doing things she didn't want to. Her bum knee twinged, a physical reminder of that fact. And no matter how much she tried to contort reality, no matter how blurry her math was, she couldn't find a way to rationalize continuing to sleep with him. Beyond the fact that her friends would be onto her—she was sharing a room with Wendy for the few nights that were left before the wedding—it was profoundly unwise. Her "stupid rules," as he'd called them last night, kept her safe.

If she kept sleeping with Bennett, pretty soon she would be upending her life for him. It wasn't that she thought Bennett was anything like Lukas—or like that Wall Street guy who'd balked at her sweatpants or any of the other men who'd failed her various tests. She was pretty sure Bennett didn't give a shit that she was a model. But he would try to collect her all the same—or, worse, to "save" her—if she let him. Serious, atoning Bennett would try to make whatever it was between them more than casual, because that was what he did. He would try to make himself fall in love with her. He would try to make *her* fall in love with *him*. And she wasn't doing that again.

She waited until Bennett went to the bathroom, flagged down the server, and had her take away her barely touched salad.

—Ꮬ—

By the time they drove through Tampa on the final stretch of their journey that afternoon, Gia had steeled herself to do what needed to be done. It wasn't like Bennett was going to be surprised. She'd been perfectly up-front with him from the start.

He pulled over suddenly, turned to her, and said, "I have a proposition for you."

Here we are. This was the perfect opportunity to make sure they were on the same page about how things were going to unfold—or, more accurately, not unfold—over the next few days. He was going to push things, and she was going to have to shut him down.

Say it. Open your mouth and say it: "We can't sleep together anymore."

"How about we take the top down for the final stretch?"

She blinked. The way he'd pulled over right on the side of the highway rather than exit and find somewhere reasonable to stop, and the way he was looking at her—so earnestly and with such happiness in his eyes—had primed her to expect something more.

"We just have to cross the bay on the causeway, then drive a bit through the city to the hotel," he said. "So the wind won't be as bad as it would have been on the interstate."

Say it. Say it.

It wasn't like she was breaking up with him—they had never been together. She was just . . . clarifying things.

She opened her mouth. Closed it.

"But it will probably still turn your hair into a rat's nest." He turned back to start the car again.

"No!" she said, too loudly. "No, I think it's a great idea. Why else do we have this ridiculous convertible?" That was true, regardless of what else needed to be said. Driving the final stretch with the top down would be fun.

He was back facing her, beaming. "Right? We started this wack journey in the snowstorm of the century, and we'll finish it cruising to our ocean-side destination under sunny blue skies."

He hit the button that started the roof retracting, and she tilted her head up. He was right. The sky was almost the same turquoise as their car, and there wasn't a cloud in it.

As the roof did its thing, she pulled a scarf out of her purse and tied it over her head. "Our destination is a giant pink hotel, did you know that? It's nicknamed the Pink Palace."

"Even better."

They both slid on their sunglasses, and she couldn't help but mirror his grin.

He held his hand up for her to high-five. She raised hers and slapped it.

He caught it before she could take it back, drew it to his mouth, and kissed her palm.

She snatched her hand back like he'd burned it.

Say it.

Undisturbed, he started the car and gunned it, still smiling like he didn't have a care in the world.

And then it was too late. Too loud. The wind whishing at them and the little engine struggling to keep up with his lead foot made it impossible to talk.

Or that was her excuse, anyway.

Chapter Thirteen

$\mathcal{I}$t was sort of blowing Bennett's mind that mere days ago he'd been snowed in in New York, barking at his staff and as estranged from his parents as ever. Look at him now: pulling up to a pink hotel in a turquoise mini car with an amazing woman next to him, and said woman's friends, having been texted about their imminent arrival, jumping up and down and screaming like it was 1964 and they were witnessing the arrival of the Beatles.

What had he called it earlier? The Gia effect.

"Happy birthday, Ladybug!" one of them—must be Elise, since she was the only one he didn't recognize—shouted.

"Look at you!" Gia exclaimed as she hustled out of the car and threw her arms around Elise. She then transferred her attention to Elise's belly, which Bennett hadn't initially noticed was of the pregnant variety.

"Hi, baby!" Gia rubbed her friend's gently protruding tummy. "How's it cooking in there?"

Jane and Wendy were there, too, and a full-on frenzied

group hug commenced, everyone jumping up and down and admiring Gia's blue hair.

They were ignoring him. Everyone only had eyes for Gia, which, frankly, he could understand. He had half a mind to steal her camera and take another picture of her. He patted the pocket where he'd stashed the one he'd taken of her at the salad bar. She'd been so alive, so lit up, as she'd been talking to that employee, he couldn't help it.

But then Noah approached, a smile on his face. "Hey. You finally made it."

Noah enveloped him in a hug, and Bennett forgot about his photographic urges. He was once again surprised by the force of his feeling for his missing friend, whom he hadn't seen since the ring-shopping trip last summer. Noah, as both a friend and a neighbor, had gone a long way toward filling the void in Bennett's life caused by his being essentially an orphan.

They parted, and their attention was inevitably drawn to the women, who were still talking a mile a minute about spa appointments and beaches but clearly preparing to depart—Jane had Gia's suitcase and Wendy had her shoulder bag. Gia herself was pulling some trash out of the car to throw away.

Noah made a move like he was going to try to introduce Bennett, but no one noticed. Bennett cracked up and waved Noah off. "Hey, I know my place in the pecking order."

Noah shook his head in disagreement and cleared his throat loudly, which drew the women's attention.

"Oh my gosh! I'm sorry!" Wendy came over and patted Bennett on the shoulder—Wendy wasn't a hugger, so that was a gesture of affection from her. "Bennett." She drew his name out and looked at him... Well, she looked at him like she knew what had happened between him and

Gia, which was a distinct possibility. Whatever. He wasn't embarrassed. "I think you know everyone except Elise." Wendy introduced them, and Elise made polite inquiries about the trip while Jane greeted him warmly, but they were clearly preoccupied by Gia's appearance.

After the introductions, a bit of awkwardness settled on the group. The women clearly wanted to leave. Gia in particular was looking at him funny, almost like she'd never seen him before.

"Should we all...have lunch or something?" Jane asked.

"Nah." Bennett waved them off with a smile. "You go. You're excused." Gia, who had an arm slung around Elise's shoulders, flashed him an apologetic look. He winked at her, in part to cover the swell of emotion in his chest at seeing her so happy, so supported. It wasn't like any of her problems would magically evaporate simply because she was with her friends, but seeing the strength of those friendships firsthand made him happy and grateful.

But then they started walking away, and it hit him that their trip was over. They'd made it. No more forced proximity. No more meandering conversations on the highway. No more late-night confessions.

Gia looked over her shoulder at him, her face completely unreadable as she got farther and farther away.

He switched from feeling grateful to feeling...fucking *bereft*.

What the hell?

He turned and caught Noah staring at him. His friend's mouth opened like he was going to ask a question.

Bennett went ahead and answered it preemptively, vocalizing in real time the truth bomb that had just detonated inside him.

"I'm in love with her."

Gia always experienced such a sense of relief when she saw her friends. When she flew to Toronto for a visit, one or more of them always picked her up at the airport, and they'd all get together.

Relief. That was the only way she could think to describe it. Profound relief. The cessation of effort. Part of it was, of course, that when she saw them, she'd usually just come from working, so there was a literal cessation of effort, but it was more than that. It was a giving over of herself to the care of her friends. To the people who would do right by her. See her. Fill her back up.

Sometimes she got a little jealous that since they all lived in Toronto, they got to see each other all the time. She missed stuff. But she never doubted their devotion to her. Their friendship always clicked immediately back into place, no matter how long she'd been away. And it weathered everything: Elise's bridezilla phase in the lead-up to her wedding, Wendy's crisis when her aunt—and only surviving family member—nearly died. They were a sister-hood, and there was nothing they couldn't handle. Plus they had a ridiculous amount of fun.

So yes. Relief. That was the feeling a reunion with her friends always brought.

As they enveloped her in hugs, she waited for it to hit, warm and sedating, like a drug.

And there it was, but…it wasn't as strong as usual. It wasn't as happily overwhelming. That was because there was also something else in there, tempering the usual reaction.

As they bore her away on a sea of chatter and smiles, she realized what it was. Regret.

The very thing Bennett had told her not to do anymore.

Reflexively she looked over her shoulder at him, wanting some sign that they were still connected, that he hadn't forgotten all that had passed between them.

He looked back at her, his face completely unreadable.

⎯ↄ

When Noah managed to pick his jaw up off the ground, he started laughing.

Not exactly the reaction Bennett was looking for. He waited it out. It wasn't like there was anything to add to his unexpected declaration, and to be honest, he was still reeling from it himself.

When Noah got control of himself, he said, "Yeah, good luck with that."

"I know."

Noah would know. As Jane's brother and as Wendy's fiancé, he had an insider's view of Gia's band of friends.

And for fuck's sake, Gia had outright *told* Bennett that the surest way for a guy to get her to bolt was to declare genuine feelings. He started to panic. "You can't tell her."

What was he? Thirteen?

"Or Wendy."

Yes, he was officially thirteen. It was just that... "If she finds out, that'll be it. She'll never speak to me again."

"If she finds out, she'll probably raise an Amazonian army and tear you limb from limb," Noah said.

"So you won't tell?"

Noah cracked up again. "No. I won't tell. But dude. How did this happen?"

Good question. A week ago, he'd been completely in control of his life, his future. Now everything was turned upside down.

"Because it sort of seems to me like you can't fall in love with someone in a matter of days," Noah added. "Lust, maybe. Infatuation."

Bennett rolled his eyes. "We can't all marry our childhood crushes." Noah and Wendy had been fated since their teens, basically, but they'd both been too pig-headed to see it.

"So explain it to me. You're in love with Gia? Why?"

"Because…" He had to think of a way to articulate it rationally. Noah was a lawyer. He dealt in facts. And Bennett had surprised himself as much as Noah just then. He'd blurted out that news in real time as the realization came over him, the moment he was able to name the confusing swirl of emotions cresting inside him as he watched Gia walk away.

"Because she solved all my problems."

Shit. That sounded lame. And vague. He tried to be more specific. "We stopped in Charleston. I saw my parents. My dad apologized."

"What?"

Bennett chuckled. He'd shocked his friend. "None of that would have happened without her. She also solved this nagging problem with the restaurant. And she had this great idea for the community restaurant, if I can ever manage to get it off the ground."

"You make it sound like she's a combination of a therapist and a management consultant."

Bennett shook his head, frustrated at the inadequacy of that assessment and of his own ability to articulate what was in his heart. He tried once more. "I love her because she's the most amazing person I've ever met, and I hate how much she doesn't realize that."

That sobered Noah right up, probably because he'd never heard such a serious declaration from Bennett before—and he'd met Bennett's last few girlfriends.

"Okay, then," Noah said. "My initial reaction is to say, 'You, my friend, are fucked.' But on the other hand, if it's possible to crack Gia—and I'm not saying it is—maybe you're the man to do it."

"So what do I do?"

"Well, to start with, don't tell her any of this shit you just told me."

"Obviously."

"I think maybe with Gia, you have to *show* her, you know? Extremely incrementally. It has to be a stealth campaign."

Bennett nodded. That accorded with his take on the situation. Gia, by her own admission, didn't respond to declarations of love. He suddenly remembered her saying, in the Baltimore airport, that she admired men of action.

Time to shut up and become one of those. But first...

He dug in his pocket and produced the little velvet bag that contained the rings. "Take these. I was starting to fear that I wouldn't get them here on time."

"Thanks, man. Sorry the trip was so..." Noah looked in the direction in which the women had gone. "Stressful."

"I'm not sure *stressful* is really the right word." He followed Noah's gaze. "Actually, maybe it is. But it was also...Shit. I don't know." Gia had apparently robbed him of the ability to form coherent sentences.

"Confusing?" Noah supplied. "Exhilarating? Life changing?"

"Pretty much."

Noah clapped him on the back and answered the unspoken question. "Welcome to the club, my friend." He nodded at the door Gia and her friends had disappeared through. "Those women will do that to you."

"But it's worth it, right?" Bennett was alarmed at how uncertain his voice sounded.

And even more so when Noah just threw his head back and laughed.

———◦———

"I think everyone knows each other except for Tobias," Wendy said as she stood at the head of the table at dinner that night in the hotel's restaurant. She gestured at a tall blond guy wearing a blue blazer with gold buttons. He reminded Bennett of a cruise ship captain.

"Tobias is Noah's friend from NYU, but he lives in London now."

"Yes, hopped across the pond after law school." Tobias gave the table a lame little salute. "Salutations to all."

Bennett had to actively concentrate on not rolling his eyes.

Wendy went around the table and introduced everyone to Tobias. "Bennett's from New York, too," she said when she got to him.

"Ah! Upper East Side born and bred. You?"

Bennett couldn't pretend to be some kind of salt of the earth guy from modest beginnings, but he sure wished he was in that moment, because damn, the entitlement that radiated off this dude was not something he wanted to be associated with. If there was one thing his rough past made him grateful for, it was shifting his views about money. Money was great. You could do things with it, as he hoped to, once he got some more of it. But it wasn't something you deserved simply because you were born with a lot of it. It wasn't an inherent personality trait, like kindness or humor.

"Born in Charleston," he said, schooling his tone to neutrality. "I live in Washington Heights now."

"Oh," said Tobias, who had probably never been above Central Park. "How...enterprising of you."

When Wendy got to Gia, who was sitting on the other side of the table and down one spot from Bennett, Captain Cruise Ship responded by saying, "Ah, the only single lady among us." Then he made a show of looking at Bennett and saying, with jokey, exaggerated theatricality, "I guess it's down to the two of us single gents to compete for the favor of this fair maiden."

Gia's eyebrows shot up, and she exchanged a look with Wendy.

What Bennett *wanted* to say was, "Well, Tobias, I've made the 'fair maiden' scream with pleasure several times now, and in fact, the 'fair maiden' informs me that my dick was *made for her*, but sure, go ahead and give it your best shot, asshole."

What he actually said was, "Since it's the twenty-first century, I'm thinking the fair maiden is probably fine without anyone competing for her favor."

His retort inspired a muttered "Amen" from Elise, who was seated next to Bennett. Across the table, Gia's eyes widened.

After that, dinner was uneventful. When it was over, a server arrived with a tray of tiny pie-like things, one of them with a lit candle stuck in it.

Elise said to Gia, "I brought them from Toronto! And there's a whole other box for you in your room." She turned to Bennett. "Gia loves butter tarts."

"Should I be embarrassed that I'm a chef who has no idea what a butter tart is?"

"Nope," Noah said. "I've never seen them outside of Canada. They're basically mini pecan pies without the pecans."

They actually sounded—and tasted—southern. Caramelized sugar and pastry. He was down with it.

Gia, he noticed, was not. She only had a bite of hers after blowing out her candle.

As the evening wound down, he turned the conversation to the picnic lunch he'd offered to make to follow Saturday's beachside wedding ceremony.

"I was thinking we'd build it around local seafood. Crab cakes, Gulf snapper." He cleared his throat and added, "Oysters," his gaze flickering to Gia as his mind flashed the image of her slurping oysters and "Oh my God"-ing in his kitchen.

"I didn't know you were cooking for the wedding," Gia said.

"He offered to do a picnic for on the beach after the ceremony, and how could I say no?" Wendy turned to him with a stern look. "But you're only cooking, remember? We have staff to serve and clean up. You're literally going to make everything, then do a mic drop and walk away."

Bennett chuckled. He'd been tickled when they'd taken him up on his offer. He loved feeding people generally, and feeding people he loved—he sneaked another glance at Gia—was the best thing in the world.

"Understood. I'm meeting with a friend tomorrow who has a restaurant down the beach. So if I have your blessing on the menu, he'll hook me up with suppliers, and we'll be good. You've got, what? You two and the wedding party, which makes eight. Plus..." He scanned the table, doing a head count. "Jay?" As Elise's husband, Jay was attending, but he wasn't actually in the wedding—he and Noah didn't really know each other. Which was unfortunate, because if Jay *had* been in the wedding, perhaps he could have displaced Tobias, the other "single gent."

"Yep," Noah said. "And my mom and her boyfriend and Wendy's aunt—those are the only other guests."

"We should probably feed the officiant, too," Wendy said. "So that brings us to lucky thirteen. And seafood is great. Anything you make will be great. You don't need my blessing." She made a dismissive gesture with her hand. "Consider any menu you come up with approved."

"Wow." Jane giggled. "You are the chillest bride I've ever seen."

Both Wendy and Jane looked at Elise, who rolled her eyes and said, "Whatever. You love me."

"Who's this friend of yours with a beachside restaurant?" Gia asked.

"A friend of a friend," Bennett said. "A guy Lalande knows. He's going to let me use his kitchen."

"Best present you could give us." Wendy beamed.

"Oh, I brought you another present," he said, thinking of the Toronto Blue Jays tickets he had in his bag for the baseball-loving couple who would be settling in Toronto permanently after the wedding.

"Damn right you did." Elise slung an arm around Gia, who was next to her. "You brought our girl."

Our girl.

If only.

Chapter Fourteen

TWO DAYS BEFORE THE WEDDING

Gia had done few things in her life she was as proud of as delivering Wendy's wedding dress to Florida.

She had surrendered the dress to Wendy last night, just after they arrived, of course. They'd hung it up in the room they were sharing. But as she waited for Wendy to come out of the bathroom the next morning, she got a little emotional. She was so happy for Wendy. They'd both had long journeys here, Gia with the dress and Wendy with...everything. To think she'd been in love with Noah since she was a teenager. And now she was *marrying* him.

Wendy emerged from the bathroom in her underwear, her hands on her hips. "How come we didn't talk last night about you and Bennett?"

So much for getting all emotional over the final dress fitting.

"What about Bennett and me?" Gia feigned ignorance.

"You texted me that you fooled around with him. But

you don't appear to have told Elise this. If you had, she would have brought it up first thing and beat you over the head until you spilled all the details."

Wendy was right. It was super weird for Gia not to have told Elise that she'd "fooled around" with Bennett. And none of the girls knew that she'd subsequently done a lot more than "fool around."

"Why didn't *you* tell Elise about it?" Gia asked. She'd been aiming for a teasing tone, but feared she'd fallen short. Usually the deal was that if you told one girl something, you told them all.

Wendy tilted her head and squinted at Gia. "When she didn't bring it up, I figured it was because you didn't tell her. And I assumed you had a reason for that. I just don't know what it is."

Shit. Wendy was onto her.

When she didn't respond, Wendy said, "I'm left to conclude that either you've already forgotten about it, or there's something going on that you don't want us to know about."

"I've already forgotten about it," Gia said quickly. Maybe too quickly.

"Then why the secrecy?"

Normally Gia wasn't shy about discussing her exploits with her friends, and Wendy knew it.

"I just didn't want to inject any drama into the wedding." There. That sounded reasonable. "The other two weddings had enough of that, don't you think? I've decided to stay away from the wedding party."

And *that* was turning out to be easier than she would have thought. Yesterday she'd been angry with herself for not making her little "we're done" speech to Bennett when she'd had her chance, but it was proving not to have been necessary. Bennett had pretty much ignored her since they arrived, huddling with Noah and then going out with the guys after their group dinner last night when the girls had swept her away for drinks and dancing to celebrate her birthday.

"Can't say I blame you on the whole 'staying away from the wedding party' front when it comes to Tobias," Wendy said, "but it would be kind of hilarious to see him and Bennett all dressed up in armor and, like, jousting over the right to hold your handkerchief or something." She threw her head back and performed her signature Wendy cackle, and Gia couldn't help but join in.

"All right." Gia crossed the room and picked up the dress with a reverence she had not exactly shown consistently when it had been in her care—her mind flashed back to the snowball fight in which she'd used it as a shield. "You ready?"

"Yeah, I guess I shouldn't keep standing here in my skivvies. They'll be here any minute."

Gia carefully unzipped the garment bag and then the dress inside it. "You want to step into it or have it go over your head?"

"Step into it."

Gia held the dress steady as Wendy shimmied into it. Then she moved behind her and zipped her up.

There was a knock on the door as soon as she'd done up the clasp at the top of the zipper, so she moved to answer it, stepping aside for Jane and Elise, who'd gone down to the lobby to meet the tailor and escort her up.

The other girls squeed and exclaimed—they hadn't seen the dress because they hadn't been in New York for the initial tailoring appointment like Gia had.

The tailor helped Wendy onto a small box she had positioned in front of the room's full-length mirror, and the chattering died down. Jane drew in an audible breath, then covered her mouth with her hand.

"It's *beautiful*," Elise breathed. Gia was gratified that she wasn't the only one a little overcome with emotion.

"Just like your mom was." Jane hugged Wendy so hard, Gia could see her arm muscles straining.

When Jane retreated, Wendy cleared her throat and eyed herself in the mirror. "It's not very on trend, but..."

"It is, too," Gia declared. The dress was ivory lace, with a short, swingy skirt and a wide, off-the-shoulder ruffled bodice. It had originally had long sleeves, which the New York salon had removed, making it more modern-looking and also more appropriate for summer. But you'd never know to look at it that it had undergone such major surgery. "Seventies boho chic just starting to shade into eighties excess. It's *fabulous*." Gia got out her camera and took today's picture.

"How are you going to wear your hair?" the tailor asked as she did some pinning.

"I initially thought down," Wendy said. Wendy had gorgeous, midback-length, shiny black hair. "But then I thought it might get annoying if it's windy. It's not going to be a long ceremony, but I don't want to spend it fighting with my hair."

"And this low back with the lace is stunning," the tailor said. "Better to wear your hair up."

"I was actually toying with the idea of just putting it in a loose braid down my back," Wendy said. "Just kind of running with the 1970s hippie theme. Is that crazy?"

"How very *low-key* of you," Elise teased, sticking out her tongue at Jane. Jane, while not nearly the bridezilla Elise had been, had spent the run-up to her wedding, which she kept insisting would be "low-key," being anything but that.

"A braid is perfect," Gia said. "Are you doing flowers? I could totally see just some simple daisies or wildflowers. You could stick one in the braid, too."

"Honestly, I thought I'd just hit the floral section of a grocery store Saturday morning and get something *low-key* like that. Slap a ribbon around them and I'm done." It was her turn to tease Jane.

Jane rolled her eyes good-naturedly and said, "That's perfect—all of it: the flowers, the braid. Totally you. Effortlessly beautiful."

Gia got a little misty again. "Who would have thought, a year ago, that Wendy would be getting married?"

Everyone turned to her. They were perpetually worried that Gia would think they'd abandoned her or something stupid like that, and she was forever reassuring them. She didn't have any of those hang-ups. She was thrilled to see her friends so happy. Plus she genuinely liked all their husbands.

It was more that Wendy hadn't seemed the marrying type. Elise and Jane had been the romantics in their group.

Gia waved away their concerned looks. "No worries, you guys. You all getting married doesn't change anything between us. I'm sticking to you all like a freaking barnacle whether you like it or not." Then she nodded at Elise's tummy. "Besides, someone has to be the cool, single aunt when you all start procreating. I only meant that you"—she turned to Wendy again—"always had such a no-nonsense approach to love and sex. You were always on about how boring men were."

"Ah." Wendy nodded sagely. "Well, gather round, children, because I'm about to impart some great wisdom and get all philosophical and shit on you."

Jane's and Elise's faces grew serious. Gia leaned in, her curiosity piqued.

"Yeah, come right in close, because this is the only time you'll ever hear me say this." Wendy waited a few beats, probably to amp up the drama, then grinned and said, "I was totally wrong about that. Men—the right ones, mind you—are the bomb."

⌒౷

Jesus Christ. Gia in a bikini on the beach. As Bennett—who had returned from his meeting with Lalande's chef friend and changed into swim trunks—approached the wedding party, it was all he could do not to let loose an audible stream of curses.

It made no sense. He'd seen her partially or fully naked a few times. Three, to be precise. Four if you counted yesterday morning's shower. Not that he was counting.

Okay, he was counting.

There was something different about this, though. She was lying on a lounge chair wearing a tiny white bikini and a big floppy hat and reading a magazine—all that perfection existing in the world like it was no big deal. Like he was just supposed to walk over and say hi, give everyone equal attention, maybe order a tea and sip it like a goddamned normal person who wasn't losing his fucking mind.

He thought back to when he and Gia had spoken about his past girlfriends. He'd claimed that he'd come to love them. He'd thought he had.

But clearly, he'd had no idea.

If this—this savage, fruitless, excruciating *yearning* he was powerless to do anything about—was love...then he was brand new to the concept.

He considered turning around and going inside.

But no. He could do this. He was a grown-ass man. This

was what he'd wanted, all week, to get here, into the warm air. He had no idea what the hell to do about Gia, but he was pretty sure hiding from her wasn't going to achieve anything.

"Hey," he said, drawing everyone's attention, including hers—she slid her sunglasses down her nose, and her gaze raked over him.

"Everything good?" Wendy asked idly from a couple chairs over.

"Yep. We're all set. I got the lay of the land, met their seafood guy, and placed our order."

"Thanks, man," Noah said from the other side of Wendy. Their chairs had been dragged flush against each other, and he was idly playing with her hair, running his hands through it.

Elise and Jay were there, too, sitting cross-legged across from each other on the same lounge chair, a travel checkerboard between them.

And that asshole Tobias was on the other side of Gia, absorbed in his phone.

"Where are Cameron and Jane?" he asked, reaching for benign conversation.

"They drove out to Busch Gardens," Elise said with a smirk.

"God forbid there should be a roller coaster within a hundred-mile radius that they haven't made out on," Wendy said.

"Everyone's doing their own thing today," Noah said. "So don't feel like you have to waste the day on the beach with us lazy bums."

"I think wasting the day on the beach has been Bennett's main goal since we left New York." Gia yawned and idly shifted her leg so she could brush some sand off it.

He had to prevent himself from reaching out and doing it for her, from taking a firm hand to that flawless expanse of thigh and cleaning off the sand that was marring its perfection.

Then he had to move his towel in front of him.

"Pull up a chair, then," Noah said, but Bennett waved him off.

"I'm going to go in the water."

"I'd suggest the pool if you want to swim," Wendy said. "The Gulf isn't really warm enough for swimming in February."

"Especially for a tender southern gentleman such as yourself," Gia deadpanned.

"I stuck my toes in, and it is *cold*," Elise confirmed. Then she made a series of moves with a checker and said, "Ha! King me!"

Apparently satisfied with her sand-free leg, Gia extended it back along her chair as she stretched out her whole body, reaching her arms above her head and arching her back.

There was no appropriate way to respond to that other than to say, "Nah, I'm good with the ocean," and to run away. It was not escaping Bennett's notice that since realizing he was in love with Gia, he'd spent more time avoiding her than with her. Which wasn't really helping him implement Noah's whole "show her" directive. But a man had to do what a man had to do in order to survive.

The only people in the water were some kids playing in the shallows and some wet-suited kiteboarders much farther out. He walked right past the kids and into the water, and *holy God*. They'd been right. It was freezing.

But he'd escaped her.

"Eeee!"

Or not.

He knew that shriek.

He turned, but not before he'd walked out enough that he was submerged to his waist.

"Ahhh!" she squealed, jumping up and down like she was walking on lava. "I was getting borderline comatose there in the sun. Thought I'd wake myself up, and—ahh!" She'd walked a little farther in and was hugging herself and squeezing her legs together like kids do when they have to pee. The sun glinted off her blue hair.

She was adorable.

He'd calmed down sufficiently that he could walk back out to meet her.

"What's the problem, Canada? Too cold for you?"

That baited her. She shot him an exasperated look as she kept walking out. "Just taking my time, South Carolina. But don't stay out here on my account. I wouldn't want your tender southern balls to freeze off."

He snorted.

"What?" She was all fake innocence. "You have nice balls. I've tasted them, and they're delicious. Preserve them at all costs, please."

Shaking his head, he kept pace with her, stopping only when she did, when they were both in to hip height. "I don't know, Canada. You're looking a little shivery."

She splashed him.

He hadn't been expecting it, so he inhaled a bunch of water and started coughing.

She was clearly expecting him to retaliate, because when he was done sputtering, she was bracing herself, half covering her head.

He walked toward her with his hands up in a gesture of peace. "Can you swim, Canada? Is there enough open water on the frozen tundra up there that they teach you to swim?"

"I'm from Ontario, Bennett, not the North Pole. Yes, I can swim."

With that assurance, he moved like lightning, grabbing her, picking her up, and, as she laughed and shrieked, throwing her in the water.

She was mad when she resurfaced, but not really. "Hooooboy! You're in trouble now!"

And he really was. The joke was on him because of course she'd emerged from the sea drenched, her hair slicked to her body and water coursing over her perfect smooth skin. Because that was what happened when you dunked people under the water—they got wet.

She came at him and tried to push him over, but she wasn't strong enough, so he picked her up and tossed her again, a sudden tide of joy, as expansive as the ocean around them, rising in his chest in concert with the splash she made.

She didn't give up; after she resurfaced, she launched herself at him. It wasn't enough. Again he caught her easily, but instead of heaving her back into the ocean, he held on. She struggled and laughed and kept trying to generate enough momentum to tip him. He merely waited her out, laughing along with her, until eventually she gave up and went still in his arms, panting and shivering at the same time.

It was all he could do not to kiss her. He would have, were it not for the audience on the beach, who were surely already wondering what the hell was going on with them.

He'd been holding her sideways, her body across his arms the way you would carry a bride over the threshold, but she started squirming, which he took to mean she wanted down. He loosened his grip and prepared to set her down, but she held on tight with her arms while she shimmied her lower body around and, God help him, wrapped her legs around his waist.

The water made her buoyant, so she didn't need him to hold her there, but once it was clear she'd reached her desired destination and was staying there, his arms went automatically around her. The bright sunshine illuminated her smattering of freckles. He *loved* those freckles.

"Hi." Her voice was low, even though there was no one around to hear them over the rushing of the surf.

"Hi," he echoed, contemplating but ultimately holding himself back from adding *I've missed you*. Because it had been all of eighteen hours since he'd seen her at dinner last night, and all of thirty since they'd woken up together yesterday in South Carolina. Not that he was counting.

Okay, he was counting.

She smiled suddenly, like something had pleased her.

And oh, how he wanted to be that thing.

Slowly, she slid down his body. He didn't bother trying to push her away before she hit his erection—that counted as "show her," right?

Her smile got wider as she encountered the bump, and even wider still when her feet hit the ground.

He felt the corners of his mouth quirk up to mirror hers. It was like there was a thread connecting them, and all he could do was echo her: say hi when she said hi, smile when she smiled. He was enchanted by her. There was no other word for it, really. He was—

"Oooh!"

While he was mooning over her, she'd hooked her foot around the back of his knees and tripped him. Sent him falling backward into the water, which he proceeded to suck into his lungs as he gasped his shock.

By the time he recovered, she was walking away. Sashaying, really, smug in her victory. He hurried to catch up to her, intending to retaliate, but she threw him another of those drugging smiles over her shoulder as the water rained off her body and said, "You might have me beat when it comes to brawn, South Carolina, but I outsmarted you there."

"You did, Canada. You totally did."

"That's it for me," she said, her teeth chattering.

He fell into step beside her as they walked out of the water. "What are you ladies up to this afternoon?"

"I don't know." She squinted against the sun at their friends on the beach. He followed her gaze. They were packing up. "Probably lunch, and then count the minutes until it's happy hour. I wish I could talk them into a hike, but they're not going for it. What about you guys?"

"I don't know about the others, but I have to go back to the restaurant where I'll be putting together the wedding lunch. I'm trying to stay out of their way as much as possible, so I'm going to do some prep work in the postlunch lull this afternoon. Most of it I'll have to save for tomorrow or Saturday morning, but I can pick up some groceries now and stow them there—get things organized."

"Can I help?"

He turned, surprised by the offer—and also by how much everything inside him rose up and shouted *Yes!* But instead he said, "You don't have to. It won't take long."

"I just..." she whispered.

"What?" He wanted more than anything to lay a hand on her back but knew she wouldn't want him to. They'd already given their friends enough to speculate about with their little "water fight with hugging" show.

"I'm hungry, and I thought...I'd rather..."

It was hard—it was almost impossible—but he refrained from interrupting, from suggesting phrases, from trying to help her get through whatever it was she was struggling to say.

When the silence stretched just to the point of

awkwardness, she said, "I thought maybe you could make me lunch."

Yes.

"We could eat together, I was thinking. Instead of..." She was slowing down as they got closer to their friends. "Instead of with everyone else."

He realized that he hadn't said anything, that the yes that had welled up inside him just then had not, in fact, been verbal.

"I just...I like eating your food."

He was overcome for a moment by the request, the admission. He knew what it had taken for her to make it. And even beyond that, it flattered the hell out of him. She might as well be batting her eyelashes and feeling his biceps.

He tried to make it not about his ego, but about what was best for her, but in this case, since the two things coincided so handily, he was going to give himself a moment to bask in it.

"Of course." His voice came out all scratchy. He cleared his throat. "You name it, I'll make it for you."

⸺ ❦ ⸺

What was she *doing*?

A day ago, Gia had been psyching herself up to tell Bennett that whatever was between them had to end.

Because it *did*.

She knew that.

So why had she followed up that intention by cavorting with him in the ocean and then inviting herself to lunch?

Because he looked really good in swim trunks was the answer—that's all it was.

Anyway, she was here now. She looked around as

Bennett laid a steak onto a cast-iron skillet. She was getting familiar with restaurant kitchens, this being the third one she'd been in this week. She liked them—they were energizing bordering on manic in the same way a runway show was backstage.

Lalande's friend owned a café on the beach a couple miles from the hotel, and as she unpacked the groceries they'd picked up, she couldn't help but compare it to Lalande's, and to Bennett's place in New York.

"This place isn't very well organized," she whispered. Unlike in Bennett's kitchen, where all the ingredients were clearly labeled and stored in rigorously organized containers, the work surfaces here were scattered willy-nilly with herbs and other stuff she couldn't identify.

"Good eye," he whispered back. "There's definitely more of a laid-back air here than is my preference."

After making some small talk with the chef-owner, they'd been given a corner in which to work and a section of a refrigerator, and left alone.

Bennett opened a bottle of tea as he tended to the steak. When he'd asked her what she wanted for lunch, she'd deferred to him, telling him she'd like whatever he made. That she trusted him.

The astonishing thing was, she did. As she watched him unpack a grocery bag and unroll a sleeve of knives—he'd brought his own—she realized she had very little anxiety about what was about to happen. He would make her something. It would be delicious. She would eat it. Maybe not all of it, but that would be okay. He would understand.

He was making them steak salads. He pulled the small, lean filet mignon off the pan and set it aside to rest. He'd already prepared two plates with lettuce and some chopped grilled asparagus that he'd nicked from the restaurant.

"You're not getting my best here," he said as he whipped up a dressing. "This is grocery store meat, so keep that in mind, and did you know that the vast majority of the world's olive oil is tainted? Cut with cheap vegetable oil and dumped on the North American market. So unless you have an importer and you can trace the whole supply chain, you're probably getting vaguely olive-flavored garbage."

He was nervous, she realized with a jolt. He was usually so confident, so it was strange to see. He wanted to please her, which wasn't going to be hard, because as amazing as his food was, it wasn't actually about the food.

It wasn't about the food.

That was an astonishing thought. Maybe that was why she was here against her better judgment. Maybe it didn't have anything to do with how good he looked in swim trunks. Maybe it was just that she'd told him her secret, and he had not made a big deal about it.

He'd just made her lunch. A *low-key* lunch, to steal a word that had become a joke with the girls.

"It's going to be great," she said as he slid her a plate. She was talking to him, but also to herself.

He'd dressed his own salad but served her dressing in a ramekin on the side, so she could control how much went on the salad. That little gesture perfectly exemplified why she'd wanted to come here with him.

He took care of her. Automatically. He knew the small things that would ease her way, and he just did them without commentary or judgment.

It made tears prickle behind her eyes.

It was also not something she could allow herself to get used to.

She picked up the steak knife he'd handed her and sawed

off part of the steak. She hadn't had steak in years, defaulting to getting her protein from chicken breasts or egg whites.

"Oh my God." There was a crunchy, salty crust on the steak—it had been perfectly seared—that gave way to a tender, flavorful center. He'd sprinkled some kind of fancy cheese on the steaks—just a bit, but its pungent tanginess worked perfectly with the meat without overpowering it. "If this was subpar grocery store meat, it boggles the mind to think what you can do with steak that's up to your standards."

He grinned but waved away the compliment. "So what's with the big pink Florida hotel as the wedding site? Wendy's such a world traveler. Seems like a weird spot for their wedding."

"There's a story there. Wendy was, like many girls, obsessed with princesses when she was growing up. Her dad gave her a Disney princess Pez dispenser a couple days before he died suddenly, and she sort of imprinted on both princesses and Pez dispensers. Mind you, she probably wouldn't explain it like that, but that's my interpretation of the situation."

Bennett cracked up. "That's so...not Wendy. At least from what I know of her."

"I know, right? Apparently Noah won her heart with Pez dispensers. Anyway, when she found out, as a kid, that there was this big pink hotel on the beach in Florida, she always wanted to come here, which of course she did as an adult when she started doing all her globe-trotting. So when she and Noah decided to get married somewhere other than Toronto, she came right out with 'I want a princess wedding at the Pink Palace.'"

"Wow," he said. "Maybe I need to take my attire up a notch. They said khaki pants and a white shirt for the ceremony, but they didn't get specific."

"Nah, her dress is pretty casual, and so are the brides-maid dresses." Gia cocked her head, thinking about how nonfussy Wendy had been about the whole thing. "Which I guess makes no sense given what I just said about the whole princess wedding thing."

He shrugged as he cleared their plates and pulled out some bell peppers. "Someone once told me that all the best people are full of contradictions."

She smiled as she watched his talented hands make quick work of the pepper, transforming it into perfectly uniform little cubes. "Sounds like a wise person," she joked.

He stopped chopping. "She is."

Something in Gia's stomach fluttered. "You want me to help?" She nodded at the peppers. "With the disclaimer that the final product will end up looking like a kindergartener produced it?"

"Nah. I'm just gonna prep a few things that will keep until Saturday. You sit there and do your thing while I do my thing."

"What is my thing?" she asked, still in the teasing manner that befitted their bantering.

He put down the knife and cocked his head. "I don't know. That's what we need to figure out."

What *was* it about Bennett? He could shift the entire tenor of a conversation with a single sentence. He could look at her like he was seeing *inside* her, like he was shining light on stuff that had been in the dark for as long as she could remember.

She also didn't miss that he'd said *we. That's what* we *need to figure out.*

She'd been right to be wary of him. He saw her as a prob-lem to fix. Like the homeless guy outside his restaurant.

Oh, she was so messed up when it came to him. She was

a moth attracted to a flame. He was bad for her, but she craved him. She *wanted* him to fix her—deep down, that's why she'd suggested lunch in the first place, right? But it wasn't safe to want that from a man. You gave a man too much power over you and before you knew it you were alone on a beach in Ibiza with a broken heart.

She had no idea how to respond to what he'd said. She was used to testing guys. To confirming her sense that when confronted with the real her, they would find her lacking. But she usually conducted these tests by presenting herself in ways they wouldn't expect—by taking off the model mask and showing up with dirty hair and no makeup. But he had already seen her like that, and he hadn't blinked.

But there was more than one kind of mask.

So she went for the truth. He had a way of pulling the truth out of her.

She looked right into his eyes and said, "I'm afraid if I eat, I won't get work anymore."

He gazed evenly back at her and said, "I'm afraid if you don't, you'll get sick."

"What's it to you?" She didn't necessarily mean to sound confrontational, but at the same time, this was a test, right? This was the emotional version of no makeup.

He didn't answer her question. Asked her one of his own instead. "What if you just didn't go back?"

"What?"

It wasn't like she hadn't heard him, or didn't understand what he'd meant, just that what he was suggesting was so far from her reality that "What?" had been the only response she could muster.

"You told me before that you didn't have another job booked. That you're on vacation for a month. That's why you could dye your hair, right? What if you just...extend the vacation?"

He'd finished with the peppers and had moved on to chopping a bar of chocolate, which seemed like an odd next item to chop, but she had no doubt he had a master plan. A masterful plan.

"I can't do that."

She expected him to argue, but he didn't. Just handed her a shard of chocolate.

She put it on her tongue. It wasn't sweet at all. It was the darkest, bitterest chocolate she'd ever had.

Chapter Fifteen

$\mathcal{B}$ennett was starting to want things it wasn't safe to want. He had lived alone for years, essentially since he left his parents' house. Even when he was couch surfing and living on the streets, he'd still been, elementally, alone.

And yes, he'd had girlfriends. He would have moved in with any of them, had things worked out—he'd always *thought* he would have, anyway. Thought that if the woman in question had been into it, they would eventually have progressed down that road of gradually escalating commitment. A few years of dating would be followed by cohabitating. Maybe getting engaged eventually, and of course engagements were generally followed by weddings. He'd thought of it like a video game. Complete level one, unlock level two. An orderly progression. Because when you committed to someone, that's what you did.

But Gia had him turned inside out. There was no orderly progression here. There were just these great lurching

lunges, his heart dragging his shocked brain and body over
markers that were going by so fast he couldn't even get a
sense of what they signified.

He'd had sex with her on the second day he'd known her,
for God's sake. He didn't *do* that.

And now, worse, he wanted *this*. He wanted to cook
for her and feed her little bits of food while he did so. He
wanted her sitting next to him in the kitchen telling him
stories about her friends. He wanted to listen to her confide
her secret fears.

He wanted to solve all her goddamned problems.

And he was pretty sure he wanted it forever.

He had to file that want away, though, because it was too
big to think about. Its bigness was paralyzing.

And it was dangerous. He couldn't let her see these
thoughts, these wants. If she could see inside his head, she'd
get spooked and do exactly what she'd told him she did in
these sorts of situations—run for the hills.

So as they got out of the car back at the hotel, he decided
to try to do what Noah had said, to show Gia how he felt
without making a big deal about it. *Extremely incrementally*
was the phrase Noah had used.

And when Bennett looked inside himself for something
that fit the bill, it was right there. A smaller, more immediate
want that was no less powerful for its modest stature.

He wanted to hold her hand.

And, he figured, he could either overthink the hell out of
the impulse or he could just do it.

So fuck it. He did it.

He jogged around to her side of the car, where she
was still getting out, and grabbed her hand. That way, he
figured, it was sort of like helping her out of the car, and
then just . . . not letting go.

When he didn't immediately drop her hand after they got moving toward the lobby, her eyes widened. He'd surprised her. She didn't resist, exactly, but there was a stiffening of her posture that he could feel through her hand.

He didn't care. He wasn't letting go unless she did.

So they walked into the hotel like that. He could tell she was nervous. She scanned the lobby, no doubt looking for her friends, not wanting to be seen with him like this.

He got it. His heart was beating fast, too, like he was doing something a hell of a lot more transgressive than holding a woman's hand. Not that he was afraid of being seen, not inherently, but he was afraid of what *she* would do if they were. She would pull back—not just from his hand, but from *him*. But he didn't know how to "show her" how he felt without, you know…showing her.

They stepped into an empty elevator, and she breathed a sigh of relief. He responded by doubling down, which, in the Incident of the Hand-Holding Transgression, amounted to changing their grip and lacing their fingers together.

He punched the button for his floor—the fifth—which was lower than hers.

She punched hers, which was fine, although irrelevant, because if he had anything to say about it, she wasn't going there.

The elevator dinged, and the doors opened. He still didn't let go of her hand. He wasn't going to make her come with him, but what if he just…stayed silent but tugged a little as he exited the elevator?

She came with him.

He turned his head and grinned at the lime-green walls so she wouldn't see how profoundly not chill he was right now.

He dug in his pocket for his room key and scanned

them in, all without dropping her hand. It was hard not
to blurt out everything, hard not to try to build a case for
her not going back to modeling, for her being with him—
or hell, even just one of the two—but he had to play the
long game here. Choose his moments to make his points
subtly.

Not that dragging her to his room when his intent must be
obvious counted as subtle, but Gia didn't mind bold sexual
overtures—they just couldn't be accompanied by declarations or expectations. She had to be able to compartmentalize,
or at least tell herself that's what she was doing.

"Do you have condoms?" she asked, the moment the
door closed.

He threw his head back and laughed. He had her so
figured out.

"I do." He had optimistically bought some last night at the
hotel gift shop after his chat with Noah. He led her through
the room to the balcony, though. They were in no hurry.

He was still holding her hand, and she pulled back
against his grip, planting her feet like she wanted to stay
in the room.

Of course she did. She was here for one thing only.

Well, no declarations, fine, but he was going to push her
limits a little. Make her contemplate the goddamned view
with him first. How was that for incremental?

So he kept pulling until she rolled her eyes and came
with him. He plopped himself down on one of the white
wrought iron chairs and pulled her onto his lap. Wrapped
his arms around her, rested his chin on her shoulder, and
took in the vista. A majestic blue pool stretched out before
them, and beyond that the sea. It was, objectively, beautiful,
but all that blue made him think of her hair, which had
grown on him. He reached a hand up and played with it a

little, gradually moving his hands up until he was kneading the tight muscles of her neck.

After a few seconds, she sighed and relaxed against him. He loved that, being able to make her physically relax.

"You miss the ocean?" she asked.

"I think so."

"You *think* so?" She laughed.

"The ocean is magnificent and all that." He let go of her with one hand just long enough to gesture at it. "I mean, no one is going to be unhappy with that. Except maybe you, Miss I Prefer the Forest. And anyway, New York is on the ocean. Some of the oysters we source at the restaurant are from Long Island. So technically, I still have access to the ocean. I think what I really miss is warmth. The warm, sunny beach, you know?"

She nodded. "If you went back to Charleston, you could open your place on the beach. I bet even beachfront property there is cheaper than Manhattan rent. Still Cajun, but you'd have a more direct line to the seafood side of things. You could have a place kind of like your friend's here."

He nodded. She was correct on all fronts. He could have that. There was nothing stopping him.

"Except with a tidier kitchen," she said, and he could hear the smile in her voice.

"Definitely a tidier kitchen," he agreed.

There was a breeze coming in off the ocean. Gia had put on a sundress before they left for the restaurant, a cute little floral thing with a short, swingy skirt. A more powerful gust of wind caught it and nudged it up into her lap. He reflexively moved to push it back down, but then he paused halfway with a handful of the fabric. Rethought things. Reversed himself and brought the skirt back up to where it had been when the wind had taken over.

He felt her intake of breath before he even touched her skin. She stiffened a little in his arms, full of anticipation.

He had just been thinking about how much he loved it when he could make her relax.

But he loved this, too—making her come to attention.

He let his hand settle on her thigh, heavy and possessive. Willed it to say what he wasn't allowed to with his mouth.

Her next intake of breath was a little sharper. Her back arched a little, like she'd been trying to prevent herself from leaning into his touch with her lower body but had forgotten to anchor her upper body.

He let the hand slide upward, let his calloused middle finger, made rough by a lot of knife work, drag across her smooth skin. Goose bumps rose, and not just there, but on her arm, too. On the side of her throat.

With his other hand, he brushed her hair aside so he could lean down and put his mouth on the back of her neck.

Her head fell back, and her hair swung over and covered the side of his face as he continued to kiss the back of her neck. He let himself get lost in the blue, better than any ocean vista. Her skin tasted salty, like seawater. His dick, which had been stirring since her first little gasp, hardened.

"We should go inside," she whispered.

He made a wordless murmur of disagreement. He wanted, suddenly, to torture her. To *show* her.

His hand, inching ever upward, encountered the fabric of her panties. He could tell they were cotton from the feel— like the jersey kitchen towels he favored. Last time he'd been in this position, he'd wished for light to see what color her panties were.

Well, now he had light. The bright, unrelenting afternoon sun.

So he flipped her dress up.

Her panties were black. Plain black cotton.

That should not have been so sexy.

After taking in the sight of her for a moment, the dark, damp black cotton against her creamy skin, he moved her underwear aside, slowly, enjoying the juxtaposition, savoring the drag of the fabric across her skin. From there, he let lazy fingers drift over her, barely touching the heated flesh they encountered.

"Bennett," she said, his name a warning on her lips.

"Shh." He'd meant to soothe, but it came out harsher than he intended, more like a command, but hey, that worked, too. She was into dirty talk, he'd learned. That was his Gia—she didn't want you to hold her hand, but saying something like "I'm going to make you come right here, and you're going to have to be quiet about it," usually worked like a charm.

The balcony was small and flanked by neighboring ones. He followed Gia's gaze as she assessed them. They were empty, but the sliding glass door on the room to their right was open.

He chuckled.

Then he watched her assess the scene below them, the pool full of vacationers.

He chuckled again.

"You're evil," she whispered.

"Maybe," he agreed cheerfully. "Should I stop?" Even as he asked the question, he swirled his fingers over her with a little more—but not too much—pressure, just the way he'd learned she liked.

She shook her head, a wordless but vehement no.

So he shifted her a little, moving her off him enough that he could get all of her skirt out from between them. Then he shamelessly unzipped his jeans, took out his dick, and settled her back against him, snuggling his dick into the crack of her ass. Satisfied with this arrangement, he then settled her skirt back over them. You would have had to look closely to see his one hand snaking under her skirt, and as far as he was concerned, anyone looking that closely was welcome to the show.

She squirmed, whether to make herself more comfortable or to make him more *un*comfortable, he couldn't say. He let his hips rock a little, even as he repositioned his hand over her mound to tease her before he got down to business.

He floated his other hand up to her chest. Not her breasts, but the flat expanse of skin that covered her collarbones and shaded into her throat. Splayed his hand wide and let it rest there, pleased with the rapid firing of her pulse he discovered.

And fuck, this was the life. One hand resting on Gia's throat, feeling the pulsing there, and the other on her pussy.

Time to see if he could make her pulse there, too. He set up a rhythm that involved the dose of pressure she liked and the occasional skim over her clit directly. It didn't take long for her to get really riled up.

"Oh my God!" she whispered. His favorite phrase in the world. A moan escaped then, a loud one. It must have shocked her with its volume, because she grabbed his hand, the one that had been resting at her throat, and pasted it over her mouth. Then pressed both her own hands over it, like she was trying to make sure she obeyed his directive to be silent but didn't trust herself to do it on her own.

Fuck. His hips, which he'd been allowing to rock gently, surged forward. She made an inarticulate noise and scraped her teeth against his palm, like she was trying to bite him but couldn't get a hold on him.

Her hands left his then and came down and clamped on

to the arms of the chair. She pressed against it, using it as leverage to lift her hips more firmly toward the hand that was working her.

He toyed with the idea of backing off, of bringing her back from the edge and making her wait, but honestly, he didn't want to. He wanted her to come, then he wanted to go inside and make her come again. Let himself come with her.

So he whispered in her ear, low and dirty. "Yeah, Gia. Fuck yourself on my hand." She liked that directive, judging by how furiously her hips bucked, so he kept it up, keeping his voice so quiet he could barely hear himself over the rush of the ocean and the din from the pool below them. "That's right. Take what you need, Gia."

He kept his hand over her mouth, because she seemed to want it there, but only lightly, so she could easily push it away or turn her head.

"Make yourself come. Use my hand to make your-self come."

And she did, biting back a scream he would have given anything to hear. He let his hand fall from her mouth back to her throat and rest there lightly so he could feel the thundering of her pulse in concert with the shuddering of her pussy.

He held her for a long time, eventually removing both hands and just hugging her while her breathing returned to normal.

She'd gone limp in his arms. He'd felt her relax before, but this was beyond that. She was heavy and vulnerable, and, he flattered himself, sated.

"Oh my God," she whispered, her tone tinged this time with equal parts amusement and awe.

He smiled and kissed her cheek.

Bennett was always doing that—kissing her after sex. Dropping these affectionate, seemingly innocuous little kisses on totally innocent body parts.

It wasn't called for.

It didn't freak her out like it had last time, though. She wasn't holding back panic, which was…interesting. It was more a minor annoyance, like a bug she hadn't managed to swat away before it bit her.

She would have objected—purely on principle—except for the fact that after that kiss, he swatted her thigh and said, "Let's go inside and do that again, and this time, you can make as much noise as you like."

And dammit if she didn't want that more than she wanted to object to that kiss. *A lot* more.

Still, she wasn't going to pass up an opportunity to tease him, so she stretched, making sure to writhe strategically as she did so, huffed a satisfied, purring sigh, and said, "I don't know. I think I'm good. I should probably go find the girls now."

He responded by picking her up, like he had earlier in the water, taking her back inside, and dropping her on the bed.

She tried not to laugh, but once it became clear she was going to lose that battle, she surrendered and cracked up.

He rolled his eyes, but he was holding back laughter. He stared at her for a moment before reaching back and pulling off his T-shirt. Then he shoved his still-unbuttoned jeans down, grabbing his underwear on the way, and stepped out of them.

The sight of him like that, naked and hard, sobered her up pretty quick.

"Still want to leave?"

She shook her head no.

He climbed onto the bed and crawled over her, resting

one knee and one hand on each side of her, caging her in against the bed. "What about now?"

"What if I did?" she teased. "This"—she gestured at him as well as she could, given how hemmed in she was—"isn't very conducive to me leaving."

Without a word he pushed himself up and rolled over, landing on his back next to her, no part of him touching her. She felt the loss of his body heat.

She'd been teasing, but of course he had taken her seriously. He would never want her to feel pressured. It was interesting. In the short time she'd known him, she'd come to understand him as a person who exerted control over every situation he encountered. It was how he'd gotten sober. How he'd built his restaurant from nothing. How he'd gotten them to Florida when she was freaking out at airline employees.

So to see him so easily ceding control to her was... puzzling.

But also not worth thinking about right now—she had more important items on her agenda. So she did her own roll, aiming for the reverse of their previous positions as she planted one knee on either side of him. Kneeling up, she mimicked him from earlier, kicking out of her panties and grabbing her dress and working it up over her head. Then, completing the mirror-image maneuver, she placed a hand on each side of the bed and lowered herself so she was hovering over but not touching him.

"You weren't wearing a bra today," he remarked. On the surface of things, he spoke mildly, like he was making an idle observation about the weather. But when you looked close—and she was looking close—his nostrils were doing a flaring thing.

"I don't really need to." There had been a period when

she was younger when she'd lamented her small breasts, but now they just seemed like the kind of breasts she was supposed to have. And they were good for modeling. "In a sundress, I'll usually just forget it. No need to worry about bra straps showing."

He nodded like that made sense, but once again, careful observation suggested that he was not as placid as he seemed. He had to visibly unclench his jaw to get his next sentence out. "So you weren't wearing a bra earlier, at the restaurant."

She grinned. He liked the idea of her braless. "That is correct."

He nodded.

She decided to keep fanning the flame. "I also wasn't wearing a bra the day we met. I'd been preparing for plane travel. You know, going for maximum comfort. But then with that storm, there were a few times when I was so cold, my nipples got all puckered up, and I thought maybe I should have gone with a bra. I wondered if you noticed."

He gave up the façade then, groaned and closed his eyes as if he was imagining it. "I noticed." He sounded almost comically displeased at the memory.

She giggled. The weird thing about sex with Bennett was that it was sometimes funny. She wouldn't have thought it possible to mix such bone-shattering pleasure with joking around, but it came so easily with him. So she kept laying it on. "Yeah, too bad you brushed off my slutty advances that night, or you could have seen for yourself."

His eyes flew open. "I was a fucking idiot, Gia. An idiot."

Then his arms banded around her, and he pulled her down on top of him.

His eyes burned. The joking was done. He was dead serious. "An *idiot*," he said once more, before kissing her.

He slid his tongue inside her mouth, and her bones liquefied. She was already lying on top of him, but she gave up any pretense of holding herself up and melted into him, into his relentless kisses.

His hands came to her cheeks and he repositioned her head, deepening the angle of their kiss before letting his hands slide up to tangle in her hair. She moaned and ground herself on him. It had taken no time at all for moisture to gather again between her legs, for the breasts that were so small to take on an out-of-proportion role in her consciousness, as pressure and pleasure both gathered in them. She rubbed them shamelessly against his chest. He grunted, and his hands left her hair and came down with a satisfying slap on her ass.

"Stop moving or this is going to be over before it starts," he ordered, which, of course, only made her speed up.

Another grunt, a distinctly unsatisfied one this time, and he sat up, taking her with him, and physically set her aside. She landed on her back on the bed—the bed he heaved himself out of.

"Where are you going?"

He didn't answer, just went over to the desk and started rummaging around in a plastic bag. When he turned, he had already ripped open a condom package.

"Oh!" she said, belatedly approving of this interruption, and then again—"*Oh!*"—as he sheathed himself while walking toward her.

"This still cool?"

Though in theory she appreciated that he was asking, she couldn't help rolling her eyes. "What part of anything I've said or done is telegraphing to you that this is not cool?"

He shrugged, the casual gesture at odds with the glittering fire of his eyes. "Just checking."

Her eyeballs were no longer under her conscious control, apparently, because they rolled again without her even trying.

Also not under her control? Her thighs. Because her second response to his question—her nonverbal, involuntary response—was to spread them. To let them fall open so she could display herself to him—all of herself.

Not that she objected to this response—her thighs were smart. Go, thighs!

That bold little move achieved her desired aim. It shouldn't have been possible, but his eyes burned even brighter. "Fuck, Gia," he muttered as he arrived at the edge of the bed. "You're killing me."

Instead of climbing onto the bed and coming toward her, he reached for her, wrapping his arms under and around her thighs, and pulled her toward him—right to the edge of the mattress. Then, the whole maneuver one smooth motion, he slid right in.

"Oh!" she said again. Maybe that was the only word she knew. It sure seemed like it, because once he was fully seated, buried in her to the hilt, his feet planted on the floor and a sheen of sweat rising on his brow, she said it again, but this time it wasn't a surprised, "Oh!" It was a satisfied, dirty exhortation.

"This," he said, his voice sounding so pained she would have been concerned in any other context.

She waited for more, but that was all he said. Then he said it again. "This."

Maybe that was the only word *he* knew.

Whatever, she loved hearing it. Loved that he was losing himself so much in the sensations they were creating, in *her*, that he'd lost his ability to form complete sentences. So, wanting more, both because her own need was rising again and also because she was getting off on the power she had over him, she lifted her knees to her chest and wrapped her forearms around her shins, opening herself to him as much as possible. It was obscene, and she loved it.

He did, too, judging by the inhuman sound that ripped from his throat in the second before he lost it, jerking his hips back violently and then pounding into her. Then he did it again and again and again.

"Oh my God, Bennett!" She'd thought a moment ago that she was approaching another orgasm. It was on the horizon. Her body was responding to him in the usual way—heat gathering between her legs, at her breasts. Her body was straining toward his.

But the thing about Bennett was that the normal road map didn't apply—to anything. Not to revealing big secret truths, and not to orgasms, either.

In the case of the latter, it was like he'd ripped it out of her. Just reached in and taken it before she'd expected its arrival. One second it was on the horizon, the next it was *there*.

"Yes," he said, in that way he had. He liked to narrate her orgasms, she'd noticed, and she wasn't complaining. The way he exhorted her, how *invested* he was, made everything hotter. "Come for me, Gia. Come for me."

She did, laughing because he'd said it like she had a damn choice in the matter.

She went limp, a noodle on the bed, and he hopped off and started rummaging around out of her sight. Was he going for another condom?

She couldn't believe she was going to say this, but, "I don't think I'm up for—"

He reappeared with her camera. "Have you taken a picture today yet?"

"Yep, of Wendy trying on her dress."

"Let's take another one." He was advancing toward her, his eyes dancing.

She tried to be annoyed but failed as he hopped onto the bed next to her and started tickling her. "I just *told* you," she said through her giggles. "I already took my picture for today!"

"Well, maybe *I* want to remember this. Maybe this is *my* picture for today."

He was still teasing, but he was also...arranging her. Pulling the sheet up so her breasts were covered.

"Bennett!" she laughingly protested when he stepped back and lifted the viewfinder to his eye.

She tried to put her hands up to shield her face, but he was fast—and she was still laughing.

Dammit.

Chapter Sixteen

Getting herself out of Bennett's room was hard. Out of his room, out of his bed, out of his arms. Not hard like he was objecting, or trying to detain her. No, he just lay there on the bed all sprawled out like the king of the castle and watched her silently as she got dressed and attempted to fix her makeup.

It was more like...she really, really didn't want to leave.

Which was exactly why she forced herself.

She couldn't just stay there after they'd had sex. After she'd let him take her picture. No way. So she made it a point to get out of there before the photo developed.

Anyway, regardless of what was—or *wasn't*—happening between her and Bennett, this trip was about Wendy. Catching up with the girls. So she went in search of them.

And did not find them. Wendy texted that she was "busy," which was code for getting it on with her fiancé. Elise was "playing Scrabble with Jay," which, in the weird board game foreplay those two did, was also code for getting it on. Jane and Cameron were still at Busch Gardens, and the way *those* two operated, when they got back, the sexual tension would be running so high that they'd disappear into their room and not emerge until morning.

So, yeah, everyone else was getting it on.

She should have just stayed with Bennett.

But no. *No.* Bennett might be a lot nicer than most guys she encountered. He might be trying to save her with amazing food and amazing sex, but he was still trying to save her. And *save* was a verb not that different from *control*.

So after idly flipping through TV channels in her room for a while, she wandered down to the hotel's spa. A couple hours later she emerged with a new platinum blond hairdo. Wendy had confirmed that she didn't care about the blue hair, but this would look better in the pictures. There was nothing like new hair to put a spring in her step, to remind her that she was in control of her destiny. She headed for the pool bar, book in hand.

She ordered an iced tea.

He'd worn off on her. It was unsweetened, though.

She was only on page twelve when a voice spoke low in her ear. "Let's go for a walk."

Damn.

Damn *him* for showing up like this, all handsome and cocky and every inch the Reese Witherspoon rom-com hero.

And damn *her* and her stupid body for jumping to attention. She sighed; she couldn't not. He was just so…delicious.

When she didn't answer, he said, "Come on. I won't even make you hold my hand." When she didn't answer— on account of the ever-present internal struggle she waged when it came to him—he added, "Everyone's doing their own thing this evening."

Oh, that drawl. What had she called it, nonsensically, before? Scratchy honey? "I think everyone's doing *each other* this evening."

His hint of a smile exploded into the real thing. "Well, there *is* always that. Twist my arm." He hitched his head toward the hotel. "Let's go. Your room or mine?"

"Shhh!" She looked around with paranoia even though she hadn't seen any of their friends for hours.

"Come on. Let's walk. It's a gorgeous evening. Only a few days left, and it's back to the snow." His brow furrowed, just a little, but she was examining him closely enough to notice it.

"I can't," she said automatically. Having sex with him was one thing—and continuing to do even that was a pretty severe violation of her rules. Sunset walks on the beach were a whole other thing.

She couldn't just dismiss him, though, because…he hadn't said anything about her hair.

And, yes, she was apparently no more mature than the nineteen-year-old in Ibiza, hoping her crush would approve of her new, blond hair.

She ran her fingers through the strands, made coarser by today's processing. She wanted him to notice it. Which was total hypocritical bullshit because she couldn't want him to notice her hair at the same time she was proclaiming walks on the beach too relationship-y.

But that was Bennett—he had her totally mixed up, riding a roller coaster of contradictory impulses.

"You can't?" The corner of his mouth quirked upward as he twisted his neck to check out the cover of her book, which was a pulpy murder mystery thing she'd bought in the hotel gift shop. "Too busy?"

Was he going to make her say it? Well, why not? A

day ago she'd been sternly coaching herself to say this very thing but not quite able to make herself, and here was the perfect opportunity. Time to woman up and stop fucking around—literally but also metaphorically.

"Bennett, we can't just—"

The brow furrow deepened. Something had drawn his attention over her shoulder. She took a peek. It was Tobias. Incoming.

Well, she might not be the most academically gifted person on the planet, but she could recognize the lesser of two evils here.

She hopped off the stool. "Forget it. A walk sounds great. Let's go."

The smile he gave her in response was so stupidly, toothpaste-commercial big—though still endearingly lopsided—it almost blinded her.

He pressed his hand to the small of her back as they exited the bar, which was fine because it wouldn't hurt Tobias to see that. They were on the same page regarding the urgency of their escape, because they walked at quite the clip, weaving between lounge chairs and charting a path around the pool.

When they got onto the beach and really got going, she tried to speed up enough to shake off that hand. He did remove it, but, undaunted, he did so in favor of grabbing her hand. She was about to object—he had *just said* he wasn't going to hold her hand—when he stopped them and turned, pointing them back toward the hotel.

"This place is ridiculous."

It really was. The sun was on its way to setting over the ocean, but warm light reflected back on the pink art deco building, making it glow with an almost otherworldly beauty.

They stood silently for a minute, taking it all in. When they started up again, he didn't drop her hand.

And she didn't make him.

This was her fault. She should have said something this afternoon, when he'd held her hand on the way upstairs, after they'd gotten back from the restaurant. There was a precedent now.

It was just that his hand felt so *good*. Warm and comforting and protective.

"Do you like my hair?" she blurted and immediately wanted to slap herself. It didn't matter whether he liked her hair. She didn't need his approval, and more importantly, she didn't *want* it.

So why was she asking?

"It's nice."

Nice? It wasn't nice. It was *amazing*—the colorist had done a bang-up job. Bleach, especially on hair as processed as hers, was tricky.

"Anyway, I'm going to have to change it back to my usual browny blond soon. This is too stark for whatever my next job is going to be."

"Why does it matter? Isn't modeling about selling clothes? What does your hair color have to do with it?"

He was testy, all of a sudden. She thought back to his recent suggestion that she quit modeling. "Modeling is about selling clothes—or watches, or makeup, or whatever—but unless you're doing a runway show where they want an extreme look, the point is to disappear into the clothes, not to distract from them. You become what you're selling. I'm a cipher."

"No you're not. You're slippery as fuck, but you're not a cipher."

Huh? What did *that* mean? She'd agreed to this stupid

walk, but she didn't need career advice from someone who knew nothing about the industry she worked in. She tried to tug her hand out of his grip—better late than never—but he held fast.

"I'm all for the crazy hair changes if they make you happy," he went on. "But if they're supposed to be covering up the real you—if the point of them is disguise, which part of me thinks it is—then I fucking *hate* them. I'd rather take a razor to your head and shave you bald myself. It wouldn't make you any less beautiful. Or any less amazing."

She gasped.

So did someone else.

She whirled. And there, about ten feet off, were Cameron and Jane. Not in their room for some post–Busch Gardens boning, but walking on the beach. Hand in hand.

Just like Bennett and her.

She yanked her hand out of Bennett's, with enough force this time that she was actually successful.

But it was too late. Jane had seen. She'd heard, too, judging by that initial gasp, and the fact that Bennett had essentially been yelling when he'd delivered his speech about her hair. About *her*.

Goddammit. She was backed into a corner. There was no way to explain this away. There was no way Jane wouldn't make this into a big freaking thing.

So, screw it, if that was the case, she was just going to say what she needed to say to Bennett. What she should have said to him yesterday. And today. "I'm not your girlfriend."

"Okay." But he shrugged in a way that suggested his agreement wasn't genuine.

"What?" she said. "I *told* you how I roll."

He nodded, infuriating in his mild-mannered agreement

that wasn't really agreement. She wanted to punch him, suddenly.

"You told me you have sex with the same person once," he said. "Twice in extreme cases. We've had sex a whole bunch of times now. You've had six orgasms in my presence."

She reared back like he'd struck her. How could he be saying this in front of an audience? "So, what? You're keeping a tally? And we've passed some objective threshold that makes me your girlfriend?"

He held his hands up defensively. Good. At least he was finally reacting with something other than that maddening calmness of his. "That's not what I'm saying."

"Then what *are* you saying?"

"I'm saying you can deny it as much as you want, but it doesn't change the reality of the situation, which is that we *are* engaged in some kind of relationship."

She thought back to that night in North Carolina. They'd *explicitly agreed* that they were just having sex. She'd told him: *I'm not going to be your girlfriend.* She had used those very words, and he had agreed. Yes, maybe she should have reminded him of that caveat more often, but that didn't change the fact that he'd known the rules from the outset. She was starting to panic. Had this all been part of some twisted plan? Had he been manipulating her all along?

Of course he was. He was trying to control her. Because that's what Bennett did—the girlfriends he broke up with preemptively "for their own good," his refusal to accept help with the community restaurant, his long estrangement from his parents. It was all about control, about setting things up to achieve the outcome he wanted.

Gia was not going to be controlled. It was just as bad as being collected. It was a variation on the same thing, actually. And, in a sinister twist, she was on a beach. Again.

"You lied to me," she said, her voice shaking. "You've been lying to me all along."

"Gia, sweetie." It was Jane, who had disengaged herself from her husband and was walking toward her with her hands held up. Why was everyone treating her like an armed criminal? Like a flight risk?

"I didn't lie," Bennett said. "We're just interpreting the same situation, the same set of facts, differently. An evolving set of facts, I might add."

"The same set of *facts*? This isn't a potayto-potahto thing, Bennett! This is an 'are you my boyfriend or are you my fuck buddy' thing!"

"You can call me whatever you like. It doesn't change anything. That's all I'm saying. I don't care what you call it."

"Gia," Jane started again. She'd reached her side and had attempted to lay a hand on her forearm. Gia bucked her off like she was a venomous snake.

"I'm not your doll," she shouted at Bennett. "You can't just unilaterally decide we're in a relationship."

"I'm not! I'm just trying to call a spade a spade."

All right. That was it. If they were treating her like a flight risk, why not be one?

She was out of here.

She turned and ran.

⟿

Of course, she'd been naive to think she could outrun Jane. Gia could, and had, *physically* outrun Jane, but there was no way she was going to be able to genuinely evade her friends in any real way. It was the dark side of their sisterhood, of them being there for her.

They were there *all the damned time*, whether you wanted them or not. You couldn't be selective with the sisterhood.

She'd been in her room for all of ten minutes before they started knocking on the door.

"Gia! Open up! You don't honestly think I could witness that and not demand an audience, do you?"

"I need some time to myself, Jane!" she called.

"Sweetie…"

Aww, shit. It was Elise. Using her RA voice. It was hard to ignore the potent combination of best friend and resident assistant.

"You guys, just give me a—"

The door clicked open all of a sudden, and Wendy walked in, holding a key card over her head in triumph, like it was a trophy.

Right. She and Wendy were sharing a room until the wedding night. She'd forgotten about that little detail.

"What happened to everyone doing their own thing this evening?" Gia asked weakly as the girls tromped inside.

"I was *just* thinking that this wedding was a little low on drama," said Wendy, who was holding a box of wine in her other hand.

"Classy," Elise said as Wendy set the box down on the table.

"Oh shut up," Wendy said. "We're doing boxed wine for the picnic Saturday. Easier, lighter, more environmentally friendly. And…" She swiveled to face Gia. "*Bennett* suggested this as a perfectly respectable vintage."

Jane had gone to the bathroom to procure the drinking glasses there and set about filling them along with a mug from the main room. She filled the other mug with water for Elise and passed them out. The girls quickly made themselves comfortable—Elise on one of the beds with Gia and Wendy and Jane at the table.

No one said anything. Gia took a big gulp of her wine. It was actually really delicious. Damn Bennett. He didn't even drink, but somehow he could select the best wine.

She looked around at her friends, who regarded her with airs of tried patience. And because she knew them, she knew they would wait *forever* for her to talk. She took another gulp, then handed her cup to Wendy for refilling. Bring on the buzz. Hell, bring on total and utter inebriation.

"The nice thing about today being unscheduled is we can sit here *all* night," said Elise with artificial sweetness.

"Yup." Wendy handed Gia back her cup filled to the brim.

Gia threw back half of her second glass and sighed. "I slept with him a bunch of times."

Jane barked a laugh. "We kind of gathered that much."

Gia's phone buzzed. Normally she would ignore it, but hey, she was not above postponing the inevitable. It was on the desk near the door, so she hopped off the bed, and whooo boy, the wine had taken effect quickly. She stumbled a bit and rammed into the desk. "Whoa!" Steadying herself, she picked up the phone.

Elise, who was closest to her, popped off the bed. "Are you okay?"

"Yeah, yeah." But she lurched some more as she headed back to the bed, which was embarrassing. "I'm an easy drunk tonight because I didn't eat dinner."

"As opposed to all the other regular, healthy meals you eat," Wendy said.

Her voice had been devoid of inflection, but she might as well have screamed those words at Gia while wielding a weapon.

"What does that mean?" Elise whirled to face Wendy, sounding equal parts concerned and annoyed.

All right. So it was time for Wendy, Wendy Who Noticed Everything, to call in her chips. Gia tried to brace herself. At least they wouldn't have to talk about Bennett.

"It means she doesn't eat. She pushes the food around on her plate, and takes a bite only if she catches you looking."

Gia lost her breath. She couldn't speak. She'd known Wendy knew, she just hadn't expected her to be so…direct about it.

Wendy walked over to the white bakery box on the desk that contained the butter tarts Elise had brought her. She hadn't eaten them, of course.

Wendy opened the box and showed its contents to the others like it was a courtroom exhibit she was unveiling for a jury.

"I was going to confront her about it, but I was going to wait until after the wedding."

"She's right here." Jane gestured at Gia. "We shouldn't be talking about her like she can't hear us."

Wendy's face was blank as she turned to Gia, her voice even as she repeated herself. "I was going to confront you about it, but I was going to wait until after the wedding."

"Sweetie, is this true?" Elise asked, concern etched across her face.

A million excuses rose up inside Gia. Deflections. *I was getting ready for a job. I eat a big breakfast and less toward the end of the day. Yes, I watch what I eat when I'm working, but I pig out when I have a day off.*

But then she thought about how after she told Bennett, the world didn't end. He hadn't been disgusted with her. He hadn't tried to "reason" with her. In fact, after she told him, she'd felt better. Telling him had created a space in which he could help her—in which she could, having shared her secret, help herself.

Was it possible it could work that way with her girls, too?

She took a deep breath. Held it for a long moment. Then, on the exhalation: "Yes. It's true."

The room exploded.

Okay, it wasn't going to work like that with the girls.

Jane was exclaiming in disbelief. Elise clearly felt betrayed, judging by the way her face crumpled. Then she started talking over Jane.

After a few seconds, Wendy, who had remained silent, staring at Gia, clapped her hands and said, "Let her talk."

Which was the last thing she wanted to do, but realistically, she couldn't drop a bomb like that and expect to just end it there.

"I eat when he cooks for me, though."

Judging by the confusion on their faces, that piece of information hadn't been what they were looking for. She had only meant it as a consolation prize of sorts to cushion the blow she'd dealt them. *Look! Here is a circumstance in which I do eat!*

"Which I know is dumb. It's not like he's my magical savior. He came along during this monthlong break from work, and he's *such* a good cook. He's more like…a life raft that seems to be working right now."

"Or *was* working, until you broke up with him on the beach," Jane said.

"I didn't break up with him. We were never together."

"That's not what it seemed like when you—"

"Whoa, whoa, wait." Elise lifted her palms. "Back up. Forget Bennett for a minute. How long has this been going on?"

Gia wasn't sure she *could* forget Bennett for a minute. That was the problem.

"You've always said how you have the metabolism of a volcano," Elise said when Gia didn't answer her question.

"You're always eating tons of..." Jane couldn't seem to finish the sentence.

Wendy inserted herself into the space left as Jane trailed off. "Not lately, though. Not since at least Elise's wedding. Have you seen her eat anything of substance lately?"

"Oh my God," Elise breathed. "How did I not notice this?"

Gia ground her teeth, annoyed. Now she was going to have to make Elise feel better? "Look, this isn't some after-school special. I'm not anorexic."

Right? She honestly didn't think she was. She had never had that tendency before. You didn't just *become* anorexic, did you? She had a problem with food. That's how she thought of it, when she forced herself to confront it.

"Then what are you?" Wendy said.

Geez. Gia usually appreciated Wendy's "take no prisoners and also no bullshit" attitude, but having it turned on you was harrowing. She could see why Wendy was such a good litigator. It was easier to just tell her the truth, if only to get her off your back.

So she did. "I'm desperate to not have to quit my job, and my metabolism isn't what it used to be—no more volcanoes."

That shut Wendy up. That shut everyone up. Gia smirked. Not that she was happy, but there was an absurd relief in having it out there.

They talked then. For a long time. She told them about the too-small dress and about how stuff like that had been happening more and more lately. They were incredulous— civilians always were about her industry, no matter how close to her they were—but ultimately they accepted her anxieties as legitimate. The more they talked, the better Gia felt. Why had she kept this from them for so long?

"I think you should quit," Elise finally said, after several minutes of insisting that the industry had never appreciated Gia as much as was warranted.

Gia smiled. "I appreciate the loyalty, hon, but what the hell else would I do? That's exactly the problem. I *can't* quit. I don't want to just stop working at age thirty."

"Really?" Jane joked. "Sounds like the dream."

She looked around at her three talented, professionally accomplished, ambitious friends. Unlike her, they had skills. Educations. "Come on. Can any of you honestly tell me that if you had a choice, you'd just hang it up right now? Retire?" Maybe most people would, but not this crew. When no one answered, she said, "See? And since I have no other skills or qualities I can fall back on to transition into another career, I'm stuck."

"Hang on now," Elise said. "I didn't know you back in your pageant days, but to hear it told, you always aced the interview."

"Right?" Jane said. "Your mom is always telling that story about the time a judge asked you about world peace and you said world peace was not the point, that even if violence could be magically eradicated, personal suffering would endure."

Gia smiled weakly. "I probably read that in a magazine."

"The point is," Elise said, ignoring Gia's attempt to downplay the anecdote, "that even in the pageant circuit, where beauty is paramount, you were routinely recognized for other qualities."

Was that...true? She did have a big storage bin full of Miss Congeniality trophies at home.

"I've always thought you should get an MBA," Wendy said, and once again, she might as well have been brandishing a weapon, given the force with which that pronouncement shocked Gia. It was a pretty big leap from Miss Congeniality to an MBA.

"What?"

"You're smart. You think strategically. You haven't wanted to be involved in the business side of modeling, in lifestyle or whatever, but you have a good head on your shoulders and an eye for style. You could parlay that into a lot of different things, things you wouldn't necessarily need to be the face of."

"I can't get an MBA without a BA," Gia offered, as if that were her only objection.

"So get a BA," Elise said. "Go back to school, and I can say, 'I told you so' about my advice back in the day! I told you you'd regret quitting!"

"Or skip the school thing altogether and just do the job thing," Jane said. "I mean, I agree—business would be a great fit, but why do all that school? You're smart and rich and well connected. You'll be able to make your own opportunities."

Gia was aware that she was gaping at everyone. It was just so weird, to hear them talking about her like this. Calmly assessing her qualities like employment counselors. But the really shocking part was that they *weren't* employment counselors. They were her best friends. They *knew* her. And they still thought she could viably do something besides modeling?

"I guess the real question," Wendy said, drilling down to the heart of the matter in her usual Wendy way, "is do you *want* to keep modeling? Because we can talk till we're blue in the face about what else you're suited for, but if you don't want to stop, or if you don't want to at least stop the kind of jobs you're doing, then this problem isn't going to go away. So to my mind, that's the real question. Do you want to keep modeling?"

No.

The answer welled up in her, as clear as it was shocking. She'd spent her whole life modeling and now she was just...done.

"I don't know."

Why the lie? Because she couldn't quite cop to the truth. Because the truth didn't change anything elementally, didn't magically bestow other skills upon her. Didn't make her qualified to do anything else.

"Well, I guess that's fair enough, but maybe you should think about it," Wendy said.

"I will," Gia promised. "But can we please talk about something else now?" She was exhausted.

"We sure can," Elise said with overly theatrical enthusiasm. "Let's talk about Bennett. Let's talk about this 'I eat when he cooks for me' business."

"I'm not really sure that counts as something else, because—"

Elise ignored her protest and kept talking. "All in favor of talking about Bennett, raise your hand."

Everyone's hand—except Gia's, of course—shot up.

Elise smirked. "Motion carries."

Chapter Seventeen

*B*ennett mentally rehearsed an apology speech while he chopped dill.

It wasn't going well.

I'm sorry I made you hold my hand?

I'm sorry I like you?

He was having trouble crafting a credible apology because he didn't think he should *have* to apologize. He *was* sorry for causing Gia pain. Watching her run off last night, hurt because of things he had said, had gutted him. But the tricky part was that he meant what he'd said, even if he hadn't said it in the most diplomatic way.

He and Gia *did* have some kind of a relationship, no matter how much the prospect freaked her out. He hadn't thought about it like that until he'd verbalized it, until they'd been fighting—but he stood by the content of everything he'd said. He and Gia had something great, and it wasn't just the sex—though that was beyond great.

He wanted to be with her. He was, to his utter shock,

all in. In a way he never had been before, with any other woman.

Even worse? He would take what he could get. Yes, he wished they were on the same page, but he was so far gone that he would accept whatever label—or lack of a label— she wanted to slap on it.

So basically he needed to find a way to say: *I'm sorry I pushed you too far. It's because I'm in love with you but I know that freaks you out so I won't say it anymore and we can just go back to baring our souls and having bone-shattering sex without putting a label on it, okay?*

"Hey."

It was Noah, making his way through the crowded kitchen. With Cameron and Jay trailing behind him.

Christ. What was this? *Intervention: Groomsmen Edition*?

He had managed to avoid them last night by ignoring their texts and hiding in his room. He wasn't in the mood to talk—not even with Noah, which was saying something. But of course they'd known where to find him this morning. He couldn't bail on the wedding cooking.

He held his hands up as they approached as if he could physically deflect whatever it was they were going to say.

To his surprise, though, no one said anything about last night's scene on the beach. "We're going for a hike," Noah said mildly. "Thought you might want to come."

"Oh." Given that the last Bennett had heard from Noah was a string of texts along the lines of What the fuck? Where are you? What happened? he had expected the Inquisition once they were finally face-to-face. "Uh, okay." He could do a hike. Things were mostly under control on the catering front, and frankly, spending the rest of the day in his own company wasn't an appealing prospect. As long as they didn't have to talk about Gia, he was in.

"Gia was keen to hike this park," he said a few minutes later as they got out of the car at Boyd Hill Nature Preserve.

"Was she now?" Noah said. He shot a look at Cameron that Bennett couldn't decode.

"Yeah. She's not much of a beach person. More of a forest person." He looked around at the palms and magnolias. "They don't have these kinds of trees where she's from. She'd be into this."

"Aww. You know what kind of trees she likes," Cameron said, amusement in his tone.

Right. Performing a monologue about Gia's horticultural heritage was probably not Bennett's most dignified moment. The guys were all looking at him like he was a cute kid they were humoring.

Also, talking about Gia was not the way to achieve his goal of *not talking about Gia*.

"Where's Tobias?" he asked, in an attempt to change the subject. "Also, why is he such an asshole?"

Noah winced. "He didn't used to be such a prig. We met in undergrad. His family always invited me over for holidays." Noah and Jane hadn't had a lot of money growing up, and to hear it told, Noah had never been able to afford to go home for the holidays when he was in school in New York.

"He made a friend," Jay said. "Passed on the hike."

Bennett snapped his head around to try to read Jay's expression.

Cameron snorted. "He's not talking about Gia. Tobias is hooking up with a waitress from the lobby bar. She fell for his fake English accent."

"How do y'all know all this?" Bennett asked. Just because Tobias had been hooking up with a waitress didn't necessarily mean his interest in the "fair maiden" Gia had gone away.

"Gia is getting her nails done," Noah said, reading his

mind. He was speaking slowly, like he was trying to reassure a child. "The girls are taking my mom and Wendy's aunt out for a spa day." When Bennett didn't say anything, Noah continued. "Dude. Do we need to talk about this shit? Here I thought we were going to partake in the time-honored masculine tradition of engaging in physical activity instead of talking about our feelings. But by all means, don't let me stop you."

Bennett shook his head. "There's nothing to talk about. I'm into her. It's not mutual. End of story."

"What does that mean, you're 'into her'?" Cameron asked.

"He's in love with her," Noah said quickly, before Bennett could answer. "I've never seen him like this."

"Okay, well, then what are you going to do about it?" Jay asked, getting all elder-statesman-y.

As if it were that easy. As if all he had to do was decide. Jesus Christ. Bennett *knew* he was in love with her. It was the whole "the feeling is mutual" thing that was the stumbling block.

"What can I do?" he asked, trying to tamp down his irritation even as he surrendered to the notion that he wasn't going to be able to avoid talking about this whole clusterfuck. He turned to Cameron. "You heard her. She doesn't want me."

"That's not what I heard."

"Excuse me, what?" he scoffed, no longer bothering to try to hide his annoyance.

"I heard you getting all weirdly bossy and telling her how things were—"

"That's not—"

"Except 'how things were' did not include a declaration of love. Mostly you just insulted her hair and got all high-handed."

Wait. *What?* "That's not what happened. I told her—"

"You told her you guys were in a 'relationship.'" Cam made quotation marks with his fingers as he kept blithely talking over Bennett. "What does *that* mean?"

"If you stop interrupting me, maybe I'll be able to answer you," Bennett shot back, not caring that he really didn't know Cameron well enough to be this rude.

Jay put his arm around Cameron. "What my baby bro forgets sometimes is that we all had a rocky path to love." He shot a quelling look at Cameron. "Let the man speak, Cam."

Bennett sighed and motioned for them to start walking. If they were going to have a powwow about his goddamned feelings, they could at least hike while doing so, so he could bare his fucking soul without eye contact.

"What I meant," he said, once they got moving, "was that we do all the stuff that people do when they're in a relationship."

"And what is that stuff?" Jay, walking at the head of the line, seemed to have taken over as the facilitator of this group therapy session.

"Well, okay, in a very short period of time, she knows all my shit, and I know all her shit." He held up a hand preemptively. "And that's all I'm going to say about that. Confidences were exchanged, and I'm not going to break them."

"Fair enough," Jay said. "What else?"

"Well, you know..." He wasn't getting into that, either. A southern gentleman didn't kiss and tell.

Cameron chuckled from behind him.

"My point is, all the pieces are there, but she thinks she's relationship averse. She's just scared, though."

"Isn't that kind of presumptuous?" Noah said. "You're

just assigning her all these feelings? Has she *told* you she's scared?"

"She doesn't have to. I know."

"That's my point," Cameron said. "You might not have meant to, but you did sound pretty presumptuous last night, just telling her the way things were between you."

"I'm just saying that what she says does not match up with what she does. With how she…"

Comes apart in my arms.

He cleared his throat. "So I don't really care what we call it—that's all I'm trying to say. If she wants to label it casual, I don't really give a fuck. I just want to be with her."

"Because you love her," Noah said.

"Yes." Part of him felt like maybe he should be embarrassed to cop to it in front of these guys he barely knew, but he was too far gone to care.

"Then tell her, man." Cameron slapped a tree as he passed it.

"I *can't*." They weren't listening. "That's exactly what she *doesn't* want, what's guaranteed to scare her off for good. I shouldn't even have said as much as I did last night. I should have just let things be what they were without trying to label them."

"Because you don't 'give a fuck' about labels," Jay said, and the way they kept repeating what Bennett had just said reminded Bennett of his time in recovery. They had tricked him. They'd made him think this was just a hike, but they'd gotten him after all.

Bennett stopped walking, huffed a frustrated breath, and lifted his head. Stared at the moss-covered oaks that reminded him of home. Of Gia ribbing him about the size of his parents' "yard." "All right. That's enough. The sharing circle is closed."

"Fine," said Cameron, getting pissy, "but it sounds like you haven't outright told her how you feel. Maybe give her a chance to reject you instead of doing it preemptively on her behalf."

Bennett felt a hand on his shoulder. Noah.

"He's not wrong, my friend."

———

The prewedding dinner that night was held at a small Indian restaurant. Wendy was known for sniffing out the best restaurants when she traveled, and Bennett was right there with her. She generally eschewed the usual trappings of fine dining in favor of local gems, and the night before her wedding was no different.

Bennett inhaled the inviting aroma of cardamom and cumin as the guys—they'd come separately from the women, who were wrapping up their spa day—were ushered through the main restaurant to a back room, trying to will the warm spices to soothe his jitters.

Nope. Wasn't working.

There was no way around it. He was about to see Gia for the first time since their beach blowup, and he was nervous as hell. "Clammy hands, dry mouth, thundering pulse" nervous.

He picked up a glass of water and took a big gulp. Which of course was the moment the women appeared in the doorway of the room.

And there she was.

He choked on his water.

"Are you okay, man?" Noah clapped him on the back when his coughing didn't immediately resolve itself.

He nodded and got control of himself. Stood up, because that's what the other guys were doing, and tried to let his gaze take in all of them with an equal degree of scrutiny. Tried to let it sweep over Gia without lingering any longer than on anyone else.

Nope.

It got majorly stuck.

She was still platinum blond. It actually looked really good on her. His comments last night, the ones Cameron had said sounded like insults, hadn't meant that he didn't like her hair, just that his liking her hair was beside the point.

She was wearing another sundress, this one a plain, pale blue with skinny spaghetti straps.

No bra straps visible.

Dammit.

His gaze fell to her hands. They'd gotten their nails done today, Noah had said. Hers were a bright cherry red that popped against the pastel dress.

He couldn't shake the thought that he wanted to grab a couple of those lacquered fingers and stick them in his mouth. Or, worse, twine his own around them and hold her damn hand some more.

He was so fucked.

The women were finding seats and getting Noah's mom and her boyfriend and Wendy's aunt settled. The guys had sort of spaced themselves out. In his haste to avoid Tobias, Bennett had left an empty seat between them, but of course all the other women went to sit next to their husbands and older family members, which left the spot for Gia. He watched her assess the situation, take in her fate. She rolled her eyes slightly as she came over.

He leaned over and whispered in her ear. "I can swap with you." He didn't know if she was speaking to him, but he wanted to give her the opportunity to not sit by Tobias.

Hell, *he* wanted her to not sit by Tobias.

"I'm fine," she said, not looking at him.

As Wendy performed introductions, it occurred to him that probably he had a job to do here as best man. This wasn't a formal rehearsal dinner in the sense that there was anything to rehearse—the beach nuptials would take all of five minutes. But still, it was a moment to be commemorated. And of course, he had nothing prepared. He'd been too caught up in his own drama.

"Shit," he muttered.

He felt her attention. Well, at least she was finally looking at him.

"I'm supposed to give a toast, right?" he whispered. "I completely forgot."

"Just wish them well," she said.

"I can't do that. It should be something not generic. It should be—"

"You want me to do it?"

"Would you? Or at least start, and then I'll come up with something while you're talking?"

She clinked a knife against her wineglass and stood.

"Ladies and gentlemen, if I could have your attention for a few moments..." The conversation died and everyone turned smiling, anticipatory faces to Gia.

"Noah Denning," she began, placing her hands on her hips and glaring at the groom like she was a teacher and he a wayward pupil. "You're the brother of one of my best friends. And you're about to be the husband of one of my other best friends." Her eyes narrowed in mock anger. "So you understand that this means that I'm watching you, because if you mess with either of those ladies, I'll be all up in your face so far you won't know what hit you."

Noah nodded and grinned. "Got it." His mother laughed and kissed him on the cheek.

"But..." Gia drew out the word. She wasn't done yet. "I think maybe it also means that I'm almost related to you?" Her tone had turned soft, almost yearning. "I hope so, because I honestly can't think of anyone I'd rather have for an almost-big-brother-slash-almost-brother-in-law."

Noah's smile turned fond, and he nodded again, more vigorously this time, as the women let out a collective "Aww."

"Because you, Noah, are all the things a man should be. You're loyal and kind and protective—" She stopped so abruptly, it seemed like she'd meant to say more. Her hand—those cherry-topped fingers—came down to grip the edge of the table. "And I can't think of anyone else in the world who's good enough to deserve our..." She turned to the bride. "Wendy."

Wendy, definitely the badass among the circle of friends, looked like she was going to cry.

Probably because it sounded like *Gia* was going to cry as she kept going. "Wendy, I don't even know what to say to you."

Her voice was shaking so much that Bennett wanted to stand up, pry that hand from its death grip on the table, and hold it in his to try to bolster her.

She cleared her throat and started over. "I've been lucky enough to have the three most amazing friends in the world." She made a gesture that encompassed all the women at the table. "And I'm so happy you've all found love. But, Wendy, I think maybe you had to work harder than the others to find yours."

Wendy's aunt sniffed loudly, and Jane and Elise nodded vehemently.

"You deserve love, Wendy." She lifted her glass. "You all do."

Bennett noticed she didn't say, *We* all do.

"To Wendy and Noah."

Oh, fuck, he loved her. He loved her so much it was astonishing. It took his breath away when he contemplated it straight on.

He looked at Cam, whose arm was slung around Jane. Had Cam been...right?

He didn't have time to contemplate the question, though, because it was his turn.

The plan had been for him to use the time of Gia's toast to come up with something of his own to say, but of course he'd been so captivated by her, by her loyalty and the raw vulnerability that no one else seemed to appreciate, that his brain had stuttered to a halt.

Thankfully, Jane hopped up and made her maid of honor toast, and then the server came. He was off the hook.

It was difficult to get through dinner. All he could do was sit there next to Gia, his heart positively busting at the seams with love, and try not to die of it. Try to think of something to say that wouldn't scare her off, but also wouldn't be presumptuous, domineering crap like the guys were accusing him of spouting yesterday. It used to be so easy to talk to Gia. Now it felt like the opposite of easy.

He had just about worked up his nerve to open his mouth and say something—*anything*—when Tobias spoke to her. She turned and shifted away from Bennett—only slightly, but he was paying enough attention to notice—so she could answer Tobias.

He'd missed his chance. Now Tobias had her attention, and he was talking about...hedge funds?

For fuck's sake.

"We went hiking this morning," he said, his voice artificially loud. It was enough to get her attention. She swung around to face him, and he just barely refrained from giving Tobias the finger. "The guys, I mean. While y'all were getting your nails done. We went to that nature preserve you were showing me before, on your phone."

"And how was it?" Her voice was completely neutral. He couldn't get a read on her.

He had no idea. He hadn't seen any of it, had taken nothing in. He'd been too busy with the bro group therapy.

Too busy wondering if he'd fucked everything up with her irredeemably.

"Great! There were lots of...trees." Then he started rambling stupidly about everything he did remember. The preserve was really close to here! Just up the road a bit to the entrance! She should check it out later!

God, he was an idiot. He could see her glazing over. Retreating from him. Which made him start to panic.

So he stopped talking and regrouped. Tried to get a grip. Tobias was conversing with Jay across the table, but he was only giving Jay his partial attention. He kept glancing over at Gia.

Pitching his voice low so only she could hear, Bennett said, "Are you sure you don't want to switch places with me?"

"I'm fine, Bennett."

He glanced at her still-full plate. "Because if you sat over here, I could—"

"I'm fine."

She was not fine. She wasn't eating. He had tried not to notice, but he couldn't *not* notice. That was the way things were when you fucking loved someone.

"Okay." He lowered his voice again. "Let's go to the restaurant later. Just you and me. I'll make you something."

"I don't need you to make me anything." She was whispering, but it was that kind of fierce, overly loud stage whispering. Tobias was oblivious, but she'd drawn Elise's attention from across the table.

"I just thought—"

"I don't need you to arrange my life," she hissed, and now Wendy was eyeing them, too.

Heat bloomed up his neck. "I know."

"Do you, though? I'm not one of your atonement projects."

"My *atonement* projects? What?" He could maybe concede that the guys had been right and he had been kind of steamrolling over her opinions about the nature of their relationship, and he needed to fix that, but she wasn't a *project*. How could she think that, after everything that had happened between them?

"Oh, come off it. You know what I mean. You're still atoning for that car crash—feeding the hungry, denying yourself simple pleasures, doing your white knight thing with your girlfriends."

He held up a hand. "Excuse me?" How could she presume to know anything about his former girlfriends based on what little he'd told her?

"I mean, come on. You hang on until you decide they're better off without you and then you break up with them to spare them the pain? Who *does* that? Presumptuous much?"

Presumptuous. Exactly the word Jay and Cameron had used. The word that had been rolling around in his head ever since. It wasn't that, though. She was misunderstanding. He opened his mouth to protest, but she wasn't done.

"And then along comes Gia, and she's like a hybrid! You can feed the hungry *and* be Mr. Perfect Boyfriend with Gia! I must have been a total jackpot for you."

The whole table was watching them now, but he couldn't make himself care because the mocking tone Gia was using was razoring him to shreds.

"Well, you know what?" she went on. "I don't need your opinion about my hair. I don't need you to monitor my food intake. I don't need you to be my career counselor."

"That's not what I'm doing."

Wait. *Was* that what he'd been doing?

Suddenly he could see it from her perspective. On the surface of things, maybe it did look like he was doing all that stuff for the wrong reasons, because he had a savior complex or something. Because she was right about the atonement stuff—in general, though not as it applied to her.

And...shit. If what Cam had said was *also* true—that she didn't know he loved her—she was misunderstanding *everything*.

"I don't need a savior, Bennett."

"No." He was struggling for words way more than he had with the toast. "I know that. That's not what I'm doing."

"Isn't it? Because I think we have a pretty serious case here of looks like a duck, walks like a duck."

"Okay, well, that's not *why* I'm doing it then. You're not a project." *God.* Everything in him rebelled against that idea.

"I'm not one of your downtrodden."

"Well, we agree on that. You're *not* one of my 'downtrodden.' Whatever *that* means."

She scoffed. "You know what it means."

"No!" he shouted. He couldn't hear any more. Well, he'd listen to whatever she wanted to say, but not before she heard him say the missing piece, the thing that might change everything. "What you are, Gia, is the woman I want to spend the rest of my life with. The one I love. I'm *in love* with you."

She blinked rapidly. He'd shocked her. She truly hadn't known.

He'd shocked the rest of the table, too. He could hear them whispering, but he kept his focus on Gia. "*That's* why I'm doing all this shit. And, okay, maybe I need to knock it off. I wasn't seeing it the way you see it, and that's on me. Maybe I *have* been atoning for my past with the restaurant, with my exes. But not with *you.* Jesus Christ, Gia, what I'm trying to do with you is about the *future.*"

She kept blinking. He thought he saw a tear forming in the corner of one eye. Yes, there it was, a bit of moisture coalescing and gathering. It felt like the perfect metaphor for that moment. They were at the precipice of something. Would the tear fall?

No. No, it would not.

Because her face turned to stone as she looked him straight in the eye and said, "What did I tell you about how I would respond to a declaration of love?"

"You said you would run for the hills."

And then she did just that.

Chapter Eighteen

Gia's mind was all over the place. *Feverish*—wasn't that the word people used for moments like this, when you were so upset you weren't sure what was real and what wasn't? When you didn't know whom to trust—including yourself?

All she knew was that she had to get away. So she fled the restaurant, stopping briefly in front of Elise, looking deep into her eyes and saying, "Please let me go. I promise I'll talk to you later, but please let me go now."

She'd tried to imbue the plea with all the fervor in her heart, and it seemed to have worked. She kept looking over her shoulder, but by the time she was two blocks from the restaurant and no one had emerged from it to follow her, she relaxed a little.

The problem was that she didn't know where to go. Not back to the hotel—they'd all be there, and even if they gave her the space she'd requested, she'd still *feel* them everywhere. And she wasn't just talking about Bennett.

She hadn't resolved things with her friends last night—they'd merely respected her wish to change the subject after she promised to give their thoughts on her career some consideration.

She hadn't resolved *anything*.

She paused and forced herself to look at her surroundings. She was on a main road, unremarkable and studded with restaurants and strip malls.

But wait. What had he said? The nature preserve was "just up the road."

He probably meant "with a car."

She started to get out her phone, intending to order an Uber, but of course, she had no phone. It was in her bag, which was hanging on the back of her chair at the restaurant.

Well, fuck it. One of the girls would grab it.

She started walking, this time with a purpose.

It wasn't lost on her that Bennett had saved her even though he wasn't physically present, by giving her a destination.

Saved her *again*.

Bennett.

Bennett, who was *in love* with her.

Did that make a difference, as he seemed to think?

She tried to think of other people who loved her. It wasn't a long list. Her parents, she supposed, but at the same time, her mother was still constantly saying stuff that made Gia feel bad. And her dad, like Bennett's all those years, just kind of hovered in the background.

She narrowed her criteria: people who loved her and actively wanted her to be happy. Her brother, Dante. Though not super actively. If you asked him, he'd want her to be happy, but it wasn't like he was out there campaigning for it.

Wendy. Wendy with her love-motivated righteous anger.

Jane and Elise. Elise had been actively invested in the idea of Gia being happy since her RA years, when she was professionally obliged to care.

Bennett.

Was it possible that his actions could mean something different than they otherwise might if the intention beneath them were different?

If, for example, he was doing all that stuff not because he was filling some hole in himself, but because, as he said, he *loved* her?

It was astonishing. It was too much.

She turned off her brain and kept walking.

But there was something there that hadn't been there before, something in her chest. It was light and heavy at the same time. It felt a little bit like...hope?

When she finally reached the park, she passed a closed education center and started down a trail. She didn't stop to read anything or to look at the map. Right now she needed to move. Move unthinkingly. She'd face the world later.

She forced herself to take deep breaths of the warm, moist air as she walked. As she'd expected, the landscape was completely different from at home—palms and more of those freaky moss-covered trees instead of the maples and pines of Ontario. But the effect was the same. The act of walking through nature calmed her jangly nerves.

So, since it was working, she did more of it. Just kept going, farther and farther along the path.

Until she rounded a corner, stepped wrong on a squishy, mossy patch of earth, and twisted the hell out of her bum knee. She tried and failed to regain her footing and cried out when she heard something crack in her ankle. Pain—much worse than the initial knee pain—slammed into her as she tumbled to the ground.

—❧—

"Go away."

Bennett was lying on the bed in his dark room staring at the ceiling. He didn't want to talk to anyone. He was beyond talking. Talking was for people whose hearts were intact. There was no amount of talking that could repair his. Watching Gia run away earlier that evening, he'd understood that it was the last time. That she'd meant what she said. Meant what she'd *done*.

"Bennett!"

It was Wendy.

He sighed. Ignoring the guys was easy. Wendy was harder. It was probably sexist, probably some vestige of his southern upbringing, but he couldn't tell a woman to fuck off the way he had Noah and Cam and Jay when they'd tried to talk to him after the dinner. Even Wendy, who, unfazed, would probably respond by telling him to fuck right off in return and then breaking the door down.

Didn't anyone around here have any respect for the concept of a broken heart? "Wendy," he called. "Please leave me alone."

There was a pause, but he was pretty sure she hadn't gone away.

"Bennett, Gia hasn't come back. It's been hours. We're really worried about her."

He vaulted up off the bed. Wendy's voice had been small. Scared. And Wendy didn't *do* small and scared.

"I'm sorry," she said when he yanked open the door. "We've looked everywhere for her. Everyone else is still out combing the beach. I thought—hoped—that you might have an idea of where she's gone."

"She's an adult. She can call a taxi. Or you." *She doesn't need my help.* Wasn't that what she had told him earlier in no uncertain terms?

"She can't, though—that's the problem. She left her bag, with her phone in it, at the restaurant. She doesn't have any money or any way to get in touch with us."

His first reaction was to panic. He had no goddamn idea where Gia would go in St. Petersburg, Florida.

"It's dark now. She's upset, and she could be anywhere. My aunt is after me to call the police, and I'm starting to think she might be right."

Fuck. *Fuck.* Fear surged through Bennett. Wild, animalistic, pure fear.

If she—wait. He *did* know where Gia would go in St. Petersburg, Florida.

He grabbed his keys. "Let's go."

"You don't need to come," she said, but he was already at the elevator punching the call button.

She kept protesting, but he ignored her as they descended. She started typing on her phone, and by the time they'd reached the parking lot, the other girls were there, too.

Elise must have been able to read his face, because she held up a hand as he and Wendy approached. "She isn't going to want to see you."

He did not, at this point, give a shit. "Well, then she shouldn't have run off and gotten herself lost in the woods."

"She's lost in the woods?" Elise's eyes widened.

They were standing in front of the driver's door of the turquoise toy car. Instead of answering, he motioned for them to move.

"Bennett," Jane tried, "we get where you're coming from, but let us go get her. If you charge in all Tarzan-like, it's only going to freak her out more. Haven't you noticed there's a pattern here?"

"Yes," he ground out. "I am well aware of the pattern. The fact remains that if Gia is lost in the woods—or worse—you're not keeping me away."

It sounded like someone else was talking, some calm but determined stranger who lived inside him.

"Listen," said Wendy. "We can compromise." She turned to Bennett. "We'll all go, but you wait in your car. I promise, if we can't find her, or if we find her and we need your help, we will let you know. But Jane's right. You have to stop pushing her. I get where you're coming from. Believe me"—she gestured to encompass the others—"we're on your side. But you continuing to push her is not going to work."

"Let *us* push her," Elise said softly. He would have thought she was kidding, but she was looking at him intently, her expression utterly serious. "But we have to *get* her first."

Some of the fight left him, then. And it left a vacancy.

He should have been too jaded or too smart—or too something—to entertain any more hope where Gia was concerned, but..."Y'all are on my side?"

All three of them nodded.

Well, shit. He could do a lot worse. With Gia, this sisterhood might actually be the secret weapon.

———Ꮗ———

After an hour, Gia started to panic. She'd been telling herself that someone would eventually come by. And surely someone would. It was just a question of how long it was going to take.

And who that someone was going to be.

The truth was, she wanted it to be Bennett.

She'd had ample time to sit—she'd tried to stand up, but she was pretty sure that in addition to aggravating her knee, she'd broken her ankle—and contemplate the question she'd posed earlier but had put off thinking about in her frenzy to get out of the restaurant. If Bennett was trying to save her, did his reason for doing so matter?

That led to another question. Maybe he wasn't trying to control her so much as trying to *help* her? Just like she had helped him, maybe—with the trip to Charleston, with seeing his parents? And maybe his interest in helping her really *was* rooted in love.

And maybe that context made all the difference. She'd been reflexively lumping him with Lukas, and all the douchebags who'd come after Lukas, but maybe she should have been lumping him in with Elise and Wendy and Jane. She didn't freak out when they tried to help her. She was seriously thinking about the stuff they'd said last night.

And the most astonishing question of all: Did she love him back? Was that possible? The longer she sat and thought about it, the more likely it seemed. Why else would she have flipped out so utterly—and more than once? Her normal modus operandi was to just…not care. She'd have her fun with a guy and move on. One-and-done. Two-and-through. She had done it so many times that she'd built herself up into believing she just wasn't wired for love.

She'd certainly never been *in* it. Which might explain why she wouldn't recognize it.

Really, why else all the anger and defensiveness? If she truly didn't care, she would have mentally moved on a long time ago, right?

So, yeah, she wanted Bennett to save her right about now.

Though she shouldn't be so picky. She needed *someone* to come to her rescue—anyone. The longer she sat there, the colder she got. The more frightened she became. She told herself she was being unreasonable. She was in Florida, for heaven's sake. Yeah, she was cold, but people didn't die of exposure in Florida. What's more, she was in a nature preserve on the edge of an inhabited place. People must come here to hike all the time, right? But damn, what she wouldn't give for Bennett's cozy, broken-in leather jacket right now.

She was so tired, too. Like, suddenly to-the-bone exhausted. Her eyes felt like they couldn't focus anymore.

"Gia!"

She had no idea how long she'd been asleep when she heard her name. Her first reaction to the familiar voice was a rush of relief and gratitude.

"Gia!"

Her second reaction was disappointment that the voice didn't belong to Bennett.

"Wendy!" She raised her voice as much as she could. "Wendy, I fell!"

There was a rustling in the underbrush around the corner— unseen, but she could hear it. Footsteps getting closer.

"Oh my God!"

It was the girls—all of them.

It should have been a relief. And it was.

But it was also not lost on her that this was the first time in her life she'd ever been disappointed to see her girls. Wished for someone else instead of them.

That was...telling.

She should probably do something about that.

But first she needed to work on keeping her eyes open.

That was proving increasingly difficult. It was as if, once she'd spotted the girls and known she was safe, her body had just given up.

So she gave in, closed her eyes, and, even though it was futile, wished for Bennett.

——⟨ఎ

Gia's friends had been in the woods for fifteen minutes. Fifteen minutes and seven seconds, to be precise. Bennett knew because after promising them he'd wait in the car, he'd set a twenty-minute alarm on his phone. When it went off, he was going in.

He jumped about a foot when the phone—the actual phone, not the alarm—rang. He didn't recognize the number and so normally would not have picked up, but he rushed to answer it now. He had Wendy's number in his phone, but it could be Elise or Jane.

"Hello?"

"Bennett."

It was his father.

The last thing he needed was more adrenaline flooding his system, but his body reacted predictably.

"I can't talk right now." That had come out wrong—much sharper than he'd intended.

"Oh, okay." His dad sounded chastened.

"I'm sorry, Dad. I actually would really like to talk, I just...am possibly in the middle of an emergency here." Then, seized with the impulse to give something back—it probably hadn't been easy for his dad to call him—he said, "Gia is missing."

"Oh no."

"She went hiking alone." Which was technically true, but that didn't exactly capture the spirit of what had happened. So, feeling either brave or foolish, he wasn't sure which, he added, "We had a pretty big fight."

"You love this woman."

It wasn't a question. Part of him wanted to object, to say that his father knew nothing about him or his life and so could not reasonably draw that conclusion, but what was the point? He was right.

And he had called.

"Yes."

"Then let me clear the line. But..."

"Yes?"

"Never mind. You don't need my advice."

"I'd like to hear it, though." It was the truth—and he was as surprised as anyone.

There was a long pause, long enough that Bennett thought maybe his father was going to backpedal. "If you love her, and she loves you, fight for that."

Shit. His throat clenched so badly he could only whisper. "I will."

"I just wanted to thank you for visiting," his dad said. He cleared his throat. "But you go now. Let me know how it goes... if you don't mind."

"I will."

He hung up and blew out a breath. Thought about the advice he'd gotten this evening. His dad saying, "Fight." Wendy saying, "Stop pushing."

Maybe they were both right.

He thought about Gia, bristling against declarations of love. Gia and her daily Polaroids. Noah saying, "Show her."

The seed of an idea took root.

And just then, they burst into the parking area—all of them. Elise and Jane had crossed their arms and made a chair for Gia, who was balanced on it with her arms around their necks. Wendy ran ahead.

"She's okay!"

He stumbled out of the car and lurched toward her. Grabbed her hand. It was clammy. He ducked down so he could look into her eyes—she was staring at the ground.

She smiled at him, but it was a sort of spaced-out smile. Something was wrong.

"She's *not* okay," he said urgently—he wasn't even sure who he was talking to. "She's not...herself."

Wendy tried to tug his hand from Gia's. He resisted.

"I'm pretty sure she's broken her ankle, and that she's in shock," Elise said gently. "But she's going to be fine. We're taking her to the hospital."

Yes. Hospital. That was what needed to happen next.

"And for us to do that, you need to let go of her." Wendy, having given up on the tugging, slapped the back of his hand.

He let go reluctantly. "Okay. But promise you'll keep me in the loop." He looked at each of Gia's friends in turn, trying to will them to understand how important this was to him.

They agreed, and he transferred his gaze to Gia. Smiled. Her expression went from spaced out to adorably bewildered. His love. His stubborn, wounded love. She didn't know what to make of his smile, he supposed.

It was difficult to take a step back, to make room to let them go. But he had things to do suddenly. "You all take care of my girl. I have something brewing."

Wendy narrowed her eyes. "You'd better. And it better be good." But then she softened and said, "Let me know if you need any help."

He nodded, flashed another smile at Gia, got back into the stupid toy car, and hit the road.

Chapter Nineteen

THE WEDDING DAY

*W*here the hell was everyone?

Okay, yes, Gia would admit that the events of yesterday had perhaps meant that this morning was not destined to go exactly the way they had planned it.

They had gotten home from the hospital after midnight, Gia hopped up on painkillers and wearing an ankle-to-knee cast. She had tried to talk to Wendy last night as she'd hobbled to bed on her crutches, but Wendy just handed her water—she'd been diagnosed with mild dehydration and shock—and a couple more painkillers, and that had been game over for Gia.

And this morning she'd awakened to a note that said, "G, wanted you to sleep in. Just out doing some last-minute prep. I'll be in touch."

Where *was* everyone? It was late—like, "thirty minutes until the ceremony was supposed to begin" late. Gia had seriously slept in.

Her phone dinged. It was Wendy.

How are you? Are you up for the wedding?

Are you KIDDING me? I could be in a full-body cast and have to be wheeled in on a gurney and I'd be "up for it." I could be dead and I'd still haunt your wedding from beyond the grave. (Seriously, I slept great and feel fine today, just a bit embarrassed. I need to talk to Bennett. But after the wedding. I have brought enough drama.)

How long ago had she been pledging Wendy's wedding would be drama-free?

Yes. Totally talk to him. But after.

Gia heaved a big sigh. What the hell was she going to say? *I'm sorry I ran away twice? I hope it's not too late? I love you, too?*

Well, yes. She would say all those things. Probably not very articulately. She would just cross her fingers and say them.

But after. As Wendy had said. In the meantime...

Where IS everyone? We have to get ready. I have to do your hair.

We had a little problem with the officiant, so we've been out trying to rustle up another one. Go ahead and get ready. We'll be there soon.

Gia's first impulse was to protest that Wendy couldn't

get ready *alone*. This was her wedding, not just a run-of-the-mill night on the town. Gia was a bridesmaid, and she took that shit seriously.

But this was also not about her.

"Drama-free, drama-free, drama-free." She whispered it to herself like a mantra, still mortified that *she* was the one who needed to hear that message. Then she got dressed, did her makeup, and, as she hobbled over to the mirror on the back of the door to assess herself, cursed her cast and crutches for ruining her look.

A knock at the door made her jump.

"It's about time!" She swung open the door and hopped back to make room for her friends.

Except it wasn't the friends she'd expected, but Cameron and Jay. Cameron was dressed in his groomsman uniform of ecru linen pants and a white button-down shirt, and Jay was looking sharp in white pants and a pale-blue polo shirt.

Bennett was not with them. Of course.

"Hey, guys. Where are the girls?"

"We're here to escort you to the wedding," Cameron said, completely not answering her question. He and his brother crossed their arms and joined their hands.

"I'm supposed to be doing Wendy's hair."

"I think that's already taken care of," Cameron said, and even though she tried not to be, Gia was a little hurt.

"Wendy doesn't want you exacerbating your injury, so we're at your service," Jay said, and they hunched over, clearly intending for her to sit on the basket made by their arms.

Okay, well, once again, this was not about her—drama-free!—so she needed to get over herself.

She rested her crutches against the wall and hopped onto the chair they'd made. Then she leaned back over and grabbed her crutches. Which, of course, would not work at all on sand, now that she came to think of it. Leave it to Wendy to think of everything.

She laughed as they set off down the hall. But then—

"Wait! I need my bag!"

Cameron and Jay looked at each other, and she headed them off by saying, "*Don't* roll your eyes at me! My whole life is in that bag."

They struggled their way back for the bag. Cameron slung it over his shoulder, which was kind of comical, and they were off again.

The guys walked her away from the hotel, carefully coordinating their steps on the pool deck as they threaded through the hotel's blue lounge chairs.

"We could have probably gotten a wheelchair from the hotel?" she ventured at one point, but they acted like they hadn't heard her.

As they emerged onto the beach, she could see the girls up ahead, Elise and Jane like beacons in their emerald-green bridesmaid dresses, and Wendy's dark hair—apparently braided by someone else—set off by her lovely white dress. Noah's mom and her boyfriend and Wendy's aunt all looked great, too, dressed up and smiling and chatting.

The plan had been for everyone to stand for the duration of the ceremony and then move to big picnic blankets for the lunch, but there was one big, cushy chair up there that looked like it had been stolen from the hotel. She would like to think it was for Wendy's aunt, but though she was in her late sixties, she was in great shape. The chair was probably for Gia and her nonfunctioning leg.

There was also...a screen?

The kind you project movies onto. Was Wendy doing some kind of slide show? You sometimes saw that at weddings—embarrassing pictures of the bride and groom as kids. Well, knock her over with a feather. Wendy seemed like the last person who would be into something schmaltzy like that.

The guys set her down on the chair in front of the screen, and everyone greeted her.

"I thought I was gonna braid your hair?" she said to Wendy. She'd watched a bunch of YouTube tutorials and was confident she could have produced something a lot cooler than the basic version Wendy was sporting.

"Eh, too much going on!" Wendy trilled dismissively, which was weird because Wendy didn't trill.

Bennett, however, was nowhere to be seen. She'd tried not to be too obvious about it, but she had surveyed the entire scene.

She had a momentary spike of fear that he had taken off, and that it was her fault. Surely he wouldn't abandon his best friend on his wedding day out of fear of facing her?

But no. There was no way he'd bail on the lunch he was catering. He was too obsessive about his food.

But whatever. She needed to bank...whatever the hell she was going to say for later.

Drama-free! Drama-free! Drama-free!

Wendy clapped her hands. "Okay! We're going to go get ready to walk down the aisle, but you're off the hook, Tiny Tim."

"What? There's no aisle." There weren't even any chairs to make an aisle. Wendy and Noah had decided not to have a formal procession, just to be surrounded by their friends without all the trappings of pairing off attendants and all that.

"See you soon, sweetie." Elise bent to kiss Gia.

Huh? How long was their imaginary aisle going to be that she needed a farewell kiss?

Jane waved and skipped off, and Gia twisted after her retreating friends. They and the guys were indeed walking away from the spot where the wedding was presumably taking place, although the only items marking the spot were that screen and an accompanying computer and projector on a stand. Maybe the computer would play music and the projector would project…rainbows and shit? Also very not Wendy.

Also, why were the older folks retreating? If there was aisle-walking happening, they wouldn't be doing it, would they?

Well, whatever. She sighed and settled into her chair to wait.

All of a sudden, an image appeared on the screen. It wasn't a rainbow; it was…a PowerPoint presentation?

She squinted at the first slide.

It was an image of a restaurant, a sort of generic-looking one. There was a big sign on it that had been inexpertly photoshopped. It read "A Community Restaurant."

"Good morning."

She whirled.

"Bennett!" He was standing by the computer and projector, impossibly handsome in his beachy groomsman outfit. "What are you—"

He held up a hand to silence her, and once he'd achieved his aim, he pointed to the screen.

The next slide said, "A proposal in two parts."

The next said, "Part A: Business."

"Why are you giving me a PowerPoint presentation?" she asked, truly bewildered.

"Because you're not the kind of woman flash mobs

work on?" He cracked up. "Or words. At least not mushy ones."

Huh? Bewilderment gave way to full-on confusion.

Then he started talking, the way you would if you were actually making a serious, professional presentation. She forced herself to set aside her questions about why he was doing this and to pay attention to what was happening. He was showing her plans for a community restaurant. But it didn't look like he was talking about Boudin. Several things were different about this proposal—there were more tables than Boudin could accommodate, for one.

"Wait," she said. "Where is this going to happen? Are you asking for money?" Because she would totally give him money—without any strings attached.

He smiled but spoke sternly. "I know you think I'm a controlling dick, but just hear me out. I'll take questions at the end." He shot her one of his crooked smiles. "And then I promise I'll stop talking for a really long time."

"Okay, but can you just—"

"I'll take questions at the end," he kept saying, every time she tried to interrupt or seek clarification. So eventually she gave up, sat back, and let him do his thing.

She'd been right. He was outlining plans for a community restaurant, like he'd always imagined for Boudin, but *not* Boudin. A new place.

"I don't know why this didn't occur to me before, but it's perfect. I'm the chef, and you're the operations person."

"Wait. *What?* I'm the *what*?"

"I hate that stuff anyway, and you'd be a natural at it."

"What are you *talking* about?" she couldn't help asking. "Natural how?"

Somehow he allowed that question. "You're business-minded. You have great ideas."

"What ideas?"

And then eff her if he didn't proceed to list every off-hand thing she'd ever said about the restaurant business, from the outdoor refrigerator to her thoughts about the restaurant makeover show they'd watched to the stupid truck stop salad bar.

"And you're good with people. It will be pay-what-you-can. No prices listed—just like you said. So if we do it right, we'll get a mix of clientele. If you do the front-of-house stuff, you'll put everyone at ease." He grinned. "Also, you're much prettier than I am. No one wants to see my ugly mug at the host stand."

She could not *believe* this. She opened her mouth to protest, to object, or...something, but nothing came out.

Then, God help her, he flipped to a slide that was a picture of her. A scan of a Polaroid. She leaned forward. It was...her at the truck stop salad bar.

"I took this picture while you were just casually dropping your wisdom on that manager guy. Of course, I didn't know at the time that's what you were doing. I just thought you looked..." He rolled his eyes. "You aren't going to like this, but I thought you looked radiant. Animated. Alive."

"But—"

He flipped to another picture of her, from the other day in his room. The one he'd taken of her that she hadn't stuck around long enough to see.

She sucked in a breath.

She looked...so happy. She was half hiding her face, but it wasn't enough to obscure a big, impossible-to-fake grin. She might even say that despite the fact that she was slightly sunburned and was wearing no makeup that she looked...beautiful?

She hardly had time to process the image—and he said

nothing about it—before he flipped to the next slide. It said, "Financials."

"This is the part where I'm supposed to have a bunch of charts and projections. I don't have that. I'm just suggesting we pool our money and our skills and go for it. Well, actually, I'm *not* suggesting that. I'm suggesting you're smarter than I am about this shit, so *you* make a bunch of charts, and then we'll go for it."

"Holy shit."

He continued like he hadn't heard her, but it didn't feel like the kind of steamrolling he'd been doing at the rehearsal dinner, when he'd been insisting she listen to him. "There's no way around the fact that you have more money than I do. If this were a for-profit business, I'd suggest you take a bigger share, but of course it's not. But I think we can figure out a way to work that out."

She blinked rapidly. Had they given her too many pain meds last night? Or was she just *crazy*?

Or was *he*?

"So that's part A." He flipped to a slide that said, "Part A: Summary," which was, in fact, a summary of the main points of his argument, complete with bullet points. There was even one that said, "Charts: Gia to fill in."

She twisted to look at him. "What's part B?"

He smiled a slow, knowing smile that sent a lance of heat through her.

Then he flipped the slide. She turned back to the screen. It was blank.

"I don't have visual aids for this." He walked from the projector to stand near her chair. "But part B is us. I've been trying to talk less and just…show you stuff. But I don't know how to show you this. You have to use your imagination. Can you do that?"

No. But she swallowed that answer. That was the scaredy-cat answer. Instead she said, "I can try?"

"Close your eyes, then."

She heaved a shaky sigh and bit back the automatic, defensive protest that wanted to surface.

And then she did the scariest thing she'd ever done. She closed her eyes.

"You're right. I *was* trying to control you. Control *us*."

She rushed to speak, ordering herself not to open her eyes. "In some ways, you were good at it." She thought back to what a relief it had been, that morning after her confession, to join him in the hotel restaurant to find he'd ordered her an egg.

There was a Polaroid of that, too, of her perfect birthday egg, but he didn't have it. It was in her bag.

"And you were right that a lot of what I've done in my life has been about atonement," he said. "I'm not sure I think that's inherently a bad thing. I did something terrible, and I turned my life around as a result. It's good to remember that. But you were right—I'd taken it to an extreme. It had become all consuming."

"I wasn't saying *that* necessarily. I was just—"

"*But*," he interrupted—and *oh*, it was so hard to keep her eyes closed—"in this case, the two things are unrelated. I was trying to control you, but it wasn't because I was atoning. It was because I didn't want to see you hurting. Or taken advantage of in your job. You threw terms like *sexual harassment* around so casually, and it made me crazy. I just wanted to...help. Like you helped me with my parents, and with my restaurant, and with...everything. I wanted to help you because I love you." His voice broke. "I love you so much."

She couldn't do it anymore. She opened her eyes.

She was ready for him to scold her, but he just smiled, her beloved Bennett, and kept talking. "It should be impossible. I just met you, for God's sake. But I do. So in this case, trying to fix everything, to rearrange your life, was selfish. I want you around. I want you healthy. I want you with me."

She started to talk, but he held up a hand and fell back on his refrain from Part A. "I'll take questions at the end."

It was nearly impossible to hold her tongue, but he clearly needed to get through what he was saying, so she nodded.

"And before I say anything more, just for the record, I don't give a *flying fuck* what you look like."

She sucked in a breath. He was angry, but not at her. It was like he was... angry at everything that had ever hurt her.

He leaned forward, staring at her so intently it was like he was trying to *make* her believe what he was saying by *boring* the words into her with his eyes.

"Blue hair, brown hair, no hair. I don't care. One hundred pounds, two hundred pounds, I do not give one *single* fuck."

She couldn't speak. Partly because of the boulder-size lump in her throat but partly because there were no words. This was beyond words. It didn't seem to matter, though, because he kept talking. He spoke loud and a little bit quickly, like he wanted to get it over with as fast as possible but also to make sure she heard—really heard.

"What I'm proposing here comes in two parts: a restaurant and us. Option A and option B. You can choose one or the other, or neither." He swallowed hard. "Or you can choose both. I hope you choose both. But I want you to know that I know even though I'm making this massively long speech, I'm not going to try to control you. I know it's not my job to fix you. I don't even think you're broken. I think you've backed yourself into a corner career-wise, and that option A—entering into a restaurant partnership with me—might give you the space to...rediscover yourself. See what happens when the pressure is off. When you unhinge your professional fate from what you look like. And if that doesn't help, we—*you*—can go from there."

We. She wanted that *we*, now that she knew what it meant.

"But I'm also a selfish motherfucker, Gia. I want you as my business partner, but I want you as *my partner* more. I know this probably looks on the surface like it isn't any different than my past relationships, but it is. Those probably *were* about atoning. I was determined not to use people, so I went through the motions of being the perfect boyfriend without actually *feeling* the shit underneath the motions."

She had to talk now. It didn't matter if she couldn't say the right things, if she wasn't as articulate as he was. She had to let him know he wasn't in this alone. That even though it might seem like he was delivering a monologue, he was actually having a conversation.

"But you feel the shit now?" she whispered. She smiled at the phrase, which was both clunky and perfect.

"I feel the shit." He laughed, and it drained some of the tension away. "Do I ever feel the shit. You're so deep under my skin. Look what you did in a week: You brought me back to Lalande. You fixed my relationship with my *parents*, for God's sake."

"I don't think I fixed those things. You did. I just nudged you in the right direction." She got it now, though. She'd done for him a version of what he did for her—they made each other better. "Kind of like you did with me, right? Before I freaked out on you?"

"Right. And what I was going to say is it's not just that stuff. You're like this angel-being who makes everything in my life better, but damn, I also want to jump you pretty much 24-7. I'm not used to that. I'm used to putting a leash on lust. But with you, all my discipline just goes out the fucking window. So everything's all jumbled up."

"Maybe it's okay for everything to be all jumbled up."

"Yes! That's my big revelation. And that's what this is about." He pointed back to the screen. "Maybe I needed to give you the space to decide what you want—professionally and personally. And if that's what you want, I get that. I respect that. But on the other hand—and I had some help from your friends here, to arrive at this conclusion—maybe it's *okay* for everything to be all intertwined."

He cleared his throat and stood straighter, like he was delivering a closing argument before a jury. "I want to be with you. I hope you want to be with me. I think the restaurant will achieve both our professional aims, and that will make us happy. And better."

"It's like doing both might create something that's more than the sum of its parts."

"Yes, exactly. And I'm sorry if this slideshow was a stupid idea. If you hated it, I can still do a flash mob."

Gia let loose a big belly laugh.

"I didn't hate it. I loved it." She dipped her head a little as her cheeks heated. "And I love you."

"That's scary for you to say."

"Yeah. They're just three little words, but..."

"They're not little, actually. They're pretty big."

She nodded. He understood. "When you've spent your whole life—personally and professionally—being valued solely for the way you look, it's hard to trust people. It's easier to just assume the worst. It becomes a habit. It becomes armor."

"Hence the 'two times max' rule."

"Hence the 'two times max' rule. Which worked just fine until you came along, you jerk."

He started to move toward her, but she held up a hand. "Are you taking questions now?"

He grinned. "Yes."

"Where is this restaurant going to be?"

He didn't hesitate. "Toronto."

"What? Why not Charleston?"

"Your idea that I could do the restaurant somewhere else was sort of shocking in its rightness. I'd never considered it, but the moment you said it, my world tilted on its axis—another example of how good you are at this clear-thinking business. I do love Charleston—you're right about that. But I also miss Noah. And I see you with your friends, and I think, if you're going to make a career change, to move into doing something that situates you in one place, I want you to be with them."

Gia choked up, her throat growing so tight she could barely whisper her next question. "But your parents..."

"Can visit us. And vice versa. Anyway, you saw my mother. Do you really want to live in the same city as her?"

"You would do this? You would uproot yourself for me?"

He made a dismissive gesture. "A million times over."

And that was it. She couldn't hold back the tears anymore. She took a big heaving breath in, and it came out as a sob.

He'd been standing near her, but he hadn't touched her. Now, though, he came closer and took one of her hands in one of his. "And hey, if you don't want to go back to Toronto, name your place. If I have you, and I have my restaurant, and if I feel like I'm doing something moderately worthwhile in the world, I'm good. We can go to the middle of Bumfuck, Nowhere, for all I care."

Another sob—a louder one this time. He looked dismayed. He was getting the wrong impression. So she grabbed him. She couldn't stand, on account of her leg, so she inelegantly clutched his arms and pulled him toward her.

His eyes widened as he stabilized in a crouching position in the sand at her feet with his head a few inches from hers.

"Okay, I'm gonna go with both option A and option B," she whispered, just before kissing him.

He groaned and slid his tongue into her mouth. She reveled in the feeling of his hands threading through her hair.

It was over too soon, though, rudely interrupted by a shout. "Can I have my goddamned wedding now?" Then, "Sorry, Aunt Mary!"

Laughing, Gia pushed Bennett off her. He did not go happily, and she loved the grunt of displeasure he made as he stepped away. She twisted in her chair. Everyone was hanging back twenty feet or so, and they were all grinning.

"I'm sorry I hijacked your wedding!" she called back to Wendy.

"Eh." Wendy waved dismissively as she led the group toward them. "We all did it to each other, right?"

It was true. Both Elise's and Jane's weddings had ended in pretty spectacular—and unplanned—theatrics. In that sense, a little slide show on the beach was nothing.

"But can we get this show on the road?" Wendy said, having come to a halt about ten feet away. "You guys good?"

Gia smiled and took Bennett's hand. Took *her boyfriend's* hand. "We're good."

"All right. Hit it!" Wendy yelled. The three of them— Wendy, Jane, and Elise—linked arms and started trooping toward Gia.

"Dun, dun, dun, dun," Jane sang, belting out a silly rendition of "Bridal Chorus." Elise and Wendy joined in.

The guys followed the girls, not singing, but smiling—even Tobias, who'd somehow taken it upon himself to escort Wendy's aunt, which was actually kind of decent of him.

A confused-looking officiant brought up the rear.

Everyone got situated, and Gia sat in her chair and watched Wendy and Noah get married.

It was the perfect wedding. It was, as Wendy had wanted, short and to the point, but it was also packed full of emotion. Ballsy, dauntless Wendy cried like a baby, which made Noah cry. Which made his sister Jane cry. Which made Jane's husband Cameron cry. Which made Cameron's brother Jay cry. Which made Jay's wife Elise cry. So pretty soon, Gia and Bennett were the only ones with dry eyes—which was actually kind of hilarious considering the circumstances.

So she laughed. Just let it rip.

Bennett, who was standing next to her chair holding her hand, squeezed it as Wendy and Noah kissed.

And hoo boy, did they kiss. It went on and on. Finally Bennett called, "Get a room!" The officiant looked scandalized, and everyone cracked up—even all the crybabies.

"All right!" Wendy pulled away from her husband as everyone whooped and hollered. She wiped away her tears, grinned, and shouted, "Enough of that. Let's eat!"

Bennett crouched down next to Gia. "I made us a separate picnic."

It was, on the surface of things, an unremarkable sentence: *I made us a separate picnic.* But his drawl had come on *strong*. And there was no escaping his meaning, not with the way his heated gaze moved all over her. Not with the way he gave her a lazy wink.

She decided to play dumb. "What do you mean?"

He leaned right over so he could whisper in her ear. "I mean the minute we can credibly get away from here, we're going to go do our own thing."

"And by 'do our own thing,' you mean 'eat lunch'?" She batted her eyelashes with false innocence.

"Among other things," he said, and bit down on her ladybug earring before he pulled away.

Chapter Twenty

I know how you hate to waste food." Gia hobbled into the elevator after they'd put in enough time at the postwedding picnic. She jammed her hand down on the button for her floor and turned. The doors shut, and by some stroke of luck, no one else had gotten on the elevator.

He swooped right in, aiming for her lips, but she twisted out of his reach so his mouth landed on her neck.

"So I'm thinking we should probably eat first," she teased. "While everything is fresh. I would *hate* to have to throw something away because it spoiled because our sex marathon took too long."

"Whatever you want," he said, and the small picnic basket he'd been holding hit the floor with a *thunk*, as did her bag, which he'd slung over a shoulder. He grabbed her ass and carefully scooted her backward, lifting her up enough that she didn't have to put any pressure on her bad leg as she went. Once she was pinned against the wall, he moved his hands to her head, using them to keep her in place as he crashed his mouth down on hers.

God. He just lit her up. Every single time. And the idea that he was *hers*. That she was never going to have to give him up. That they could do this as often as they wanted. It was—

Ding.

The doors opened on the second floor. With a whispered curse, he pulled away, settled an arm over her shoulder, and tucked her against his side.

An older woman in a caftan and flip-flops got on. She moved to press a button, and Gia's gaze followed, only for her to discover that every single floor was lit up. Ha! The "wall" that Bennett had pushed her against had actually been the bank of buttons, and her back had hit all of them.

Bennett made a strangled noise as the elevator stopped at three.

Gia giggled.

The woman glanced at them as the doors opened for what felt like an eternity.

Four.

"Oh my God," Bennett muttered.

When five finally rolled around, he stuck his hand out to hold the door. He was on five, but she wanted to go to her room. "Let's go to my room. I want to take my dress off."

As soon as the sentence was out of her mouth, she realized how it sounded. She'd meant she wanted to swap the bridesmaid's dress for something more comfy, but judging by his raised eyebrows and flaring nostrils, he hadn't taken it that way. And he must have decided he didn't care about propriety in front of their audience, because he said, "I'm pretty sure that dress is coming off no matter which room we're headed to, but okay."

Caftan Lady gasped.

Bennett punched the door close button to speed things up. When it stopped again at Gia's floor, he grabbed Gia's crutches—and Gia. He bent down, hoisted her over his shoulder firefighter-style, and hoofed it down the hall.

Laughing, Gia waved at Caftan Lady, whose mouth had fallen open.

Inside her room he lowered her to the bed. A look of extreme tenderness crossed his face—followed by a look of extreme irritation.

"Goddammit."

"What?"

"I left the picnic basket on the elevator."

"Oh no." She mock-pouted as she slipped the straps of her dress off her shoulders and tried not to laugh. "You'd better go try to find it. We can't let all that food go to *waste*."

He glared at her. In another context, that look would have unsettled her. Well, it *did* unsettle her, but not in the way he intended. She finished wiggling out of her dress. She wasn't wearing a bra, and she knew how that tortured him. And sure enough, he let out a strangled groan as his eyes raked over her. She kept her eyes on him, like they were playing another game of truth or dare—a silent one— and when his gaze rose again to meet hers, she raised her eyebrows.

"Truth or dare?" she said.

"Truth."

She hadn't been expecting that. She'd expected him to choose dare, and then of course she'd been planning to dare him to take his clothes off.

He was off script.

"Oh, um ... " She didn't have anything ready.

"Here's a truth," he said. "I love you so fucking much."

Her face heated. She was still unused to allowing that kind of declaration.

"Here's another one. I want you like crazy. Sometimes I'm worried about how this restaurant thing is going to work, because I want to fuck you all the damn time."

She smiled. "So what are you waiting for, then? Why are you still dressed?"

That lit a fire under his ass. Within seconds he was naked, kneeling on the bed next to her. "How do we work around this?" he said, indicating the cast.

"Right." She wanted to climb him like a mountain, to claim him in a crazed session of lovemaking, but the damn cast was cramping her style. "I don't think I can be on top. I think I just need to lie on my back and try to keep the leg out of the way."

He nodded, assessing her like she was a plate he couldn't decide how to garnish. Then, seemingly settled on a course of action, he stuffed some pillows behind her back and moved one more over from the other bed to prop up her leg.

Then he sat back on his haunches and nodded, a master pleased with his work. "Do you have condoms here? Are there still some in that makeup bag of yours, or should I eat you out?"

The directness of the question shot a bolt of lust through her. "Condoms in my makeup bag in the bathroom," she managed.

There was some rustling from the bathroom, then him shouting from it. "Of course, you can always elect for *both* option A and option B."

"I think I vote for option A. Or whatever the option is that involves the condom."

God. She needed him so badly. Her body was vibrating. Moisture was pooling between her legs. She cursed her damn leg again. She wanted to launch herself at him, but all she could do was wait.

At first she thought he'd decided to ignore her vote for option A, because he started at her ankles. He kissed up along her good leg, lingering a bit at her knee before kissing and nipping up her thigh.

When he got close enough to grab, she twined her fingers in his hair and tugged. "Kiss me," she ordered, and he obeyed, but only sort of. He sped up his progress, kissing his way up her belly and breasts and neck. When he got to her mouth, he stretched himself out along her, rolling them so she was half on her back, half on her good side. Then, seemingly satisfied that he'd found a good, safe angle, he pulled back enough to sheathe himself in the condom he'd brought. Pausing between her legs, he said, "Okay?"

"Yes," she said, laughing at the inadequacy of the word.

And then he proceeded to make love to her.

He went slow and steady, kissing her and moving inside her and touching her all over. She'd been disappointed before, because she'd been imagining an athletic romp, a claiming of sorts, with lots of effort and shouting. But this was *more* intense, somehow. Its deliberateness, the utter care he was taking with her. It…undid her. The fire he was painstakingly stoking in her lapped at the edges of her being, slowly but surely consuming her.

"Gia," he breathed at one point, and it made her realize that whatever was happening to her was happening to him, too. That was the thing about Bennett. He was always right there with her.

His gaze was locked on hers.

"Do you think you can come?" he asked, grinding his hips even harder into hers, adding to the almost unbearably delicious pressure on her center. "Can you come for me?" Even as he ground against her so wonderfully filthily, he rested a hand lightly on the back of her bad knee—not with any pressure, just with a...presence.

She nodded. Yes. Because it was already happening. Tears gathered in her eyes, and she came on a big, shuddering sob.

⌒ↄ

The picnic basket wasn't in the elevator, so Bennett feared that the woman who'd been on the elevator with them had nicked it. And why shouldn't she have? They'd scandalized her sufficiently that she'd probably earned the amazing lunch he'd put together.

But that was *Gia's* lunch, goddammit.

But then, on a whim, he went down to the concierge to ask after it, and amazingly, it had been turned in.

When he got back to his room, Gia was wearing his leather jacket. And nothing else.

He sucked in a breath.

She must have thought it was lust—and it was, but it was also...something else. That shitty mixture of shame and guilt and regret that always overtook him when he looked at the jacket he'd worn the night of the accident.

"Can I have this jacket?" she asked.

"Yes," he said unhesitatingly. But then he realized that since they apparently, and against the odds, were going to move to Toronto together to open a restaurant, he was going to be seeing that jacket a lot.

And hell, they'd dealt with his family shit and her career shit. So why not this, too?

"That was the jacket I was wearing the night of the

accident. It's the only thing I have left from that time in my life. I pretty much hate it, but I could never make myself throw it away."

She sat bolt upright and started to shrug out of it, but he sat on the bed next to her and said, "No, it's okay. I'm glad you like it. It might as well get a new, happier life."

"Bennett, do you know what happened to her? Is she okay today?"

He didn't have to ask who "her" was. "Yes. I google her a couple times a year. She doesn't have her Facebook privacy settings set very stringently, so I can see that she's a teacher. She has a couple grandkids now." He paused, feeling like a stalker. "Is that creepy?

She shook her head. "No. I'd be doing the same thing."

"She was in the hospital for a long time after the accident—that I know from the lawyers my parents hired—but she recovered. I'm still not sure why she didn't bring a civil suit. I wrote her a letter to apologize, but she never replied. I sometimes wonder if I should try to do more. But then I think it's not up to me to control how or whether she speaks to me."

"I guess all you can do is try to keep facing it. You did something bad. You can't change that. You can't undo it by controlling everything else in your life, but you can—and you did—let it change who you are."

He cleared his throat. "You are an amazing woman."

She smiled at him, and there was so much love in her eyes that he thought he might actually lose the battle with the tears that were threatening.

But then she said, "True, but I am also a hungry woman."

So he laid a towel out on the mattress and unpacked his carefully prepared meal. He'd made a simple egg salad—she liked eggs, right? Had selected two perfectly ripe mangoes and a small wedge of Comté. And he'd added a bottle of champagne, which he reached for now and uncorked.

"This is...perfect," she pronounced.

He sagged a little in relief. He hadn't realized how on edge he'd been about making their first meal together— really *together*—special.

She grabbed a fork and contemplated the spread. "I want you to know, though, that I don't know if I'm suddenly going to be fine now that I'm not going to be modeling anymore."

"I wouldn't expect that. I don't know that much about it, but I doubt that's how it works."

"I'm not sure I have an *eating disorder* eating disorder, if that makes any sense. I do think it was pretty circumstantial, but I...I have deeply ingrained habits."

"And I don't ever want you to think that I'm monitoring you."

She shot him a look. "Oh, come on. You are monitoring me."

"Okay, busted. I can't help it."

"But I appreciate that you don't make a big deal out of it. You just...make it easy for me to eat."

That was exactly what he'd been trying to do, all this time.

"But you can't save me. You can't be Mr. White Knight here. I have to save myself." She grinned. "With maybe a *little* help from you, Elise, Wendy, and Jane."

"I wouldn't have it any other way."

She brought a forkful of egg salad to her mouth. "Oh my God."

He chuckled. If he could get an "Oh my God" from humble egg salad, then damn. The woman had to legitimately be into him. He sighed happily.

"Partly," she said, talking with her mouth full, "by

making such ridiculously delicious food. It's like it's not just food; it's...an elevated experience."

And that right there was the best compliment he'd ever received.

Their little egg-salad-and-happy-hormone-fueled cocoon was suddenly burst by the beeping sound of someone keying their way into the room.

What the hell?

Gia, who hadn't bothered to get dressed, grabbed a pillow and covered herself with it. "Wendy still has a key!" she whispered.

They heard the unmistakable sound of the door creaking open.

Also the unmistakable sound of feminine giggling.

"She's totally in there," said a voice he recognized as Elise's.

"Even if she's not, she'll get it later." Jane.

"Shhh." For some reason he'd become so embedded with Gia's friends that he could recognize Wendy just from her "Shhh."

And then, a bouquet of daisies came sailing into the room.

Wendy must have a pitching arm to rival Carl Mays's, because those flowers hit the TV so hard, they knocked it over. A freestanding flat screen, it fell back against the wall.

"Subtle!" Gia shouted, cracking up.

"We love you!" Elise called.

"I love you all, too, you nut bars!"

The door clicked closed, and she turned to Bennett. "And you. I love you, too."

Then she got out her camera and turned it around, snuggled up against him, ordered him to say cheese, and shot a selfie of them.

Epilogue

TWO AND A HALF YEARS LATER

To: Elise Maxwell, Jane Denning, Wendy Liu

From: Gia Gallo

Subject: What are you doing today at four?

Whatever you're doing, cancel it, because it's not as important as coming to my wedding. SURPRISE! City Hall elopement. Four p.m. sharp. Wedding chapel is on the third floor of the east tower of city hall. Bring men and kids. Dinner to follow at the restaurant.

xo G

Wendy arrived first. "Gia! What the—"
Noah, holding a little girl in his arms, elbowed Wendy.

"Fudge!" Wendy said pointedly. "I was *going* to say fudge!"

She turned so Noah couldn't see her and rolled her eyes at Gia. "He says I have to stop swearing now so that by the time the spawn is in school, only sunshine and rainbows will come out of my mouth. But honestly, Gia. What? The? Fudge?"

Gia hugged Wendy. "Oh, you know, I decided to try to one-up you on the whole low-key front."

Then she pecked Noah's cheek and held out her hands for squirmy eighteen-month-old Jasmine—yes, Wendy had named her daughter after her favorite Disney princess. "But I would like to inform you that even though I'm getting married, I'm still the cool aunt."

As if to ratify her declaration, Jasmine, who had been fussing, reached for Gia and laughed as Gia lifted her so they were eye to eye and made funny faces at her. It was still kind of weird—awesome, but weird—to contemplate Wendy's having a kid. Gia had always sort of imagined Elise as a mother, even though Elise was the one for whom it was supposed to have been biologically impossible. But Wendy and Noah had surprised everyone by getting pregnant immediately after their wedding. ("Hey," Wendy had said, "I just thought, if I'm going to get knocked up, it might as well be at the Pink Palace.")

"Jasmine," said Gia. "We were wondering if you would like to be our flower girl."

Instead of answering, Jasmine grabbed a hunk of Gia's hair and pulled. "Pink!" she wailed, letting loose a sob of betrayal. Gia had recently dyed her hair bright pink. She hadn't kept it for long, but Jasmine had loved it, and was still angry it had been covered with something close to Gia's natural honey brown. Gia still loved dyeing her hair—and though it had never been about disguising herself, as Bennett had once accused her of doing, even she could see the wisdom of getting married in her natural color.

"And that is my cue." Gia held the little one out at arm's length for one of her parents to take. "One of the benefits of being the cool aunt is you get to give them back."

Wendy was closer, but she nodded at her husband, so Gia aimed the now-wailing Jasmine at Noah, who made an exaggerated smiley face at the girl as he took her and said, "Does someone need a treat?" in full-on cooing baby talk.

Gia cracked up. There was something so incongruous about the juxtaposition of the hotshot lawyer Noah, who had always bristled at the idea of taking on additional family responsibility beyond his mom and sister, and the gooey, besotted dad Noah.

"Yeah, good luck with that flower girl thing." Wendy linked her arm through Gia's. "If you can get her to walk in a straight line for more than three steps, I'll give you a hundred bucks. But she'll love the flowers. Especially if she gets to throw them."

Before Gia could answer, the elevator opened and Elise came running out ahead of Jay and their daughter.

"Oh my God!" She yanked Gia from Wendy, placed a hand on each of her upper arms, and looked her up and down. Gia felt like she was a missing person returned to her mom, and her mom was assessing her for damages.

On one of her passes of eyeing Gia from head to toe, Elise grabbed her hand and brought it up to eye level. Gia was wearing a ring with a ruby surrounded by smaller, black stones. It was unusual and pretty, and she loved it. Her face still heated when she thought about the night last week Bennett had given it to her and asked her to marry him.

"It's sort of an abstract ladybug," Gia explained. "Ruby and onyx."

"Did Bennett do this all by himself?" Elise demanded.

"Bennett did this all by himself," said the man in question—her husband-to-be, which still threw her for a loop—as he came up to join their circle and slung an arm over Gia's shoulder.

"Well, damn. Good job." Elise narrowed her eyes. "But since you guys didn't give us any notice, Bennett, now you're going to have to stand here and listen to me make a 'So help me God, if you hurt my best friend in any way, I will end you,' speech. Normally I'd have the courtesy to make it in private, but..."

Gia thought about shushing Elise, but there was no point. Bennett grinned. "Noted."

"Hey, Mia." Gia crouched down to talk to Elise's daughter, who was almost two. A rush of love filled her. Gia was Mia's godmother, and though there was supposedly some long story to do with Jay naming Mia after some Lego thing, Gia always tuned out when he told it, teasing him that that was just his cover story—because clearly *Mia* was an homage to *Gia*.

"We were wondering if you would like to be our ring bearer." She had thought initially of asking Mia to be a flower girl, but Mia was a serious kid with a major aversion to traditionally girly stuff, so she thought the responsibility of being the ring bearer might be a better fit. "It's a really important job. You get to hold on to the rings until we need them."

Mia smiled like Gia had just delivered her heart's desire, clutched her dad's hand, and nodded.

"Wow!" Jay said. "What an honor! You're going to be great."

Mia turned to her dad and whispered, "Daddy help?"

"Of course." There was so much love in Jay's eyes for the kid they'd all thought was an impossibility that it almost made Gia choke up.

Luckily Jane and Cam arrived at that moment, so no tears needed to be shed.

Jane swooped off the elevator, and there was more squealing and shrieking. Cameron greeted his brother, Jay, warmly and scooped up his niece. Jane and Cameron were childless by choice—as Jane said about her life, "If it ain't broke, and it very much ain't broke, don't fix it." And honestly, to look at them, still all googly-eyed, over-the-top in love, it was hard to disagree. Jane's books were as popular as ever, and Cameron had just finished his university program and started working at a civil engineering firm. They were both crazy about Mia and Jasmine.

"Unca Cam help!" Mia shrieked in delight as Cameron spun her around. Cameron seemed to be uniquely able to get serious Mia to loosen up, and he took every chance he got to do just that.

Jay laughed. "Forever upstaged by my cooler brother."

"Help with what?" Cam asked, dangling Mia upside down to great effect—Mia laughed and laughed, but managed to say, "I ring bear."

"Ah." Cameron set down his niece and nodded seriously. "Ring bear. Yes. Of course I'll help. Should we go practice our growling?"

"Yeah." Gia made a shooing motion. "All you men and offspring, make yourselves scarce for a minute." She wanted some time alone with her girls.

"You look amazing," Jane said, taking in Gia's dress. Gia had called around to some old fashion industry friends and, even with such short notice, managed to get her hands on a gorgeous vintage Givenchy gown—a classic, simple silk number with capped sleeves that fit her perfectly.

"It's a size six," Gia whispered, and they all knew what that meant. She had gained weight since the big career shift. As she'd predicted to Bennett, it hadn't been easy. But at the same time, it hasn't been as difficult as she'd feared to break the hold that food had over her. She'd started seeing a shrink who specialized in eating disorders. And, strangely, what helped as much as anything was that she and Bennett worked all the time. She loved it. It had felt like they were building something real, something important, with the restaurant, and she was able to see that she was a critical part of that process. Bennett really *did* want her to be the business brains of the operation, and she was *good* at it.

Given all that, she'd been able to grasp the importance of fueling her body, of keeping herself healthy. So when Bennett, who had made her a soft-boiled egg every damn morning since they'd been together, put food in front of her, she ate it. It had been nerve-racking at first to see the numbers inch up, but then Bennett had thrown her scale out. Just put it out with the garbage one morning before she'd woken up. She'd been gobsmacked at first, and a little indignant, but she'd come around to seeing things his way. And she seemed to have stabilized at a size six.

And she did look pretty incredible in the dress, if she did say so herself.

"So has Bennett been slaving over the wedding dinner on his one day of rest?" Elise asked.

The restaurant was closed on Mondays, which was why they'd chosen today for their wedding.

"Nope. I wouldn't let him. We're going there, but we're ordering pizza and having butter tarts for dessert."

"All right!" Jane said, delighted by this pronouncement.

"You *definitely* win the prize for lowest-key wedding," Wendy said.

"Yeah." Gia, a little overcome with emotion, smiled at her girls. "No offense, but I think we've had enough wedding drama for a while. Bennett's parents are coming tomorrow, and we'll do a big elaborate meal at the restaurant with them. We'll save the drama for then."

"Ohhh," said Wendy ominously, and Gia had to kind of agree. Bennett's parents had visited once before, about a year ago, and though it was clear his dad was trying—and he and Bennett talked pretty frequently these days—his mom had been as bitchy and cold as ever. But continuing to try to build a relationship with them was important to Bennett, so Gia was right there with him. She'd suggested they invite his parents to the actual wedding, but he'd shut that down, insisting that he wanted only their closest, most supportive friends there.

"Yep," Gia said. "It will probably suck, but I'm prepared to be pleasantly surprised. My family is coming, too." She hadn't even told them about the wedding yet—she planned to spring that on them tomorrow. When Bennett had decided not to invite his family to the actual wedding, she'd followed suit. She loved them, but she wanted it to be just her and her best friends—her chosen family.

"Marc Lalande is coming, too," she added, "so hopefully he'll provide a bit of a buffer. Can you imagine? The two families and the big mentor chef? Bennett is going to go so overboard. He's been plotting and grumbling for weeks, but he won't tell me anything about his plans."

"Yeah, but on the other hand, it will probably be the best meal you've ever had in your life," Wendy said. "If you love me at all, you'll save me a doggie bag."

"Oh! I almost forgot!" Elise produced a magazine

from her bag—*Toronto Life*, the hipster lifestyle rag. "I'm redesigning their offices, and I snagged this advance copy." It was the magazine's annual "where to eat" issue, the local bible of restaurants. Elise flipped through and handed it to Gia open to a page in the middle. "Look! You guys got best start-up!"

Goose bumps rose on Gia's skin as she read the glowing review of the Ladybug Café. It praised the "fresh, sophisticated but unfussy" food but also the concept. They had gone ahead with Gia's idea of not listing prices but delivering itemized "bills" to the table and encouraging people to pay what they could or wanted to. To her delight, the place was drawing a mixed clientele. It didn't feel at all like a "charity" restaurant, but like a funky, friendly neighborhood place where anyone was welcome. And the best part about the article was that it name-checked Bennett as the "ridiculously talented southern transplant" and her as the "business and creative force" behind the place.

She sniffed. Okay, now she really was going to cry.

"Aww!" said Elise.

"We're so proud of you!"

"We love you!"

They all rushed her, and Gia let herself sink into a big, teary group hug.

"Hey." Bennett's approach broke up their lovefest. "We're up in ten minutes." He looked at Gia's friends with obvious affection in his eyes. "Mind if I steal my girl away for a minute?"

"Of course," Jane said.

"But mind yourself there," Wendy said. "She's not *your* girl."

"Right!" Elise said. "She's *our* girl."

"As long as I'm part of that 'our,' I'm cool with that."

Bennett threaded his fingers through Gia's and walked her away from the busy area outside the chapel where an assembly line of weddings was being performed.

"Hi," he said, when he'd found them an empty corner. He twirled her around so they were facing each other.

"Hi." Her mouth quirked up into an almost involuntary smile, as it so often did when he was near.

"Hi," he said again, his tone more serious this time, lower, as he pressed her up against the wall and planted a kiss on her. She could tell he'd meant it to be a quick peck, but she wrapped her arms around him and held tight. He only resisted for a second before groaning in a mixture of defeat and pleasure and letting his mouth go slack. She seized the moment and feasted on him, relishing the way he always made her insides feel like they were liquefying and getting heavy at the same time.

"Uhh," he grunted as he overpowered her a few seconds later, levering her arms off him and stepping away. "We gotta get going or we're going to miss our own wedding."

She made a vague noise of displeasure as he pressed his forehead against hers. He was panting a bit. She loved that she could get him so riled up, even after all this time. There was certainly something to be said for his way of doing things—for learning a man's body and, not to be too schmaltzy, his soul. For letting yourself fall deeper and deeper every day.

"Truth or dare?" he whispered, his forehead still touching hers. His eyes were closed, and his face was screwed up like he was thinking really hard about something. It almost looked like he was praying.

"Dare," she said, her voice overcome with emotion.

His eyes flew open, and even though she'd seen them a million times, smiling at her when she woke in the morning, flashing as he dominated the restaurant kitchen, it was still a shock to see them *right there*, so brilliantly blue and so kind, and so utterly focused on her.

"Marry me," he whispered. "Be mine forever."

She smiled, pulled away, and extended her ladybug-bedecked hand.

"I don't know. I might rather do twenty push-ups, but..." She pretended to think about it as he swatted her butt, then took her hand. "Okay. If you insist."

And then they got married. There were tears. There was a kid named after a princess who made it halfway down the aisle before she sat on the floor and dumped her entire basket of flower petals over her head. There was a bear, complete with growls, who managed to drop both rings and needed some help from her bear uncle to finish the job. There was sassy back talk from Jane, raucous laughter from Wendy, and very loud shushing from Elise.

There was a group Polaroid.

Then Gia slung her husband's leather jacket over her dress and they all went to the Ladybug Café and ate pizza and butter tarts.

In other words, it was perfect.

Did you miss Jane and Cameron's story?

Please keep reading for an excerpt from

ONE AND ONLY

Available now!

With her bridezilla friend on a DIY project rampage, bridesmaid Jane Denning will do anything to escape—even if it means babysitting the groom's troublemaker brother before the wedding. It should be a piece of cake, except the "cake" is a sarcastic former soldier who is 100% wicked hotness and absolutely off-limits.

Cameron MacKinnon is ready to let loose after returning from his deployment. But first he'll have to sweet talk the ultra-responsible Jane into taking a walk on the wild side. Turns out, riling her up is the best time he's had in years. But what happens when the fun and games start to turn into something real?

Chapter One

*J*ane! I thought you were *never* going to get here!"

"I came as quickly as I could," Jane said, trying to keep the annoyance out of her tone as she allowed herself to be herded into her friend Elise's house. She exchanged resigned smiles with her fellow bridesmaids—the ones who had obviously taken Elise's "Emergency bridesmaids meeting at my house NOW!" text more seriously than Jane had. Gia and Wendy were sprawled on Elise's couch, braiding some kind of dried grass–type thing. Wendy, Jane's best friend, blew her a kiss.

Jane tried to perform her traditional catching of Wendy's kiss—it was their thing, dating back to childhood—but Elise thrust a mug of tea into Jane's hand before it could close over the imaginary kiss. Earlier that summer, Elise had embraced and then discarded a plan to start her wedding reception with some kind of complicated cocktail involving tea, and as a result, Jane feared she and the girls were doomed to a lifetime of Earl Grey. Their beloved bridezilla had thought nothing of special ordering twenty-seven un-returnable boxes of premium English tea leaves. She also apparently thought nothing of forcing her friends to endure the rejected reception beverage again and again. And again.

"Jane's here, so now you can tell us about the big emergency," Gia said. "And whatever it is, I'm sure she'll figure out a solution." She smiled at Jane. "You're so...smart."

Jane had a feeling that *smart* wasn't the word Gia initially meant to use. The girls—well, Gia and Elise, anyway—were always telling Jane to loosen up. But they also relied on her to solve their problems. They liked having it both ways. She was the den mother, but they were forever teasing her about being too rigid. Which was kind of rich, lately, coming from Elise, who had turned into a matrimonial drill sergeant. Jane put up with it because she loved them. Besides, *somebody* had to be the responsible one.

"Well," Jane teased, "this had better be a capital-E emergency because I was in the middle of having my costume for Toronto Comicon fitted when you texted." She opened the calf-length trench coat she'd thrown over her costume at the seamstress's when Elise's text arrived. It was the kind of coat women wore when seducing their boyfriends—or so she assumed, not having personally attempted to seduce anyone since Felix. She should probably just get rid of the coat because there were likely no seductions in her future, either.

"Hello!" Gia exclaimed. "*What* is that?"

"Xena: Warrior Princess," Wendy answered before Jane could.

"I have no idea what that means, but you look hot," Gia said.

Jane did a little twirl. The costume was really coming

together. The seamstress had done a kick-ass job with the leather dress, armor, and arm bands, and all Jane needed to do was figure out something for Xena's signature weapon and she'd be set. "It was a cult TV show from the 1990s," she explained. Gia was a bit younger than the rest of them. But who was Jane kidding? The real reason Gia didn't know about Xena was that she was a Cool Girl. As a model—an honest-to-goodness, catwalk-strutting, appearing-in-Calvin-Klein-ads model—she was too busy with her fabulous life to have time to watch syndicated late-night TV. "It's set in a sort of alternative ancient Greece, but it's leavened with other mythologies..." She trailed off because the explanation sounded lame even to her fantasy-novelist, geek-girl ears.

"Xena basically goes around kicking ass, and then she and her sidekick get it on with some lesbian action," Wendy said, summing things up in her characteristically concise way.

"Really?" Gia narrowed her eyes at Jane. "Is there something you're trying to tell us?"

"No!" Jane protested.

"Because you haven't had a boyfriend since Felix," Gia went on. "And you guys broke up, what? Four years ago?"

"Five," Wendy said.

It was true. But what her friends refused to accept was that she was single by choice. She had made a sincere effort, with Felix, whom she'd met halfway through university and stayed with until she was twenty-six, to enter the world of love and relationships that everyone was always insisting was so important. Felix had taught her many things, foremost among them that she was better off alone.

"You know we'll love you no matter what," Gia said. "Who you sleep with doesn't make a whit of difference."

"I'm not gay, Gia! I just admire Xena. She didn't need men to get shit done. We could all—"

A very loud episode of throat clearing from Elise interrupted Jane's speech on the merits of independence, whether you were a pseudo-Greek warrior princess or a modern girl trying to get along in the world.

"Sorry." Jane sometimes forgot that most people did not share her views of love and relationships.

"I'm sure this is all super interesting, you guys?" Elise said. "But we have a serious problem on our hands?" She was talking fast and ending declarative statements with question marks—sure signs she was stressed. Elise always sounded like an auctioneer on uppers when she was upset. "I need to grab my phone because I'm expecting the cake people to call? So sit down and brace yourselves and I'll be right back?"

Jane sank into a chair and warily eyed a basket of spools of those brown string-like ribbon things—the kind that were always showing up tied around Mason jars of layered salads on Pinterest. She wasn't really sure how or why Elise had decided not to outsource this stuff like normal people did when they got married. The whole wedding had become a DIY-fest. "What are we doing with this stuff?" she asked the others.

"No idea," said Wendy, performing a little eye roll. "I'm just doing what I'm told."

Jane grinned. Although she, Wendy, Gia, and Elise were a tightly knit foursome, they also sorted into pairs of best friends: Jane and Wendy had grown up together and had met Elise during freshman orientation at university. They'd picked up Gia when they were seniors and Gia was a freshman—Elise had been her resident assistant—RA—and the pair had become fast friends despite the age difference.

"We are weaving table runners out of raffia ribbon," Gia said. She dropped her strands and reached for her purse. "Slide that tea over here—quick, before she gets back."

"God bless you," Jane said when Gia pulled a flask of whiskey out of her purse and tipped some into Jane's mug. If the "emergency" that had pulled Jane away from her cosplay fitting—not to mention a planned evening of writing—was going to involve table runners, she was going to need something to dull the edges a bit.

Elise reappeared. Jane practiced her nonchalant face as she sipped her "tea" and tried not to cough. She wasn't normally much of a drinker, but desperate times and all that.

"I didn't want to repeat myself, so I've been holding out on Gia and Wendy?" Elise said. "But there's been a...disruption to the wedding plans?"

I love you, but God help me, those are declarative sentences. Sometimes Jane had trouble turning off her inner editor. Job hazard.

"Oh my God, are you leaving Jay?" Wendy asked.

"Why would you say that?" Elise turned to Wendy in bewilderment.

Now, that was a legitimate question, the inner editor said—at least in the sense that it was meant to end with a question mark. The actual content of Wendy's question was kind of insensitive. But Wendy had trouble with change, and Elise pairing off and doing the whole till-death-do-us-part thing? That was some major change for their little friend group. Jane might have had trouble with it, too, except it was plainly obvious to anyone with eyeballs that Elise was head-over-heels, one hundred percent gaga for her fiancé.

"I'm kidding!" Wendy said, a little too vehemently. Elise looked like she might have to call for smelling salts.

"Take a breath," Gia said to Elise, "and tell us what's wrong."

Elise did as instructed, then flopped into a chair. "Jay's brother is coming to the wedding."

"Jay has a brother?" Jane asked. Though she was guilty of maybe not paying one hundred percent attention to every single wedding-related detail—for example, she'd recused herself from the debate over the merits of sage green versus grass green for the ribbons that would adorn the welcome bags left in the guests' hotel rooms—she was pretty sure she had a handle on all the major players.

"His name is Cameron MacKinnon."

That didn't clear things up. "Jay Smith has a brother named Cameron MacKinnon?" she asked. Was that even possible?

"Half brother," Elise said. "You know how Jay's mom is single?" It was true. There had been no "father of the groom" in Elise's carefully drafted program. "Well, she split from Jay's dad when Jay was nine. Then a couple years later, she had a brief relationship with another man. Cameron is the product of that—that's why his last name is MacKinnon and Jay's is Smith."

"But he wasn't always going to come to the wedding?" Gia asked. "Were they estranged?"

"They're not particularly close. There are eleven years between them—Cameron was in first grade when Jay left for school—but they're not estranged," Elise said. "He wasn't going to be able to make it to the wedding because he was supposed to be in Iraq. He was in the army. But now he's...not."

"That sounds ominous," Wendy said.

"Look, here's the thing," Elise said, sitting up straight, her voice suddenly and uncharacteristically commanding.

"Cameron is a problem. He's wild. He drives too fast, drinks too much, sleeps around. You name it—if it's sketchy, he's into it."

"And this is *Jay's* brother," Jane said. Because no offense, she liked Jay fine, but Jay was…a tad underwhelming. He was an accountant. No matter what they were doing— football game, barbecue, hiking—he dressed in dark jeans and a polo shirt, like it was casual Friday at the office. To be honest, Jane had never really been sure what Elise saw in him. The girls were always telling *her* to loosen up, but compared to Jay, she was the life of the party.

"Yes," Elise said. "Cameron is Jay's brother, and he must be stopped."

"Dun, dun, dun!" Wendy mock-sang.

"Hey, I can totally switch gears and weave this thing into a noose," Gia said, holding up a lopsided raffia braid.

"I'm not kidding."

Elise's tone made everyone stop laughing and look up. The upspeak was gone, and the bride had become a warrior, eyes narrowed, lips pursed. "He's a high school dropout. He burned down a barn outside Thunder Bay when he was seventeen. He was charged with arson, the whole deal. Jay says his mother still hasn't lived it down. And there's talk he got a girl pregnant in high school."

"What happened?" asked a rapt Gia.

Elise shrugged. "Her family moved out of town, so no one really knows."

"Wow," Wendy said, echoing Jane's thoughts. Jane had initially assumed Elise was being melodramatic about this black-sheep brother—as she was about nearly everything wedding related—but this guy *did* sound like bad news.

"Anyway." Elise brandished an iPad in front of her like it was a weapon. "Cameron MacKinnon is *not* ruining my wedding. And if he's left to his own devices, he will. From what Jay says, he won't be able to help it." She poked at the iPad. "This changes everything. We need to redo the schedule—and the job list."

The words *job list* practically gave Jane hives. Elise had turned into a total bridezilla, but by unspoken agreement, the bridesmaids had been going along with whatever she wanted. It was the path of least resistance. But also, they truly wanted Elise to have the wedding of her dreams. Even if it was painful for everyone else.

But, oh, the *job list*. The job list was like the Hydra, a serpentine monster you could never get on top of. You crossed off a job, and two more sprouted to take its place. Jane had already hand-stenciled three hundred invitations, planned and executed two showers, joined Pinterest as instructed for the express purpose of searching out "homemade bunting," tried on no fewer than twenty-three dresses—all purple— and this Cameron thing aside, it looked like today was going to be spent weaving table runners. And they still had the bachelorette party and the rehearsal dinner to get through, never mind the main event.

It boggled the mind. Elise was an interior designer, so of course she cared how things looked, but even so, Jane was continuously surprised at how much the wedding was preoccupying her friend. She could only hope they would get their funny, creative, sweet friend back after it was all over.

"Cameron is coming to town tomorrow," Elise said. "I don't know why he couldn't just arrive a day ahead of the wedding like the rest of the out-of-town guests, but it is what it is." She let the iPad clatter onto the coffee table. "I don't even know how to add this to the job list, but somehow, we have to babysit Cameron for the next week and a half."

"We?" Wendy echoed.

"Yes. He needs to be supervised at all times until the wedding—until after the post-wedding breakfast, actually. Then he can wreak whatever havoc he wants."

"Hang on," Jane said. "I agree that he sounds like bad news. But let's say, for the sake of argument, he did something horrible and got arrested tomorrow. I don't really see how that would have an impact on your wedding at all, because—"

Elise looked up, either ignoring or legitimately not hearing Jane. "You can't do it, Gia. You're my maid of honor, and I need you at my side at all times."

"Sure thing," Gia said.

Easy for her to say. Gia had purposely not taken any modeling jobs the two weeks before the wedding. She had plenty of time to lounge around braiding dried foliage and looking effortlessly beautiful in sweatpants. Also, there was the part where she was a millionaire.

Elise started scrolling through some kind of calendar app on her iPad. "Now, tomorrow we're supposed to be spray-painting the tea sets gold."

Jane looked around. *Spray-painting the tea sets gold?* Why was no one else confused by that sentence?

"But we'll have to do that in the afternoon," Elise went on, "because—"

"I have to work tomorrow," Wendy said. And when Elise looked up blankly, she added, "Tomorrow is Wednesday."

Jane was about to protest that she had to work tomorrow, too. Book seven of the Clouded Cave series wasn't going to write itself. Just because she didn't have to be in court like Wendy didn't mean her job wasn't important. She had an inbox full of fan mail from readers clamoring for the next book, not to mention a contractual deadline that got closer every day.

Elise continued, seemingly oblivious to her friends' weekday employment obligations. "Tomorrow we also need to do a practice run of boutonniere, corsage, and bouquet making. I finagled a vendor pass to the commercial fruit and flower market, but we need to get there early. So we should do the flowers in the morning and paint the tea sets in the afternoon. We'll meet in Mississauga at five thirty, but someone needs to pick up Cameron and make sure he behaves all day."

"I'll do it," said Jane, mentally calculating that to be at the suburban flower market by five thirty, she'd have to get up at four a.m. Also, there was the part about spending the afternoon spray-painting tea sets. It didn't take a genius to figure out which was the lesser of the two proverbial evils. She could babysit this Cameron dude. She'd treat him like a character in one of her books—figure him out, then make him do her bidding. "Give me the wild man's flight info, and I'll pick him up."

"I thought it would be best if you did it," Elise said, still scrolling and tapping like a maniac. "I mean, your job is so—"

Wait for it.

"Flexible."

But at least she hadn't said anything about—

"And you're so responsible. I feel like this is your kind of task."

Jane stifled a sigh. Everyone always called her responsible, but they made it sound so...boring. She preferred to think of herself as conscientious.

"I really, really appreciate this, Jane," Elise said, finally looking up from her iPad and gracing Jane with a smile so wide and sincere that it almost made her breath catch.

Yes. Right. That was why she was voluntarily submitting

to this bridesmaid torture-gig. Her friend Elise was still somewhere inside the bridezilla that was currently manning the controls, and she was so, so happy to be marrying the love of her life. That was the important thing. It made even Jane's heart, which was usually immune to these kinds of sentiments, twist a little. A wedding wasn't in her future, and she was fine with that, but all of this planning made her think of her parents' wedding pictures, the pair of them all decked out in their shaggy 1970s glory. Had they been in love like Elise and Jay, before the accident? Maybe at the start, but probably not for long, given her father's addiction. He was never violent, but he wasn't very...lovable.

But now was not the time for a pity party, so she smiled back at Elise. "No problem."

"You need to meet his plane, take him to Jay's, and make sure he doesn't do anything crazy. Jay will be home as soon as he can after work, and then you can leave for the evening and we'll figure out the rest of the schedule from there."

"Got it."

Elise reached out and squeezed her hand. "Seriously. Making sure Cameron doesn't ruin my wedding is the best present you could give me."

She waved away Elise's thanks. This was going to be a piece of cake. Or at least better than tea set spray-painting duty. After all, how bad could this Cameron MacKinnon guy be?

About the Author

Jenny Holiday is a *USA Today* bestselling author who started writing at age nine when her awesome fourth-grade teacher gave her a notebook and told her to start writing some stories. That first batch featured mass murderers on the loose, alien invasions, and hauntings. (Looking back, she's amazed no one sent her to a shrink.) She's been writing ever since. After a detour to get a PhD in geography, she worked as a professional writer, producing everything from speeches to magazine articles. Later, her tastes having evolved from alien invasions to happily-ever-afters, she tried her hand at romance. She lives in London, Ontario, with her family.

Learn more at:
   Jennyholiday.com
   Twitter @jennyholi
   Facebook.com/jennyholidaybooks

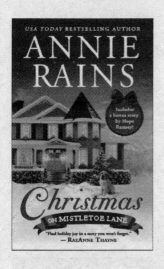
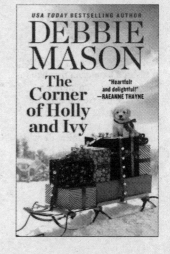

Discover exclusive content and more on forever-romance.com.

CHRISTMAS WISHES AND MISTLETOE KISSES
By Jenny Hale

Single mother Abbey Fuller doesn't regret putting her dreams on hold to raise her son. Now that Max is older, she jumps at the chance to work on a small design job. But when she arrives at the Sinclair mansion, she feels out of her element—and her gorgeous but brooding boss Nicholas Sinclair is not exactly in the holiday spirit.

THE AMISH MIDWIFE'S SECRET
By Rachel J. Good

When *Englischer* Kyle Miller is offered a medical practice in his hometown, he knows he must face the painful past he left behind. Except he's not prepared for Leah Stoltzfus, the pretty Amish midwife who refuses to compromise her traditions with his modern medicine...

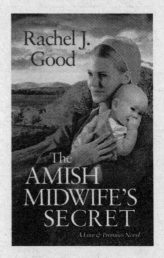

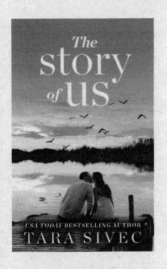
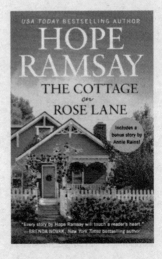

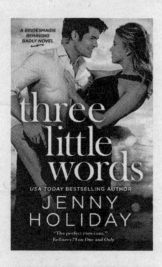